THE
RENEGADE
EQUATION

KENNETH TAM

SAVANNA FELIX
ADMIRAL, THIRD FLEET

THE
RENEGADE
EQUATION

THE THIRD EQUATIONS NOVEL

KENNETH TAM

ICEBERG

Published in Canada by Iceberg Publishing, Waterloo

Library and Archives Canada Cataloguing in Publication
Tam, Kenneth, 1984-
    The renegade equation : the third equations novel / Kenneth Tam.
ISBN 978-0-9865017-3-9
    I. Title.
PS8589.A7676R46 2010   C813'.6   C2010-900085-4

Iceberg Publishing
55 Northfield Drive East, Suite 171
Waterloo ON N2K 3T6
contact@icebergpublishing.com
www.icebergpublishing.com

First trade paperback printing: December 2004
First pocket paperback printing: May 2005
Special international edition: January 2010

Cover Artwork: Wesley Prewer
Cover Design: Kenneth Tam

For Peter,

My father, the best I could ask for.
Because I owe my common sense,
in no small part, to him.

Even if I don't use it all the time!

Many thanks.

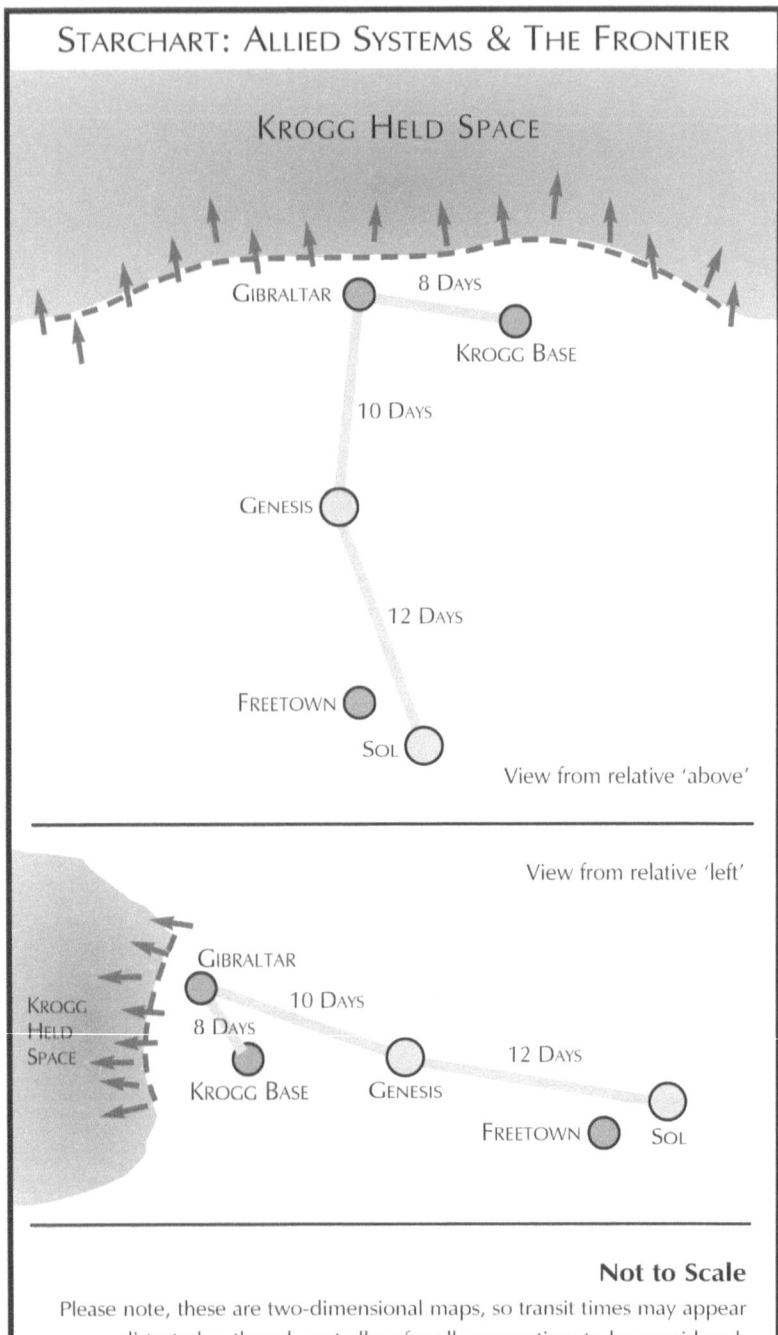

STARCHART: ALLIED SYSTEMS & THE FRONTIER

KROGG HELD SPACE

GIBRALTAR — 8 DAYS — KROGG BASE

10 DAYS

GENESIS

12 DAYS

FREETOWN

SOL

View from relative 'above'

View from relative 'left'

GIBRALTAR

KROGG HELD SPACE

10 DAYS

8 DAYS

12 DAYS

KROGG BASE   GENESIS

FREETOWN   SOL

Not to Scale

Please note, these are two-dimensional maps, so transit times may appear distorted as they do not allow for all perspectives to be considered.

Travel times are approximate based on average Earther ship cruise time.

FOREWORD

I may be mistaken in this, but I tend to find there are few people more irritating than the ones who storm through life with some naive or pre-packaged philosophy (usually ones they don't really understand), and who never seem to clue into reality. Often these individuals have never really faced up to a challenge that would test their beliefs, and they usually avoid or marginalize any opinions contrary to their own.

When I come across these people, I do find it difficult to interact with them. I like the question 'why' too much, and it's often the one that stops them in their tracks.

It's important, though, to recognize the difference between these sorts of people, and those whose perspectives — even if apparently naive — are informed by a genuinely deeper philosophy, or by hard experiences that have forged them. The distinction between these wiser people and the flimsier types is often difficult — sometimes impossible — to detect, at least until the going gets tough.

But there's certainly a difference, and that's what *The Renegade Equation* is largely about.

The Earthers have been enjoying a great deal of success in the war against the Kroggs, and being technologically inferior, the humans aren't having such an 'easy' go. Thanks to their natural bitterness and cynicism in the face of heavy losses, our fellows from Genesis are also starting to do what I think comes naturally to many of us: they're turning against those who they believe have it easier.

What do the stupid idealistic Earthers know, anyway? They're goody-goodies and they don't really suffer!

Well, the body counts from the last two books might disagree, but still, we humans have a startling ability to look past evidence when it doesn't conform to our angry and irrational claims. So to hell with them, the Earthers are having an easier time of it, and they're looking down their noses at us!

It's at this point when the Earthers sort of look at each other and shrug. Then, true to their 'alien' form, they don't give up trying to be our friends. We're just human, after all. One day we might wisen up — they're in no hurry, they'll wait an let us evolve.

Of course, the humans might have a point: by the time the story reaches this book, the Earth-born species has been part of the war against the Kroggs for close to a year, and the Earthers seem to send the Kroggs running at every turn. Their military successes are a function of their military prowess... and probably a lot of luck. I suppose one could have made similar observations about Japanese successes between December of 1941 and June of 1942.

But runs of luck like that seldom last.

When an enemy has a lot of territory, one of the best tactics they can utilize is retreat — they can force their opponent to over-extend by falling back. The Russians did this against Napoleon, and against Hitler. Worked rather well.

At the same time, they should be adapting to cope with the enemy who is having these successes, particularly if they've spent centuries fighting another foe, and in that time have tailored all their tactics and weapons to deal with the old enemy. What works against the Larosians and the humans won't necessarily work against the Earthers, so alterations should be made.

I wonder if the Krogg Queen would be wise enough to realize all this...

So after all of those cryptic historical allusions, you might get a sense of what's about to happen. Let's just say the going is about to get tougher, and we'll get to see how flimsy Earther resolve really is...

Several acknowledgments must be given before we wade into the war against the Kroggs, though.

Cody Herauf leads off the thanks yet again, because his Kroggs and Larosians are obviously crucial to this book. The rich history and tapestry he produced for those two races was such an invaluable resource to these stories, I remain hugely grateful to him. One of the specific plots in this book was also derived from a conversation he and I once had. I believe a story about Earthers stalking adversaries through the woods has indeed proved as effective as he and I thought it might.

This book introduces ENS *Engadine*, and the first generation of a new Earther weapon system: gunboats. If you're ever wondering what these craft and their mothership look like, just go ahead and close the book. Wes Prewer continues his graphic arts wizardry for this cover, and once again, his image fails to disappoint. Wes' skill and his commitment has provided so much important support to this series that I still can't say enough about it.

And in this volume, we do come across another hint of his written contribution to the series. Ami Cairn's 141st Flying Squadron is at the heart of his spinoff novel *Retaliation*, and that book is actually set around the events of this one. As such, you might come across a reference to Cairn in pages to come. Keep an eye out.

My good friend Peter Caron, as I've said before, has made fundamental contributions to this series, and in *The Renegade Equation* we see how some of these essential contributions create opportunities that simply wouldn't exist without his sound and most welcome advice. What would this book be if not for *Archangel Sword* and the Freetown privateers? It'd be different, that's for damned sure. So as usual, I want to thank him profusely for his efforts, and his insight. I'm very much obliged to my friend.

And once again, we turn finally to my family. Jacqui and Peter Tam, my parents and partners in Iceberg Publishing, have long been a driving force and a steadying hand. They've made this series, and so many other things, possible. Thanks guys.

Atlas is last, because these Earthers still owe him a great deal. Many thanks to my bygone friend.

PROLOGUE

Deckplates shuddered softly as the Earther First Rate ship of the line *Agamemnon* decelerated from energy drive and gradually slid into the uncharted system. On its bridge, Admiral Andra Ursla sighed — the 150-gun First Rate hadn't been in port for seven months, and the vibrations during what should have been a smooth translation to normal drive were clear evidence of the wear on the ship's machinery over that time.

Wear and tear, Ursla thought quietly. *Hallmarks of this protracted campaign...*

But at least a shudder wasn't significant enough to worry about — such signs of materiel fatigue weren't uncommon in the Earther Navy these days. Indeed, part of *Agamemnon's* mission in this system was to try to find some relief for the exhausted Allied Fleet. Though the ship's 150 guns could still be worked with customary ease, and its shields were a match for its Krogg opponents, *Agamemnon* needed a place to rest. Like the rest of the fleet, it could only be sustained for so long out of port. And with Genesis over a week behind Ursla's squadron, and Earth another twelve days behind Genesis, they needed to find a system to fortify on the line of advance against the Kroggs.

"Squadron has exited energy drive," Artemis Tigar said softly. *Agamemnon's* Flag Captain sat in his traditional place next to Ursla, his humanoid-tiger body being eclipsed by his Admiral's bulk.

Ursla nodded in reply, twisting her neck through a slow rotation to work out a series of kinks that had built up over the past few hours. She was finding new creaks throughout her three-meter-tall kodiak bear-humanoid frame — many more than she was accustomed to. Stress-related, she supposed.

Andra Ursla held command of the Earther Second Fleet, but over the past eight months, the Krogg Fleet had not once collected itself into a single fighting force to challenge her. Instead, her 600 ships had been separated into many dozens of eight-ship squadrons and detailed to prowl along the vast front line, hunting for the enemy and fighting relatively small single-ship and squadron-sized battles while dropping battalions of marines to clear innocent worlds of Krogg infestation.

Caine's First Fleet and Felix's Third were both being deployed with the same strategy, as was Sarah Manchester's Genesis Fourth Fleet. So while the Kroggs continued to cover their long retreat with guerrilla attacks, the front lines were pushed out further from Genesis, spreading wider and wider as they went.

Much wider, in fact — travel straight from one flank of the advance to the other actually took a *month,* meaning it would take slightly less time for an Earther ship to go home from this place than it would to go from one end of the front line to the other.

But that statistic seemed more overwhelming than it really was, and Ursla understood that better than most. Caine had planned this campaign, and so far things were working out well. The Kroggs were running, and they showed no signs of turning to mount a concentrated challenge.

That meant the Allies had breathing room — time to consolidate their advance... So after fighting her twenty-second action with her veteran 201st Battle Squadron, Ursla had volunteered to find a good planet for a forward base, and now as *Agamemnon* cruised out of energy drive at a moderate pace, the battle plot revealed just such a system before her.

It was a nice — and *desolate* — enough place. They could set up here without endangering a local ecosystem, and because it was so lifeless the Kroggs probably wouldn't expect an Earther presence.

Since the Battle of Genesis, only eight months past, there had been numerous fights between Kroggs and Earthers, both in space and on the ground. The Kroggs had hopefully grown accustomed to the Earther tendency to set life-bearing systems as objectives — planets with life and ecosystems that the Kroggs were destroying. The Earther fleets had found many dead worlds that had once been lifebearing, clearly ravaged by Krogg 'science'. They were determined to prevent the repetition of such destruction wherever possible — being mutant wolves, cats, and bears, they had inherited a sympathy for exploited biology.

But today sympathy wasn't part of the equation.

And you're musing an awful lot about it. Might be better if you just do your job.

With an inward groan, Ursla shifted her focus to the battle plot, and watched as deep scans displayed the system in the holo tank.

"Local space looks clean, ma'am," the Sensor Chief announced after a moment. "Just like Commodore Nightclaw said."

Ursla nodded and smiled briefly; her former Flag Captain from her frigate days had come through this place as he advanced up to the front lines with his Flying Squadron. Nightclaw still flew his flag from Ursla's old Fifth Rate *Cerberus,* and his 111th Flying Squadron remained the best cruiser formation in the Alliance. Considering the competition, that was no minor boast.

Indeed, the entire Earther Navy was fast proving itself to be a dedicated and deadly fighting force. It was almost unsettling in some ways — the Earthers had never been keen on war, their fleet had been built to halt human aggression... but long-term defense and a promise to help protect Genesis had mixed them up in this war. And now that they were in, they were doing *very* well — certainly pulling their weight in the Alliance.

The Earthers were partnered, of course, with the Larosians, though those veterans of the Krogg campaigns had removed all their ships from this galaxy to fuel a major drive in their home space. As such, support for the Earthers came from the much more familiar and originally-terrestrial humans. Under Sarah Manchester, the Genesis Fleet had become quite a deadly instrument — a great asset to the Allied advance — though it had been suffering more sharply from Krogg action than the Earther Navy had been of late.

The Kroggs helped build the human fleet, they obviously know its weaknesses... stop musing already!

Of course, Andra Ursla hadn't seen a human ship in about three months, a human being in five months, or a human planet in eight. She'd been out of port too long — as much as she loved her ship and her command, this campaign was starting to wear on everyone, even her.

Ursla's chair groaned in seeming response to that thought. While it was only ten days of hard travel back to the docks at Genesis, the trip seemed virtually impossible for any combat commander on this front. Ships of the line were always needed to deal with Krogg raiding forces, and frigates were always needed to *find* the Kroggs. There was no opportunity to get back, at least not without a desperate need. The front line was simply spread over too large an area — to deprive it of too many ships would create massive breaches.

This solar system, perhaps, would offer an important alternative base, a place to collect forces, affect repairs, and *recover* from campaign, all sufficiently closer to the front line of advance.

"Yep... readings look good, ma'am. One small star, a dense asteroid belt, one planetoid about the size of Pluto. Its orbit keeps it just inside the belt... no danger of collision with the asteroids. No atmosphere, but its surface is mainly a granite-compound," the Sensor Chief reported the information as it came up on his screen, then he looked up as the data stream ended, "It's perfect, ma'am."

Ursla smiled, "Very good. Dispatch *Match* to Nebula Anchorage. Let the engineers know we've found a place for them to go to work."

"Yes ma'am," the Signal Officer replied easily, relaying orders to the nearby sloop. "Should I transmit a designation for the system?"

Ursla frowned and glanced at Tigar. On the charts, this giant rock was simply recognized by an alpha-numeric code, and somehow Z10-46 didn't have a good ring to it. It didn't even correspond to the old alpha-numeric codes they'd used for systems between Earth and Genesis... as if that mattered. She'd have to name it then... but *what*? 'Giant Rock' didn't quite seem fitting...

"How about... Graniteworld?"

Ursla blinked and glanced sideways at Artie Tigar, who smiled sheepishly and shrugged, "So I'm bad with names. But come on, it's just a *rock*."

With a slow nod, Ursla let out a breath, "I guess it's 'the rock' then..."

Tigar frowned, "What rock?"

"Well..." Ursla paused, remembering a story she'd once read about a human sea Navy during one of the world wars. Actually, many of the wars had prominently featured 'the rock', if she recalled correctly, though today the place on Earth was surprisingly not referred to by its natural feature.

"Let's call it Gibraltar."

Tigar cocked an eyebrow, shrugged, and then bobbed his head to the Signal Officer.

Minutes later, *Match* hurtled from Gibraltar space, and *Agamemnon* and the 201st dropped grav anchors.

CHAPTER 1

It was just a little over a month later when First Lord Setter Caine of the Earther Navy sat down in a lounge aboard *Gibraltar One* and stifled a yawn. The station, the first of six to be put in orbit around the Gibraltar planetoid, had been prefabricated and was assembled with relative ease by the Earther Corps of Engineers just two weeks prior. More stations and weapons platforms were still on their way up from Earth, so *Gibraltar One* was on its own for the time being. It would take a few months to fully fortify this system, but when everything came together it would serve as a particularly strong anchor for the Earther line of advance.

That, as far as Caine was concerned, was absolutely crucial. The Allied Navies had surged forward for eight months, and their line of supply was getting dangerously long. While Earther vessels were essentially self-sufficient, convoys of human munition ships carrying Genesis missiles and equipment had become increasingly vulnerable in their open-space rendezvous with warships — the Kroggs were getting clever and had begun hunting for those rendezvous points.

Gibraltar was thus vital as a supply base to maintain the momentum of the continued drive, and the Allies had to keep pushing to ensure the Kroggs couldn't regroup and retaliate against Genesis or Earth.

So far, that plan was working. Although the advance of Battle Squadrons in this sector of space had slowed slightly, with a number of units consolidating around the new base, the ultimate drive was still going strong. On a front that was actually broader than the distance from Gibraltar to Earth, Allied ships were sweeping the Kroggs from space.

They'd find the Krogg homeworld in no time, by the looks of it.

And yet despite that progress, the Krogg home planet wasn't the first thing on Caine's mind. Like Ursla, he'd spent the last eight months aboard the 175-gun First Rate *Orion*, flagship of his 101st Battle Squadron, giving close support to the dozens of Flying Squadrons cruising against the Krogg front. This was the first reprieve from open space duty he'd had in all that time.

And since Gibraltar was drawing many flag officers to its new station for a small conference about the continuing advance, Caine would have a chance to catch up with his old friends.

Glancing now at the lounge's chronometer, Caine sighed. Ursla was due to meet him any minute...

...

In *Gibraltar One's* landing bay, the flag pinnace from *ENS Agamemnon* lowered itself gently to the deck. Andra Ursla watched from the side window, noting the various small craft already occupying the acre-sized landing cavern. A nearby pinnace had *Orion Flag One* painted proudly on its side — Caine had gotten here before her. In the distance she saw another flag pinnace... aha, from *Tonnant*. So Savanna Felix was aboard as well; this would be a good reunion.

There was plenty to talk about, not least the state of over 3,000 Allied ships spread weeks apart on this frontier. With Gibraltar in place, it might be time to start drawing forces together and reestablishing formations larger than battle groups.

But the deployment issues would be discussed after they spent a little time catching up, and after some important humans arrived.

Where is Sarah, anyway... well she must be on her way, Joseph Barron's *in orbit out there.*

Sarah Manchester, ArcGeneral commanding the Genesis Navy, let her head loll back on her chair's headrest. She was *bloody* tired. Her 401ˢᵗ Battle Squadron had arrived in Gibraltar just the day before and everyone aboard was looking forward to a bit of a break from the rigors of campaign duty. But she still hadn't caught up on her sleep... and she probably wouldn't get to.

Fatigue seemed to be an accepted part of her job these days. The Genesis Fleet was scattered all through space, divided usually into formations of seventy-five ships to serve as heavy support for Earther forces. Keeping those widespread units properly supplied was little short of a nightmare; the Genesis Navy Office had been forced to requisition any human ship that could haul equipment or ordnance and integrate it into the supply convoy system... and even with these acquisitions she was short of vessels. Earther-built haulers were taking up most of the slack, and thank Gods for the plentiful output of the Naval yards in Earth space. Without those Earther-built ships hauling munitions and supplies, the Genesis Navy would have been sitting in its home system, waiting for a single big battle to fight. But the Kroggs hadn't given them a really large action for months — no climactic battle that could settle the war.

Instead, the aliens were fighting guerrilla-style, and while the Earthers could successfully meet them toe-to-toe in small squadron actions, Sarah had discovered months before that single squadrons of Genesis ships were little more than inviting targets for the alien menace. That said, the Genesis battle groups she'd created tended to be large enough to fend off Krogg raiders, and there were few enough of them to allow for simpler supply lines, but the problem remained pressing.

For the most part, the Earthers got into action first these days, and they were just kind enough to call in the Genesis ships when there was something worth cleaning up. Sarah was still trying to decide whether they simply saw her force as dead weight on their advance, what with its poorer combat ability, but she somehow doubted the Earthers would be so mean-spirited as to call her ships combat-ineffective.

Anyway, minor inferiority complex aside, Sarah *was* exhausted. Between commanding her own ships in action and orchestrating arrangements for fleet supply, she was getting dangerously close to physical collapse. So Gibraltar was a Gods-send.

Supply troubles about to end...

Oh right, and Pat was here too. That had definitely improved her spirits...

Just to clarify for anyone unfamiliar with the realities of the Genesis Navy, ArcBrigadier Patrick Conroy was something of a celebrity. Barring Earthers (and only *certain* Earthers), he was the best cruiser commander in the Alliance. His squadron, the 444th, was the most notorious human formation in the fleet, with the lowest casualty rating and the highest number of kills.

And he and Sarah were the featured players in the Allied Navy's recruiting-poster romance. They'd stumbled into love, not having realized their feelings for each other for a period of some sixteen months, but now that they were together the fleets cheered them on... whenever duty allowed, anyway.

Pat's Battlecruisers spent most of their time advancing with Earther Flying Squadrons, well out ahead of the main fleet's advance. Sarah thus didn't get to see much of him, her 401st usually being trapped in the rear with the battleships.

So yesterday, when *Pope Joseph Barron*, Sarah's Superdreadnought, had pulled into Gibraltar and found *Harbinger Bishop*, Pat's intrepid Battlecruiser, she had been most excited. Pat's pinnace had reached the flagship's flight deck in about fifteen minutes, and for the next fourteen hours the pair didn't come out of Sarah's cabin.

They'd actually been asleep. The whole time. People could say whatever they liked, but exhaustion had a way of beating romance in the end.

In any case, today was the first time the commanders of the four Allied Fleets on this front were in the same system. Sarah would be happy to see them all — Ursla, Caine and Felix were all good friends, and there was quite a lot to talk about after eight months of hard campaigning. She was going to meet with them all now, and Pat was with her.

Pat had earned the title of 'Evil Irishman' in his actions thus far, and his venerable 444th was known to one and all as 'Pat's Pirates'. Though he wasn't a fleet commander, he could sit at any Earther meeting he chose, and Ursla, Caine and Felix would all be glad to see him...

Yes, Pat would be there. Sarah smiled at that thought, and closed her eyes for just a second.

• • •

Pat looked sideways at Sarah as she dozed off, trying to estimate just how much sleep she had actually been getting over the past months. Not enough, it seemed. He'd talked to her flag staff, and they'd evidently offered to take on some of her administrative work — that being the job of the staff, after all — but she had insisted in retaining total control.

And while she'd managed so far to shoo away her fatigue when battle called, earning an excellent record for her BatRon 401, she seemed to be edging into breakdown territory. Just *edging*, and she wasn't showing any obvious signs yet, but he could see some warning markers.

This break would hopefully refresh her. A rest at Gibraltar, and then the shift of supply responsibilities to a new officer coming out from Genesis, and she'd be able to restore some balance to her life.

Then her head flopped onto his shoulder with a dull thud.

Sarah jumped, "What the... Pat, that wasn't very nice!"

The Irishman frowned, "You hit me with that *big head* of yours, don't blame me."

With a long blink Sarah slowly drew a smile to her face, then put her head back on his shoulder.

The pinnace touched down a few minutes later.

Coming down her pinnace's ramp, Ursla watched the rust-colored Genesis shuttle slide through the energy shield at the far side of the bay, immediately recognizing it as Sarah's craft from *Joseph Barron*. Everyone had now arrived.

"Andra!"

The call came from a hundred meters down the deck, and Ursla turned her three-meter tall body towards the origin. A two-meter tall cat hustled across the distance at a swift walk, the trim on his uniform giving him away even before Ursla's gaze shifted to his face.

"Savanna, by the Earth it's good to see you!" Ursla grinned as he came to stop in front of her.

"And you! I heard about that scuffle off the Castorvan Nebula," he grinned with just a little bit of glee, putting out his hand. "A Mothership, I heard."

Ursla shook his hand with a smile, recalling the action: she'd run across an unescorted Krogg Mothership and had destroyed it without a single Earther casualty. Throughout the whole of the campaign to this point, Motherships had been rare finds. She'd been awfully lucky to come across one on its own in deep space — luck and what they believed was Krogg overextension had just worked in her favor. But she wasn't the only one scoring victories...

"You've been doing your own bit, I hear. The battle group at the Arbalest Pulsar, right?"

Savanna Felix smiled and nodded, "Luck."

"Somehow we seem to be having a lot of that these days. Let's hope it holds up, eh?" Ursla added, and Felix chuckled.

"Whatever works. I'm not going to look a gift horse in the mouth."

As the pair turned to face the landing Genesis craft, a thought crossed Ursla's mind, "Do you think that saying got started at Troy?"

Felix bobbed his eyebrows and elected not to answer.

Sarah consciously forced herself not to drag her feet as she descended her pinnace's ramp, and she offered a bright smile to the two Admirals waiting for her, "Good to see both of you!"

Pat came down behind her, "Yes, yes I suppose it is. Though I did see you two months ago at Grendel's Belt, Savanna, so you don't get a hug."

Savanna grinned in reply, "I suppose that's fair... you two are looking well."

He shook Sarah's hand as she offered it.

"So *I* get a hug Pat?" Ursla smiled down at the burly Irishman and he grinned back.

"Nothing personal, dear Andra, but I like my spinal arrangement as it is, thanks."

Ursla laughed.

A few minutes later, Setter Caine came to his feet as the lounge doors opened and a group of his finest flag officers and best friends arrived, jesting amongst themselves. They fanned out as they entered the bright room, and Caine offered them a smile, "Well, it's very good to see you all!"

And it most certainly was.

CHAPTER 2

Captain Audrey DeBrooke awoke slowly as sunlight cascaded through the window and onto her bed. It was a refreshing thing, sunlight, and something she was still becoming accustomed to again after so long in space. Despite a few months planetside, her body hadn't yet fully acclimatized to the realities of orbiting a star. It was odd, trying to shake off space legs after a decade in the service.

But at least living in a veritable resort-paradise helped take the edge off that strangeness.

It had been just about seven months since Audrey and then-ArcColonel James Stanton had found this system. It was located only a few stars down from NV 214X, a planetary solar system that had seen action eight months before... unofficial action, that was, since they'd been renegades at the time. After dealing with some unseemly 'Coalition' pirates, they'd run across then-Commander Fox Magnus and his sloop *Flame* when he'd been on an urgent courier mission from Genesis to Earth. And at the moment they'd found him, he was about to be destroyed by a large Krogg force.

Luck had smiled on the renegades that day. They'd rendered assistance — the best their two cruisers, *Archangel Sword* and *Grendelsbane City*, could when faced with Krogg Superdreadnoughts — and then when the situation had seemed beyond hope, they'd all been saved by Admiral Savanna Felix. That incident had led to both Audrey and James being commissioned as Earther privateers — a win-win arrangement, to be sure.

Now they were completely independent of the Genesis and Earther Fleet commands, but had the absolute support of the latter, and thus a certain defacto legitimacy. Those Earthers really had great ways of doing things.

Audrey and James had assisted at the Battle of Genesis, then had found this place rather quickly after leaving that system. After the privateers had announced their intention to settle it, an Earther hauler had dropped off a rather substantial pre-fab base kit that the human engineers were still constructing.

It was an amazing base, with many houses and public buildings, and all the mobile industry plants needed to keep ships and populations in service on their own. Best of all, it was situated on what could best be described as a tropical-paradise island.

The renegades had named their new home Freetown, after the settlement in Africa that had become a haven for freed slaves in the nineteenth century on Earth... though they were certainly planning on avoiding the political and social trouble that had beset the original city before the rise of Omega. So far everything was going well, but there'd be many years of work ahead...

It's a beautiful morning and I'm thinking about societal problems when we don't even have any. There's something very wrong with this picture...

Slowly sitting up in bed, Audrey squinted at the sunlight and yawned. Today would be another one filled with meetings — several new ships had joined their Freetown settlement in the last few months, and another Light Cruiser had shown up just three days ago. There wasn't much worry that the wrong sorts of people would come to Freetown — the Earthers weren't handing letters of marquee out to just anyone — but the privateers did have to watch for the remnants of that outcast Coalition... and, of course, there were some differing ideas regarding the formation of a government for this planet.

Such questions inevitably led to everyone having plenty of *talks*... and while the process wasn't *too* frustrating, it was complex enough to keep Audrey and James busy. So that would be the plan for today. There'd also probably be more construction work, and talk of resources and trade...

Essentially, it'd be another day of plain administration. Not exactly Audrey's favorite pastime, but she'd suffered through far worse. James was the sort of fellow who thrived on challenges like this one — he was happy to build a strong base, and even happier to be doing it with her. And it was really, *really* nice not to be separated on different ships... though even James was beginning to wonder how he could get *Sword* out to aid the Allied Fleet once or twice...

And as much as she liked paradise, Audrey was eager to go with him. For a couple of reasons she could reflect on later. For now it was time to get out of bed.

"Get up James. Come on..." she planted her feet on the floor and stood, "...society to build remember."

Shifting a little, James Stanton grumbled something, pulled the sheets up around his chin a bit further, and didn't get out of bed. Audrey went to fill a bucket with cold water.

ENS Highlander slid out of energy drive alongside the long string of haulers it was escorting — a convoy of cargo ships lugging gear from Sol to the new base at Gibraltar. Because this line of ships carried such important equipment, Captain Garvin Jardaw had been assigned to protect it... and unfortunately, that mission wouldn't be as easy as an outside observer might have expected.

Due to the strain of the long supply lines, the Earther Navy was being forced to rely on some older haulers to augment its modest number of long-range cargo vessels. The ships traveling with *Highlander* were perfect examples; at over a century old, they were almost the same age as Jardaw, and had only been recently retrofitted with new energy drives. With so many Earther yards committed to building 74s and 44s, there simply weren't enough slips available to build a fleet of new haulers — these old ones would have to do for the time being.

And that meant it would be a somewhat complicated trip to Gibraltar.

While the energy drives fitted to the old haulers were new, the power systems on the ships weren't. That might not have been a problem had they been warships — *Highlander* was a sixty-year-old ship, and vessels like Admiral Felix's *Tonnant* were older still. No, the problem was caused by the mass of the cargo they were carrying. The strains of that mass on the energy drive were immense, and the old reactors were fighting to cope with the overload. Thus, a pause from energy drive didn't hurt now and then — mainly to swap out half-cooked flow regulators for new ones.

Indeed, they'd be halting every two or three days during the entire trip to Gibraltar — almost a month away from Earth.

It could prove to be a very tedious run for all involved.

On *Highlander's* bridge Jardaw sat patiently, watching the thirteen First Rate-sized haulers signal the beginning of their maintenance cycles. The polar bear had been Captain Draco Maximane's First Lieutenant in *Apollo* during the Battle of Genesis months earlier, but when that 74 had been severely battered in one of the few bad exchanges after the First Fleet's arrival, it had been returned to Earth for repair and he'd been reassigned. *Highlander* was his first command, and he was pleased with it... and with this task.

What some would consider mundane jobs really could be quite interesting, if you happened to like the operational practicalities of a Navy. Garvin Jardaw did; this was a real intellectual treat for him. And the threat of action was small — even though the Coalition was reportedly still out there in some force *somewhere*, he didn't expect they'd cause any trouble.

Wait a moment, I actually had the audacity to think that. Which means...

"Captain, I've got eight ships coming out from behind a planetoid deeper in the system," the cougar Second Lieutenant made the alert sound subdued. "No friendly colors on their transponders."

Aha, interesting timing, as ever it seems.

Jardaw sat up in his chair and his eyes narrowed as he nodded; perhaps the Coalition was more audacious than he'd first thought. It'd be their greatest mistake if they tried to make trouble for *Highlander* and the convoy, even with superior numbers of warships... Glancing to one of the nearby holo screens, however, Jardaw realized that the haulers he was escorting were certainly *not* in a position to make a stand. Their drives were offline, and one of the ships wouldn't be active for at least ten minutes because of the number of coils it was swapping.

"ETA on the unknowns?" he turned back to the Second Lieutenant.

There was a pause, "Two minutes, thirty seconds to weapons range."

Well that wasn't promising. Coming to his feet, the polar bear made his way forward to *Highlander's* main battle tank, and the ratings in control of the holographic projection immediately obliged him with a map of local space.

"They're not Coalition, sir. They're Krogg," the Second Lieutenant continued to report from his post behind the sensor consoles.

That revelation brought silence to the bridge — what were Kroggs doing back *here*? Up to this point they had shown no indication of knowing where Earth was... indeed, Kroggs had never been seen this close to Earth — the Allied squadrons were supposedly keeping them under pressure at the front.

Jardaw's quiet confidence abruptly turned to deep concern.

"Very well. Classes, please," his voice remained even, and the bridge crew seemed to draw some solace from his seeming confidence. Instinctive bursts of anxiety still traveled between officers and ratings, but they were ignored.

"Seven large Destroyers... one Dreadnought."

Well then. Jardaw linked his hands behind his back and took a deep breath — 64s such as *Highlander* weren't necessarily matches for that sort of firepower. As Jax Furgus had discovered twice at the Battle of Pluto's Orbital Plane and once at the Battle of Genesis, close action by a Fourth Rate in a capital ship fight often led to that ship's destruction. Jax survived by some minor miracle, and for whatever odd reason he kept going back to his 64s, but the Admiralty had long ago chosen to shift construction emphasis to the disproportionately tougher 74-gun Third Rates...

Facts which all surfaced in Jardaw's mind in the first few seconds of thought. *Highlander* could have handled Coalition ships, but not this.

There'd be no standup fight on this occasion... he needed to buy time so his convoy could escape. And warn Earth.

But how. And where to go?

Quickly keying up a star chart on his pad, Jardaw checked for the nearest hiding place. They were only recently out of Sol — four days travel at a low cruising speed — but they'd never reach the home system with their fragile drives being pressured by pursuit.

There was a nebula nearby... NV 296X. No, too far...

Aha.

"Signal Officer. All ships to make best speed for NV 217X as soon as they are able. We'll cover their retreat."

The signal raced out almost immediately, and seven of the cargo haulers entered energy drive within a dozen seconds. Three more reported momentary readiness, but the last one — caught with four of its energy reactors in the middle of a restart cycle — would be at least six minutes more.

Highlander would be staying for a while.

As the first haulers made their escape, Jardaw's First Lieutenant came to stand alongside him at the plot, "What's in 217, sir?"

Jardaw took a deep breath, "The Freetown Privateers... let's just hope they're home."

The Lieutenant nodded slowly, and then after another few seconds of thought, Jardaw looked to the cougar, "Beat to quarters now, I think."

Highlander's crew cleared the ship for action.

Audrey felt an immature glee as she modeled her new uniform in front of the mirror. The royal blue Earther-style garment had been adopted by the privateers without much debate — they had wanted to get out of Genesis green, and since the Earthers were essentially legitimizing their status as renegades, it seemed only fair to give them a nod in the uniform department.

That and they *really* looked *good*. Much more pleasantly form-fitting than the Genesis greens, as James kept telling her. Apparently the Earther garment-manufacturing machines were particularly adept at scanning their subjects and supplying clothes that fit perfectly... which made sense since this was the same equipment that could make uniforms for both Andra Ursla and Fox Magnus in half an hour. Flexibility was built in. And so the double-breasted tunics with the two rows of squared gold snaps and tasteful amounts of gold trim could be cut to fit a human figure most flatteringly.

Just as Audrey was admiring her physique, James emerged from the bathroom with his tunic half buttoned, the top flap hanging down on a diagonal.

"I think this looks appropriately rebellious!" he grinned, and Audrey turned and began tugging at his uniform's shoulders to make sure it was fitting him properly.

For James' part, he was loving his new life at Freetown. Only months before all he could think about was getting a piece of the Kroggs. He and Audrey had done that at Genesis; now they could move on with their lives, and it felt right.

Not that he would mind going back out there and getting into more trouble with the Kroggs, if circumstances demanded, but still...

The comm chirped.

Turning back to the panel on the wall and quickly pulling her long brown hair back into a pony tail, Audrey hit the appropriate button, "DeBrooke."

"Ma'am, Earther convoy approaching system at high speed, asking for immediate assistance!"

Highlander cleared for action and charged its guns just as the first salvoes of spines hit space. Jardaw wasn't pleased by the size of the volley, but the two additional barrages he expected to follow the first didn't come — the Krogg ships usually had three complete salvoes of spines ready to fire at a time, but they were probably saving the rest for when they closed range.

Against these odds, Jardaw's first inclination would be to deny them that chance — were he and *Highlander* alone, he'd already be in energy drive. But there was still a vulnerable hauler here, recalibrating its aged reactors. Five more minutes and it'd be ready to move... he just needed that long.

"Keep us between them and the hauler... make the Dreadnought the priority for gunners. Signal Officer, prepare a pod to warn Earth... in case it starts to look like we're not going to get through this," Jardaw's words were cool and professional. "Make full speed now. Starboard broadside run out and fire as you bear. Carronades stand by for point defense."

The orders forced *Highlander* into abrupt motion. The Krogg ships spat another volley of spines at the 64, but Jardaw's ship was moving too quickly, closing fast on the high side of the alien vessels. Neuro pulses began to lance out at the 64 as it entered range, grazing its shields with angry heat.

Then the Earther gunners released their shot, and twenty-five cannon on the Fourth Rate's starboard broadside crashed out. The Krogg ship started to evade, swinging hard to starboard in a bid to avoid the solid wall of energy, but to no avail.

Though not as potent as a 74's broadside, the guns still tore viciously into the Krogg carapace, throwing it to one side as if it had been slapped by a great hand. Jardaw's eyes narrowed as the targeted Krogg righted itself quickly and began to angle up, but before the Dreadnought could restore its direction, its consort Destroyers were sweeping up into *Highlander's* wake.

"They're coming up after us, skipper," the Second Lieutenant reported from sensors, and Jardaw nodded, turning immediately to the Master.

"Reverse drives and present the port broadside, 80 pls."

The veteran canine offered a nod, then barked quick orders. The 64 came around and backwards with respectable handiness, its port-side gunners watching the Destroyers appear in their sights.

Shot crashed out almost immediately and without specific order, Gun Captains loosing their energy as soon as they had a firm lock. Jardaw frowned at his plot as the ragged 25-gun broadside cruised out — the Kroggs, instead of attempting to barrel through, broke their formation and scattered around it.

They hadn't been doing *that* at Genesis... or a couple of months ago, even.

"Ahead full, get us into carronade range, and starboard guns present on that Dreadnought..."

The Krogg capital ship had charged up the other side, and Jardaw's eyes noted its course in the plot just as three full salvoes of spines spat from it at near point-blank range, heading directly for the starboard broadside.

"Up angle ninety, give me 90 pls..." Jardaw ground his jaw at the orders — there was no way his 64 could get out of the way in time... "Starboard gun crews activate shields. Carronade crews get ready for when it passes us."

There was a second of fateful silence, and then the better part of the

Dreadnought's salvo hammered into *Highlander's* starboard broadside. Energy shields held fast for the first two waves of projectiles, but the third battered through, and the entire broadside was ravaged.

Gunports had been open, and so several spines got through those hatches and slammed into guns. Some tore through the hull between hatches, some glanced off. The entire deck depressurized, but the gun crews, under orders, had their platform shields up, saving most of them from death. Two of the guns were blown off their tracks, but emergency grav anchors kept the fifty-ton weapons from sliding about.

The entire ship trembled, and Jardaw took a deep breath... "Carronades."

The Dreadnought thought to pass beneath *Highlander*, but as it did the carronade crews tracked it. Long lances of powerful energy slashed out, and the capital ship's upper carapace was split in two, blood erupting from the long gash.

"Port broadside to bear please, Master."

Just as the cannon finished recharging, the Gun Captains laid their sights on the rear of the wounded Dreadnought. At nearly point-blank range they let go their shot, and the ship bucked as almost the entire salvo struck home.

But the fire wasn't one-way; the neuro blasts of the Dreadnought's point-blank armament hammered hard at the 64's shields, and though not as concentrated as carronade shot, they cut through the energy barriers and tore into the Earther ship's hull.

The carronade crews were already set to respond. From mounts all over *Highlander's* outer hull, the crews of those weapons marked target points on the Krogg Dreadnought, and even as the energy shot from the Fourth Rate's broadside tore into the carapace of the greater capital ship, these long lances of energy again cut viciously at the vessel's hull. On the unengaged side, similar carronades ripped two Krogg Destroyers limb from limb.

But the Dreadnought righted itself and changed course to come back in for close action, and the remaining Krogg Destroyers began to circle the wounded 64...

"Enough of this," Jardaw turned quickly from his plot to the Master, even as the ship bucked again beneath his feet. "Give me an evasive course — angle away from the hauler."

Despite its wounded starboard quarter, *Highlander* swung with respectable quickness, bringing its charged and shielded port broadside to bear on the attackers. As each gun flared and rolled back on its track, the 64's engines came to full life.

Though energy shot tore through the armor of two more Krogg Destroyers, overwhelming them and spattering their innards, the rest of the Krogg force came on angrily. A partially injured Dreadnought and three Destroyers... *Highlander* was seriously outclassed right now.

And then, in a burst of good timing, the hauler icon in the holo tank collapsed into energy drive and hurtled away from the fight. It escaped unmolested, thanks to *Highlander's* efforts.

Jardaw resisted a sigh of relief and nodded to the Master even as the veteran Earther was ordering the helm over towards 217 and the energy drives were spinning up.

"Get us out of here!"

James dropped into his chair on the bridge of *Archangel Sword* only twenty-two minutes after the comm call, and immediately sent to *Grendelsbane City*. Audrey had gotten to her bridge first, and now she appeared on the monitor.

"Ready?" James made the question quick and friendly.

She bobbed her eyebrows and smiled, "Of course."

"Good," his replying smile was of the 'ate the canary' variety, and as Audrey disappeared he turned to his Signal Officer, "Orders to squadron: ships to accelerate towards the convoy's arrival vector."

The orders cascaded outward in short order, and in addition to *Sword* and *Grendelsbane*, the recently-joined ships *Torcott City*, *New Cashtown*, *Lagarand*, *Jesuit*, *Forton* and *Vance* began to accelerate outward, arming their weapons as they went.

Highlander crashed out of energy drive in the Freetown system with a noticeable shudder — courtesy of the Krogg-inflicted damage to its starboard side. The hull was a mess of twisted alloy, hardly conducive to a smooth reconstitution from energy state.

"The last four Kroggs are still chasing us, skipper. Closing now... weapons range in just under a minute."

Jardaw ground his jaw — the Kroggs were persistent...

"Ready the port broadside. Master, bring it to bear."

Hopefully this dramatic little scrap hadn't been futile...

"Order the haulers to make directly for the planet, we'll stay between them and whoever's after them," James nodded to his Signal Officer and the orders lanced out through space.

On *Sword's* main bridge screen, a map showed the large Earther ships accelerating sluggishly, and then the privateer squadron passed them on the way to the system rim. Now, what were they about to face...

"Incoming, a wounded Krogg DN and three large DDs," the Sensor Chief abbreviated the class names in his rapid report, but James knew what he was talking about. Kroggs, out here...

Must remember not to think about things I 'want'.

As *Highlander's* transponder came up on *Sword's* screen James frowned at the situation, then took a steadying breath and put his mind on battle footing, "Give me flank speed. Squadron to engage the Destroyers, we'll look after that Dreadnought..." he frowned at the Earther Fourth Rate's icon — it indicated damage... "What's the status of that 64?"

The Sensor Officer paused as she consulted her readouts, "It's *Highlander*, 64, under Garvin Jardaw. Starboard broadside's been beat to hell... looks like he's waiting to give them the port shot when they get into range."

James only nodded in reply — a tough ship, but clearly outgunned. Jardaw had done well to get here at all against that sort of Krogg force.

Well, the Earther Captain was about to reap the rewards of persistence and good escape tactics.

"Here they come..."

Jardaw took a breath, "Target the Dreadnought and fire as you bear."

As the 64's broadside put to space the plot chirped, and from the direction of the planet a line abreast of privateer ships appeared in the battle plot. The ships were cruisers and Destroyers only, but their missiles, guided by Earther tracking suites, were more than adequate to the task of killing Krogg Destroyers...

Jardaw let out the breath he'd been holding.

As *Highlander's* shot drove home, enhanced missiles from *Archangel Sword* followed closely, and the Dreadnought was swallowed in a fireball. The Destroyer trio attempted to scatter, but one ventured into range of *Highlander's* carronades, and two others were set upon by Freetown's Heavy and Light Cruisers.

Highlander's broadside fired a last time at one of the fleeing ships before missiles from *Grendelsbane* incinerated its flesh, and then the last Krogg Destroyers collapsed under the weight of the lasers from four human vessels.

Space calmed, and Garvin Jardaw rubbed his neck and let out a sigh. That had ended up going rather well. Job done... ship beaten to hell, but job done.

"Call coming in from *Archangel Sword*, sir," the Signal Officer reported quietly, and Jardaw looked up through the tank and nodded.

"Give it to me here," he nodded to the holo plot.

A few seconds later James Stanton appeared on a screen in the glowing blue projection, "Good day, Captain. Need a hand?"

CHAPTER 3

Gibraltar One's lounge was home to high spirits as the Allied leaders split their time between recounting their stories and considering their present circumstances.

"So, we'll continue to press them. We can ease off on the pressure to consolidate for now, but we'll begin advancing again within two weeks. Sound about right?" Felix leaned back in his armchair and looked to his fellow flag officers.

Caine nodded first, "About right. We've got what... sixty warships here now? A good portion of the First Fleet is within a week of us, and some of the Second is no more than eight days out."

"A good section of the Fourth can be here in that time," Sarah added with a subconscious wince. Her head was starting to hurt, but she hoped her discomfort didn't show through her British-accented words.

"The Third will take a bit longer," Felix finished with a frown. "A lot are out on deep scouting patrol, and some are watching Krogg forces in systems further out."

Caine concurred, "We'd best leave them there then. We can relieve them in short order, as soon as we get the squadrons rotated. We'll be receiving new ships from the yards soon too. The first Carriers are on trials now. They'll be useful, I expect."

Nods were exchanged between the commanders.

"Now that we have a forward base, we should really start rotating back for repair more often," Ursla commented after a moment. "A good couple of hours' tune-up in the yard could certainly help keep our ships in fighting trim. We can probably even rotate them back two at a time as needed."

Again the officers nodded thoughtfully. It was an appealing concept — keeping ships in top condition would be quite useful, as the attrition of months in space could hamper a vessel's performance just enough to give the Kroggs an edge.

Pat grinned, "I can get *Bishop's* hydroponic gardens tweaked then. They always go finicky and give some damned pink potatoes."

Being from a great race of potato eaters, some of the Earthers put on expressions of mock horror, while Sarah snorted a laugh, "How un-Irish of them."

Pat, sitting next to her on a couch, put a playful arm around her, "That's the problem!"

Chuckling, Ursla turned to Caine, "The local squadron can be made up of whatever ships are being rotated in here then, plus a squadron of 74s, I think."

Caine nodded again slowly, "One squadron of 74s and one of frigates. Sarah, any hope of getting some cruisers or Dreadnoughts from you?"

"I can scrounge some up, I think. I have some good skippers verging on breakdowns from stress, and they could do well here. Give them time to get their legs back under them before I send them back into action."

"Good," Caine was already mentally assigning ships to the garrison flotilla. Most of the veteran but under-crewed 74s that had suffered high casualties and needed time away from the action to recover and replenish their companies.

There was silence after his word, though Caine didn't realize it for a few moments. They'd been chatting for over two hours now, but shop talk was starting to darken the happy reunion.

"So, I suppose the operative question is where do we head next?" Felix piped up in the vacuum.

Ursla's eyebrows rose and she cast a glance at Caine, who tilted his head and squinted thoughtfully.

Sarah frowned, "We've been heading on that straight line axis, haven't we? Right down the Kroggs' throats."

There was a series of nods, and Sarah continued, "I say keep going, but I'd also recommend we try fanning out on the flanks a bit more. I know your fleets are spread thin as it is, but I think I could send a couple of Flying Squadrons out to the fringes to see if the Kroggs are planning anything unpleasant for us." She nudged Pat, "You could go find some of them, couldn't you *honey*?"

Pat reddened a little and frowned, "Of course... *piglet*."

The Earthers in the room laughed outright, and Sarah drove a stiff elbow into Pat's ribs. He gasped sharply and whispered a mock threat in her ear while Caine exchanged amused glances with Ursla and Felix. Those two really *were* made for each other.

"Sounds good to me," Ursla interrupted the friendly human bickering.

Caine nodded with put-on (but legitimate) enthusiasm, "Certainly!"

It was good to have family.

Some hours later, the flag officers of the Alliance Fleet filed out of *Gibraltar One's* lounge and walked slowly back towards their pinnaces. Ursla and Caine trailed behind, watching Sarah and Pat sway together in somewhat obvious (at least to Earther senses) exhaustion.

"The kids are worn out," Caine smiled up at Ursla.

She laughed softly, "I think so. Speaking of which, heard from Elandra lately?"

Caine nodded, surprisingly solemn thoughts of the wife and son he hadn't seen in eight months coming to mind. There were comm messages, of course, but that wasn't the same as...

He stopped the line of thought.

"She's doing fine, as is Phealan. She says he misses me a lot, but that he understands why I'm not home."

Ursla nodded with a smile, "He's a smart cub."

Caine indulged his pang of loneliness for a second, recalling the abrupt circumstances of his departure and the lack of time he'd had since... but then he blinked the emotions away. He'd find time to get home soon enough, now that Gibraltar was out here to service the fleet. He wasn't sure how the two were connected — Gibraltar and going home — but he was somehow sure they were.

Or maybe he just hoped they were.

Several minutes later, Ursla arrived in *Gibraltar One's* main flight bay, and came to a stop alongside her fellow fleet Admiral Felix as Sarah's pinnace rose slowly off the deck and cruised out of the bay. After watching the departure of her friends, she glanced down at the cat, "So, how long do you think?"

Felix hadn't exactly been paying attention at that instant, so it took him a few seconds to realize what his friend was referring to. He cocked an eyebrow, "A year, maybe."

Ursla frowned, "To the Krogg homeworld? A year?"

Felix nodded and looked up, "The Larosians are pressing from the flank, but the Kroggs know how to slow them down. They've been fighting each other for centuries, after all. But I get the sense we're close to cracking them — we just need to find whatever installation they're using out here as a forward base."

Ursla scratched her neck absently, "Forward base... yes, I suppose they must have one. Their ships need to graze after all... they're harder to keep in space than ours. And I think you're right about them breaking, too. With the number of Motherships we've been catching out in the open, it seems like they aren't even coordinating properly anymore..."

Her voice trailed off as her companion nodded, and she frowned at the thought of the chaotic Krogg frontier — there were dozens of minor fights happening across the war zone every day, so Felix was surely correct: a base had to be supporting the Krogg raiders. It was up to the Allies to find that base before it could stage an attack more substantial than the raids they were seeing. There was no reason that should be a great problem, either, based on the lack of coherence the Kroggs had been showing of late...

Ursla nodded slowly to herself at the thought, then glanced again at Felix, "It *seems* like we've got them over a barrel, anyway. We can consolidate here over the next month and then get out with a dozen Flying Squadrons on the flanks. We should be able to track down their forward base quickly enough."

Felix tilted his head a bit, "I get the feeling that finding them won't be the problem, Andra. With us spread so thin advancing, I'm more worried about *dealing* with them when we do find them."

Ursla's ear twitched and she looked down at her fellow Admiral, "Sheesh. Optimist."

Felix shrugged, "I'm a tiger."

Ursla frowned, "What's that have to do with anything?"

"Umm. Nothing, really, but it would've made for a convenient end to this conversation. Now you've wrecked it!"

The pair smiled irreverently and waited as their pinnaces were made ready to take them to their ships.

Sarah slid into bed with some relief, ignoring the nagging soreness in favor of the comfortable warmth of her blankets. The reunion had lasted almost eight hours, just about half of which had actually been spent working on strategic questions. She'd hoped the gathering would be more relaxing... instead it had just run late and increased her level of tiredness, and now she was desperately in need of sleep. She was also troubled.

Well what else was new? She'd been looking after fleet logistics *and* fleet deployment *and* squadron tactics... the Genesis Navy needed a better staff corps. Sure, they *said* she could delegate to her current staff, but she couldn't trust those particular people with the lifelines that kept her fleet going... so to make sure things stayed intact, she just had to do it herself. Fine, it was her job...

Of course, there were other things to worry about, too, and those were bothering her more right now. Pat was actually going to go poking around on the flanks of the front with just a squadron of Battlecruisers... Ursla had once come across a Mothership out on the flanks, what if Pat did too? His cruisers wouldn't be able to deliver enough punishment to put it out of commission — Ursla had been with a full Battle Squadron, Pat would have only twelve *Battlecruisers*. Asking him to go was seeming like a bad idea...

What if he got killed?

Logically, that was a question she was supposed to have prepared herself to answer long ago — they were both officers in a war, and death was an accepted risk. But for the eight months of this advance Pat had always been cruising with someone else, always been in the center of the lines, ready and able to call up support...

This was a different sort of job, and while she didn't quite know why, she had a bad feeling about it... it was as though she sensed that the momentum of the war was destined to change, and Pat's mission might be the turning point.

Maybe it wasn't a good idea to send him...

"Pat," Sarah nudged Pat as he slumbered beside her. "Pat!"

The Irishman opened his eyes groggily, "What? Too bloody tired..."

"I don't know if you should go out there..."

Pat's eyes opened narrowly, "What are you talking about now?"

"The flank... I'm not sure you should go out there... I have a... *bad* feeling..."

"I'll be careful, Sarah... you're just getting jitters because it's 03:00. Go to sleep."

Sarah bit her lip and rolled away from him. He was right — pessimism plagued her at night. This mission wouldn't be any different than the rest. She wouldn't lose Pat... she simply couldn't. With all the other stresses of life, he was the single most important factor keeping her going. Even when he was absent, the personal life they had created together was a powerful counterweight to all-consuming work...

So he'd just *have* to be fine.

And with that decision, Sarah went directly to sleep.

CHAPTER 4

Audrey DeBrooke leaned back in her chair and brought her knee-high leather boots up onto the table in the Freetown Government House's main conference room. The bright lounge — Earther pre-fab with high enough ceilings for bears and one wall a window looking out onto the sunny, sandy beaches of the capital city — was the room in which the two leading Captains of the privateer squadron did most of their administrative business. It was also where they'd meet their unexpected but most welcome guest.

Highlander and the Earther convoy were currently lying in orbit, with the rest of the Freetown Squadron drawn up around them as escort in case of more serious trouble. And the 64's Captain was due to arrive presently...

Just as Audrey thought of the austere polar bear, the door opened and Captain Garvin Jardaw entered, James at his side. Audrey had just shifted to ensure her boots were comfortably set on the table, so with hidden disappointment she hauled them down again and got to her feet. Come to think of it, she wasn't entirely sure why she'd put them up there in the first place... it just seemed privateer-worthy.

"Captain Jardaw," James said formally, "may I present Captain Audrey DeBrooke, *Grendelsbane City*."

Audrey smiled and extended a hand to the two-and-a-half meter tall bear, "Pleased to meet you."

Jardaw offered a smile in reply, "And you, Captain. As I've told Captain Stanton, I was most glad that you were willing to help."

Audrey waved the trio back into seats around the table, "We're glad to be of service. We fly Earther pennants, after all."

Jardaw bobbed his head slowly, "But you remain an independent force. And even if you weren't wearing our pennant, I'd owe you my thanks."

Audrey settled herself in her chair and looked to James, who was now sitting across from her. He cocked a pleased eyebrow at Jardaw's remark and she gave a quick eyebrow twitch of her own in reply, silently conveying her pride. Jardaw noticed both subtle gestures, his Earther senses picking up the private by-play, but he said nothing. Earthers exchanged such wordless messages all the time — it was nice to see these privateers were picking up on the practice.

"Well," James said after a moment of silence, "I'm afraid we lack the facilities to repair *Highlander's* damage here, Captain Jardaw. We deal in cruiser size and down, nothing so grand as a 64."

Jardaw grinned, "A 64 is not all that grand, Captain, but I appreciate your generous description. My Cruising Master assures me he can have us ready to put to space in a day, but we won't be able to bring the starboard broadside back online without some dock time. That's why I requested this meeting."

Audrey frowned at the last remark, "What can we do for you? We don't have a dock."

Jardaw nodded, "True, but you do have a good cruiser squadron. And when we get closer to Genesis we may run into trouble that *Highlander* can't handle. The Kroggs have come this far, there's no telling what's going on further out. I've sent a pod to the Admiralty, but I haven't asked for any reinforcements to my escort force — I know they won't have the ships available, what with Earth and Freetown to guard. But the parts we're hauling are crucial to Gibraltar, and if the Kroggs are resurging they'll certainly be needed soon..."

James held up a hand and frowned, "Gibraltar?"

Jardaw looked at him with a cocked eyebrow, "You haven't heard? We're hauling five pre-fab stations for a new forward base about ten days out of Genesis. They're calling it Gibraltar."

James shot a brief glance to Audrey, then looked back at Jardaw, "Aha..."

"Sol space is only lightly protected right now, but I'm sure the Admiralty can get a strong enough force out here to watch Freetown — in the meantime, I must take the convoy out of your system with all possible speed. If you'd be willing to come with us, you might well make the difference to our reaching Gibraltar intact."

Considering that description of the situation, James cast a curious look at his co-commander. She shrugged, "Well now that the Kroggs might know we're here, it's probably better if we clear out for a while — at least until the Admiralty can secure the area. There's not much chance of us stopping a major Krogg raid alone, and there's nothing down here we couldn't rebuild."

Nodding slowly, James narrowed his eyes, "And by going we take a load off the Admiralty's plate — they can focus on local defense... which is probably much more reasonable for ships just out of the yards than a convoy run, anyway..."

Altogether, it didn't seem like a bad option. And the privateers could make a difference again.

So with a last confirming glance to James, Audrey smiled casually at Jardaw, trying to appear to be a comfortable swashbuckler, "Sure. I wouldn't mind seeing this new place, and we could pick up supplies on the way back. Leave this matter to Admiralty, they can do a better job of it than we ever could."

The polar bear nodded slowly, "Indeed. Much of what's in Sol is in for repairs, but even if they're forced to put partially refitted ships back into service, they should be able to patrol both this system and Earth for further raiders.

Freetown itself might even bait a trap for the Kroggs."

"And with the whole squadron gone there'll be nobody left planetside — if the Kroggs flatten some buildings out of spite we'll put up new ones," James leaned back in his chair. "I'd rather be mobile, honestly, if the Kroggs are buzzing around here causing trouble. Not like we could stop a heavy squadron ourselves, especially if we're tied to the planet."

His eyes met Audrey's and she slowly nodded, "Alright. I'll pass the word along that we're packing up. Captain Jardaw, I believe you've got yourself an escort squadron."

The bear smiled, "I must renew my thanks, then. We'll be ready to put to space in about twenty-eight hours. Is that enough time for you?"

James nodded with a brief glance to Audrey, "Should do nicely. Maybe some of your crew would like to come down to Freetown while you wait. It's really quite pleasant around here."

Standing slowly, Jardaw smiled, "I'll pass the invitation on to my crew, but not to be rude, I'll decline. Warm climates don't tend to agree with me... I think it's genetic."

James began to rise but Jardaw stopped him with a hand, "It's alright, I'll see myself out. Have to get back to *Highlander* and see about repairs... but once again, thank you both. I imagine we'll be well protected with your squadron along."

With a last nod to each of them, Jardaw ducked out the door and lumbered down the Earther-fabricated corridor.

As he left the room Audrey brought her boots up onto the table again and leaned back, unbuttoning one flap of her jacket, "Well, we're about to get a change of scenery then."

James nodded, leaning forward with his chin cradled in the palm of his hand. His eyes strayed to Audrey's boot-bottoms, "Why are your boots on the table?"

She smiled and shrugged, "Seems the right image for a privateer, doesn't it?"

James grinned.

The junior captains of the privateer squadron expressed certain enthusiasm for their new mission when they were called into the briefing room twelve hours later. The tropical paradise they'd enjoyed on Freetown certainly wasn't unpleasant, but they were all spacers at heart. They were itching for more action, especially after having their appetites whetted by the skirmish with the Kroggs.

By the time twenty-eight hours had passed, the Freetown ships were crewed and fully loaded. The entire capital city settlement was being vacated — a central computer would run a shield grid to protect the buildings from weather and any attack, while the orbiting defense batteries which were set to automatic would keep the system safe from just about everything it could've resisted had the squadron still been there.

With all those arrangements safely looked after, James found himself back on the bridge of *Archangel Sword*, tapping his foot on the deckplate as he watched the Earth haulers — lumbering vessels clearly not designed for maneuverability — slide elegantly into their formation. Like all Earther operations, it appeared to him an extraordinarily simple movement, though he knew better. Trying to get luggers into formation was like getting cattle into single file... it took a lot of skill.

Fortunately, Earthers were brilliant ship-handlers and the vessels were in line-ahead formation after only ten minutes, their reactors spinning up to activate energy drive.

"Message coming in from Captain Jardaw, sir," the Signal Officer spoke up as the line of cargo ships formed on *Sword's* plot screen.

James nodded and straightened himself in his chair. He'd been slouching subconsciously, and it'd never do to show that sort of unprofessional behavior... even if he happened to be a privateer, "Put him on."

The Signal Officer complied and the main screen activated.

"The convoy is in formation and ready to enter energy drive, Captain Stanton," Jardaw reported with an austere smile.

"Very good... you guys head on into energy drive and hold at 2,000 pls. We'll accelerate into flux and catch up to you," James recalled his past operations with Earther ships as he spoke, and Jardaw nodded comfortably. Despite different drive technologies, they'd manage a cohesive convoy.

"Certainly."

Jardaw gave a quick nod, then the screen blanked and James slouched back into his chair. His posture wasn't as rigid as it had been in years past — he'd spent too long now as a renegade. But the Earthers probably had a cure for the lower back trouble that would come from slouching...

"*Grendelsbane City* hailing, skipper," the Signal Officer called out again.

James considered straightening up but decided not to.

"Put her on."

Audrey appeared on the screen, "Ready to move out then?"

James nodded, "They'll go to energy drive, we'll enter flux behind them and catch up. All clear on your side?"

She nodded, "Yep, we're good. So I'll talk to you later."

James smiled, "See you then."

They twitched eyebrows at each other, and then the screen blanked once more. James heaved a bit of a sigh — they'd spent so much time together on Freetown he'd almost forgotten what it was like to be alone on his own ship. Now he was about to get a twenty-odd day reminder.

"The Earthers are entering energy drive, skipper."

James watched on the screen as the line of Earther ships accelerated to faster-than-light speeds. They did it smoothly, with the first ship in the line collapsing into a ball of energy, followed by the next three seconds later, then each successive ship following in its own interval.

A well-trained Genesis Battle Squadron would never have done it so well, let alone a convoy of Genesis merchant cruisers.

In less than a minute, the convoy disappeared, and *Highlander* accelerated to follow.

"Send to squadron, let's move out."

Archangel Sword, the most advanced vessel in the privateer force, was the first to accelerate to flux, followed quickly by *Grendelsbane City*. The remaining vessels — the Heavy Cruiser *Torcott City*, the Light Cruiser *New Cashtown*, and the Destroyers *Lagarand*, *Jesuit*, *Forton* and *Vance* — accelerated in close order, forming a diagonal line trailing to port. They reached flux simultaneously, and James grinned as they rushed away from Freetown.

Well we're not too shabby ourselves. Not too shabby at all...

The Kroggs might have agreed with James' thought, in their own alien way. Their force of fourteen Dreadnoughts and a Mothership was sitting just beyond the system, watching the departure through the eyes of a lone corvette. The small ship had avoided detection by blending into the Freetown system's asteroid belt, and now that its reconnaissance task was complete, the Krogg Telepaths controlling it ordered its death — there was no time to recover it anyway. There was a bloody explosion in the belt, leaving the Mothership short one corvette... one that could easily be regrown before the squadron reached its destination.

While the large attack force could overwhelm the pathetic base in this system, there was a far more important target only a few days away. Earth had sent its Home Fleet out to support operations on the Gibraltar front — only ships in need of overhaul were left in the home system.

This was the information the Kroggs had extracted from a human prisoner taken in battle on a planet some eight weeks earlier.

And it was essentially correct.

CHAPTER 5

To Commodore Draco Maximane, former Captain the 74-gun ship of the line *Apollo*, Earth space felt particularly empty. Maximane missed the security of having an entire fleet standing by, ready to react to any threat. Though Earth's fixed defenses were extensive, the fleet was out on the front, and only a handful of ships remained in full fighting trim in the system. That meant the strength of the Earther Navy was almost a month away from Earth, centering its efforts around Gibraltar.

The lion hadn't actually seen any action since the Battle of Genesis, where he'd suffered some dramatic wounds when *Apollo* had been battered by a Krogg Superdreadnought squadron. He'd been caught out in that fight because of corvettes — *Apollo* had been swarmed by about thirty of those small ships, and the Krogg capital ships had pounced in the confusion.

Once Maximane had gotten back to Earth to have his limbs restored, he'd reflected a great deal on the impact of corvettes — they were damned annoying and particularly dangerous tools in the Krogg arsenal, and he'd become determined to find a way to counter them. During his recovery he'd sifted through everything he could find in human historical records of the airplane-fighter craft, and also taken a look at any Larosian information he could access. The conclusions he'd drawn had led him to make a suggestion to the Bureau of Research and Development — the Earthers needed *Carriers*, and *gunboats* to go with them.

After reading so much and completing as thorough an analysis of the Krogg Motherships as possible, he'd come to the conclusion that the best way to counter Krogg corvettes would be for the Earthers to deploy their own light craft in battle. Fleet R&D took his recommendation under advisement, promising to consult him on a decision. Of course, the fact that what Maximane was suggesting had long been a proven element of the Larosian Navy's strategy helped immensely.

So after only a month of evaluating the proposal and studying its viability, it was decided to take older Earther ships that had been held in mothballs for a *very* rainy day and immediately begin converting them to Carriers. Maximane had suggested the concept first, so he was promoted to Commodore, and temporarily seconded to the R&D department to lead the team that would design a Carrier program for the Earther Navy...

From the lion's point of view, he had little business being put in charge of the Carrier program. He didn't really know any more than the rest of the Earther populace on the subject — he'd just made a suggestion based on theory and some histories of human wars. Which, he supposed, did give him a base of knowledge, and that was ultimately why the Admiralty had handed the job to him.

He was determined to do well with it.

As soon as he'd taken on his new role, Maximane had rushed to the fleet mothball yards. Many older ships from that floating graveyard had been pulled by the Navy Board and modernized to compensate for Ursla's losses at Genesis, but many were simply too antiquated to serve as gun-carrying ships against the Kroggs. He'd found two classes of those old ships and ordered conversions on all of them.

The first, larger type of these soon-to-be Carriers was the ninety-year-old *Boadecia*-class. Once the elite First Rates of the fleet, their aged generators were too weak to power the new guns that were now the Navy's standard, and their smaller hulls left little room to install the extra reactors necessary for a 90-gun ship. However, by reducing their ninety guns to thirty and hollowing out flight deck space to accommodate eighty-five small craft, the strains on the refurbished reactors would be far less. Ninety guns required a *lot* more energy than several sets of flight deck doors and some structural reinforcement fields.

Six of the *Boadecias* had been slotted for conversion, in company with nine 70-gun *Diadem*-class ships. The *Diadems* were only sixty years old, but their guns were distinctly underpowered as well. Since seventy guns also drew more power than flight deck doors, Maximane chose the *Diadems* to be Light Carriers supplementing the large *Boadecias*. Outfitted with twenty guns and sixty craft, they would hopefully protect Battle Squadrons against the small, fast Krogg corvettes.

After he'd chosen the vessels for conversion, the Admiralty offered to build twenty-five new Carriers alongside the conventional construction in Naval docks. Receiving the news, Maximane had then teamed with Commander Tor Protus, the famed shipwright, for two weeks of intense discussions that ended with the design for the new *Engadine*-class Carrier. Larger than an *Orion*-type First Rate, each *Engadine* would hold 120 craft and mount thirty-five Second Rate-sized guns. With Earther construction being as efficient as it was, the entire order of *Engadines* was due within fifteen months, and the first vessel was shaking down right now.

In fact, as Maximane pondered all this, he was sitting on its bridge, staring at its two battle plots.

The Earther Provisional Carrier Squadron (temporarily numbered the 901st), was executing maneuvers in the Sol system. Led by *Engadine*, the force had five additional vessels: *Boadecia*, *Godetia* and *Galatea* of the *Boadecia*-class, and *Diadem* and *Monarch* of the *Diadem*-class. The plan was to send the force for orientation and combat trials at Gibraltar within one month, and Maximane fully intended to be at its head.

"Gunboats are in formation and are making their run."

The report came from across *Engadine's* bridge, and Maximane nodded in reply.

The 901st could, at present, put 510 gunboats into space. Each boat carried a single Mark XV cannon — the sort of weapon usually found in 74s — slung under its bow. To charge these massive guns, the pinnace-sized vessels were built with disproportionately large reactors, and with the benefit of their firepower it was predicted that a single boat would be a match for a corvette. In preparation for such an engagement, the squadron's boat crews were thus participating in a week of war-games.

"Enemy squadron launching corvettes," the 'Skywatch' Officer on *Engadine's* bridge reported.

"Our boats are formed?" Maximane looked at the Lieutenant.

The panther nodded, "Yes sir. They'll meet the corvettes half way to target."

Maximane matched the nod and watched the battle plots. *Engadine's* bridge was unique in the fleet — it was equipped both as a Flight Operations Center and as a warship's nerve center. As such it had *two* main battle tanks, the second one exclusively for displaying holo projections of the gunboats in flight. It tracked them now as they accelerated toward the simulated corvettes.

Those corvettes, in reported Krogg style, advanced haphazardly, while the significantly smaller and wholly outnumbered boats moved in twenty-ship formations that resembled giant claws. One such claw stayed back with the Carriers as a combat patrol, just in case any corvettes slipped through.

None did.

This was the third time these boat crews had trained together, and even more in sync than average Earthers, they acted as if they were one entity. Claws of boats sheered off from their greater combined formation every few seconds, and as the simulated corvettes tried a disorganized swarm they were split apart and thoroughly annihilated.

And it only took half the Earther boats to do it.

The other half of the gunboat force kept driving on, quickly reaching the 'Motherships'. The two 74s acting in that role — the only two Earther ships of the line in full fighting trim in Earth space, and both just recently repaired — were rapidly overcome by the simulated heavy fire of the boats' guns.

Maximane watched with some satisfaction. The theories he'd suggested seemed to be panning out quite well. Gunboats offered high maneuverability, independent fire ability, and an abundance of firepower — a combination that ensured they'd be more than ready to deal with everything the Kroggs had shown the Allies so far.

•••

ENS Kite, an 18-gun sloop only recently out of the builders' yards, cruised at a leisurely pace across the Pluto Orbital Plane. Aboard the diminutive ship, Commander Fern Graywisker felt nervous energy coursing through him. This was the young wolf's first cruise as a Commander, and even though he'd only been tasked with picket duty, he was feeling a heightened obligation to perform well.

Graywisker had been promoted to the post a few weeks before, having come back to Sol as First Lieutenant of the 16-gun *Flier*. While that little ship had its drives overhauled and its port broadside rebuilt, he'd been singled out for command of the new *Kite*. He was still feeling a bit awkward about the job... but that would pass. Eventually.

It would have to — in about a month's time, he'd almost certainly be joining the new Carriers and the two 74s now pretending to be Motherships in those war-games, as well as a number of other recently finished or restored ships, in cruising to the front lines. Between now and then, he'd certainly have to become–

"Sir," the Sensor Chief interrupted Graywisker's musings with a frown, "my deep scans are showing a hyper footprint..."

It took a second for the young wolf to process that report — a hyper footprint near *Sol*? The young Commander's brow furrowed, "Confirm that again for me... *hyper*?"

The rating behind the sensor console nodded, "I'm certain sir... it's odd..."

Then the automatically-triggered alarms aboard the sloop began to scream.

"Sir... it's a Krogg force. Fourteen Dreadnoughts... and a *Mothership*!"

Graywisker's eyes widened despite his efforts to control his shock, "What's the range?"

"They're coming out right on top of us!" the Sensor Chief betrayed his lack of his experience with the outburst.

"Energy drive. Back to Mars *now*!" Graywisker's order didn't sound quite as calm as he thought it should have, but given the circumstances he quickly decided that was excusable... and *Kite* lost only a fraction of a second's efficiency due to shock as it hurtled into energy drive.

Even as the first spines spat from the Dreadnoughts, the sloop was reaching the dangerous speed of 400 pls on its way back to Mars.

CHAPTER 6

Maximane was watching the recovery operations when an unexpected vessel turned up in his battle plot. An 18-gun sloop... *Kite*, according to its icon... appeared in the middle of the Earther boat formations, causing chaos as the gunboats swerved to avoid collision.

A frown crossed Maximane's face — no Earther would be so reckless without cause...

"General alert from *Kite*... Krogg force of fourteen Dreadnoughts and a Mothership sighted on the Pluto Orbital Plane... Confirmed, this is not a drill..." *Engadine's* veteran Signal Officer calmly repeated the message as it reached his screen.

Maximane froze. That warning would have also reached the two 74s playing Motherships in his own boat exercise, as well as the Earth and Mars defense stations and the three frigates being tended to in the slips at Io.

"Message from Commodore Peregrine... text only," the Signal Officer continued. "Setting rendezvous at Io for all warships. Join me?"

Maximane cocked an eyebrow. Peregrine was a line officer who'd returned from the front aboard her battered 74, *Gargoyle*. She'd been kind enough to offer both her ship and its fellow *Minotaur* as dummy Motherships for the exercise, but the two 74s could never stop a Krogg force like that alone. Even with the frigates at Io they'd stand little chance...

"Send 'Will join when boats recovered,'" Maximane ordered after a second of thought. "Get the boats in as quick as you can... Boat Officer, how long?"

The Lieutenant in charge of the gunboats looked at the numbers and consulted the Deck Chiefs in each of *Engadine's* six boat bays, "Ninety seconds, sir."

Maximane nodded. Each bay could land five boats at once, a feature which made *Engadine* and others of its class ideal for strike operations. The *Diadems* and *Boadecias* were less capable, as their reconstructed hulls had only two bays each, and they could only take aboard three boats at once...

"All ships to meet at Io as soon as they have their boats. We move independently... we have to be ready for the Mothership."

Commodore Kylie Peregrine was a veteran of the Battle of Genesis, and she'd also been involved in a few scuffles with a Battle Squadron since that time. Those experiences had taught her how to deal with Kroggs... and had convinced her that, wherever possible, it was a good idea to avoid odds as bad as these.

Her preference, then, would have been to just collect her small force and make a run for it. But the particulars of this situation forbade such action; abandoning Earth was hardly an option.

So she'd have to make do with her two 74s, two 38-gun frigates, one 32, and four sloops. Nine vessels that were altogether no match for those Dreadnoughts, let alone the Mothership.

The one edge she did have working for her was the presence of the 901ˢᵗ Carrier Squadron — she was extremely impressed with the Carriers. They might offer an advantage...

The mixed squadron of Earther warships, all that was available in a system so far from the front lines, left their slips and assembled within two minutes. Having no better option, Peregrine led them out of Io's orbit and formed them into a loose line ahead.

Standing at *Engadine's* battle plot, Maximane's eyes narrowed. Kylie Peregrine wasn't waiting — it seemed she was hoping to knock the Kroggs off balance before they realized just how substantial an advantage they had.

The last boats had just hit the deck, the doors were closing, and he could move as soon as they shut. Maximane turned quickly to *Engadine's* Master as the lights in the boat plot flashed green and the ship was secured for maneuver, "Energy drive, right now. Head straight for an intercept with the Kroggs. Squadron to follow."

With a single nod from the Master, *Engadine* dropped into energy drive, followed seconds later by *Monarch* as that converted Carrier landed the last of its boats. The rest of the Carriers continued their recovery operations.

Gargoyle and *Minotaur* led the Earther attack, with the frigates *Cambridge*, *Caesar* and *Daffodil* and the sloops *Kite*, *Flier*, *Dasher* and *Orca* bringing up the rear. With their usual precision, the Earther ships emerged from energy drive with guns already running out of their ports.

The Kroggs, having been in-system for over five minutes, were expecting just such an attack, and were ready to counter. Twelve of their smaller Dreadnoughts met the defenders head-on, spines lashing out as soon as the Earthers turned back into matter. Volleys of canister were loosed from Earther broadsides in quick reply, the entire squadron trying to deflect the spines with clouds of destructive energy.

As sensor screens clouded with the fog of canister energy, Commodore Peregrine rolled her squadron to present its second line of broadsides. Gun Captains focused the next salvo on the only Dreadnought not eclipsed by the canister on their scopes, and concentrated energy shot was fired. As the mixed squadron sheered away to avoid further spines, that unfortunate Dreadnought released a horrid telepathic shriek and died in a fountain of blood.

But the rest of the Krogg formation still came on strong, and spines continued to race from its leading ships. One caught *Gargoyle* in the port side; the 74's shields took most of the impact, but the spattering of super-powerful acid that reached the hull burned into its power relays and overloaded its internal coolant system. In a twist of bad fortune, one of the ship's reactors had just begun to cycle up to charge a broadside, and with the excess heat the system overloaded.

The resulting explosion blew out most of the power relays on the ship, and as one went on the bridge, it killed three officers, including the Captain. Kylie Peregrine turned from her plot to catch one of the falling officers just as a shower of shrapnel leapt out, and she landed hard on the deck as both of her legs were quite literally sliced out from under her. The ship's First Lieutenant roared to the Master, "Hard to starboard, get us out of the way!"

Squadron command was deferred immediately to the Captain of *Minotaur*, and *Gargoyle* limped away from the fight as medics tended the Commodore.

Maximane ground his jaw as he watched the exchange of fire in *Engadine's* battle plot, and he let out a frustrated sigh as he saw Kylie Peregrine's pennant begin to flash over the icon of her wounded ship. She was out of the fight, then — a very lucky shot had sparked an unfortunate chain reaction in the freshly refitted *Gargoyle*.

The situation wasn't looking too promising — *Engadine* was heading for the Krogg force with *Monarch* close behind, but would they really make a difference...

"Sir, have a look... the Mothership's breaking formation..."

The report of the Second Lieutenant compelled Maximane to shift his attention. Sure enough, the Mothership and two of the larger Dreadnoughts were slipping by the defenders, heading for Jupiter.

A Mothership would have a tough time completely overwhelming the orbital defenses of Earth or Mars, but of the Sol system's 230 shipyards, only seventy resided in the essentially safe orbits of those two planets. Jupiter and the asteroid belt, relatively devoid of heavy orbital forts, held most of the rest.

And the Mothership was evidently aware of that vulnerability.

Maximane scowled at the plot, wondering just how the Kroggs could have learned of that particular defensive weakness without close scans... The enemy clearly had the information edge in this little encounter.

But did they know about *Engadine* and the Carriers? Well, whether they did or didn't, they were moving in on Jupiter at low hyper speed, and he'd have to stop them.

Krogg in-system hyper being less precise than energy drive, they wouldn't be in range of Io for seven minutes... *Engadine* could reverse course and be there in two.

"Adjust course, let's head to Io. *Monarch* and *Diadem* to join us, the *Boadecias* to join the squadron in defense of the Pluto Orbital Plane," Maximane gave the orders as he turned and nodded to his Boat Officer. "Get your crews ready for launch, Lieutenant Ramsay."

The Carriers might be new to war, but Maximane had faith in them nonetheless. A Mothership could launch anywhere between 600 and 700 corvettes at a time, depending on how many were aboard. Jupiter, like all installations, had a battery of Mark XVIII heavy guns, as well as a point-defense network of medium carronades. Those would be able to take care of some of the corvettes, and the 240 boats Maximane's half of the Carrier Group would launch should be able to handle the rest...

It wasn't a conventional plan, but he didn't have any alternatives right now.

The two Dreadnoughts were another matter... one thing that Maximane had not intended when he'd designed his Carriers was to have them go gun-to-gun with enemy ships. *Engadine* could outgun any frigate, but a capital ship was too much for even the Carrier's heavy guns.

"Boats from *Monarch* and *Diadem* should focus their initial strikes on the Dreadnoughts. We'll keep the corvettes busy. Let Jupiter know they should watch their targets — we'll be deploying boats."

Maximane laced his fingers and held his hands behind his back, then watched in the battle plot as *Engadine* headed back towards Jupiter. The Krogg Dreadnoughts and Mothership seemed to realize they were being pursued... Maximane's best hope was that they expected the vessels intercepting them to be members of the traditional classes dictated by their sizes. Surely, they couldn't be expecting Carriers — as far as they could see, three 90s, two 74s and a ship large enough to be a 200 were coming for them.

As Io appeared under *Engadine* and *Monarch*'s hulls, Maximane's plot showed an abrupt increase in the aliens' speed.

"They're taking a big hyper risk... ETA thirty *seconds* sir..."

The Commodore nodded slowly as he watched the Kroggs' approach — he'd have to wait for them to close range before he launched his boats...

"Bring us around behind the moon, Master. Signal to *Monarch* to keep company with us."

His two Carriers began to shift their orbits, hoping to disappear from Krogg sensors as they hid in Io's grav shear. Indeed, as the Krogg detached force ran down on the moon, it appeared that the other Carriers — seemingly three 90-gun ships — made no move to intercept the attackers. Perhaps the Kroggs were encouraged by that shortsightedness... and as far as they could tell, only one 70 was giving chase from the rear.

Well, hopefully they wouldn't see a single 70 as a major threat — they would envision themselves ravaging Jupiter's local orbital yards and falling upon whatever Earther ships presented themselves.

With that goal guiding its actions, the great eye that was the Krogg Mothership began to open, the night-black eyelid peeling back to reveal 700 corvettes as they launched.

On *Engadine's* bridge, Maximane watched with his jaw set. Here came the big test…

"*Engadine, Monarch,* launch all boats."

Between them, Maximane's two Carriers put 180 gunboats into space, and Io base added its newly delivered squadron of twenty of the craft as well. The Carriers' boats hurtled around Io in ten large claw formations, aiming directly at the Mothership as they sprinted through space at near-light speed. The Io-based flight stayed back from this large wave, forming its own claw and holding position as a defensive reserve around the moon.

Krogg corvettes were being spat from the Mothership as these strange Earther vessels appeared, but as the alien small craft unraveled themselves and surged ahead they scarcely paused to consider their new opposition. Though these Earther ships were far larger than Larosian fighters, they were still much smaller than corvettes, and they were dramatically outnumbered, 700 to 200.

Maximane felt his breath catch as he watched the two clouds of small craft close with each other in the boat plot, and everyone on the bridge of *Engadine* shared his apprehension.

"Closing to engagement range in five seconds."

Maximane's eyes were fixed on the markers representing his boats as they closed to attack range…

And then the Kroggs were abruptly introduced to Earther gunboats. Fully-charged Mark XV Earther cannon began to fire in staggered salvos, hurtling from the formed boat claws into the tight mass of corvettes. Each gun required nineteen seconds to recharge so only ten boats in a squadron fired at one time, allowing for a continuous stream of fire to pour from the formations.

The assault was unlike anything the corvettes could have expected; designed as gunships to shoot down swarms of light Larosian fighters, they had no protection against capital ship-powered shot… their formation rapidly tore apart in a gruesome wake of gore and telepathic screams.

"Break by Gun Squadron and engage," Maximane looked through the plot at the Boat Officer as the latter passed those orders to the captains of the gunboats. In the holo tank, icons immediately displayed a reaction to the commands, and the Earther attack ships slashed into the Krogg hordes.

Apprehension again tugged at Maximane as the corvettes lashed out at this offensive move, but the Krogg small craft were doing virtually no damage to their opponents. Again the boats benefited from the fast-tracking, low-intensity weapons the Kroggs had developed for anti-Larosian work — the corvettes couldn't concentrate enough energy fire on any one boat at a time to crack its sturdy shield. Only six of the Earther craft were destroyed by spine shots, while over 100 Krogg ships had been eliminated.

Things, then, were going well. And as Maximane let out a long breath he realized they were about to get even better...

Diadem appeared on the flank of the Krogg force, opening launch bay doors as soon as it emerged from energy drive. Just a moment later, sixty fresh boats lashed outward, targeting the Krogg capital ships. Simultaneously, *Monarch's* boats detached themselves from their fight with the corvettes, and unopposed by small craft, both flight groups fell upon the nearest Dreadnought.

So here would be another test of theory — Maximane ground his jaw as the two boat groups converged on the Krogg ships. Surely these aliens were used to anti-fighter work... How would his small craft fare...?

Quite well, in fact.

Half the boat plot swelled to display the action in every detail, and as Maximane watched silently, the Dreadnought's weapons either missed the boats, or bounced off shields built to be more robust than their Larosian counterparts' models.

Neuro pulses, the traditional anti-fighter weapons on Krogg ships, glanced off the boats without inflicting significant damage. Only prolonged contact with a boat's shields proved harmful, but the neuro burst emitters pivoted in their mounts too quickly, and couldn't keep in contact with the maneuvering Earther small craft. Three boats took damage from the glancing strikes, but none were destroyed.

All that war-gaming was paying off.

As the claw formations got themselves into point-blank range, firepower equivalent to both broadsides of a 74 pounded the Krogg Dreadnought. With fire coming from all sides, the ship was given no avenue of escape, and in a scant moment its hull collapsed in the withering maelstrom. The second Dreadnought turned to engage the boats, but the scenario repeated itself. Both escorts crumpled under the encompassing fire, and the 120 gunboats of *Monarch* and *Diadem* turned on the corvettes now caught in the fire of both Io and *Engadine's* forces.

Two additional boats had been lost in that fight, as compared to 130 additional corvettes. Unlike Earthers, the Kroggs were not adapting to the unexpected circumstances — the mindless drones commanding the corvettes were attempting to return to their original mission against Io's repair and building slips. The chaos caused within their ranks by the attack of the boats precluded any effective counter-orders, so ignoring the Earther small craft, the corvettes tried to run straight in to attack the base and its sixty shipyards.

While mounting only twenty guns, Io battery's of Mark XVIII's were, when set to canister, more than capable of driving back this smaller disorganized group of Kroggs. When combined with the carronades and the defensive fire of *Engadine's* and *Monarch's* broadsides, these guns shattered any corvettes that reached the moon long before they were in range to inflict harm of their own. What few survived were caught in the open, proving easy prey for the 232 boats that weaved among them.

With the corvette attack beaten, Io's guns turned on the Mothership. The huge vessel was preparing to abandon its corvettes and beat a hasty retreat when the shot of the moon's battery first slammed into it. A number of boat groups turned on it as well, and *Diadem* closed to engage with guns. The Mothership, overwhelmed, exploded in a bloody flurry.

Draco Maximane, with his concept of boat warfare more than adequately proven, took a deep breath and then turned to the Boat Officer, "Get the boats back. Master, mark a course for the fight on the plane."

Out on the Pluto Orbital Plane, the other three Earther Carriers arrived on the scene just in time to catch the open flanks of ten Krogg Dreadnoughts. *Boadecia*, *Godetia*, and *Galatea* released 270 boats into space as those Krogg ships dove after the remnants of the Earther mixed squadron, and the alien capital ships weren't ready for the interruption. Indeed, all they seemed to see was the plight of the conventional Earther force: *Gargoyle* was dead in space, its drives crippled but its guns still dealing a great deal of damage, while *Minotaur* and the three frigates, though continuing to move rapidly and strike back at the attackers, were slowly absorbing punishment as well.

The Earther sloops on the scene tried to shoot down as many of the volleys of spines launched against *Gargoyle* as they could, though *Flier* itself was now heavily damaged.

Aboard *Kite*, Commander Graywisker was feeling a certain strain — he grasped the side of his battle plot to hold himself upright as his little sloop heeled in various directions and destroyed volley after volley of spines. He was pleased that the small ship wasn't suffering a great deal of damage, but he didn't know just how long he could keep his eighteen guns in action under this withering fire...

Then the boats hit the Kroggs.

As had been the case with the Mothership escorts, confusion broke out at the arrival of what could only be compared to Larosian fighters. Neuro-electric blasts grazed off the boats, spines proving too slow to hit them, and as capital ship-sized energy shot slammed from the small craft formations, the tide of the battle turned.

In the next five minutes, the boats of the three Carriers, in combination with *Minotaur* and the frigates, pinned the Krogg capital ships in what had been open space. The aliens were shocked by their enemy's new tool, and the large ships began to crumple under intense fire.

Nine Dreadnoughts were destroyed by the time *Engadine, Diadem* and *Monarch* were able to arrive on the scene with boats ready for re-launch, but as Maximane turned from his battle plot to his boat plot to supervise a new launch, his First Lieutenant stopped him, "Sir, it's running!"

Maximane looked back to the holo tank and, as he watched, the last Dreadnought, sheltering itself in the wreckage of its dead fellows, managed to surge through a gap between *Boadecia* and *Galatea's* Gun Squadrons.

Then before the frigates could surge ahead and get their broadsides into its drives, the ship accelerated off into hyper.

"Damn..." the word escaped under Maximane's breath as his head filled with three potential problems.

First, that ship had both located Earth and seen how open the system would be to heavier attack. Second, it knew about Carriers and gunboats, essentially removing any of the surprise advantage from their introduction. Third...

Well, alright. There were just two problems — but between them they were more than important enough to warrant his response. They'd have to hunt down that Dreadnought. None of his ships had been expecting a cruise, but they were supplied for one in case of emergency. This qualified.

Examining his battle plot, Maximane determined which ships were fit to join *Engadine*... "Make to Admiralty: 'Pursuing Krogg Dreadnought in order to prevent betrayal of Sol location and Carrier existence. Following ships accompanying: *Engadine, Monarch, Diadem, Boadecia, Godetia, Galatea, Minotaur, Caesar, Cambridge, Daffodil, Kite, Orca, Dasher.* Expect intercept within a day.' Send it."

The message shot through energy comm to Admiralty House in London, and the listed ships dropped into energy drive to pursue the Krogg survivor.

CHAPTER 7

Harbinger Bishop was still the flagship of the 444ᵗʰ Allied Flying Squadron — a force happily dubbed 'Pat's Pirates' by the officers and crews of its ships. This formation seldom saw a quiet and uneventful cruise, as ArcBrigadier Patrick Conroy's ability to locate Kroggs seemed almost clairvoyant at times.

Of course, when he did locate them, they usually outnumbered him at least three-to-one.

Despite this tradition of finding the enemy and being badly outnumbered, the 444ᵗʰ had lost only one ship in the past seven months, and almost the entire crew of that ship had been saved. Pat was immensely proud of the squadron, and he was completely confident in its abilities.

The Pirates had departed from Gibraltar on their flank-scouting mission eight days earlier, and they were now some ways from that new base. Pat's instincts were telling him the Kroggs were hiding out here, on the far right of the Allied front lines, and actually 'behind' Gibraltar relative to Genesis. His hunch didn't seem beyond the realm of possibility, and he had to admit a certain anxiety when it came to thinking about what he might find.

Still, the presence of the 444ᵗʰ was more than enough security to compensate for that concern. As an added bonus, *Bishop* had taken aboard a squad of Earther marines under an old friend, Sergeant Major Lupus, in case planetside scouting missions were called for. For some reason, Pat always felt a little better with Earthers around... and Lupus was a special Earther. Almost two years earlier he'd been instrumental in keeping Sarah alive at the Antarctic Plain.

"Ready to drop from flux, sir," one of the officers on *Bishop's* bridge said softly.

Pat shook himself out of his pondering and nodded, "Which system?"

"That binary one with the strange magnetic field," the Sensor Officer reported as Pat turned to him.

"The one our sensors couldn't penetrate?" Pat asked with a cocked eyebrow.

The chief nodded.

Well this would be interesting. They'd been cruising out on the flank for all this time, checking occasional systems that looked suitable for hiding. Any system with an odd grav or magnetic field, or for that matter an abnormal asteroid belt, could potentially hide a Krogg base. As such they were examining anything they found that happened to be suspicious. Granted, they were so far out from Gibraltar that logic deemed it unlikely the Kroggs would bother to commit to building a base, but prudence was still important.

There was a bit of a war on, after all.

Pat leaned back in his chair and ground his jaw, "Right, let's do this carefully now. All ships to action stations, we'll have to be ready if we find something."

The orders generated little tension — the veteran crews of the 444th were accustomed to action. They'd faced everything up to and including a Mothership — albeit with well-timed Earther help now and then — so there wasn't much the Kroggs could throw their way that wouldn't bounce off or that they couldn't avoid.

"All ships decelerating, sir," the Sensor Officer continued reporting as the ArcColonels of the squadron maneuvered their ships towards the system in question. "We're entering system… running deep scans. Picking up…"

The man stopped suddenly.

Pat frowned and turned to the officer… the ArcLieutenant was pale. Pale as a ghost.

"Report," Pat's tone was firm.

The officer swallowed hard, "Nineteen Motherships, over 200 Dreadnoughts and 400 Destroyers…"

A hush fell over the bridge.

You could've heard a pin drop.

Pat sat frozen in his chair. So he'd been right then — the Kroggs were out here. Lots of them. And they were preparing for a flank attack. A big one. *Damn.*

A rush of panic surged through him, his confidence melting in a split second. This was the sort of attack fleet that could roll up the entire front, or just go on and wipe out Genesis and Sol. And it went without saying that the Pirates were entirely outmatched.

Gods wept, they had to get the word out…

"All ships, reverse course right now! Charge flux drives!" Pat roared the orders at a stunned bridge, and the crew, veteran as they were, responded with near-Earther speed.

"Gods! Dreadnoughts right here now, sir! Twelve of them… incoming fire!"

The ships of the 444th had charged their armor when they decelerated, but Battlecruisers were no match for Dreadnoughts. The Pirates' success had always been derived from forcing Kroggs to fight on Pat's terms — the Irishman was expert at using Krogg weaknesses against them. But this time the Pirates had put their heads right on the block just as a rather large axe was falling…

And two Battlecruisers blossomed into mighty fireballs as their armor buckled under the massive onslaught.

"Return fire! Evasive maneuvers! All ships break into divisions and get the bloody hell out of here!" *Harbinger Bishop* swerved hard as Pat barked the next set of orders. The Battlecruisers began to pair off into their squadron divisions, but it all seemed hopeless.

Paladin Saint fell in alongside *Bishop* just in time to absorb a salvo of forty spines meant for the flagship. A veteran of the days when Sarah had commanded the squadron, *Saint* shattered in a bright flame.

Pat drove his big fist into the arm of his chair with such intensity that the chair arm flew off as he connected, leaving his hand smarting and bloody from a gash. He grunted.

Three more Battlecruisers were shredded just as *Saint* had been, and then from somewhere Krogg corvettes arrived and got in amongst the Genesis ships. A Mothership had closed range and launched its fleet of small attack ships, and now they swarmed around the disorganized and virtually helpless survivors of the 444th. Another four of the veteran ships burst into silent fireballs... leaving just *Bishop* and *Cardinal Herald*.

Flux drives had recharged by now — what seemed an eternity to Pat had actually been only thirty seconds. *Herald* accelerated safely, just avoiding a massive salvo directed towards it.

Bishop was less fortunate.

A spine slashed through the armor protecting the Battlecruiser's engines and inflicted crippling damage. Despite the grievous wound, *Bishop* managed to accelerate sluggishly into flux, but as the ship settled into its usual cruising pace of 24.5 cee, it was racked by tremors.

"Damage?" Pat gritted his teeth to contain his frustration as one of his bridge spacers got him some bandages for his hand.

"Engineering reports the drives are heavily damaged... they say we're going to lose flux very soon... any minute."

Pat ground his jaw. To have flux cut out suddenly would mean the crew would be killed by the massive deceleration.

"Find a system we can decelerate into. Are we being followed?"

The Sensor Officer paused to consult his panel, then nodded, "At least fifteen Dreadnoughts."

The Kroggs don't want us to get word out...

Pat ground his jaw and came out of his chair, narrowing his eyes at the main plot screen at the front of his bridge. *Cardinal Herald* was intact — they could get away, warn Gibraltar... *Bishop* would stay and try to slow down a squadron of Krogg capital ships.

Well as deaths go it's pretty noble... of course, I wanted to make it to at least 100 before I made a concession like that. So much for the porch and rocking chair at the retirement home...

Pat frowned against the very badly timed burst of inner wit and turned to his Comm Officer, "Signal *Herald* to run straight for Gibraltar, alert the fleet. We'll try to draw heat off them. Helm, decelerate into the next system."

A deathly calm settled over the bridge as the realization began to spread that this was going to be *Bishop's* last action. So this was what the certainty of death was like... they'd never really contemplated it before, but now it seemed painfully straightforward.

"Engineering, can you get the drives back online?" Pat asked in a subdued tone, returning to his seat.

There was a pause as the engineer on the bridge consulted teams in the wrecked engine deck, "We can. Give us two hours and we can give you 14 cee."

Pat cocked an eyebrow, "Our regular drives are alright?"

"Yes sir."

"Fine, we'll make a fight of it. Decelerate, maintain battle ready."

Cardinal Herald sped away at 26 cee... and ran head first into a group of Krogg Destroyers that had been sent out on picket duty. There were only three of the small ships, and they'd probably been hiding in nearby systems in case a force like Pat's came along. While normally they'd pose no problem to the 444th they qualified as a significant threat to the lone *Herald*, and to make matters worse they didn't attack in any conventional manner.

In flux, a Genesis warship was fragile beyond reason — any attack made on it could only be avoided at such high speed. The Destroyers used this to their advantage, and came out of hyper just in front of the running human ship.

Instead of trying to fire, they simply maneuvered directly into its flight path, then accelerated before the Battlecruiser's ArcColonel could adjust course. Deeming the human ship's destruction worth their sacrifice, the three Destroyers rammed *Herald*, and in the collision, all four vessels were duly disintegrated.

Only *Bishop* remained of the 444th.

"Sir... I think they just got *Herald*," *Bishop's* Sensor Officer offered a grim scowl.

Pat turned quickly to the man, and instinctively raised his bandaged fist to drive it into something... but then thought better of it.

"Fine, it's up to us then. We've done cat-and-mouse before."

"Decelerating," the Helm Officer's report followed on the heels of Pat's comment.

"System has four planets... two of them habitable. No asteroid belt..." the Sensor Officer's voice was not cheerful.

Like trying to play hide-and-seek in an open field. Bloody great... Pat silenced his mind.

"Head for the nearest habitable planet; squeeze out every bit of speed you can."

Bishop put on a great deal of normal-space speed despite its damaged state, and as it neared the chosen planet, Pat grew hopeful again.

Then the Krogg Dreadnoughts came out of hyper.

There were ten — what a turn of luck, only *ten* now — of the Krogg behemoths and they'd come much deeper into the system than was usually recommended before exiting hyper. They entered normal space well within weapons range of the Battlecruiser.

Bishop's missile tubes fountained counter-missiles and its laser turrets activated for point defense, but the little Battlecruiser had no hope. For every counter-missile deployed, fifty spines were rushing in.

"Download the log to all our message drones and launch! Hurry, dammit!" Pat came to his feet as he barked the orders, and then the first spines slashed in angrily.

As *Bishop* bucked, six long-range flux drones spilled from its tubes. They were hidden amongst the mass of counter-missiles, but the Kroggs still noticed the distinct drive signatures. Neuro-energy bursts rapidly destroyed four of the message carriers, but two made it to flux. Pat hoped one would reach Gibraltar...

Bishop bucked again, and fourteen spines passed through the ship's hull. The veteran Battlecruiser, a ship that had seen so much action in its life, seemed unwilling to die.

At least not until it let its crew off.

"All hands, abandon ship. Head for that planet."

As he gave the orders, Pat realized over half his crew was probably already dead, but the rest had to be responding immediately. They'd take last looks at their ship and their comrades, then go running for the nearest life pods. Pat stood on the shaking bridge and watched his command crew go.

"Goodbye old girl," his hand touched the back of his chair.

It was a sentimental moment — he'd been through a lot with this ship. Starting back when–

Really not the time to reminisce, you imbecile!

Pat blinked at the mental kick, and with a last longing look he sprinted from the bridge.

He slid to a halt as the corridor beyond the bridge bucked; all the pods on this deck had been launched.

He turned and sprinted down the corridor — he might have time to find another one.

Harbinger Bishop, flagship of the 444th Flying Squadron, took almost 100 spines before succumbing to the punishment. Having vented all its pods, the valiant old Battlecruiser finally rolled and let its reactors go critical.

Anyone left aboard met a swift end.

CHAPTER 8

Sarah's patience this morning wasn't exactly limitless. She was pacing the flight deck of *Pope Joseph Barron* waiting for a pinnace that was already a few minutes late, and stockpiling frustration at a rate that would let her fill a warehouse with it, if she so wished...

To make matters worse, the unsettling cloud of concern that had been hanging persistently around her head since Pat's departure was still there, seemingly omnipresent just now, and she was having the damnedest time trying to get herself past it.

Why am I letting a pinnace frustrate me? And what's behind this bad feeling about Pat's mission? Gods, I need to get a handle on this agitation...

Fatigue might have something to do with her problem. Soon she could stop worrying about fleet logistics, thank Gods, and so she'd be able to get more rest. The pinnace she was waiting for was carrying the solution to her workload and delegation problems... though it was also probably carrying the catalyst to other, albeit *better* ones.

The sound of the pinnace in question gliding into the bay's far end finally reached Sarah's ears, and she came to a stop on the deck as she watched the small craft crawl through the air in search of a landing pad. With no ceremony at all, the ship dropped smoothly from its hover to land firmly on the deck, its weight taken by its landing skids. The counter-grav fields installed along the deck grabbed it as it came down, assuring a soft stop. They then taxied it over to its parking slot.

Coming to a dead stop, the pinnace began to hiss as it vented coolant, and Sarah was abruptly shrouded in thick mist. She tried to wave it from in front of her, but this pinnace seemingly hadn't been in a repair dock for a while and was also now shrouded in gray. She couldn't see a thing...

By this time Graham Manchester, who had also been trying vainly to bat the gray mist out of his way with his hand, managed to step clear of the fog.

But he was going the wrong way.

"Graham! Over here!" Sarah called to her younger brother and waved her arms broadly just as the hissing stopped and the deck began to clear.

Turning at the call, Graham was treated to the somewhat absurd sight of his sister trying to signal him down with broadly-flapping arms. She almost looked like a bird... Then she realized she'd been spotted — by everyone on the deck — and stopped.

Graham grinned and trotted over, offering a hug as he stopped in front of her. Sarah accepted the embrace without trepidation, even in front of the eyes of the deck crew. She was too glad to have Graham here to be stoic just now...

Which seemed odd to her, because she would have expected more self-control. Oh well...

"Sarah, Sarah, Sarah!" Graham released his sister after a second. "How have you been keeping? I heard about Trelest Star. Hot work, they told me..."

Sarah shook her head, "I really don't need to retell war stories right now, Graham. Come on, tell me about Genesis. I've been away for so long..."

Twenty minutes later Graham collapsed back into the armchair in his sister's flag cabin, "Gods, this place is a bit of a disaster."

He swirled a glass of ice water in his hand, examining the ArcGeneral's large cabin. Sarah had once been scrupulous about her housekeeping — many a time Graham had been compelled to make his bed at the threat of his elder sister's formidable wrath — but his cabin was markedly neater than this one.

And that was setting a rather low bar for cleanliness.

There were pads and stacks of papers and books all over, along with empty water and juice bottles, a couple of plates with the remains of food on them... the place was a mess.

"Logistics. I don't have time to worry about how I live just now..." Sarah let out a long sigh after she spoke, then brushed a half dozen pads off her couch and dropped onto it. "I'm certainly going to be glad to hand this chaos to you."

Graham cocked an eyebrow and started to wish there was something older and stronger than fresh water in his glass, "I look forward to it."

A small, tired smile crossed Sarah's face, "I suppose this isn't a great advert for the job. Really though, it shouldn't be too bad if you're not trying to run the whole fleet's campaign at the same time."

"Ah, well since I'm no line officer then, I'll keep myself occupied in *Gibraltar Two*, take care of this and spend most of my time dining in pleasant company."

Sarah almost failed to register the comment as she laid her head against the headrest and closed her eyes. Of course Graham was going to be setting up in *Gibraltar Two* once the station showed up...

Dining, though? Sarah cocked an eyebrow before she managed to open her eyes... yep, she definitely needed a bit more sleep.

"You don't 'dine' unless you're..." Sarah's cocked eyebrow collapsed into a frown. "Graham, it's wartime. I highly recommend avoiding relationships, otherwise you'll end up a basket case if something happens..."

Despite her fatigue, her mind was prudent enough to delete 'like me' from any part of that sentence.

Graham smiled and shrugged, "Relationship isn't the word for it, I just started having dinner now and then with Gillian Hodge back when we were both posted to *Genesis One*. You know, she's extremely refined for a marine..."

Sarah frowned, "*Gillian?*"

Hodge was the Commandant of the Genesis Marine Corps — the senior field commander whose main task in the past eight months had been keeping her troops ready to counter a Church insurgency on Genesis. Harvey Bingham's government had made certain she never had to do so, and Liz must have moved Hodge up to Gibraltar in hopes of promoting the deployment of human marines during the campaign...

But what the *hell* was she doing dining with Graham?

"There's no way she'd make time for you — you're lying," Sarah almost scowled at her little brother, but he arched his eyebrows and shrugged.

"I asked nicely and she wasn't all that disinterested. Believe it or not, Sarah, I'm not 'little brother' in every woman's eyes!" Graham's grin twitched into a smile.

Sarah harrumphed and let her head fall back against the headrest again, "You brainwashed her. Admit it."

Graham chuckled and took a long drink of water, "Believe what you will. I'm not actually that undesirable, even to a woman as noticeable as Gillian."

With a sisterly glare, Sarah rocked her head side to side against the headrest, "You're so immature."

The younger brother frowned at the comment, "That from the woman who didn't see true love staring her in the face, even after he saved your life a number of times. Want me to run a tally?"

Sarah opened her mouth to say something, then thought better of it. He had her with that one — she was in love with only one man, and had only ever really been in love with one man. Maybe shopping around was just normal for some people, Graham being one of them...

"So," she changed the subject for more reasons than Graham knew, "when's *Gibraltar Two* arriving?"

Hiding a triumphant smile behind his glass, Graham frowned, "Well from what Liz told me, the convoy left Earth a couple of weeks ago. They'll be cruising smooth, I expect, so it shouldn't be too long now..."

CHAPTER 9

Highlander turned hard to starboard and let lose its port broadside, the shot lancing out viciously and catching four Krogg Destroyers as they attempted to close the range. Two of the ships swung away in time to avoid the heavy onslaught, but two more were too slow in their bid to slide out of its path. The shot ruptured their hulls in a flurry of blood and gore.

The surviving alien attackers from that group fled back to their consorts — eight more Krogg Destroyers — and then the whole group turned back toward the Earther convoy. Garvin Jardaw ground his jaw as he watched the maneuvers in his plot aboard *Highlander*. They were just four hours outside Genesis, and only minutes from the detection range of the system's outer globe of pickets.

How exactly had these Destroyers gotten into position to mount a raid like this? This space should have been safe...

The Kroggs *had* to have a forward base nearby.

Jardaw contained a deep sigh as that thought passed again through his mind. The convoy had already faced other Krogg raids on the way to Genesis — usually of three Destroyers only, but raids nonetheless. Such long-range strikes simply couldn't be coming from Krogg space on the far side of the known frontiers...

Where the ships were coming from was a moot issue for the convoy right now, however; the first priority was to weather this little scuffle.

Jardaw's eyes narrowed at his battle plot as ten Krogg Destroyers came at *Highlander* in a single huddled mass. They plainly sought to overwhelm the wounded 64 and they'd only need to get to the ship's starboard side to find its weakness. The convoy, still in energy drive, could be caught later...

A volley of advanced missiles from *Grendelsbane City* spoiled the alien effort. With *New Cashtown* and *Vance* in a close line abreast, Audrey DeBrooke's ship dove at the Kroggs from above. Simultaneously, James Stanton appeared below them with the rest of the Freetown force, and as Jardaw watched in the plot, missiles lashed out from each of the privateers' bows.

The range was absurdly close — the humans had used a few Earther bits of stealth kit retrofitted to their existing systems to allow for such close maneuvering. Their missiles were flying at nearly light speed — they'd been made almost as effective as Earther energy shot. Six of the Krogg ships vanished immediately in the crossfire, and the rest had the sense to peel off and jump to hyper before they shared their companions' fate.

Jardaw released the sigh he'd been holding and offered a nod to his First Lieutenant, noting silently to himself that the trade routes simply weren't safe any longer — this was the seventh attack they'd been subject to since leaving Freetown. With this much activity in the space between Genesis and Freetown perhaps it was time to strengthen the Home Fleet again; a raid on Earth wasn't inconceivable.

James sat quietly on *Archangel Sword's* bridge as the ship decelerated from flux into Genesis just ahead of the first hauler in the convoy. He'd left this system on good terms the last time — he'd just helped the Earthers defend it against the Kroggs. But human memories could be short, and he still felt uneasy about being in the same space as so many of his former comrades.

The Genesis Navy seemed to tolerate his privateer nature when an Earther Fleet was in system, but there weren't many Earthers around just now... and the last time he'd met with Liz Hastings, James hadn't much enjoyed the encounter.

As a picket cruiser approached the convoy to offer the standard query, James found himself tensing — he really didn't want to be the one answering for this Earther group, even though he was wearing an Earther pennant.

Highlander saved him the trouble, erupting from energy drive just ahead of *Sword* and coming between the two human ships.

"They're querying *Highlander*, sir," James' Signal Officer reported with a noticeable sigh of relief. "Captain Jardaw just called us part of his escort force... we've got permission to enter the system."

James nodded evenly in reply, keeping his feelings on the matter to himself, "Master, bring us into line behind *Highlander*. Signals, order the squadron to follow."

The convoy slowly shook itself into order and began to cruise in-system. The busy space surrounding the haulers and their escorts seemed to take no notice of them — there was too much else going on, what with war-games, maneuvers, shakedown cruises, and resource transports... Genesis was busier than James had ever seen it.

It was still a front line base in an intergalactic war, so that probably made sense. When Gibraltar took over most of that role, Genesis would likely settle down as Earth had.

If this convoy got through, that was.

James and Audrey stayed close to each other as they walked through the busy corridors of *Genesis One*, the premier Genesis orbital defense station. Jardaw was walking with them, conscious of their anxiousness and silently using his polar bear mass to shield them from any glares sent their way.

In the months since the Battle of Genesis, he'd heard that the humans of the Genesis Fleet had lost their tolerance for the privateers of Freetown — unkind words were apparently the only ones spoken whenever the renegades came up in conversation, rare though that was. They were shirkers, not doing their part, not helping fight the Kroggs or restructure Genesis... Jardaw found it interesting how quickly humans could turn on those who had once been their very own. It was another of those human characteristics that simply didn't fit the Earther mindset.

In any case, he wasn't about to let such negativity overwhelm the people who had done so much to get *Highlander* this far. And he was a polar bear — even as he crouched to pass through corridors, he was big enough to have a quieting effect on those who would be less than courteous.

When the trio of Earther-uniformed Captains reached the Administrator's Office after a few minutes, Jardaw led them into the waiting area, speaking to Liz Hastings' aides while the privateers uneasily took seats and watched the Genesis Navy personnel bustling around the outer office.

The wait was mercifully brief, the ArcGeneral having expected them. An aide approached only a moment after Jardaw had decided none of the chairs could hold his weight, then waved them towards the tall, broad doors leading to the Genesis Navy Command and Control Centre. They filed into that room, and as Jardaw straightened up under the higher-ceilings of the compartment, Liz Hastings turned from a set of screens that were running lists of fleet inventory and let her eyes settle on the newcomers.

"Captain Jardaw," she nodded to the bear, who nodded back immediately. Then, with a noticeable sigh, Liz looked to the privateers. "*Captain* Stanton, *Captain* DeBrooke."

She almost bit her lip when she realized how icily those last two names had come out — she'd promised herself moments before that she'd be courteous to the renegades. They were friends of the Earthers, and thus friends of hers... but they were also, by human standards, traitors. As much as she forced herself to be courteous, that continued to gnaw at her.

Yes, that fact still stung her, and it stung her more now than it had eight months before because she'd spent that time watching the casualty figures from the campaign roll in. Numerically speaking, the Earthers were suffering just under a third of Genesis' losses on this campaign. For every three or four good officers Liz lost, only one Earther was killed... or more likely sent home invalided. Genesis had lost more people than she cared to count, and it was Liz who got to see the broken hulls of ships come in time and again.

She'd somehow thought that with the Earthers joining this war, the days of enormous casualties to her fleet were at an end. There were supposed to be no more slaughters like those the Larosians had inflicted on Genesis Fleet so many times... But no, the war was hotter now than ever, and more humans were dying than she'd ever projected. Foolish and bitter officers within her ranks claimed the Earthers were using Genesis ships as fodder. Based on the casualty numbers, Liz supposed that was a somewhat understandable mistake to make.

But she knew the deployments, and she saw the plans. The Earthers were doing more than their share of the hard fighting, and the only reason they weren't dying as handily as the Genesis Fleet was simple: they were much better fighters.

It tore at her to watch, because every time a casualty list came in, she'd inevitably find herself looking in the mirror and asking herself how she could send those poor unsuspecting humans out to try to fight a war at the level of the Earthers and the Kroggs.

The humans of Genesis had been fighting for centuries, and this war was reminding them of their average war record... Only the newcomers to fighting, the idealistic Earthers, seemed able to excel.

A hell of a lot of irony in that. And bitterness for some too...

All that said, the Genesis Navy was determined to fight on. Most realized that to pull their weight in these circumstances, they'd have to work harder than ever before... And here, sitting before Liz, were two Captains who'd spent the last months happily and safely building a resort on a sandy beach, far from the front lines.

She had every right to think they were traitors... so long as she recognized they were still Allies.

It was a tough sell, even to herself.

So now, as the two humans nodded curtly to her, she ground her jaw against saying anything foolish, and instead forced herself into a straight observation, "I understand you had a number of run-ins on your way here?"

"Indeed," Jardaw replied with a nod. "Eight separate attacks, two including Dreadnoughts and the rest made exclusively by Destroyers."

Hastings frowned, "That many? I'd heard rumors about raiding groups, but there's relatively little travel between here and Earth, so there was no confirmation. I'll scrape together a provisional squadron to go hunting, but I don't have much that isn't slotted to go to the front in the near future..."

Virtually nothing, in fact. The front line had gotten so badly extended that every squadron of ships that could be spared was being thrown forward, hopefully to plug any gaps in the advance.

Jardaw cocked an eyebrow, "Aye ma'am... if I could make a suggestion, it might be wise to look for the source. There must be a Krogg forward base serving as a central operation point for these forces, and I would suspect it must be somewhere out here. It would doubtless be easier to find than any individual raiding groups on the move."

Hastings 'hmmed' and turned from the Captains to study a map of the relative positions of Genesis, Earth and Gibraltar. There was a lot of space between all of them... far too much to make random sweeps effective.

"Yes... I'll look into it, thank you Captain. I should also send a courier back to Earth with word of the danger — there aren't many ships in Sol space, are there?" Hastings turned back to the bear as he shook his head.

"No ma'am. *Highlander* was one of only three operational ships of the line when we departed, and if I'm not mistaken, only three 74s were near ready in repair yards."

Hastings nodded, "I'll send a courier today then..." She paused, looking at the map as she called up some numbers on its screen, "I take it you'll want to put *Highlander* in dock now that you're here?"

Jardaw nodded, "If you can spare the ships to send on with the convoy to Gibraltar. My engineers have rigged us for cruising, but we're not particularly combat-effective just now. They say a few days in the yards and we'll be back in fighting trim."

With a short nod Hastings let her eyes drift to James and Audrey, "I'm pretty tight for ships, especially if I'm sending some back towards Earth. Would you two be willing to pitch in?"

The question had a neatly concealed undertone of bitterness, but James and Audrey both managed to detect it. They ignored it as best they could.

"Your ships can either go work with my hunter group on the sweep back toward Earth or keep going with the convoy... if you're interested, that is..." Liz managed to solidify her control over her tone.

James tilted his head slightly, glanced at Audrey, then offered a single, jerked nod, "We'd been planning to stay with the convoy out to Gibraltar."

Liz looked from James' face of resolve to Audrey's and back. Fair enough, they wanted to pull their weight, and she wasn't in any position to tell them they couldn't — for a number of reasons, in fact.

So she nodded silently, trying not to hope these *privateers* ran into the sorts of odds that were slaughtering Genesis crews... "Fair enough. I'll send a supply ship to your squadron this afternoon. Take what you need. I want the convoy to move out this evening... meanwhile I'll scrape together some ships to go up with you."

James nodded stoically, but Audrey frowned, "Who are we to be joined by, ma'am?"

Liz cocked an eyebrow — perhaps these two wanted as little to do with Genesis ships as she wanted her ships to have to do with them, "*Earther* ships, Captain. Just back in for tune-ups after their operations at the Galahad Belt. Two 74s and a sloop — *Atlas*, *Vulcan* and *Flame*. Under Fox Magnus."

Audrey and James brightened almost instantly. Fox Magnus was an old friend — they went back to the days before the Battle of Genesis, when they'd saved each other several times. Neither Audrey nor James had seen the dapper little Fox since that time, though word was he'd gotten a number of plum independent assignments from Admiral Felix.

"He's on the station if you want to talk with him," Liz was speaking absently, unaware of their prior relationship, and inclined to have the renegades out of her office as quickly as possible. "He's become a bit of a famed storyteller down at the *Bloody Pulsar*."

The two human Captains nodded simultaneously, James speaking first, "Yes, thank you ma'am."

Liz cocked an eyebrow and nodded, "Fair enough. If that'll be all, I've got plenty of business to get back to. Captain Jardaw, take your ship to Repair Forty-Three. Good day."

The three Captains nodded in turn and then left the C&C chamber at an even step, James and Audrey doing their best to hide their smiles from the Genesis officers as they paused in the hall outside the offices. It'd be good to see Fox again.

Neither human noticed at first as the now-crouching figure of Garvin Jardaw extended his large, white hand towards them, "Thank you again for your help out there."

Audrey blinked first and carefully took his hand, nodding in reply, "Glad to."

As James took his turn he nodded as well, "Our pleasure."

The bear smiled in reply, "Well if you need anything, I'll likely be with *Highlander*. I take it you're going to find Captain Magnus?"

Audrey and James nodded again in near unison, "He's an old friend."

Jardaw cocked an eyebrow, "Indeed. Well, best of luck to both of you. I'll doubtless meet you again."

"If you're ever passing by Freetown, you're always welcome," James smiled at the Earther.

"Kroggs or no," Audrey put in with a smile of her own.

Jardaw chuckled, "I'll look forward to it. And until then, good luck, and goodbye."

They parted ways, the Earther proceeding to the launch bay while the humans headed down to the *Bloody Pulsar*, the station's notorious spacer bar.

The *Bloody Pulsar* didn't fulfill any historical human stereotypes of what a bar should be. It was clean and bright, though still somewhat noisy when nearly full. Of course, human historical stereotypes really didn't concern Captain Fox Magnus just now as he sat back and lifted a mug of water to his friends, Commander Chronos Claw and Lieutenant Lang Sandpelt.

Fox had served aboard the sloop *Flame* with both these fellows — they'd been his two subordinate officers while he was the Commander. Now he'd made the jump up to *Atlas*, one of the most famous 74s in the Earther Fleet, and they'd each taken promotions in *Flame*.

The trio's two ships were polished and out of the yards, so they'd soon be heading back up to Gibraltar to take on their new assignments. This could be their last drink together for a while, and given their affinity for banter, it seemed prudent enough to get a lot in when they had the chance.

As their mugs clanked together, Claw grinned at his old skipper, "So you think life in the big ship's going to make you rusty, Fox?"

Fox laughed loudly, Sandpelt joining in, "You weren't asking that when I got between you and that Dreadnought. My Cruising Master nearly smacked me for trying that move with a 74."

Claw chuckled, "Yes, well we were doing just fine against that Dreadnought on our own."

Sandpelt chuckled, "Yeah, we had a solid minute left to live."

Fox smiled — there certainly had been some misadventures at the Galahad Belt. They'd been a small force sent to clean out that section of space while Admiral Felix's 301st pressed on towards Gibraltar, and it'd been a little more dramatic than anyone had expected. But then *Flame* seemed to have a habit of finding the most overdramatic ways of doing things — it was as though some cosmic fate was fluffing up the sloop's life to make it into a more entertaining story.

Yeah right, and one day I'll be First Space Lord...

Fox grinned in spite of his musings, recalling the little sloop's impressive history of daring.

"Remember back when we were after that Queen's Hive? We put a few scratches on the paint then, didn't we?" Two new Earther uniforms were standing next to the table, the wearer of one of them having just spoken.

The Earthers grinned and Claw opened his mouth... then his eyes shifted to the newcomers as they both dropped into empty seats at the table... "You certainly managed to bail me out in the process."

The Earthers at the table found their smiles broadening instantly.

"Audrey! James! By the Earth, what are you doing out here?" Fox expressed his delight while the two *Flame* officers grinned and extended their hands.

Audrey, who had spoken, shrugged, "Escorting a convoy with you, it seems. Came from Freetown with it. Plenty of Krogg raids along the way."

Fox took his turn to grin broadly, "I see! Well, certainly glad to have you with us — it'll be like old times. And you can help me put these cheeky sloop officers in their place. Go ahead, Chronos, tell them that wacky idea of yours — 'energy-hyper' or whatever you call it. Go on..."

Laughter quickly followed, and while human patrons of the bar tossed occasional curious or even disapproving glances towards the Earthers and their renegade compatriots, they seemed to know better than to interrupt.

CHAPTER 10

Engadine, despite its considerable size, was the fastest Earther capital ship in the service. Powered by five high-yield energy reactors, it had more available power than *Orion*, and it lacked the large number of thirsty guns to drain that energy away. As such, it could channel unprecedented amounts of energy into its drives, producing a forced speed of nearly 2,900 pls.

Maximane had hoped this would have allowed him to overtake the Krogg Dreadnought within a day, but it hadn't been so easy. In fact, it had been six days now. The Krogg ship must have been of a new breed, designed to run faster through hyper, because it was moving more quickly than any other Krogg Dreadnought on record.

The Dreadnought hadn't headed directly out towards Genesis. Instead its course had angled off the traditional transit route, moving towards what seemed to be the flank of the Allied front lines. After chasing for a day, Maximane had ordered the slowest ships in his force back to Earth to help defend in the event of any further attacks. *Minotaur*, *Daffodil* and *Cambridge*, all having suffered battle damage, led this slower group, with the sloop *Orca* serving as escort. The Carriers had remained together, but after three days even they were being divided by their respective speeds. Maximane had thus been compelled to part ways with *Caesar* and the three slower *Boadecias*.

He'd been torn as to where to send those ships — Earth could use the protection, but as a major forward fleet base, Genesis *had* to know about the raid, and he couldn't chance splitting the Carriers up lest they be detected and attacked when they were vulnerable and alone. So *Caesar* and the Carriers were heading to Genesis first, to be redeployed from there. That left only three Carriers and two sloops hot on the trail of the Krogg Dreadnought.

From his bridge, Maximane watched the running Dreadnought somewhat anxiously. He wanted to catch that ship and return to Earth — he felt as though he'd left his home system helpless, despite having sent some of his forces back. The *Boadecias* would doubtless return there with support from Genesis, but they wouldn't even arrive at Genesis for another five days. *Engadine* and the *Diadems*, far faster, could make it back to Earth in six.

If only the Krogg would stop.

"Sir... strange readings... it looks like the Dreadnought is getting ready to exit hyper."

Wow. I should absently review events in my head and make impossible requests like that more often.

Silencing those musings, Maximane turned to the Sensor Chief, "Which system?"

"In open space, sir."

Maximane frowned. Was the Dreadnought blown? Had they tired it out with this high speed run?

"Sir, I'm getting other readings... I think it's a Krogg squadron. At least three Dreadnoughts, another half dozen Destroyers."

Aha. Maximane's eyes narrowed — was this a designated rendezvous point or had they just happened across each other? And why were there so many Krogg ships out here anyway — this was still about ten days from the front...

"Should we beat to quarters, sir?" *Engadine's* Captain, a fellow cat named Ronax Hobbes, came to stand next to Maximane.

The lion Commodore paused, looking at the battle plot in the bridge's center. His Carriers could probably take quite a strip off that squadron... but did they want to?

"It's out of hyper, sir... the squadron is forming around it. Looks like they're getting ready to re-enter hyper."

Maximane frowned. Past experience with Kroggs suggested they'd usually make a fight in circumstances like this — they had a strong force, he had a weaker-seeming one. So far in this war, such odds had seemed to be more than good enough reason for the Kroggs to join action... but in this case they were apparently siding more with prudence. The Dreadnought he'd been chasing must have let them know these new Earther ships were dangerous, and that there was important information to bring back to their commanders.

They couldn't transmit their information telepathically until they were much closer to their base — the Earthers had enough experience with Krogg telepathic communication now to realize how relatively limited it was. They had to carry messages as intricate as scans and navigation plots to within a system of their message destination, or important details would be lost in transit... at least that was the conclusion of the Admiralty science section after examining reports from the last eight months of campaign.

Well if these Kroggs wanted to escape with crucial intelligence, perhaps he'd just have to let them go. Turning to *Engadine's* Second Lieutenant, Maximane let his eyes narrow, "How far can we stretch our drive field at this speed?"

The Lieutenant frowned thoughtfully and paused, reviewing pertinent statistics in his mind, "I could give you 180 percent I think. Sustained for a long cruise, that is."

Maximane nodded to the Lieutenant and then turned back to the Sensor Chief, "Do you think that'd be enough to avoid detection?"

The Chief glanced up at his supervising Sensor Officer and then with a confirming nod looked back to Maximane, "Aye sir, I think so."

Draco Maximane smiled — that was it then. They hadn't stretched their drive fields as they'd chased the lone Dreadnought since there'd been no reason to risk potential speed in order to be covert. But now, while the Kroggs paused to reassemble, their pursuers would apparently break off.

"Signal Officer," he turned to the coyote running the communications system, "order *Monarch* and *Diadem* to reverse course immediately and drop out of sensor range. Ron," Maximane turned to Captain Hobbes, "we'll go with them. Once we're out of sight we'll stretch drive fields to maximum safe size for long-distance cruising and catch up while the Kroggs work themselves up to full speed. Repeat those orders to the sloops."

The Sensor Officer nodded in acknowledgement, while Captain Hobbes ordered the Master and the helm to produce an abrupt reverse of course. *Engadine* began to fall rapidly off the pace — as though expecting an attack from the combined Krogg force.

A common message beamed through energy comm and reached each of the pursuing vessels, and as it did they too dropped back alongside their flagship. Maximane turned to *Engadine's* Captain, "We're going to follow them and see where they're headed. I have a feeling there's a base out here somewhere. If we can find it we'll either be able to take it out ourselves or at least give it a beating and get word out of its existence."

Hobbes nodded, "Very good, sir."

"Sir," the Signal Officer spoke as Maximane turned from his Flag Captain, "*Monarch* reports able to go to 170 percent. *Diadem* reports its field can only be stretched to 130 percent. They're facing reactor trouble over there... looks like this speed is wearing on them."

Maximane frowned again — he didn't want to give up another ship with the prospect of finding a base on the horizon, but he couldn't risk losing a Carrier to engine trouble either.

"Send to *Diadem*, 'Maintain field size and head for Genesis. Alert them of our situation and explain to them that we are following this squadron to what we hope will be a Krogg forward base.'"

As the message was sent, Maximane ground his jaw. He couldn't afford to send his sloops with *Diadem* — not with the prospect of a bigger fight to come. The two little ships might prove too crucial to *Engadine* and *Monarch*...

So *Diadem* would just have to cruise alone. Hopefully there weren't more Krogg groups out there waiting to pounce on lonely Allied ships.

Engadine and *Monarch* led their pair of accompanying sloops back into the chase, drive fields stretched as they raced through space.

CHAPTER 11

His head was ringing.

Not his ears, his head.

Of all damned things to have, a ringing head.

Typical.

"Gods wept," he tried to sit up.

"Easy there, ArcBrigadier, your head got hit pretty hard."

Pat Conroy grunted and pushed off the restraining hand, "Bloody hell to that... oh *Gods*. What hit me? A Gods-damned planet?"

He forced his eyes open despite the painful light, and blinked several times until his vision cleared. The scene around him was unfamiliar... he was seeing a planet, not a ship... and a planet covered in lush vegetation that seemed to be more blue than green. The sky was an unhealthy shade of pink, and another planet seemed to be hanging in the sky overhead, keeping company with the sun.

"Where the bloody hell am I?"

A familiar face appeared in front of him, "I don't believe this planet's been charted, sir. But you're... well... *here*."

Pat squinted, "Lupus, that's you isn't it?"

Sergeant Major Beckett Lupus nodded, "It is, ArcBrigadier."

Pat absently rubbed his forehead with one hand and pushed himself to his feet with the other. The ringing eased, though a massive headache was suddenly blaring through the din.

"And how did I get *here*, then, Sergeant Major?"

Lupus stood next to the sore Irishman, "You came down to the flight deck looking for an escape pod. We found you knocked out just outside the bay when we were leaving, so we took you off with us."

Ah right, his ship had been blown up. And he'd been running to and fro, looking for a pod... well then...

Pat nodded painfully, "Ha, 'leaving'. You make it sound like the ship wasn't going to pieces around you... well thanks for pulling me off, Sergeant Major."

"Sir, please call me Beckett."

Pat grinned with some determination, "Right, and I'm Pat. Now what's our situation?"

Lupus frowned thoughtfully, "Well, my squad is here, entirely intact. We got our dropship off *Harbinger Bishop's* flight deck before it was destroyed, and we made a smooth landing."

Pat nodded, "Good. How many others from my crew?"

Lupus frowned, "The Kroggs were shooting down escape pods, Pat. We've been here five days and we haven't found anyone else yet, but I do believe there are survivors out there."

Pat's eyes widened, "You haven't seen anyone... five days, you say? Well, we'd better get looking — if there are wounded..."

Lupus nodded, "I've had Corporal Howler and half the squad sweep the area for fifty kilometers around us, nothing so far. But now that you're up and about we can start pulling up camp and looking in earnest. "

Pat stiffened and held up his hand, "Fifty kilometers?"

Nodding again, Lupus bobbed his head towards the exit hatch of the dropship, "But it's dense jungle, they might have missed something. And any survivors from *Bishop* would probably be on the move."

Pat blinked a couple of times, rubbing his forehead, "Right. So we lift off and start broader sweeps."

Lupus shook his head, "Not quite that easy — the Kroggs have a pair of Destroyers in orbit so we've been forced to hide our ship under the brush and stay close. We've seen a number of their landing craft going back and forth overhead."

"The bastards are hunting my crew," Pat's headache abated temporarily with the realization. "How many in your squad, Beckett?"

"Seven, aside from myself."

"And you're loaded for bear with plenty of supplies and guns enough to wipe out a small army?" Pat said the words angrily.

"A *very* small army, yes."

"And you're trained to avoid Kroggs?"

Lupus cocked an eyebrow, "I can pull up our résumés if you'd like to have a look at them."

Pat scowled, "When did you get funny?"

Lupus shrugged, "Always have been, I suppose."

"Well that's dandy. Now let's start looking for survivors to save."

On cue, a console inside the dropship beeped and interrupted them.

Spacer First Class Raymond Keats fought to control his trembling as he hid in the underbrush. His buddies hadn't seen his predicament yet. Or the Kroggs in the clearing, by the looks of it, though those black monsters were searching... and searching hard.

Being chased by a four-armed, heavily bladed, shiny black creature with one eye was more than just unsettling. Facing a whole squad of the things qualified as absolutely terrifying... and he'd been doing it for five days now.

Indeed, it had been five days since Keats had boarded a pod that had survived the destruction of *Bishop*. His pod had landed within a few kilometers of two others, and so he'd been able to join up with a group of fourteen survivors, including one officer, ArcLieutenant Jakes from engineering. They'd picked up what looked like an Earther beacon on the handheld pod scanners, and they'd figured the Earther recon team aboard *Bishop* had managed to make it down in one piece.

It'd be true to form for those wolves to have survived the destruction — they were elite, even by Earther standards. So with Kroggs after them, Keats' group of survivors had elected to go in search of that squad, their best hope for survival. They'd already covered about sixty kilometers on their trek through the brush...

But the Kroggs were stalking them. And the aliens' numbers were growing.

The pods had provided small arms and supplies, but the auto-guns they carried simply weren't up to cracking Krogg carapaces. Jakes, a resourceful officer, had thought to grab a case of Earther-made pistols from the armory before escaping *Bishop*. Still, it only supplied four guns with their extra power cells.

During the first attack, after the Kroggs had literally dismembered one of the engineering techs, Jakes took two of these guns and made a heroic charge at one of the aliens, firing like an ancient cowboy. The maneuver shot the blade off one of the Krogg's arms, but didn't stop the soldier. Or its companion.

While the rest of the party ran, Jakes' head came flying after them. They never got the two pistols back. And the horrifying mental picture wasn't going anywhere either...

Since that time, the survivors' number had been reduced by three more, the majority always managing to flee into the thick underbrush while an unlucky man or woman bought them time.

They hoped they were only a kilometer or two from the beacon, but Keats was fast losing faith. Not that he'd admit that to his mates — he'd been left in charge when the last Petty Officer had been halved by the Kroggs... and so now he was tightly clutching one of the Earther pistols, praying that his rank didn't automatically make fate single him out to be the next victim.

The five Kroggs stalking his party carefully prowled the clearing, their shimmering bone-blades reflecting strange patterns of light onto the blue trees. Keats held his breath — one was turning to look right at him.

None of the Kroggs had noticed the rest of the *Bishop* party on the other side of the clearing — the other spacers had already crossed by the time the Kroggs had shown up. He was the only one cut off. It appeared as though it was his turn to be the decoy... to give the rest of his group time to escape.

Yes, it was his turn. So clutching his pistol tightly and drawing a bead on the eye of the Krogg facing him, he opened his mouth, took a deep breath, and–

The furry hand of an Earther suddenly clasped over his mouth, and he jumped in surprise. It came away as Keats turned to look at its owner, the Sergeant Major of the recon team. True to form, the Earther had appeared from *nowhere*.

A deep sigh of relief escaped the spacer as Lupus pointed to the clearing and then silently slipped towards it. The Sergeant Major came to a stop just at the edge, hidden from the Kroggs by a thick patch of underbrush.

The perimeter sensors laid days prior by Corporal Cadmus Howler's patrol had detected these approaching humans — and their pursuers — ten minutes earlier. There had been no debate as to the course of action; the ten Kroggs would die, the humans would be rescued.

So the recon team had made exceptional time from the dropship, and they now surrounded the section of the clearing holding the Kroggs. Having evolved from predators, the tactic was second nature to these Earthers — indeed, ancestry combined with training allowed Lupus' all-wolf team to operate much as a wolf pack would in the wild... a pack with modern combat equipment.

Lupus waited a moment, watching the Kroggs look slowly around the terrain. Howler would be moving any time now...

Cadmus Howler stepped calmly into the clearing and casually twirled his enhanced sword umbrella-style. The weapon, originally of Larosian design, had been adapted by Earther R&D specifically for recon teams like Lupus'. Unlike the regular infantry pattern swords, the blade of this weapon measured only two feet, but that made it much handier and more lethal in the close situations this squad's wolves were usually involved in.

Howler glanced at the five soldiers as they turned to face him. They seemed to straighten their postures in the face of this new adversary — trying to intimidate him in an animalistic way. It really *didn't* work.

Howler keyed his sword to life, its blade subtly glowing red as the atoms along its sharpened edge began moving rapidly. It was now a veritable chainsaw with an atom-wide cutting surface — thin enough to slice right through a Krogg.

In the next split second, the Kroggs tensed themselves for action, raising their four-bladed arms and broadening their stances.

Then Lupus and the rest of the team lunged into the clearing.

In just a second, Howler was among the much larger Kroggs. His blade, swinging fast at the nearest soldier, was deflected by a quick downward sweep of the soldier's upper blades. As this happened, Howler's right leg came around in a sturdy roundhouse that knocked the Krogg off balance. The sword swung around again, this time going right through the Krogg and slicing off his torso.

Lupus' own blade removed one head from its shoulders, then drove into a second stomach. The rest of the Kroggs were caught unaware from behind, Earther swords hacking them apart with disturbing cleanliness.

As the Kroggs fell into a heap, the members of the squad drew themselves up carefully at the center of the clearing. It wasn't over... they knew from past experience that Kroggs never sent *all* their forces into a clearing at once.

The rush came from somewhere to Keats' left. Another five Kroggs, the other half of the platoon, made a mad charge at the eight wolves. The Earthers met them smoothly, their blades singing as they deflected the heavy Krogg blows.

One Krogg soldier's swing managed to lance through the Earther defenses, connecting blade-first with Private Pawman's chest, but it was instantly deflected by the Earther's personal shield. The blow stunned the smaller wolf, but didn't slice him in half as the Krogg expected. The wolf struck back a second later, one shielded fist putting the Krogg back on his heels while the other hand brought his sword through the Krogg's legs.

With the last rush finished, Lupus straightened his uniform and sheathed his sword.

"Cadmus, you, Pawman, and Canit, deploy across the clearing, watch for follow-ups. Everyone else, get these people back to camp."

CHAPTER 12

Setter Caine leaned back in a chair in his cabin in *Orion*, sipping on an orange juice. In front of him was an interesting book: *Garnan on Human History: Naval Warfare, 1730 – 1950.* Garnan was an Earther historian — a great fellow with particularly useful insights into humanity's past. Caine had already read this particular volume twice, but he felt like consulting it again.

Of late, he was finding himself drawing all sorts of parallels between the actions of the Allied Fleet and those of the U.S. Pacific Fleet during Earth's Second World War. Having caught their enemy by surprise at just the wrong moment, as the United States Carriers had at Midway, the Earthers and humans were now hopping from system to system along the axis of advance...

Carriers. Caine paused to think on that new development — they were going to have Carriers out here on the front line soon, though Carriers in space would be employed rather differently than those at sea. Modern-day gunboats simply didn't have the same decisive advantages that human aircraft once did...

In any case, it was the concept of the gunboats and the Krogg corvettes that had prompted Caine to pull this volume from his shelf. While he doubted the long-term decisiveness of corvettes, even after having faced them occasionally over the past months, Caine was worried the Kroggs might find some way to improve their breed of the swarming vessels.

The concern had led him to look at a Second World War naval battle in the Mediterranean, when the British Royal Navy — a later version of the service upon which the Earther Navy had been modeled — attempted to evacuate Crete by ship without control of the skies.

The British ships had been woefully unprepared to defend against large numbers of attack planes, and they'd suffered enormous casualties as a result. Caine nursed a nagging worry that the same would happen to the Earther Fleet. Designed to go toe-to-toe with enemy battleships, most ships of the line had only a dozen carronades to protect them against corvettes — adequate for the time being, but perhaps not in future, if the Kroggs adjusted their designs to exploit the weakness.

Gunboats would offer cover, of course, meeting the corvettes on their own terms, but the Admiralty was only planning on commissioning forty Carriers within the next year and a half. Under the current system of Battle and Flying Squadrons, many small forces would simply be left without boat protection. And quite honestly, it seemed difficult to justify the construction of more Carriers when ships of the line were so desperately needed...

Caine frowned as he re-read the pages that documented how Stuka dive-bombers had menaced British cruisers a number of times. Those British ships had been built in an era when attack planes had existed, but before the time when such planes had been recognized as much of a threat. The Earthers had long ago learned how to neutralize corvettes — well-timed broadsides, canister, and carronades — but the Kroggs were good at adapting. Perhaps the Earthers today were underestimating gunboats as the Navies of Second World War had first underestimated aircraft...

Reports had recently described upgraded Dreadnoughts and Destroyers, bred specifically for action against Earthers, and soldiers with more speed and agility developed for the same reasons. If the Kroggs similarly enhanced their corvettes... Well, there had to be a way to toughen the Earther Fleet; the threat was there, and it could be a decisive one in the grand scheme.

The question that remained, though, was *how* to strengthen the Earther Fleet. Unfortunately even Garnan's histories couldn't provide an answer like that, and it'd take months to get the query back to Admiralty and Navy Board R&D. What could he do *right now?*

More carronades?

Hmm... no. To get every Earther ship back to Genesis for gun upgrade would be impossible. Maybe Gibraltar would facilitate such additions in time, but the base was not yet so well developed. That simply wasn't the answer.

Caine's mind seemed to stall in the face of the dilemma... he needed to talk to someone, shift his perspective and come at this from a different angle.

But Ursla, Felix and Sarah were out on maneuvers. Who was left?

Graham's temporary office on *Gibraltar One* was nothing to shake a proverbial stick at. It was big and comfortable, though the main selling feature, from his perspective, was its location just across the hall from the Marine Commandant's office.

Graham was entirely too happy about his consistent dining arrangements with the Commandant — he'd been looking for someone to spend time with, especially now that Sarah and Pat had finally gotten together.

Not that he was going to rush into anything, but he did enjoy spending time with Gillian Hodge, and that was more than he could have said about any other woman for the past six years. Yes *six.*

Of course, right now this splendid woman who he enjoyed spending time with was off reviewing marines somewhere — apparently she wanted to make certain the latest group of arriving Genesis troops was ship-shape. She was well above the ranks of the combat field commanders, but she seemed to enjoy those low-level jobs all the same.

Well that was fine, Graham had work to do too... though he wasn't in the mood to do it. There was a hefty stack of paperwork on his desk, but there was no point attacking the pile and taking three hours to get through it because he wasn't in the mood. Once he was in the right frame of mind, it'd only take him a half hour to do.

So he relaxed, and as he sat back he hauled his heavy leather boots up onto the table and leaned back in the chair, closing his eyes, and thinking about recent goings on...

"Comfortable?" Caine was standing on the other side of Graham's desk, eyebrow cocked and an amused smile on his face.

Graham's eyes flew open and as he tried to get his boots off the desk, he fell off his chair.

Well, it actually sort of fell and took him with it, though luckily the nicely carpeted floor accepted his collapse with nothing more than a dull thud.

"Bugger! Gods..." Graham struggled to his feet awkwardly, "Um... hi Setter."

Caine barely kept himself from laughing, "Getting used to luxury, I see."

Graham shrugged, "It's a nice office."

Caine released a short chuckle, and Graham reddened slightly. Well a bit more than slightly, but who was really paying attention anyway...

Clearing his throat, the junior Manchester gestured to a chair facing his desk, "Please, have a seat." He righted his own chair and sat gingerly, "What can I do for you?"

Caine, sobering, leaned back a little in the seat he was offered, "I need to talk to someone about combat theories. You familiar with our current tactics?"

Graham blanched, "I'm rather an excellent *watcher* of them. Nobody's ever put me on a bridge, though."

Caine smiled again, "Perfect. Fresh perspectives can be most useful — Savanna taught me that."

Graham brightened again, "Aha! Chair-falling-off not withstanding, I can be fresh and perspectivish..."

Caine frowned and Graham's brightened expression dimmed as he reddened even more, "Did you just make up the word 'perspectivish'?"

Scratching his forehead, Graham tried to think of something clever to say, "Yes. Well. It's ancient Greek. I mean... um... word-making-up is a privilege of rank in the Genesis Navy. Um. Well. I mean. Maybe. Yes. What's it to you?"

A smile crept back over Caine's face at the human's stumbling mock defensiveness, "You done?"

Graham shrugged, "I think so."

"Splendid. You see, I'm worried about Krogg advances in the area of corvette design. I've been thinking these first eight months have been a bit too easy... I get the sense that the Kroggs have been doing their homework on us, and if we're not careful we're going to walk head-first into a new batch of forces tailored specifically to break us. I suppose I'm worrying about our ships getting overwhelmed out there."

A frown crossed Graham's features, his mood shifting to genuinely serious, "Really? I understood that our ships have been holding out rather well against corvettes... when we run across them."

Caine nodded with a matching frown, "They have been, but I've got a feeling the Kroggs are going to improve on their corvettes — make them far more deadly."

Graham cocked an eyebrow, "Indeed?"

"They've been coming up with faster Dreadnoughts lately, and their Destroyers have gotten a whole lot tougher as well," Caine leaned back a little. "It seems likely they'll try, especially once the gunboats arrive."

Nodding slowly, Graham strummed his fingers on the desk, "More carronades?"

Caine chuckled abruptly, "My first thought too. But there's no time to upgrade the fleet. Even if we could get all our ships back to the Genesis yards, fitting them with more carronades could take weeks."

Graham rubbed his forehead again, more thoughtfully this time, "Well, you *will* have the gunboats soon. They'll be useful."

Caine nodded and absently scratched his neck, "But we'll only have forty Carriers by year's end. I'm thinking we'll need a smaller-scale solution, but I can't even come up with a way to build combat-effective Carriers for operation at the squadron level. It'd take hundreds of hulls — hulls we still need for conventional ships."

"How many Motherships do the Kroggs have, though?" Graham asked skeptically. "You won't need to worry about them turning up everywhere."

"True. But any squadron without a Carrier that happens across one..." Caine's words trailed off.

"Setter, forgive me, but aren't you seeing shadows here? I mean really, the Kroggs haven't done anything yet. It seems a bit premature to be worrying about all this. We may have encountered an unusually large number of Motherships lately, but we've beaten them all."

Caine cocked an eyebrow as Graham's suggestion struck an uncomfortable chord.

They had been seeing a great number of lone Motherships lately... and none of them had put up much of a fight. Everything he'd been seeing in the recent reports suggested that the reign of the Mothership had been ended by the Earther line of battle. If he hadn't had the free time to sit down and crack Garnan — to read about Crete and Midway again — the deaths of those Motherships might not have occurred to him as odd.

As his eyes began to narrow, Caine looked across the desk at the junior

Manchester, "Graham, before the Quest, how many Motherships do you remember seeing in Genesis?"

The human squinted thoughtfully, "There was only one they told us about. Though their fleet at that rift had... hmm, I think maybe twenty-five."

Caine nodded, "And we destroyed at least ten in that action, more likely seventeen or eighteen."

Graham frowned, "So?"

"The Larosians told us Motherships are hard to create. Take up to a year to grow. Since Genesis we've destroyed six in action. They've all been alone or only lightly escorted. Why would they send them out at us that way unless they were trying to *get rid* of them."

What an unusual thought... at first Graham didn't quite see the logic behind it. The Kroggs were being trounced, why would they intentionally add to their losses if they had...

Oh.

"Wait, you think they're wasting *Motherships* to lull us into believing in our own patent superiority? Make the shock of a new assault more pronounced?" Graham's eyes widened just a little. "I could see that, certainly. But again, could be shadows."

Caine nodded, "True. But it doesn't hurt to be prepared, just in case. Now logically, if they're sacrificing old Motherships, they could well have new ones breeding... which makes my original question more important."

Graham leaned back — more carefully this time — in his chair, "Carronades take too much time. What about anti-corvette cruisers? Send out some Light Cruisers with extra laser mounts?"

Caine frowned, "Too much time to reconfigure, and they might prove too vulnerable to conventional attack anyway."

Graham sighed and scratched his chin, eyes straying to the pads on his desk. One said 'Small Craft Manufacturing Plant' and was stamped 'Operational'. It needed his signature to confirm that *Gibraltar One*'s pinnace-building bay was up and running.

"What about..." he leaned forward and snatched the paper. "We could put boats on every ship. Cram them in — as many as each flight deck will take."

Caine looked up thoughtfully. *Orion* popped into his head... the First Rate carried fifty-five small craft in its landing bays... it could easily cut that number to twenty-five and load thirty boats... of *course*! A 74 would probably be able to hold at least fifteen boats, and in a squadron of eight ships that would provide 120 boats... as good as one of the new Carriers.

"Brilliant, Graham! Can you get the pinnace bay working on boats?"

Graham was startled by the outburst, "I imagine so. We probably have the specs on file somewhere... we've got plenty of construction equipment since they're getting the new yards online, and more than enough raw material around here with the belt to harvest."

"Good. I have to go call Andra... This could be decisive, Graham — well done!"

"No problem," Graham said simply, waving as Caine left in a hurry.

Now, what kind of mad construction project had he gotten himself into? Oh well, he'd figure it out.

"All in a day's work," he muttered to himself as he brought his legs back up onto the table.

Then he closed his eyes and leaned back in his chair.

And yes, he fell off again.

CHAPTER 13

Pope Joseph Barron slid silently through space on the outer limits of the Gibraltar system, accompanied by eleven more Superdreadnoughts of the same formidable type. On the ship's bridge, an unsettled but focused Sarah Manchester leaned forward in her chair.

The odd feeling that had been with her when she'd welcomed Graham to Gibraltar hadn't faded in the past week. If anything, it had intensified. Keeping herself busy seemed to be the only way to limit its intensity, so she'd been happy to have her 401st Battle Squadron join Ursla's 201st and Felix's 301st for maneuvers.

As the flag units of their fleets — the Fourth, Second and Third Fleets respectively — these Battle Squadrons were the Allies' elite. Particularly in the Earther case, that was quite a boast. Earther ships were *always* well handled, no matter how inexperienced the crews happened to be. Earthers instinctively knew how to work together.

For Sarah's own squadron, the elite status was less intuitive, and thus perhaps more impressive. Her well-honed ships could probably never outperform an elite Earther force, and they may even come across as only 'regular' when measured by Earther Fleet standards.

Regardless, Sarah was extremely proud of them. They always came through for her when it counted.

"Ma'am, signal from Admiral Ursla. She's changing vector to sweep the belt."

Sarah blinked at the Comm Chief's report, "Very good. We'll maintain this vector. I still think Felix is out here somewhere."

Admiral Savanna Felix was hiding in the asteroid belt, and he knew that Ursla knew he was there. It often worked out that way in this game of hide-and-seek — the Earthers knew where to look, the humans would get there in due time.

That was not to criticize the humans unfairly — they were apt spacers, and Felix would be the first to say so. But to effectively hunt an Earther, you probably needed to *be* an Earther.

"The 401st is continuing on, the 201st is coming right at us," Captain Varnia Broadpaw said in her quiet tones. The wolf was daughter of Admiral Broadpaw,

Ursla's humorous second-in-command on the mission to Genesis nine months earlier, and previous commander of the Third Fleet. Thanks to time off for reattachment of limbs, Varnon was only recently back in the war, and though he no longer commanded the Third Fleet, he was actually in charge of one of the largest concentrations of ships on the frontier, and his battle group was off on the flank making trouble...

Felix nodded to Varnia, "I thought Ursla might sniff us out."

The 80-gun ship *Tonnant*, Felix's flagship, was hardly a 'super' First Rate like Ursla's 150-gun *Agamemnon*, but that had advantages. It was rather difficult to hide a 150-gun behemoth in a scattering of asteroids. *Tonnant*, however...

"He's being clever," Captain Artemis Tigar of *Agamemnon* cocked an eyebrow as he examined the battle plot. "He knows *Tonnant* can hide just about anywhere, and he's going to force us to go in and find him."

Ursla smiled and nodded, "That's Savanna for you. Send to Sarah. Let's spring his little trap."

The ships of the 301ˢᵗ Battle Squadron were floating in a group of asteroids with their guns run out and charged for war-games use. The simulated firepower of the combined squadron was impressive, though Felix wished *Atlas* and *Vulcan* were with him. The 74s still hadn't returned from their flank-securing operation at Galahad's Belt, so his force had been reduced to only six ships.

Now Ursla's far more heavily-gunned 201ˢᵗ was creeping up on him. One 150-gun and seven 74s — more than a match for his squadron — were coming straight for him, and Sarah's 401ˢᵗ was approaching from the flank. It was all seeming quite futile just then... ha! Andra and Sarah were about to get a surprise–

"Sir, something's decelerating from flux."

Felix's eyebrow twitched and he turned to *Tonnant's* battle plot. A message drone was coming to a stop only a short distance from the 301ˢᵗ. It was a Battlecruiser-sized communications pod, and by the low energy readings on its drive, it'd come from quite a ways out.

Well... he could ignore it until after the games... or *not*. It could be important. And it wasn't as though things were going that well in the war-game world.

"Send to Ursla. End games. Tell her we've got a Genesis message drone on sensors."

"Aye," the Signal Officer began sending messages, and Varnia Broadpaw nodded to her First Lieutenant and her Cruising Master. *Tonnant* slid out of stealth mode.

Felix watched the information from the drone scroll up on the plot. It was a Type 44-3 drone, max speed 31.4 cee... yeah, yeah, yeah, the specs on the drone carrying the message always came before its data, for whatever frustrating reason. Then came a map of its flight path, and its source of... aha.

It was from *Harbinger Bishop.*

"Move us to intercept, Varnia."

The drone was scorched on one side, obviously the victim of a near-miss from a neuro blast.

Tonnant's grav tractors gently pushed it clear of the asteroid field as the first surges of information were drawn from its databanks, and slowly the 201st, 301st, and 401st clouded around it. *Agamemnon, Joseph Barron,* and *Tonnant* all came the closest, the latter ship attempting to download the messenger's database.

Felix tapped his foot anxiously on the deck as the Signal Officer queried the drone several times. Couriers were designed to lock their information unless the correct code was received over the comm, but they could be notoriously temperamental with those codes. Usually at the most awkward times too — it was like some lazy galactic force was using unexplainable technical trouble to build cheap suspense...

But then perhaps being scorched had made this little drone even more disagreeable than usual.

And perhaps that made the contents in the pod's little buffer that much more pertinent.

Sarah paced as *Tonnant* repeatedly tried its hails.

A barely-controlled sense of panic was viciously hammering through her veins. She was deathly worried about Pat, and the present signposts looked particularly negative.

"Anything yet?" she demanded abruptly, and the Comm Chief shook his head slowly.

"They keep trying, ma'am. But the signal isn't being acknowledged."

Sarah frowned, stopping her pacing, "Dead signal receiver?"

The Chief frowned and hit a couple of keys before nodding, "Maybe."

Sarah's foot tapped the deck loudly for a moment, but she forced it to stop. Alright, if they couldn't get the information out of it by remote...

"Signal Savanna. Tell him the damned thing is dead and we'll bring it into our bay and work on it. We'll probably have better luck going in manually."

The Chief nodded, "Yes, ma'am."

Sarah turned to ArcColonel Evan-Thomas, *Barron's* commanding officer, "Get me that drone."

Pope Joseph Barron edged easily towards the pod, one of its light craft exiting the starboard flight bay to retrieve it. Ursla watched with a frown.

The drone's antenna was obviously dead — that or the main computer on the tiny craft had been fried. In the latter case, information retrieval would be entirely impossible. In the former, it would be nearly so...

But the very fact that the information was going to be hard to get at probably meant it was valuable... Pat must have found something.

Ursla pictured Pat's oblique recon course in her head. Somewhere along that axis of travel, a Krogg force must have been waiting — one tough enough to give Pat's Pirates a run for their money and to keep them from escaping.

Which meant there was more trouble on the flank of this advance than anyone could have guessed...

"Send to Sarah: rejoin at *Gibraltar One* at earliest convenience. Signal all Earther ships to make way there now." Ursla turned to Tigar, "Whatever happens to be on that drone... well, I get the sense we'll need to have this base ready to receive."

The cat's ear twitched, and then he nodded to the Master.

Agamemnon led the 201st and 301st Battle Squadrons towards *Gibraltar One.*

CHAPTER 14

Pat sat back stiffly in the landing craft's single private cabin. For an assault ship, the vessel was packed with a relatively large number of amenities. The Earthers had obviously planned for a long-term stay on a hostile planet — along with any other conceivable situation — and as such they'd provided virtually everything Pat could have thought of in one pinnace-sized package.

They even had components for a Mark XII cannon stowed in the cargo hatches under the small craft's engines. They'd assemble that later.

Taken together, it was extremely impressive — it seemed Lupus' squad would have the gear to plant crops or walk on water if so needed, but even with all this to their advantage, they were still sitting here, on their bloody hands.

Despite a desperate need for sleep, Pat couldn't shed the frustration that came with the revelation: he was sitting in a fully-equipped and highly-advanced dropship, and he couldn't use it to get to his crew.

The story of *Bishop's* survivors had developed greatly in the past two days. They now *knew* there were survivors, because in order to secure a more defensible location, Lupus and his squad had risked a jump in their dropship. They'd lifted off and moved camp to a cave overlooking a nice sheltered slope beneath a belt of craggy mountains...

And in the process, they'd gotten the chance to run some longer-range scans of the continent they'd landed on. The scans weren't exhaustive — they hadn't been able to probe everywhere with the dropship's powerful Earther sensors before the threat of detection by Krogg Destroyers had forced them to ground — but they'd found the major cluster of *Bishop* escape pods.

Just about 200 of *Bishop's* fine men and women were stuck in an open plain, their camp surrounding three crashed pods near a nice river. Sounded lovely, save for the Gods-damned fact that they were sitting in an open field with Kroggs from two Destroyers looking to get in there and cut them up.

Grinding his jaw against the bitter conclusion, Pat took a calming breath and redirected his mental frustration as best he could. Based on the intensity of his headache, it wasn't working... his crew was sitting in a near-indefensible position, and he was safe and sound up here.

And — *and* — Beckett Lupus had refused to haul ass down there in the dropship to collect them. Which, logically, was a fair and rational decision — the Earther ship wouldn't be able to carry 200 survivors at once, and it would probably be shot down if it tried anyway. But aside from flying, Pat couldn't conceive of any way to reach his people.

That was due to the other detail: they were 8,000 Gods-damned kilometers from this lovely mountain range. In other words, they were on the other bloody side of the continent.

So how could the survivors be rescued? Apparently Lupus was thinking about that... well, no apparently about it. Pat again tried to blink away his frustration, because Lupus didn't deserve such unkind thoughts, but it still wasn't working. While Lupus considered the options, the wolves of the recon squad were setting up a perimeter around this camp. A secure base to bring the humans to, Beckett had explained... but there'd be no humans to save if the Earthers didn't move bloody soon...

"Damn, damn, damn," Pat muttered to himself as he rubbed his throbbing head.

"Bad time, Pat?"

The Irishman winced and frowned as he looked up at the open hatch of his small cabin, "Aren't they all? Got something?"

Lupus considered entering the cabin, but quickly realized such an attempt would have ended with both of them stuck in the confines, "How about a walk. I've got an idea about getting your crew up here."

The Earthers had set up a perimeter some 130 meters from the broad mouth of the cave, forming a semicircle around the line. The shiny steel boxes that deployed the Earther energy shields were spaced evenly along the line, though for the time being they weren't active. As long as they remained undetected, there was no reason to raise those shields — they had plenty of power thanks to the dropship's powerplant, but because the fields would likely be detectable from space, activating them would invite Krogg visitors.

That said, if this camp was found despite their caution, those shields could be raised, creating an interlaced and hopefully impenetrable energy barrier along the front. Lupus had assured Pat that, thanks to the dropship reactor, the shields could handle as much punishment as any Sixth Rate's broadside, so he was reasonably comfortable with them.

When they assembled the Mark XII cannon — another Sixth Rate-sized piece of kit — they'd put it in a gun pit somewhere out in this clearing, and cover it with brush to camouflage its obvious silver barrel. Thanks to the one-way shield, they could fire shot right through without lowering their defenses.

"Well, Beckett?" Pat adjusted to the gradual downward slope of the land as he walked.

The wolf took up an even stride next to him, "You know we've got parts to assemble an old-fashioned water boat, right Pat?"

Pat stopped and frowned, "So?"

Lupus turned and grinned at his puzzled comrade, "Boats float, Pat."

Pat scowled, "Not here for riddles, Beckett. Gods wept, I need to get my people up here!" He thrust his thumb back at the cave.

Lupus nodded with a smile, "I know. And we can get them here. *By boat*."

Pat froze. The waterfall within the perimeter had a river running from its base. They'd included a fair stretch of the winding fresh water source in the safe zone, mainly for the fish that occupied it. They weren't salmon, but the little yellow ones tasted alright.

And Pat had seen the topographical scans showing the river flowed into a larger waterway that went south...

Setting off towards that part of the compound at a slow walk, Pat spoke up, "How big's the boat?"

Lupus followed with his easy stride, "Big enough for my entire squad. Runs on a small impeller. The manual says it can get up to fifty knots when you need it too, and it has mounting brackets for two pulsars."

Pat frowned. The pulsars would be easy enough to come by. The Earthers had put at least two of every infantry weapon on their lander, heavy guns like pulsars included. And the speed made for a decent round trip time, but the capacity... "Only room for your squad? That's a lot of trips for 200 people, Beckett."

They slowed as they arrived at the river bank and Lupus cocked his eyebrow, "I was thinking we might be able to cobble together some rafts from whatever salvage they have down there. If we brought a couple of extra generators we could most likely tow the lot of them back here."

"Against the current lugging that much cargo?" Pat skeptically examined the fast moving stream, watching as the water bubbled around the rocks on the stream banks.

"Specs say the impeller can tow up to 1,000 metric tons," Lupus nodded.

Pat cocked an eyebrow, "Built to last, eh? What kind of speed though?"

Lupus shrugged, "Against the current, probably twenty-five knots. Maybe less. It'd drain a lot of power, but we should have enough reserve cells."

"And you could recharge with solar panels," Pat said thoughtfully.

Lupus nodded.

Pat sighed again. It was the best option they had just now.

"Alright, how long to get the boat together?"

"It can sail in four hours, fully loaded. It'll take us about four days of hard travel to get there, sparing the engine, and I'd bet eight or nine to get back."

Pat nodded, "You'd take your whole team?"

"I'll leave Ernile Cuttar. He's a good engineer, and he can help you assemble the gun in case we get noticed on the way back."

Pat pursed his lips and nodded, "Let's just hope you get to them before the Kroggs do."

Lupus nodded solemnly.

CHAPTER 15

"You're sure?"

Setter Caine frowned as he lowered himself into a chair facing his friend. Ursla, having arrived in the First Lord's cabin aboard *Orion* after a conspicuously hurried flight over from *Agamemnon*, shrugged at his question as she leaned back on the couch.

"I'm not *positive*... I can't possibly be," she said with a sigh. "But looking at that pod gives me a very bad feeling. I mean... well, look at it this way, Pat's drone hit the 3,000 pls mark getting here. It was sent maximum priority, and it pretty much burned out its engines. And at some point along the way it was clearly under fire from the Kroggs — those scorch marks aren't consistent with anything else we know of."

Caine cocked an eyebrow, "Aye, it does look like it's bearing bad news. Isn't Sarah trying to download its data now?"

Shifting in her seat, Ursla offered a slow nod, "She's trying. Don't know if she can salvage anything... but even if she can't... well, it just feels like trouble's on the way."

"Something hefty... a force that could roll up our flank before we can concentrate and turn to stop it," Caine settled back and ground his jaw.

Ursla nodded again, "Something heading right down the line to Gibraltar."

Caine scratched his cheek absently. It was a dire prospect... though realistically, this could simply be what Graham would just term a 'shadow'. The pod could say anything...

Caine's instincts were at last beginning to take stock of the situation, and the concern that was coursing through Ursla's veins was finding its way into his as well. Strategically, the front lines would be vulnerable to collapse if the Kroggs were able to concentrate a powerful force and sweep down from one of the extreme flanks, hitting Gibraltar as they came. Up to this point, there'd been no evidence to suggest that the Kroggs had enough force anywhere in the warzone to carry out such a daring operation...

This pod might just be the first clue.

There was nothing explicit about it so far — nothing that said beyond a shadow of a doubt that the Kroggs were coming. But every minor detail about this pod's condition, its arrival, and its sender suggested that it was reporting on a force that had been more than a match for Pat's Pirates.

That meant a force that would be a significant threat to the front lines as a whole.

And *that* meant Caine would have to act to counter it.

Of course, time might prove he was jumping to conclusions — this pod might not bring entirely dire news — but he couldn't ignore the possible warning.

"So let's assume you're right. Worst case scenario — if the Krogg force in question closely followed this drone, they'll be here soon," he said finally in quiet tones.

Ursla nodded, "My thoughts exactly. The drone's transponder said it had been in space for six and a half days... I'd guess a large Krogg Fleet would probably only transit at 2,000 pls, so that'd mean it could be here in another three."

Caine felt a growl build in his throat, but he suppressed it. Three days didn't even give him enough time to get word to Genesis. Worse, the only squadrons they could call in to bolster Gibraltar's defenses would already have to be within two days travel of the system — beyond that, word wouldn't get to Allied forces quickly enough to allow them to get back to the base in time for the fight...

"I know we aren't absolutely sure, Setter. But the last time I got this sort of feeling about something on campaign, it was connected to the arrival of the Larosians at Genesis. And shortly thereafter I was shaking Novash's hand... I don't know how or why, but I think we might be onto something here..." Ursla's words trailed off as Caine nodded.

"There's only a tiny prospect of a Krogg attack..." his mind drifted back to Garnan's history, "...but such was the case at Midway. We've got too much to lose here — if we're wrong about the Kroggs coming, we'll still have a chance to repair the fleet as it comes in. But if the Kroggs are resurging, we're going to need every ship we can get here."

Ursla frowned at the reference to Midway, certain neither of the human sea battle's context nor connotation... but both were irrelevant: Setter Caine shared her concerns.

"Start recalling ships, then?" she asked quietly, and Caine nodded again in reply.

"In for a penny, as they say... but Andra, we can't pull in just half the fleet — we'd risk having entire battle groups cut off if it's a feint. So we have to collapse the broad front right now. Let's get the word out right away, recall *all* ships to Gibraltar. I want every squadron, every battle group, *here*. It's about time we changed our tactics — I think the Kroggs are already changing theirs."

As Sarah examined the scorched casing of the drone, she felt as though her stomach was being sliced open from within. The damage was, at least in her eyes, terminal — the log computers had probably been fried, and it was remarkable the guidance systems had survived.

The prospects of recovering *anything* from this pod were disappearing fast, but though she refused to admit it to anyone, Sarah could draw some very disturbing conclusions just by looking at its battered shell.

Pat's legendary Pirates had been destroyed.

And Pat was probably dead.

That very simple revelation brought with it more of a shock than any blow she'd ever taken in the sparring ring. She winced as though she'd been struck as she failed in her attempt to suppress the thought.

What was she to do–

"Ma'am?"

Sarah's head snapped up abruptly at the interruption, her face pale and devoid of feeling, both hands clutched tightly into fists, "Spacer?"

The technician looked down at the drone and shook her head, "Can't get anything out of it. All I can tell you is that it was launched with five others, four of which its sensors report destroyed. We tried to recover the rest of the log, but the actual memory banks were wiped — that was all that was left in the short-term cache..."

Sarah nodded blankly, and then her jaw locked as a feeling of dark dread seemed to fill every inch of her. If the recovered drone had been launched with five others, Pat had dumped every available pod. That panic in dispatching the drones, combined with the substantial damage to this one, indicated a major naval encounter.

Something he couldn't handle... something he had to warn them about...

And something that had probably killed him. And would ultimately kill them all.

Damn, she *had* to work this through, personal despair or no...

"Can you tell where it was launched?" somehow the words came out evenly.

The tech shook her head slowly, "I'm sorry ma'am, the damage was too extensive. All I could suggest is that you track back along its base course for six and a half days and estimate a velocity of 30 cee. That'll probably give you a reasonable indication of where it came from."

Sarah nodded, "Thank you, spacer."

Thoughts tried to enter her mind — where had Pat died, where had this great threat originated... what was she to do...?

But she knew she couldn't answer those questions now. She needed to conference with her friends first. They had to work this through.

With that in mind, she turned and left the engineering bay.

Moments later Sarah stood on *Barron's* bridge, studying star charts with a blank expression. By now, word of the presumed fate of Pat's Pirates had reached all hands on the Superdreadnought, and a dark cloud had settled over the crew. There had been a great camaraderie between the crew of *Barron* and those Pirates, because many of the flagship's officers and spacers had served under Sarah when she'd commanded *Warlock Prophet* in the days of the Quest.

And the significance of Pat Conroy's demise wasn't lost on anyone, either.

The bridge crew was solemn, eyes on Sarah as she stared at screens of star charts. The AI had highlighted two possible systems as the originators of *Bishop's* drone... but they were so far away. It seemed impossible that anyone could do more than guess about his true fate.

Pat was notoriously hard to kill. Sarah knew that and she desperately wanted to believe he was still out there, that either things weren't as bad as the pod's condition suggested, or that he'd escaped a dire fate with his usual cunning and guile...

She desperately *wanted* to believe these things.

But reality was a firm player in Sarah's thoughts, and now it was confronting her with the slim chance of Pat's survival. The very thought terrified her: she was exhausted, weakening... how could she survive this war without him there to back her up?

What would losing him do to *her*... what would it take from her?

The potential answers to those questions horrified her. She didn't want to lose her ability to function, but somehow, after enduring so much with so few positive forces working on her behalf, it seemed as though she would collapse.

At this place, in this time, she couldn't conceive of any other outcome. If Pat was truly gone, she'd break. Soon.

And she didn't want that to happen — she couldn't let that happen. She had to focus, she had to work through this. Every action, every order... she needed to compel her mind to fight the tide of fear and sorrow: she needed to beat away her grief with duty.

Focus. Focus on the things you know you can do.

Sarah closed her eyes and tried to level the spikes in her heart rate.

Focus.

It was all she could do; it was what she *would* do. She couldn't afford to give into her pain, or her fear. The Allies were relying on her.

And, if he was out there, Pat was relying on her too.

She had to hold fast...

As she opened her eyes again, her gaze fell on the two systems highlighted by *Bishop's* AI. Those two systems would have to be examined. Someone would have to determine what was in them — if something there had been powerful enough to kill Pat.

And if it had, the Allies would need to know.

Sarah had to focus on duty, and duty might just allow her to lead a search party. To find the enemy, and gain some measure of retribution.

And maybe, just maybe, to find Pat.

●●●

Far away, a second drone raced through space. Its energy supply had been exhausted, and thanks to the battle damage it had suffered, its guidance systems were unable to ascertain just where it was along the run to its destination. It had peaked at 30.4 cee, and now it had probably overshot Gibraltar altogether.

With its energy draining fast, it would only remain detectable for moments after it exited flux — if not sighted immediately, it would be lost in space. So as it slowed from flux, the drone began to power its long-range beacon.

If only someone was out there listening...

"Picking up a beacon, skipper," the Sensor Officer reported with a frown. "A messenger pod... looks like it's come a *long* way."

James Stanton frowned and turned his chair towards *Sword's* Master, "Must have gone off course for Gibraltar. Helm, decelerate. Let's pick it up for them."

CHAPTER 16

Archangel Sword slowed ponderously from flux drive, carefully matching vectors to allow for pick-up of the drone. James sat rather comfortably on his bridge and absently strummed his fingers on the arm of his chair. Picking up an off-course drone did make for a break from the monotony of convoy duty... just not a particularly interesting one. They had encountered no Kroggs between Genesis and Gibraltar so far — apparently the space nearest the front was safer for civilian traffic than the convoy lanes between Earth and Genesis. That just seemed *wrong* somehow...

"Launch bay reports the pinnace is clearing the deck now," his Second Lieutenant reported in slightly bored tones, "Picking up the pod in eighty seconds. We're seeing tags now... its from *Harbinger Bishop.*"

Ah, that might add to the interest a bit — *Bishop* was Pat Conroy's ship. What the Irishman had been doing, and why he would send a drone so far, was something of a mystery. Such a long courier run was usually detailed to a ship. It was probably nothing, though — James could think of all sorts of situations that would warrant a drone traveling that far...

But now that he considered it more carefully, none of the scenarios that came to mind were good.

What *had* Pat been doing sending a *drone* this far? And what had he been doing so far out to begin with? Surely Sarah wouldn't have sent him over a week out of Gibraltar unless there was something serious that needed looking into. And if Pat sent a pod back the whole way, it suggested...

"They've grappled the pod," the Second Lieutenant's monotone suddenly cut through James' thoughts.

"Hail the pod," James came quickly to his feet, his urgency surprising the bridge crew. "Hail it *now.*"

The Signal Officer blinked herself into action, "Aye sir. We're querying the pod..."

James took a few steps toward the center of his bridge, "On the screen."

The Signal Officer strummed her keys and fed the transmission to the bridge monitor. James waited, grinding his jaw as the exhausted computer on the buoy accepted *Sword's* Earther codes and began dumping its information... not a simple data stream, but actual *ship logs*. That was by no means a good sign — if all the sender had time to do was dump his ship logs...

Sword's Signal Officer sifted through the information as it came in, and as she recorded it to the database she immediately projected the most pertinent feeds onto the main screen.

Logs indeed.

James' eyebrow began to climb as the screen lit up. The picture being displayed seemed to have been taken by one of the external cameras on what he presumed was *Bishop's* hull. The ship was decelerating from flux without any other ships in sight — the rest of the Battlecruisers were presumably in formation out of the shot. So far there was nothing unusual about the footage — every Naval officer in the Genesis service had seen this many times before...

The regular starscape fizzled blue-green and then returned to black, and James squinted slightly at the monitor. Visual sensors couldn't often show anything valuable in space — fighting was frequently at such long range that only enhanced images could reach human eyes. Indeed, it was enhanced visuals that allowed Earther gun crews to lock on targets with their weapons before firing...

But this picture was unenhanced–

Gods!

The screen spiraled violently off its initial course, and first one Krogg Dreadnought, then another swung into view. James could make out the spines as the Kroggs spit them, and could see the neuro pulses as they lashed out. A Battlecruiser entered the frame just in time to disintegrate.

The camera showed movement now — *Bishop* was getting up speed and running... Transfixed by the deadly ballet, James watched, as did the whole bridge crew. In short order, the stars fizzled again, but not before the ship toppled sideways.

Engine hit.

James let out a breath — *Bishop* had gotten to flux too late. He watched in utter silence for another minute before he was satisfied that was the end of the feed. He turned to the Signal Officer, "How long is this tape?"

The woman frowned, quickly scrolling ahead in the preview on her master feed console, "About four minutes. Looks like the next two are all in flux... hang on..."

She sped up the feed significantly, stopping just seconds before the stars fizzled and *Bishop* slipped out of flux drive for the last time. James turned back to the monitor and released a deep sigh. *Bishop* hadn't been able to sustain flux with the damage it had taken. But had the Kroggs followed the limping Battlecruiser?

The camera began to show the signs of rapid maneuver, and a planet came hurtling into view on the screen. Then the angle shifted to show a squadron of Krogg ships opening fire–

The signal cut and the screen blanked.

"Gods alive," he breathed. They'd smashed Pat's Pirates. "Anything else on there? Other than that feed?"

The Signal Officer's jaw ground rhythmically, and she nodded, "*Bishop's* long range sensor data of the system the Kroggs were in. Just a moment..."

The main screen came alive again, this time displaying a glowing map of a star system. James' jaw dropped and the bridge was silenced by a wave of shock. While the flotilla on the monitor might have been tiny in comparison to the ones that had grappled with each other at Genesis, it was still about the size of a full-strength Earther Navy fleet.

And it was out here. *Now.*

While the Allied Fleet was scattered half way to hell and back.

The initial data gave a count of nineteen... no *twenty* Motherships, 203 Dreadnoughts, and 414 Destroyers. That much firepower could potentially turn the tide of the war — there was certainly no concentration of Allied warships along the front lines that could match such a force.

As data scrolled across the screen, James let his eyes drift from detail to detail, taking in as much of the threat as he could...

Wait, what was that... "Anything more specific on those Motherships?"

The Signal Officer, still stunned, began to sift through the information provided by the drone and a new window popped up on the screen.

"One deep scan," she reported with a frown. "Looks like the AI ran it. Not very focused — *Bishop* was weaving by this time, I think. But that's *definitely* not your average Mothership."

The computer-generated image of the vessel more than proved the point.

Motherships were usually massive behemoths, and without their corvettes they tended to be defenseless against conventional gun attack. These were anything but; they appeared to be large enough to carry maybe 400 of their usual 700 corvettes. But the energy readings from the launch bays on the backs of the ships seemed to indicate that these 400 were together as powerful as any 700 that came before them...

And worse yet, the Mothership being scanned had begun to move during the attack — with *triple* the acceleration of a standard ship of its type... and probably twice the relative maneuverability.

Even more damning still, the monstrous ship appeared to be armed to the teeth, an analogy which James suddenly realized was far too accurate.

The great eyelid on the half-sized vessel had a serrated edge, and James watched with a sinking feeling as it opened to launch its charges. The door hurtled open with violent force, and then slammed shut like a hefty jaw after the corvettes rained out.

It was absurd to think of a Mothership trying to eat an enemy vessel... hopefully that little feature had only been developed to intimidate enemies...

There were also numerous spine batteries and neuro pulse emitters across the hull of the massive ship... these Motherships seemed to be as tough as First Rates. Grown to *fight* First Rates, probably, in less than eight months...

And they had *twenty*.

James swallowed hard and ground his jaw. There was no doubt this fleet could crush Gibraltar right now. He could only hope it didn't move to attack Earth or Genesis instead... the Kroggs might not even be aware of Gibraltar yet and the threat it posed to them.

"Pinnace has been retrieved... *Flame* is dropping out of energy drive on our port quarter," the Second Lieutenant reported.

James blinked twice as his mind considered the options. This convoy was three days out from Gibraltar at the luggers' pace... but *Flame* was both by reputation and in fact the fastest ship in the fleet.

"Message coming in from Commander Claw."

James nodded, "On the screen."

Chronos Claw appeared on the monitor just as James looked to the Signal Officer, "Beam the contents of the pod to them." He turned to *Flame's* Commander, "Chronos, not to put too fine a point on it... we've got big trouble. Looks like Pat Conroy found a Krogg Fleet out there... I need you to get this to Gibraltar *fast*. Can you do that?"

Claw had been about to give a curious greeting, but his mouth closed at James' grim expression.

Nodding, he glanced off screen for a moment, "We're receiving. What're we looking at?"

James swallowed visibly and then took a breath, "Enough Krogg firepower to wipe out this front. Go *fast* Chronos."

The cat nodded once and then disappeared. Seconds later *Flame* burst into energy drive, making brilliant speed towards Gibraltar.

James turned to his Cruising Master, "Get us under weigh."

CHAPTER 17

"Make a bloody hole! *Move damn you!*"

Graham unceremoniously drove a pair of ArcLieutenants out of his way as he sprinted down the corridor. His feet slammed loudly into the deckplates with the fast, heavy stride of a man not accustomed to running, but the noise alone wasn't warning enough for some of the idlers in the halls of *Gibraltar One*.

Well, that was the Earther term, and in the realm of human semantics it wasn't really fair — they weren't really *idling*, they were just off duty. Though they certainly seemed to be moving slowly to Graham. But so did everyone, because he was just about at a dead run right now...

As an Earther-built pre-fab station, *Gibraltar One* qualified as *huge*, even by the standards of an ArcLieutenant-General who'd made his career on the large Genesis orbitals. One thing he'd have to get used to was the running time — on *Genesis One* he'd been able to get from his cabin to C&C in less than sixty seconds, but he was already in minute three of this particular sprint.

Graham's breath was starting to catch in his chest — he really *wasn't* a runner.

Going to have to start on the treadmill at this rate...

Part of the problem had to be the dinner he'd almost finished on the concourse, and he was starting to get the feeling that if he didn't slow down he was soon going to *see* that particular meal on the floor around him.

Grinding his jaw at that rather unpleasant mental picture, Graham turned the next corner and raced past a surprised Earther Midshipman.

Now what was this he was rushing to anyway? Everyone else seemed to be getting to their stations fast enough without the dead sprint he was enduring... but then again Earthers always seemed to look like they were strolling when their pace was up to the level of a good human jog. Oh well, tough luck being human...

Caine had put the station on alert, but from his table at the mess there'd been no way for Graham to get a specific explanation as to what was going on. The only way to find out was to get to C&C.

More surprised Earther ratings blurred past as Graham launched himself through the corridors. Scowling as he tried to keep his strides long and even, Graham surged around the last gentle bend in the corridor. Only a few hundred meters more now... though the salmon from that dinner with Gillian Hodge was starting to feel *exceptionally* unstable in his stomach. Would slowing down for a minute matter? He couldn't know for certain, so he denied himself that option and instead focused on the readiness of *Gibraltar One*.

Sarah, Ursla and Felix were on maneuvers and Caine's 101st was anchored at the Gibraltar planetoid. The Boat Bay had already produced fifteen gunboats of the Mark XIV class, and was now retooling to build the slightly heavier Mark XVs. The turnaround on that production had amazed Graham — the Earthers seemed quite adept at building things with conspicuous quickness.

The C&C door finally appeared in front of Graham, and he pulled up from his run with a consuming sense of relief... between gasps. Catching his breath as he stepped through, he found the command deck cluttered with dozens of busy techs moving back and forth between stations.

As Graham vainly attempted to control his panting, his eyes searched the bustling C&C, at last coming to settle on the sturdy black-and-white bear who stood in its center. Commodore Karl Kandam had once been commander of the 236th Battle Squadron, but after a tough action near the Kesseler Cluster he'd been forced to disband that combat formation — with only two 74s left in service, one of them his own *Namur*, and with a leg missing at the time, he'd elected to take a shore posting to *Gibraltar One*. Since attacks on a forward base like this one were expected, it certainly didn't hurt to have Kandam, with his battle line experience, on hand to meet them.

"Guns are crewed and standing by," *Gibraltar One's* Second Lieutenant reported rapidly, dropping into a fire control chair on one of the center's flanks.

"Very good," Kandam had a soothing voice that meshed well with his friendly panda bear appearance. "Bring up the shields..." the Earther turned to Graham just as the junior Manchester slid to a halt on the deck.

"What's going on, Karl?"

Kandam frowned, "All I've received so far is a general alert. *Orion* broadcast it about five minutes ago, and we're not sure of the specifics."

Graham frowned momentarily as he advanced to stand next to Kandam at the plot, "Where's the rest of the in-system force?"

Karl gestured towards the holo as Graham moved closer, and the human's frown deepened as he saw the locations of the ships in the system. *Agamemnon* had returned to *Gibraltar One*, as had the rest of the Earther force. Sarah's ships were also on their way back in. The frigate squadrons — one of Fifth Rates and the other of Sixths — were forming with the Earther ships of the line...

And just then every last Sixth Rate in the system dropped into energy drive and throttled out of the holo, charging in all directions at a blistering speed. Graham cocked an eyebrow as the 28-gun ships — half the cruiser force in Gibraltar — scattered so suddenly on virtually every vector.

"What the hell haven't I been told?" he let the question slip before he could stop himself. It was hardly politic for a Genesis junior flag officer to be so abrupt in his demands for information, but Kandam merely cracked a smile at Graham. The panda shrugged, "See, I was wondering that too. But all things in time..."

"Message coming from *Orion*," the Signal Officer's voice came as if on cue, and Graham's frown was replaced with a minor grin. These Earthers had a knack for timing... hopefully that would stay with them.

As Graham's expression changed, Kandam looked over the shorter human's shoulder, "Well?"

The cat at signals held a receiver to his ear and frowned, "All squadron leaders to meet aboard *Gibraltar One* post-haste."

Graham cocked an eyebrow — he really liked not having to concern himself with travel time... "Splendid. Put them in Conference One, landing deck."

Karl nodded, then his ear twitched thoughtfully and he turned to *Gibraltar One's* First Lieutenant, "Get the crews to their boats. I want them ready to fly patrol while the pinnaces make their runs in."

Graham's other eyebrow rose along with the first, "Patrol?"

Kandam smiled again, "Since we haven't been told exactly what's going on, better safe than sorry. And good to give the crews some exercise, I think."

Graham gave a brief nod as Kandam turned back to his First Lieutenant. Taking a deep breath and looking back to the plot, the human watched as the Allied ships of the system began to collect. There'd be gunboats out there soon, too... the first squadron of those had been finished only the day before in the belly of *Gibraltar One's* mighty manufacturing plant. The boat crews were volunteer Midshipmen and ratings who already had experience in small craft and gunnery, but they were indeed new to their jobs.

Kandam was right: whatever time they could get in formation maneuvers before they reached combat would be invaluable. Thus far they'd had almost no chance to so much as crack the manuals for their new craft — some had only been assigned to their new posts the night before. But if anyone could mobilize a small craft combat force on such slim notice, it was the Earthers.

Caine's concerns still floated in the back of Graham's mind — if there was trouble on the way twenty gunboats on their first flight wouldn't be enough to cover the system. Could enough be built... soon enough...?

"Karl, who's in charge of the Boat Bay?"

The Panda turned back to Graham, "Third Lieutenant Earon."

"He up here?"

Kandam nodded, "Trax, can I borrow you for a moment?"

The sleek gray fox looked up from his console, "Skipper?"

Kandam bobbed his head to Graham, and on cue the ArcGeneral stepped forward, "How fast can you get production on those Mark XVs started, and what sort of production rate are you looking at?"

The fox frowned briefly, consulting a pad handed to him by a nearby tech, "My techs say the machinery can be ready in another four hours. Then they're counting on full-scale production... we're looking at about thirty in a twenty-four hour period."

Graham squinted slightly and did the math in his head. Twenty-eight hours from now they could have a total of forty-eight boats flying, including the ones that were now rushing into space. A third of them would be of the Mark XIV type and two thirds of the larger Mark XV... Not altogether too bad.

"I take it that's working round the clock?" he asked absently, and the fox nodded.

Graham 'hmmed' — these boats were ridiculously easy to build, their design requiring only easy-to-manufacture stock pinnace parts in many areas. Thanks to the massive Earther production plant sitting in the lower decks of *Gibraltar One*, they seemed to be having absolutely no trouble with construction.

"That'll be our capacity," Earon added helpfully. "I imagine the other five stations will be able to match that output when they're set up, and the docks will be able to double it whenever they don't have a ship to tend."

Graham nodded, "Sounds like our only shortcoming will be personnel." He glanced at Kandam, "That many boats will require a lot of crew to fly."

The panda nodded thoughtfully, "At peak production we'll need to reassign 120 personnel per day to fly them. We're carrying almost three times a standard complement right now since we're holding crews for the rest of the stations. That gives us just about 1,100 nonessentials, and I'm sure we can free up some more people if needed."

Graham nodded, "Good. So long as you're certain of production, Mister Earon."

The fox smiled, "The math is sound, sir."

"*Orion*'s pinnace is launching now, Captain," a Sensor Tech reported from the far side of C&C. "*Agamemnon*'s as well."

"The boats away yet?" Kandam turned back to Earon, who nodded again.

"I've just scrambled them. The crews were already running pre-flights because of the alert. Ten are in space now."

Graham turned back to the main plot and watched three of the gunboats form a vertical diamond around each pinnace as it cleared its base ship. It was like watching escort Dreadnoughts form around a cargo hauler... but in miniature. Perhaps history would prove these little ships irrelevant to warfare, but for now Graham was glad to have them as gun platforms.

"Very good... if you don't mind, gentlem... um...Earthers, I'll go receive the Admirals," Graham turned unceremoniously and left the C&C as Kandam chuckled at his parting words.

But as Graham stepped into the corridor, he realized something most unfortunate... he'd have to run again. And almost as though on cue, his stomach rumbled...

Well bugger... he trotted off.

CHAPTER 18

Caine sat in silence as his pinnace slipped from *Orion's* massive side. He'd be aboard *Gibraltar One* soon, where he and his trusted friends and colleagues would deal with this problem.

Well, more precisely, they'd find a way to prepare for it — they still couldn't be certain that, strictly speaking, the problem existed. Caine and Ursla believed it did, but those were just two opinions...

Halting his thoughts, Caine let his eyes sweep back into the cabin. He was tired, and as such his tactical prudence was trying to convince him not to trust his instincts.

This mightn't be anything, his mind seemed to be saying. *Be careful not to overreact.*

It was a fair point, but at the same time it did not forbid him trusting his senses. Indeed, if this turned out to be a mess, the First Lord feared it might be *failure* to follow his instincts' directives that would have brought it on.

Right now his assessment of the state of the front lines wasn't necessarily accurate. Since he'd left Genesis after the battle eight months earlier, he'd been ordering the Allied Fleet ahead in whatever way allowed him to catch the Kroggs, and he'd spread his ships all across the stars.

Even if the Kroggs *weren't* coming after the front line with some cleverly-reserved concentration of ships, the lesson had to be well learned: he'd left the war wide open for them to take.

It was a patent — and galling — mistake.

Letting his head fall back against the headrest, Caine closed his eyes at that thought. He'd failed to realize just how dangerous a situation his decisions could lead to, and now the Kroggs could be gearing up to teach him a lesson...

Hopefully a lesson at no cost. Because whether a Krogg force came this way or not, he'd be taking steps in the coming weeks to concentrate a strong strategic reserve — he'd use Gibraltar as a fortress, and put a flotilla of ships in its space to deal with any Krogg counterattacks.

But for now... he'd sincerely hope the enemy wasn't coming, because if it did, the Allies at Gibraltar were in no position to counter it.

Over the last few minutes, Caine had been considering Allied deployments; presuming the Kroggs began to do what he would — use a concentrated force on the flank of the front to blaze down the long line and wipe out the unwarned individual units of the Allied Fleet, squadron by squadron — there would be nothing powerful enough to stall them, save of course for Gibraltar base itself.

And what if they used that force to strike at the Allied production bases, Earth and Genesis?

Caine's eyes opened at that thought — it hadn't even occurred to him before, which, he supposed, was not a glowing statement in support of his clear-headedness over the past months. He'd never believed the Kroggs would be able to concentrate for an end-run attack against an Allied planet... but they did know Genesis' location, so he couldn't discount an attack there as a possibility.

Leaning forward in his chair, Caine kneaded his hands together for a moment. *Damn*.

He really hadn't planned things as well as he'd thought when he'd assumed that by driving the Kroggs before them, the Allies would naturally keep their homes safe.

Now what?

Caine blinked twice, and both his ears twitched. The possibilities were daunting — he could think of too many ways the Kroggs could catch the Allies out, find every weakness and exploit it...

The thought was a sobering one, and it forced Caine to lean back again. His eyes drifted back to the window, and as they did his gaze settled on a few of the new gunboats that had flown off *Gibraltar One* to serve as escorts. He was too preoccupied to realize just how significant their presence might be — they were, after all, a secret weapon in the Earther arsenal...

Indeed, they could be of consequence. But the circumstances right now couldn't allow him to focus on their presence; if the Kroggs were ending their period of chaotic withdrawal, it was time to get ready to meet them.

So what would the aliens do against their mortal enemies...

Caine stopped his mind. *We're not their mortal enemies. That's the Larosians...* And of course, that meant...

"Wiping *us* out isn't the Kroggs' main concern. We're a sideshow," he actually spoke to himself as the revelation fully hit him.

The Allies had been harrying the Krogg retreat in every system across a front line that was so long it took a month to travel from one end to another. Which meant the Kroggs didn't have the time free from action they would need to reassemble the thousands of ships that had fled from the Battle of Genesis — with the Earthers and humans showing up all across their old zone of occupation, the Kroggs had to resist or...

Or the Allies would arrive at the Krogg homeworld in no time.

That made sense.

If the Allies were about to face a concentration of Krogg forces, it was likely something akin to a home fleet — a force that was reserved for local defense of Krogg home space. Which meant it couldn't be sent out to attack the Allied planets without jeopardizing the safety of the Krogg homeworld... and risking safety at home probably wouldn't suit the Krogg Queen too well.

No, if he were the Kroggs — and yes, he knew full well he wasn't — this force would do what he'd already expected it to do: attack the Allied front lines and attempt to break the advance.

Because if the Allies stopped pressing forward for even a month, the Kroggs would have time to consolidate their own position... and they needed to do that even more than the Allies did. After all, in another galaxy, a Larosian Fleet over 10,000 strong was beating down their much older front lines, and the couple of thousand ships the Earthers were tying up with the wide frontier could better serve against the Kroggs' old enemies.

It made sense. If anything, this was a play to stop the advance, not to attack Genesis or Earth.

Unless you're entirely wrong. In which case we're sitting out here cut off from the homeworld we're fighting to protect.

That thought brought a long sigh. He could be wrong.

His instincts told him the theory of deployment he'd just thought up was sound... but his mind remained skeptical. The Kroggs weren't fools... the Queen was, in fact, quite cunning.

So he had to make sure he was better at this than she was.

Need to get started soon then...

As if on cue, the pinnace entered *Gibraltar One's* flight bay.

The briefing room was full when Caine arrived. Ursla had come over early, and Felix had quickly joined her. Both Admirals were standing beside the plot at the center of the large chamber, looking over the dispositions of ships on the front line.

Sarah and Graham were present too, and as Caine's eyes fell upon the elder of the siblings, he absorbed such a stab of pain that he nearly shuddered. But he fought the feeling of discomfort and advanced to Sarah's side.

"Nothing more from that drone?" his question carried multiple levels of concern, and as Sarah turned to look at her trusted Earther friend, she shook her head.

Caine's eyes caught hers very briefly, and within those wells he could see an abundance of pain and terror, thinly contained. But something was holding Sarah together, despite the stress and exhaustion and now the possibility of Pat's demise.

Duty, perhaps, and good sense; Sarah was a brilliant commander, after all. The power of her mind had been enough to coordinate the campaign of her entire Navy up to this point, including everything from the logistical side to command in action. She was relying on that strength now... and Caine was proud of her for being so steadfast.

"Andra just told me what you're thinking," Felix turned to Caine as the First Lord broke Sarah's gaze. "A force out on that flank can go one of two ways: after us or after Genesis..."

Caine cocked an eyebrow, "Indeed."

His brow descended into a frown as he noticed two flashing lights in the plot.

"*Joseph Barron's* AI says those are the systems Pat was in... probably was in, anyway," Graham offered evenly, leaning forward to look around his sister.

"They're a ways behind our front line, too," Felix added quietly. "Just far enough beyond our outermost squadrons to be passed unnoticed, and in a perfect position to menace our rear."

"Genesis could've been attacked already. We wouldn't even know for days..." Graham added dryly.

Silence descended over the chamber for a moment, and Caine's eyes shifted from the flashing systems indicated in the plot down the line to Gibraltar and back. The systems were on a tricky angle, stuck in the three dimensions of space in such a way that they could threaten Gibraltar or the home planets...

"So do you think it was a fluke they managed to find themselves in such a perfect spot as to threaten us? I mean, have a look at how well placed they are — they could go from there to Genesis, or just up the line to start knocking off squadrons... or they could come here..." Ursla took her turn to speak, and the assembled commanders nodded evenly.

"Very propitious placing... but they could be anywhere by now," Graham glanced up at the bear.

Felix was the one to reply, "Well if I were them, I'd be headed here. They can't worry about destroying our infrastructure off the top — that wouldn't solve their immediate problem on this front. Even if they hit Genesis and Earth and took out our production, we could fight on for months without letting up. With the Larosians pushing them, I doubt they have that sort of time... and, come to think of it, they'd also be trapping themselves behind our lines, with us between them and their home. And they'd be handing us a chance to consolidate our fleet at will."

It took a few seconds for everyone to fully process the cat Admiral's conclusions, but Ursla and Caine nodded almost immediately nonetheless. The bottom line was that if the Kroggs knew just how weak the Allied rear was, they mightn't turn down the chance to hit it. But they *couldn't* know that much about the rear, and they couldn't risk removing all their resistance from the front lines to go raiding towards Earth.

All they could worry about right now was stopping the Allied advance. Period.

"So they'll come here," Ursla nodded once as she said it, and Felix cocked an eyebrow.

"It's what I'd do. If they take us out it gives them some breathing room to consolidate..."

As Felix spoke, Caine's eyes shifted immediately to the tiger. His old friend, once so determined to remain at a desk at Antarctic Base, was now perhaps the most apt commander on this front line. A friendly twist of galactic irony.

"But they don't know where Gibraltar is, folks."

The simple statement drew all eyes back to Graham, and he turned and leaned with folded arms, back-on against the table, "Sorry, but this base is only six weeks old... how could they know to come out here to hit us? If they just start rolling up the line, they won't even get here until they've destroyed nearly a thousand ships."

Caine cocked a brow at that — in his analysis of this subject, he'd given the Kroggs credit for too much knowledge. If they didn't know Gibraltar existed, they wouldn't know to attack it...

"We can't know for sure, one way or the other, Graham. But it's the best option to consider right now, and anyway, if we begin consolidating here, we'll build a concentrated force capable of moving out to counter them at will. For now let's worry about Gibraltar," Caine's cautious conclusion drew thoughtful nods.

"So, we just need a defense against an enemy that may not exist, whose disposition we don't know," Graham cocked an eyebrow.

Feeling a bit of renewed energy on her own part, Ursla smiled ironically, "How can something that doesn't exist have a disposition?"

It didn't matter; the minds of the Allied Fleet leaders began to consider options.

CHAPTER 19

"Can we do it?"

Commander Chronos Claw finished his proposal with that somewhat loaded question, and First Lieutenant Lang Sandpelt shrugged in reply, "We can try, but we might blow ourselves to bits in the process."

Claw frowned and looked from his trusted friend to the main battle plot on *Flame's* bridge, "Yes, but the risk of that is *low*."

Glancing then to the chronometer, the Commander ground his jaw and started considering relative risk. Both he and Sandpelt had a great deal of experience driving their sloop to insane speeds — they'd done so on the Genesis campaign with Fox, and a half-dozen times over the past eight months of campaign. They were also doing it now — but they were still eighteen hours from Gibraltar, and the news James had sent with them certainly seemed to warrant an even quicker delivery.

Unfortunately, the only way to decrease transit time would be to try something that didn't quite qualify as *sane*, at least based on the current thinking at Earther R&D. Claw was an engineer to the core, and he'd been working on the idea since he'd first seen Larosian and Krogg hyper drives in action... he'd just needed a good reason to try it out here on the front lines. This seemed to qualify.

Granted, Sandpelt was right in suggesting this idea could blow *Flame* to pieces, but that was highly unlikely, and besides, they could send a fast pod on to Gibraltar under regular energy drive — at this range, it could get to the system just as fast as *Flame* would under normal power anyway. If Claw's idea worked, though, they'd traverse the distance in about two minutes.

So just how could Chronos Claw manage such a ridiculous jump in speed?

His idea was based on practical understandings of the way ships in the Earther Navy flew. Energy drive was super-efficient and quite quick, but it was bound by the laws of this layer of subspace. If he were to use it in *hyperspace* — a different layer of subspace where regular sub-light speed travel was relatively accelerated by different laws of physics — the projected speed increase would be near exponential. Practically, the trip shouldn't be too much more stressful on the reactors, except for the part where *Flame* exited hyperspace and energy drive all at once...

Indeed, if he got too ambitious — presuming someone didn't claim he was being too ambitious for even considering this wild idea — Claw could get his ship up to relative speeds in excess of a million pls. If he went into hyperspace at full energy drive speed, the jump would be to over *seven million* pls... just a little too fast for the first time out.

If, however, he went in at a modest 500 pls, he should be able to jump up to 270,000 pls, and arrive at Gibraltar in literally no time. It was tricky... but according to the multiple sets of numbers he'd run, it was certainly *possible*. They'd have to simulate a hyper engine's field with their Wyndhymn generators, decelerate and draw their drive field in tight... but they could do it.

Claw ground his jaw, then nodded to Sandpelt, "We should do it, Lang. Every minute could be precious with this info. Prep a pod to go on along this course with our message in case things go badly... and get the generators ready."

The holo tank in the center of *Gibraltar One's* primary flight deck briefing room glowed light blue with a map of the campaign frontier, marking all Allied units according to the color of their Admirals' pennants — white for the First Fleet, red for the Second, blue for the Third and Green for Genesis.

Unfortunately, there were precious few colored pennants around Gibraltar. Most were weeks away, maintaining the fluid front lines they'd hoped would keep the Kroggs at bay.

"We're not in great shape to receive anything unexpected," Felix observed quietly, and Caine nodded at him from across the tank.

"Putting it mildly," Ursla added softly. "We've sent frigates and drones out with recalls. Best bet is we have these..." she pointed to three squadrons "...here within four days. These..." another two squadron markers "...in five or six. That'd give us the nucleus of a rapid-response force if the Kroggs began advancing down the line."

Caine nodded again, counting the vessels in question — forty-four capital ships and eight frigates. A pittance compared to the standards the Kroggs seemed to use when assembling large forces... so he had to continue to hope there wasn't a serious enemy concentration out there.

"In the days after that we'll get another seven formations though," Felix added with a touch of optimism. "Including the First Rates of the 202nd and your old frigates from the 111th."

Ursla nodded, relieved at the thought of having her old Fifth Rates nearby. Those frigates were the best in the Alliance, still under the command of her once-Flag Captain, Dran Nightclaw. But they were eight days away with the rest of the battle group under Admiral Varnon Broadpaw, who'd been preparing to advance with them in support of the Flying Squadrons far out on the right flank. Even so, at that range, those venerable ships would not be able to assist if the Kroggs moved quickly down the frontier...

If the Kroggs didn't come too quickly, and the Allies had eight days at Gibraltar to prepare, they might be able to pull in twelve squadrons, a mix of Earthers and humans, totaling about ninety-seven warships, plus the forty-four that were already in Gibraltar space. After that, the next reinforcements from the front were eleven days away, assuming safe and speedy journeys for the ships carrying the recall orders.

"I get the sense it probably won't be enough," Caine frowned quietly at the tank.

Felix smiled sadly, "Probably? Folks, we don't know what's coming our way — we may not have enough, but we may be fine... we don't know."

Ursla leaned forward, "I know we shouldn't draw hasty conclusions, Savanna... but my instincts tell me they're coming. And we've given them a bit of an edge with our deployment, being spread out as we are..."

"Given them an *edge*?" The three Earthers turned to Graham as he looked up from the tank, cocking his eyebrow, "If it wasn't for being spread out across this frontier, there'd have been nothing keeping the Kroggs from concentrating their forces again. If we hadn't been out there causing havoc in every system we could find them in, they'd have pulled together the thousand ships that ran from Genesis in a month or less, and then they'd have come calling. So let's watch out with the pessimism there."

Felix nodded with a smile, "See, there you go. Let's not start second guessing offhand. We just need to move to counter — *if* there's something coming this way."

"A shot-up drone from parts unknown doesn't have to mean doom," Graham continued. "Does it occur to any of you that we might have *more* than enough to deal with the attack? They could be coming down with twenty Dreadnoughts and a Mothership as easily as a hundred Dreadnoughts and twenty Mother-ships. We don't *know*."

Felix smiled more brightly, "Well with two of us saying it, surely it has to sink in..."

Graham, feeling just a little too self-righteous at that moment, paused at the remark and then nodded, "Right..."

Caine arched his eyebrows, "I think that's the point we're *all* trying to make."

"Well yes, I suppose so," Graham stopped. "I was talking to Commodore Kandam this morning, and he thinks we can get thirty boats a day at peak production. That'll give us 120 in the three days it takes these..." he indicated the first three squadrons "...to get here."

Felix nodded, "They'll certainly be handy."

"We just need a better picture of what's coming at us," Ursla said quietly, sharing a subtle nod with Caine...

"Perhaps one of us should go investigate."

Sarah had been standing silently on Graham's far side for most of the meeting, and the assembled officers had let her be — she'd jump in when she was ready...

Now she turned and looked around her brother's shoulder to lock eyes with her friends.

"We can't know what's out there until we look," she repeated her thought. "I could go."

It was hard to say whether she was trying to hide what was clearly a request to go after Pat... or if she just assumed they knew she was asking.

So everyone stared rather awkwardly at her.

"Hyper footprint... by the Earth it's *big*, skipper!"

Commodore Karl Kandam looked up abruptly, "*Footprint?* All hands to action stations! Give the coordinates to the squadrons, alert the Admirals!"

"The engine power I'm tracking makes it a large fleet, skipper. The output is massive."

Kandam nodded to his sensor chief, then keyed the intercom, "All hands, large hyper footprint has been detected. Get to your stations. All idlers get to your designated quarters, non-essentials to your shelters–"

"We're unsure of numbers as yet, but the emissions make for a big group."

The intercom cut out and Caine quickly keyed the holo tank into a map of regional space, the huge hyper footprint showing up as an angry black cloud just beyond the range of *Gibraltar One's* guns.

He keyed the comm and spoke immediately, "Caine here, signal *Orion* immediately."

"Artie, I'm taking the 101st to meet them... coming along?" Labrador Forepaw dropped into his chair on the bridge of *Orion*, looking at the holo image of *Agamemnon's* Flag Captain.

The cat nodded, "No point waiting here. They're just out of range now anyway."

Another figure glowed to life in the tank — the form of Varnia Broadpaw in her chair on *Tonnant*, "We'll come out with you; I just told Evan-Thomas on *Joseph Barron* to stay put. Commodore Zar's frigates are cleared as well."

Forepaw nodded, "Let's move then. If we've got any chance, it'll have to be when they translate."

The Captains shared nods — there was no time to reclaim their Admirals, the Kroggs were too close at hand. Lab Forepaw, senior among Flag Captains in the Allied Fleet (and an Earther who would clearly have been a Vice Admiral by now if he just stopped turning down promotions) would lead these Gibraltar squadrons out. The small garrison force would just have to do its best to catch the Kroggs as they reentered normal space.

It wasn't a promising prospect — based on the size of that footprint, the attack force was going to be at least ten times the size of the Gibraltar Fleet.

Oh well, bad odds. Lab Forepaw was still going to do his job...

As the transmissions cut, the veteran canine Captain turned to his First Lieutenant, "Beat to quarters. All ships advance towards the footprint."

"The First Lord is on the line for you, skipper..."

Forepaw appeared in the briefing room tank, "Here, Setter. We've got the 101st, 201st, 212th, and 301st deploying to hit them as they come out."

Caine nodded, "Very good..."

There seemed little chance of it being enough, but perhaps in concert with the guns of *Gibraltar One* and the boats...

"The hyper point is opening skipper!"

Kandam turned to his own battle plot, "Trax, move your boats to escort the battleships. Run out our guns."

The Admirals in the briefing room held their collective breath as the massive hyper signature erupted from the lower layer of the space-time continuum, and ejected its travelers... correction, *traveler*.

Flame somersaulted out of the hyper point, its energy drive cutting out as it did.

"Fire the braking thrusters, get us under control!" Claw held himself in his chair through sheer force of will and the vice grip he had on its arms — most of his bridge crew was heaped in the forward corner of the command deck, trying to sort themselves out after that violent translation.

"We've lost generator two — the safeties shut it down when we emerged," Sandpelt reported over the rumbling of the sloop.

Claw nodded, "Signal Officer, broadcast the drone data."

The occupants of the conference room in *Gibraltar One* were shocked into silence as *Flame* emerged.

A *sloop* in hyper with that massive footprint... and *Flame* no less...

Ursla's mind was the first to grasp the curiosity, "Claw must have gone into hyper in *energy drive*. He must have blown every relay on the ship with that sort of acceleration, but probably covered a day's travel in a minute..."

She paused, and the same question occurred to everyone in the room: what sort of information would warrant that risk?

The answer came via an information dump sent from the stabilizing *Flame,* which a surprised *Gibraltar* Signal Officer had the sense to pipe directly to the

Admirals as it came in.

Well, there were the Krogg icons that Graham had moments earlier rightly claimed were no more than a possibility... They were real. And there were too many. Many too many.

Drawn up before the assembled Allied commanders was a Krogg Fleet that included twenty Motherships and over 200 Dreadnoughts. And as everyone watched, they shredded Pat's Pirates.

"Gods wept," Graham Manchester whispered.

CHAPTER 20

Liz Hastings arrived on the command deck of *Genesis One* after a reasonably slow walk. She was tired — the days seemed to be getting longer and longer while she tried to balance the logistical requirements of the campaign with her administrative responsibilities. She both needed and deserved a break, but she couldn't afford to leave her post while the war was still on.

At some point she'd be able to rest... she just couldn't hold her breath waiting for that time. And right now, pressing matters of fleet business required her presence in *Genesis One's* C&C — specifically, there was an unknown ship cruising into the outer picket zone around the human system's perimeter...

"Have we got an ID yet?" Hastings asked the question quickly as she came to a stop before the big screen that dominated the center.

"It looks like an Earther ship coming in... we *think*. It's flying a yellow pennant and it dropped from energy drive pretty abruptly just out of solid scan range. Now it looks to be limping in fairly slowly," the ArcColonel commanding the station reported with a frown.

Hastings cocked an eyebrow, "Got some picket ships moving in?"

"*Fornile* is approaching to query it now. *Pope McCreary* and *Saint Deveraux* are standing by in case there's a problem."

Hastings frowned, then glanced at her ArcColonel, "Earthers don't tend to cause problems, Paul."

The officer nodded, "I'm just worried it might be a Krogg copy, the way it's coming in so slow..."

A panel chirped to interrupt the ArcColonel's supposition, and his and Liz's eyes turned to the Comm Officer on the deck's far side.

"Signal coming in from the Earther, ma'am. *ENS Diadem*, reporting reactor trouble... it's come in from *Earth*..." the officer paused now, frowning as she pressed her earpiece deeper into her ear. She looked up after a long few seconds. "Captain Farley Karr... he's reporting a Krogg raid on Earth!"

So that was it then. Liz moved to the Comm Officer's side with a step far quicker than the one she'd used to get to the C&C, and as she came to a halt next to the junior officer she looked over the text that was scrolling up on the comm screen. Attack indeed...

"Request details..." she tried to keep the mild panic out of her voice. If Kroggs had found Earth, Genesis could well be their next target... and what if they took out Earth... what would the Alliance be without the seemingly invincible Earthers...

As the Comm Officer began querying *Diadem*, Hastings turned back to the commander of *Genesis One*, "Get orders to the 501ˢᵗ... they're to prepare to ship out for Earth. Get a courier ready to head to Gibraltar."

Her head hadn't fully wrapped itself around the news yet. Garvin Jardaw had suggested it was possible that raids would be carried out, but she hadn't really taken the threat that seriously. Damn all... well, she had a provisional squadron of repaired and recently completed ships ready to head back to Earth for trade protection... they'd just have to leave sooner than expected.

And hopefully they could get there before the Kroggs could repeat their attack...

The Comm Officer looked up at Liz just as she turned back for an update, "Captain Karr reports a Dreadnought-Mothership raid. Chased off by two 74s, some frigates and sloops and..." the ArcLieutenant frowned and looked down at her screen again, "...sorry *Diadem*, repeat your last please..."

Hastings frowned and leaned over the officer's shoulder to view the transcript of the voice conversation that was now coming up on the comm screen...

"And by *Carriers* ma'am. *Diadem* reports they gave chase, and that *Engadine* and *Monarch* are still in pursuit of Krogg forces... both ships *Carriers*. Also reports that three Carriers and a frigate should be arriving here within a day to carry this same message... they're just moving slower and from further out..."

Hastings was reading much the same on the screen as the information was delivered, "The attack was repelled, they said?"

The ArcLieutenant nodded, "Yes ma'am."

Hastings took a deep breath and turned back to the main screen. *Carriers?*

The Earthers had been developing the Carrier concept, even beginning production — but so far as she'd been told, there were only a handful in space, and they were still only shaking down. They must have been ready enough to deal with the Kroggs... but with them apparently out giving chase, Earth had to be rather slimly protected just now.

Well, she could do something about that...

Hastings stepped out from behind the Comm Officer and nodded again to her ArcColonel, "Signal Barrington to take the 501ˢᵗ to Earth immediately. They'll likely need more support there with all of these Carriers coming to us."

The ArcColonel nodded and turned to his own Ops Officer while Hastings turned to a Sensor Tech on the other side of the C&C deck, "Any sign of an incoming Earther squadron from Earth?"

After a moment the tech shook his head, "Not a thing, ma'am."

Hastings nodded slowly. They'd be coming in, soon, she imagined. Then it would just be a matter of deciding what to do with them...

• • •

Commander Chronos Claw reached the briefing room on the flight deck of *Gibraltar One* and hesitated outside the door. Inside stood the Admirals in charge of the entire Allied Fleet and the commander of the station itself. He knew them all vaguely, generally through Fox Magnus, and he felt a bit anxious to be joining them just now.

He had given them a dose of very bad news, after all. They had plenty to sort out, and it almost felt as though he was imposing... even though he'd been ordered to report.

Taking a breath, Claw opened the hatch and stepped into the room, stopping just inside the door until he was recognized. He stood still for just a moment, noting the presence of Caine, Felix, Ursla and Sarah as they carefully examined the battle plot, studying the daunting situation revealed by *Flame's* intelligence.

Graham was the first of the commanders to notice the arrival of the intrepid sloop master, "Gutsy maneuver there, Commander Claw — well done!" the junior Manchester smiled and approached the cat with an extended hand. "And damned if you didn't scare the Gods' truth out of us!"

Claw nodded in thanks to his human superior, then he took Graham's hand.

"Yes, very well done Chronos," Caine looked up through the plot at the sound of Graham's voice. "Forgive us our inattention — we're a bit mixed up in the strategy of all this right now. How's your ship?"

Claw's ear twitched, "We took some minor damage from the translation, but we've learned some lessons too. Next time should go more smoothly."

A proud smile spread onto Caine's face, and he glanced up at Ursla and then at Felix before rounding the plot to meet *Flame's* commander, "That's what I was hoping you'd say. We've got a couple of jobs for you then, if you're willing."

"Always, sir. I don't think my crew's in the business of saying 'no'..."

Graham grinned and glanced at Caine, "Now I know who to borrow money from."

Caine's smile broadened at the good-natured quip, and Claw felt a surprised smile slipping onto his face — he was feeling quite at home here, not awkward at all...

"Earthers don't use currency, Graham," Felix was staring into the plot, seemingly not paying attention as he answered on behalf of the Earthers in the room.

"Gah, you idealists and your utopia!" Graham's reply seemed harmless enough.

"Anyway," Caine looked from the junior Manchester to Claw, "I need you to get back to Genesis immediately. Show them how to work your energy-hyper, and then get any ship that thinks it can manage it up here as quickly as possible. Then you come back... but by a different route."

Frowning slightly, Claw tilted his head, "I don't think ships any bigger than a sloop will be able to manage the trip, sir — relative strength of energy drive fields being what they are. Without a lot of research, I can't vouch for anything bigger surviving an energy-hyper run without blowing its reactors."

Caine cocked an eyebrow, "Ah. Well, then get all the sloops you can. We'll have to use them for communications — at least we can halve the time it takes to recall ships."

Claw nodded, "Yes sir."

"Good," Caine bobbed his head to the holo tank, then turned to face it, Claw understanding the signal and stepping forward to stand between the First Lord and Graham. "Now here's the course I need you to take back from Genesis," Caine continued. "See the system Pat found that fleet in? I need you to stop by there and let me know whether the Kroggs are still in port. If they're not in the system, we know we've got a problem."

Both Claw's ears twitched — this was no small order. Pat's Pirates had been eviscerated in that system... but *Flame* had a reputation for not being seen or caught. Either way, he'd already said it: *Flame* didn't say 'no'. That was the legacy of Fox Magnus.

"Yes sir," Claw said without delay, then he again noticed Sarah Manchester standing on the far side of the plot. "Should we also look around for survivors from any of the 444th, sir?"

Claw immediately sensed the increased tension his question caused and he watched quietly as Graham looked to Sarah and she looked to Caine with almost pleading eyes...

But the First Lord shook his head and turned to Claw, "There's no evidence of survivors, Chronos. And, I need you back here as soon as possible — we'll need your information and your services again. Minimize your risk on this job, alright?"

Avoiding Sarah's gaze, Claw bobbed his head, "Aye sir."

A little more ponderously, Caine nodded, "Very good. I'll let you get back to your ship then — we'll have a signal for you to carry to Genesis by the time you get back aboard."

"Very good, sir," Claw nodded to Caine, then to Graham and the rest of the commanders. With that he turned on his heel and departed, relieved to leave the tension of the room behind him. *Flame* had a dangerous mission... but what else was new?

Lang Sandpelt wasn't going to be very happy.

"They're coming in now, ma'am. Three *Boadecias* and a frigate."

The ships appeared on the screen as Hastings nodded in reply to the report. They'd just sent *Diadem* to Repair Sixteen to have its engines overhauled, and the

Earther engineers seconded to that station said they could have the converted Carrier ready for space in less than two hours. Just a matter of swapping out some relays, they said — easy enough to do with a ship in dock.

ArcGeneral Barrington and the 501st Provisional Squadron — fourteen ships including two 74s and three Superdreadnoughts — had left exactly forty-two minutes before, heading for Earth with as much speed as they could muster. Hastings' intention was to send the Carrier group out in their wake, with any other ships she could pull together in a two-hour period.

Earth had to be secured.

Captain Karr of *Diadem* had explained the circumstances of the Carrier chase at some length, and had alerted Liz to Commodore Maximane's belief in a Krogg flank base. She'd pass that word on to Caine at Gibraltar — he'd ultimately have to deal with it, so it would be best to let him know before the Kroggs could mount anything.

"Signal coming in from *Boadecia*," the Comm Officer reported abruptly, and Liz shook her mind out of its musings and turned to the screen as the ArcLieutenant continued reporting. "They're sending visual this time."

"Put it up," Hastings ordered, and a black bear appeared.

"Captain Dudley Redvers, ma'am, in *Boadecia*. I have some important news—"

Hastings held up her hand, "*Diadem* arrived a little over an hour ago and reported. Captain Karr's getting his drives adjusted and then I'm going to send you all back to Earth. I sent a provisional squadron to Earth forty-five minutes ago, as well. Do your ships need anything, Captain?"

The bear showed no surprise at being preempted in his announcement, "We're quite well off, actually. Thank you, though. Might I inquire as to the state of *Engadine* and *Monarch*?"

"*Diadem* last saw them four days ago, still pursuing the Krogg ships that attacked Earth."

The Captain nodded, "Very good. If you don't mind, ma'am, I'd like to get my ships prepared to go back."

"Certainly," Hastings nodded and turned away as the signal cut.

"You really think this is going to work, Chronos?" Sandpelt leaned against the side of Claw's chair, and the Commander shrugged.

"Worked the first time. We know what to balance now, so everything should run smoothly."

Sandpelt laughed nervously, "Sure it will. But I suppose we get to set a record, don't we. Gibraltar to Genesis in what, fifteen minutes?"

Chronos took a deep breath, "Ten, maybe."

"Yeah. Ten," Sandpelt turned away slowly. "The hyper field almost set?"

The Cruising Master nodded, "Less than a minute."

With that, Claw keyed the intercom, "Alright everyone. We're going again. Hold onto something secure, we'll be in for ten minutes this time."

The Master looked up from his console and nodded to Sandpelt.

The Lieutenant turned to Claw, "We're set."

Trying not to wonder whether *Flame* would survive a second encounter with insane acceleration, Commander Chronos Claw nodded, "Go."

And they went — *really* fast.

CHAPTER 21

Watching *Flame* disappear from Gibraltar space, Ursla turned to Caine, "Funny, that's the same ship that carried my message to you from Genesis."

Caine smiled sadly, "A lucky ship, I hope."

Lucky indeed.

The Allies' hope of success was yet again carried by that 18-gun sloop, and Caine knew it. With immediate knowledge of impending attack, Genesis could send *everything* it had. And that, at least, was something...

Of course, looking again at the immense energy and grav fronts involved, Caine could see that Claw was quite right — a capital ship would simply be too large and unwieldy to attempt such a dangerous mode of travel, at least on the second or third time out. But by cutting the communication lag between Gibraltar and the scattered Allied squadrons, *Flame* might just make it possible for reinforcements to get to the system in time.

And once *Flame* returned too, the Allies would also know whether the Kroggs had already left their base. That sort of knowledge would at least confirm whether a threat was on its way. If it was, they could attempt to counter it.

"Well... assuming we're basing our estimates on the drone's direct travel time, it's going to take the Kroggs a little while to get here," Felix remarked from the other side of the holo tank. "I'd say ten days total from whenever they left, based on the number of Motherships."

Caine nodded slowly, analyzing the images and readings presented in the new information, "But keep in mind, Savanna, those are new Motherships. Smaller and tougher. Probably faster too... We'd best call it nine days... and that's from whenever they left. If they departed right after Pat's drones, we don't have long... so we best hope *Flame* finds them sitting at anchor. If they don't realize we're on to them, they mightn't have moved."

"Either way, we should try to strengthen ourselves here, eh?" Graham replied, glancing between his Earther compatriots.

Ursla nodded slowly in agreement, but Felix rounded the tank with a thoughtful frown, "We might have a bit of breathing space now, anyway. And if we can get some sloops together and let them in on Chronos' trick, we'll have time to get the word to more squadrons and tell them to get back here."

Eyeing the image of the front displayed in the large plot, Caine noted other squadrons that would be able to come to Gibraltar in time, assuming sloops could get back from Genesis to Gibraltar and replicate *Flame's* speed.

Felix was right, there was a chance now... because a junior engineer had come up with a rather fantastic idea and operationalized it just in time. For a brief second, the First Lord wondered what Garnan's history would have made of that — the commanders in chief being bailed out of a bad situation, at least in part by the ingenuity of their juniors.

He bit back the thought. This might turn out to be just what he'd hoped it could be: a lesson learned without paying the price. They were already discovering the acute dangers of being spread thin... now if they could crush a Krogg counterattack in spite of their weakness they'd gain important wisdom without great loss.

Caine nodded slowly to Felix, then glanced toward Sarah who was standing stonily on the far side of the plot, replaying *Bishop's* flight recorder... *again*.

Pat.

Caine's eyes drifted to the floor as the impact of that loss hit him again. Gone was one of their elite commanders, one of the ones who seemed destined to weather every battle, to defy death and destruction at every turn... this was part of the price he was paying for his mistake. And Sarah was paying it with him.

Her determination to go out after her partner had been forgotten with *Flame's* arrival, at least by the Earthers. There was no need... no *excuse* now. But that couldn't be any sort of consolation to Sarah... torture, perhaps, not consolation.

So now Graham stood close to her, while the three Earthers chose to give her space.

Ursla looked to Caine, then to Felix, "I'm going to head back to *Agamemnon*. I'll see what my engineer says about energy-hyper."

"Yeah... Me too," Felix sighed.

"I'll wait here," Caine said quietly, and Ursla glanced at him. Her instincts told her to go, so she took a breath and left silently.

Graham looked up at the First Lord, then returned his focus to the log playing itself out in the holo tank. He wasn't even sure there was any physical warmth left in Sarah's body — she seemed completely frozen by the images.

And in her mind things were static. She wasn't actually thinking, or hoping, or plotting, or coming up with some scheme, or *anything*. She was virtually catatonic, watching the feed and remembering that Setter Caine had told a sloop Commander there was no sign of survivors.

She knew Caine's statement had been accurate... but it still *felt* wrong.

And there was nothing she could do about it...

But she'd finally gotten things worked out with Pat. She couldn't give him up now...

Well it seemed the Kroggs had made that choice for her: *Bishop*, sole survivor of the 444th, flung itself toward a planet in a nameless system... then the ship bucked, churned, exploded... and Pat was gone.

There was nothing she could do. His life was over, and to some extent, so was hers. She'd go on, she'd do her duty, but she'd be forever different. And alone...

But even as Sarah tried to control the pain that came with those thoughts, the opposing feeling continued to churn inside her — the same sort of feeling that had warned her Pat was going to find trouble on the mission. It had been right before... and now it was telling her that, despite the fact that there was no evidence of survivors from the drone's feeds, Pat was out there.

Alive.

Sarah couldn't ignore that feeling — not this time.

And Caine immediately read that determination on her face. He knew exactly what the commander-in-chief of the Genesis Fleet was thinking — she wanted to go out.

Graham noticed too, and he looked nervously at Caine. He wasn't eager to see his sister brave enemy space to chase a faint hope and a ghost. *Bishop* and the Pirates had died out there as a warning; he couldn't let his sister follow them to the grave.

But in Sarah's mind, options other than going out after Pat were quickly falling away. What else could she do — she couldn't let her grounding force drift into oblivion when she knew, or at least when she *felt* that he was out there. She was a great fleet commander and a formidable warrior... She would use her abilities to find him... She *had to*...

As she looked up at Caine, the First Lord of the Earther Navy met her gaze with stoic sympathy.

"I'm taking *Barron* out there to find survivors, Setter," she said quietly, and Caine took a breath.

Graham interjected, "No, Sarah, you are *not*. There aren't any survivors — you've seen the readings..."

The senior Manchester turned to the junior, "I can... *feel* it Graham. Don't start with me..."

He opened his mouth, but seeing the desperate, determined expression on her face he chose to close it without replying.

Sarah turned back to Caine, her determination bolstered by Graham's failure to object, "Do *you* have a problem, Setter?"

Caine read her tone quietly, detecting both grief and determination. She wasn't ready to handle this problem rationally just yet, and he couldn't grudge her that. But he couldn't let her rush into anything she could regret later... if it didn't kill her...

"It's your decision, Sarah," he said quietly. "We need you here, and there are no signs of survivors. But it's your ship, and your mission, and your choice.

Just remember what you're leaving behind if you do go."

"One ship won't matter here, and despite what you say I don't... *feel* that he's gone..." her words drew a surprised stare from Graham.

Caine kept his eyes locked on hers, "One ship *will* make a difference, Sarah. Because I made a mistake out here, every ship will be needed to make sure it doesn't cost us the war. It's my fault, but it's the way things are."

Sarah blinked a few times as she heard the words, and taking a deep breath she started to shake her head, "No, it's... it's..."

Caine walked softly around the tank to see her more clearly, "You've put yourself in the middle of a lot of fights. This one will probably kill you, and most likely for nothing. I need you here, but I can't tell you to stay. It's really your choice, and I'll respect your decision. But *please* don't leave us."

Sarah's jaw trembled slightly at the plea, but she continued to peer into the First Lord's eyes, "But I *must* go, Setter... even... even if just to give you warning of when the attack comes."

Caine shook his head, "The Fleet Commander doesn't get picket duty."

She looked away, trying to convince herself to give up, trying to convince herself to just go anyway.

"You decide, Sarah," Caine put a gentle hand on her shoulder.

Shifting her weight anxiously, Sarah sighed — he was right. She had to stay here and command, even though there were already three brilliant fleet commanders in the system...

And she *loathed* herself for having doubted her duty.

Without a word she turned away, shrugging off Caine's hand and brushing past Graham before he could react.

"Sarah..." she was out the door before he could say anymore.

Looking back to Caine, the junior Manchester took a breath, "I... bloody bad business, eh?"

Caine nodded slowly, "Painful. Very painful... for all of us."

CHAPTER 22

"Hyper footprint ma'am — the energy output is *massive!*"

Hastings' head whipped up at the report, and she deftly stepped around the Comm Officer's console, "On screen."

The main screen in *Genesis One's* C&C lit up with a sector map that displayed a flashing black hyper point just beyond the range of the station's missile envelope. Its size was astounding... like 1,000 ships all in hyper transit at once...

Dear Gods. This was unthinkable...

"General quarters! All warships to action stations! Alert Genesis civil defense to prepare for ground incursions..." Hastings turned quickly to *Genesis One's* ArcColonel as she barked the orders, and the command deck suddenly began to buzz.

"Point's about to open..." the Sensor Officer's follow-up report drew Hastings' eyes back to the screen.

As the flashing black field began to pulse faster, Hastings felt her breath catch. The Superdreadnought *Pope Kiley McCreary* was near the exit point, and in a gallant maneuver the lone Genesis ship turned to bring its tubes to bear on the forming hyper point... for all the good one Superdreadnought was going to do against such a powerful foe. What had happened to Earth was about to happen here, but on a much larger scale...

The field coalesced and the window to a different layer of subspace opened.

A swirling ball of energy burst from the hyper point, then quickly dropped out of energy drive, returning to its traditional form...

"*Flame.* Gods dammit, it's *Flame!*"

The crew of the C&C seemed to simultaneously release a gasp of relief, and after a few seconds, messages began to flow in.

Captain Garvin Jardaw was quite pleased with the restoration of *Highlander's* broadside. The Earther crews stationed in the Genesis repair slips retained the knack for restoring ships in short order, as evidenced by the slightly larger form of *Diadem*, which was now edging out of its own repair dock after only two hours service.

Jardaw was to join the Carriers *Diadem, Godetia, Galatea, Boadecia* and the frigate *Caesar* in a Provisional Carrier Group. Sitting on *Highlander's* bridge, he quietly gave orders and watched as his ship maneuvered to join the Carrier formation just beyond the range of the repair slips. A number of other Earther vessels fresh from other Genesis slips were joining this group as well.

Two of the handsome new 44-gun *Charybdis*-class frigates — *Charybdis* and *Acheron* — were present, as were two 38s — *Penelope* and *Constitution* — and another 64, *Elephant*. Altogether this constituted a light and quick mixed squadron, save for the bulky Carriers.

All that remained to be confirmed was their final destination. Fifteen minutes earlier, Jardaw would have expected to be going right back to Earth — Captain Karr of *Diadem* had sent him information regarding the situation at the homeworld as soon as he slipped into the repair dock. But now, with *Flame's* abrupt arrival from places unknown, Jardaw couldn't be sure.

"ArcGeneral Hastings hailing," *Highlander's* Signal Officer reported abruptly.

"Very good," Jardaw sat back in his chair as a screen appeared in the main tank.

Hastings' figure glowed to life in the main holo tank, her face darkened by a frown, "Captain, you're being sent a detailed orders packet right now. And I'm making you Commodore of the Provisional Carrier Group. Get it to Gibraltar as quickly as you can."

Jardaw froze... *Commodore?* He'd been a Post Captain for barely a month, and that was in *Highlander* — what was he supposed to do with Carriers?

"Ma'am?" he asked with a raised eyebrows.

"Your ships are the fastest we have in fighting trim right now — and after your experience on the way here I'm giving you overall responsibility. You'll probably want to defer to Karr or Redvers on Carrier tactics if it comes to it, but I'm giving you complete charge of the overall force. Get it to Gibraltar within eight days, if you can."

"It's a ten-day trip, ma'am."

Hastings nodded, "I know. Do it in eight. *Flame* brings word that there could be a major battle at Gibraltar in nine... if not before."

Jardaw nodded thoughtfully, opened his mouth to ask a question, and then watched as Hastings abruptly vanished. Alright, that meant there wasn't much time to clarify.

Without any more instruction, then, Jardaw turned to his First Lieutenant, "Let's get under weigh. Signal the squadron of my appointment and hoist a broad pennant. I'll take the packet in the main tank."

"Aye sir," she replied with a smile. "Congratulations."

Jardaw blinked and nodded, "Um, thank you..."

I think...

Flame dropped grav anchors alongside *Genesis One* while the Carrier group launched quickly into energy drive. Those Carriers were fast ships, but Claw knew he'd found a way to make sloops much, much faster. A *dangerous* way to make them faster, of course, because while they'd managed to use it twice now, they had no idea just what sort of strain repetition might put on power grids and reactors.

But circumstance required the use of this innovation, so it was up to *Flame's* crew to introduce it to the engineers of the other sloops currently stationed in Genesis space for courier duty. Alongside *Flame* now were nine other equally diminutive ships: two older sloops of 16 guns, a new 20 and six of 18 guns. Their chief engineers had all just gone aboard *Genesis One* to meet with Lang Sandpelt and learn the basics of energy-hyper.

The *very* basics, that was, since *Flame's* expertise in the field amounted to two tries.

"Engineering reports the drives are fitted out and ready to go again," *Flame's* Master said as he moved to his Commander's side. "We can make the run to that base at any time."

Claw nodded, "Good. Caine's waiting for our intel... we'll leave as soon as Lang returns."

The Master nodded silently.

Hastings was still getting over her shock at *Flame's* abrupt and entirely unconventional arrival as she began to concern herself with the serious challenge at hand

There were a lot of Kroggs concentrated out there.

The main screen in *Genesis One's* C&C was filled with lists of all the ships in Genesis space, including those under repair or fresh from the construction yards. Hastings was desperately trying to pull together a solid group to send out to Gibraltar after Jardaw and the Carriers, but so far she wasn't looking at a particularly large formation.

Having sent Barrington off with an impressive chunk of her in-system force, she was sorely lacking in capital ships. She couldn't recall the Earth force because of the serious threat of another Earth raid. With the two 74s left behind by Maximane when he pursued the attackers, Barrington and the Earthers could put a reasonable defensive force into space around the Earther planet. But what about Genesis? There had to be defenders in this system too, and that meant a tricky balance between defense at home and at the front...

And while Caine's message asked for reinforcements at Gibraltar, Hastings couldn't help but wonder if, after that raid on Earth, the Krogg Fleet wouldn't look to follow up and overwhelm the Earther home... or Genesis.

Caine hadn't known of the raid on Earth when he'd sent the call for reinforcements... could she override him now to keep some ships here and send some to Earth?

No. No, if there was any Naval officer whose judgment Liz Hastings would trust with the fate of her homeworld, it was Setter Caine. He said the front, and even though he didn't have the full picture he had *enough* of it...

And war, after all, was never without risks.

Examining her lists of active ships, she selected her two capital squadrons — the remains of the Genesis Home Fleet — and ordered them to Gibraltar. Twelve Superdreadnoughts and twelve Dreadnoughts, leaving just one Destroyer squadron in system, acting as picket. She promptly selected the Destroyers and sent them as well.

Now to the wounded ships... fourteen capital ships were in dock and could be launched with relative safety at four hours' notice. She gave them that notice, then copied the orders to four more cruisers and frigates. They'd form another provisional force and head out in... five hours. That brought the total reinforcement group up to thirty-eight capital ships and sixteen escorts... all of which would try to make a ten-day trip in eight.

It was unfortunate that the energy-hyper strategy developed by Claw on *Flame* was so dangerous. The technology allowing the use of the energy-hyper configuration by capital class vessels could probably be worked out given time, but they didn't *have* time.

So that would have to wait for later.

In the meantime, Genesis was soon to be stripped of its mobile defenses.

ArcGeneral Elizabeth Hastings sighed deeply and got back to the business of mounting a reinforcement operation. For now they had to gamble and hope...

Flame weighed grav anchor as soon as Lang Sandpelt's pinnace returned to the ship from *Genesis One*. Sitting on the bridge, Chronos Claw nodded to his cruising master, "Let's go have a look out there. Signal Officer, inform the sloop group to make for Gibraltar as soon as they're confident in their drive configurations. We'll meet them there a bit later."

Shifting somewhat expectantly in his seat, Claw watched as *Flame* began to accelerate under normal drives away from the line of sloops. They just needed to gain enough open space to allow the safe forming of a hyper point...

As *Flame* got far enough out, the Master nodded to the engineer on the bridge, and a hyper field was projected from the Wyndhymn generators through the forward shield emitters. The subspace layers just ahead of the slowly-cruising sloop began to warp.

Without any need for orders, the Master then stopped the sloop in space, and the warp in the spatial layers opened a slit just before *Flame's* bow.

"Ready for entry, sir," the Master looked back to Claw, and the young commander nodded.

"Very well. Bring us to energy drive, enter hyperspace at your discretion."

Seconds later, *Flame* slammed into a different subspace layer, heading for the Krogg base at once-impossible speeds.

CHAPTER 23

The blue vegetation was calm around the lightweight Earther boat — to quote a cliché phrase, *too* calm.

Sergeant Major Beckett Lupus was lying in the rear of the boat as the shore passed, his eyes hovering just above the side and his gaze piercing the thick brush as best it could. This was their fourth day on the water and according to the positioning sensors they would reach the human camp within minutes.

The brush around the camp seemed so utterly calm it was as though something had scared away all the native fauna. And the only thing Beckett Lupus could think of that was terrifying enough to scare off that many local creatures was a force of Kroggs. The human camp was quite probably under siege.

"Port side, Beck, I see movement," the words would have been inaudible if it wasn't for Lupus' sensitive hearing. Turning his head very slightly, the Sergeant Major let his eyes track the movement that had been reported... yes, there they were. Kroggs out on the port bank, silently following the Earther boat, probably hoping the Earther arrival would cause the humans to open their defenses just long enough to strike...

Lupus' veteran eyes sought to differentiate between the signs of movement. Four... no six soldiers were barely visible. A scouting squad.

"Get on the pulsar," he replied softly.

Howler slid down the side of the boat and reached the large gun, keying its power pack to full. They'd mounted the big energy guns on the boat just in case circumstances like this arose... now it looked as though the heavy weapons would be needed...

Ahead the brush thinned into a clearing, and as far as Lupus could see there were open, sky-blue grassy plains. Looking carefully, he could also make out the silhouette of a fallen escape pod on the horizon further down the river... nearly four kilometers away, if his visual range judgment was working to its usual sharp standard.

How fast can the Kroggs cover that distance? And what about those soldiers reporting this location to the Destroyers... we have to take them down quickly.

A branch shook on the shore, and a Krogg came clearly into view. This was as good a time as any, then... Lupus barked the command, "Fire!"

The squad opened up with their rifles first, shredding vegetation with coarse energy beams, then Howler squeezed the trigger on his massive pulsar. The boat rocked slightly sideways with the recoil and the massive burst seared through the underbrush, knocking down trees and burning away plant life.

Kroggs screamed in outrage, bursting into plain view at a flat run.

Without a word, the Earthers turned their fire to the rushing aliens, immediately knocking down two, leaving four to charge towards the bank of the river in an attempt to reach the boat. Swinging his rifle inboard, Lupus reached to the command console and keyed the boat's above-waterline shields.

Just in case.

The pulsar's whine continued, and two more Kroggs exploded as the heavy gun caught them. Only two of the scouts survived to reach the water, the first one losing his lone eye to a rifle shot and his head to the pulsar. The final Krogg reached the boat and attempted to slam a blade into the side. The sharp bone bounced off the shield above the waterline, but then glanced into the unshielded hull beneath the water's surface...

Lupus turned back to the console and reached for the underwater shield key, cursing his decision not to reactivate that one for the sake of speed — he'd turned both shields off to avoid detection from orbit while they traveled... but now it was too late.

Driving into the boat engine, the Krogg's blade shattered, and its fragments ripped through the finely-machined impellers, thoroughly destroying them. The soldier screamed and collapsed back into the water where a pulsar blast cut him in two... and the sound of the running engine stopped altogether.

"We've got a bit of a problem, I think," Lupus said quietly, glancing to Howler.

The Corporal's eyes had widened at the silence, and the two wolves sighed simultaneously.

ArcColonel Jessica Forbes ran point for her fire team, stepping through the portal in the defensive shield and cautiously entering the unprotected plain at the head of her column. They'd heard the sound of energy weapons — a likely sign the Kroggs had found more survivors from her crew...

As *Harbinger Bishop's* ArcColonel, Forbes had been given a certain amount of latitude when it came to fitting out her escape pod with supplies for a hostile planet landing. That preparation had paid off: she'd stowed forty energy rifles, a pulsar, four shield generators, and an Earther minifab plant — one of the tiny units that could build anything smaller than a chair if it was supplied with the raw materials — in the hold of her pod, and now this gear was keeping her people alive. With three pods and 200 people collected on this plain, she'd managed to maximize the overall chances of survival. The mini plant was even producing a new energy rifle every day.

Unfortunately, fate hadn't granted them a particularly good location. They were wide open here — shields only afforded them modest protection — and

Forbes' ultimate hope was that once they could arm enough of the survivors to neutralize Krogg raids she could move everyone towards the mountains.

But for now, the sounds of energy rifle fire suggested that another group of crashed survivors had found the camp... and that the Kroggs were in pursuit.

"Team two is out through the starboard shield now," the voice of ArcLieutenant Kitts reached Forbes through her earpiece.

Kitts, as junior, was in command of the second fire team Forbes had assembled. Both twenty-three person teams now wielded energy weapons, and many of their members were marines who'd survived *Bishop's* destruction. Carrying their light-pattern Earther rifles they stood a chance against Kroggs, though the pulsar they'd salvaged — their most effective Krogg killer — was too heavy to be considered mobile, so it was guarding their makeshift camp.

The day was darkening — the sun was falling below the horizon and the sky was turning yellow. Forbes couldn't afford to let her people get caught out after dark — the Kroggs could slaughter the humans at will if they were caught at night in the open... well, the aliens could slaughter *Bishop's* crew during the day, too, but at night there'd be no way to see them coming.

"We'll head down to the river, you head for the brush. Don't go past the perimeter of the field, though. You could get ambushed if you go into the woods," Forbes spoke softly into her microphone, then waved her team towards the darkening riverbank.

"Movement on the plain, Beck," one of the wolves near the front of the boat spoke in low tones.

Lupus turned to see the plain fill with what he estimated to be sixty figures, moving slowly, and watching all angles for incoming attacks. The concern over the boat engine now seemed entirely unimportant... it looked as though only three quarters of those figures were human.

"The crew must have heard our weapons firing," Lupus said quietly. "They've come out to see what's going on... and there are probably Kroggs hiding in that depression in the ground in case they did."

He didn't have to say more. In the failing light, the humans wouldn't stand a chance against the Kroggs that were moving to take them. So now it was up to Beckett and his squad to stop a slaughter...

In a single motion, Lupus swept himself through the shield, over the side, and into the cool water. Howler, taking the pulsar off its mount, followed quickly, as did four more of the wolf squad. The last one remained in the boat, shifting the starboard-mounted pulsar to the port side and watching the squad advance into the twilight.

"Tim here, skipper. We're about a click out, heading for the bounce hole." Forbes heard the report and replied without thinking, "Good."

The 'bounce hole' was the place her pod had hit and bounced from during its rough landing, lying about a kilometer from the current camp. It was a good marker for the progress of the ArcLieutenant's advance, and as she watched him approach it her team fanned out and moved obliquely towards the riverbank.

Then her ear filled with static.

Stopping in surprise, she put a hand to her ear, "Tim? Tim!"

The team halted around her and the sound of energy fire crossed the plain. Ripping out the earpiece, Forbes keyed her rifle to full charge and turned for the bounce hole, knowing it was too far away for her to reach in time to do much good, but determined to try to help anyway.

"Caught," Lupus whispered to himself as the Kroggs started to rise from the depression, and he quickened his pace as the aliens swept from their hiding place. Howler was close behind him with the pulsar, but at such range he couldn't risk using the weapon lest he hit humans in the process.

No, Lupus and his squad needed to get closer. Their sprint from the boat had started just under three kilometers from the depression the Kroggs were hiding in, and the wolves almost covered the distance in four minutes... but they weren't in range. They had to go faster, but there were limits to their speed...

Howler's eyes narrowed as he came to the top of a low ridge in the field. He could manage to shoot cleanly from here, and he had to, because the Kroggs were about to eviscerate every human outside the shields of the camp...

Swinging the hundred-pound pulsar off his back, he drew the telescoping stand from his belt, drove it into the ground and mounted the weapon. As his squad ran on, he trained the great energy gun at the enemy and opened fire.

Even at such long range the energy burst batted one Krogg down in the depression and drew the attention of the rest — some of whom were now in the loose human formation, wreaking havoc.

The Kroggs immediately recognized a new and far more formidable threat on the plain, their postures changing and some of them turning to face the direction of the energy fire.

Running hard, Lupus cast his rifle aside, drawing his heavy pistol and sword instead. He moved fast and hard, his muscles aching but not failing him.

His short sword hummed to life just as the half dozen Kroggs rushed out of the depression, making a headlong sprint for the wolf and his four marines. Behind them, sitting atop what Lupus now saw was a high point on the lowly rolling plain, Howler let loose another barrage from the pulsar. One Krogg exploded, and then the wolf hefted his huge energy gun off its mount and sprinted down after the squad.

• • •

Forbes watched as the twilight lit up with a pulsar burst from the top of the next undulation — she could barely make out figures running down the gradual slope towards the bounce hole. That's where the Kroggs must have been hiding... they must have killed Kitts before he knew what hit him.

Her team was just over a kilometer away...

Lupus keyed his shield as the first Krogg neared. The soldier held his arms and blades out to slash Lupus as he went by, but the Sergeant Major was far too adept for the soldier's maneuver to meet any success. Diving into a low summersault, Lupus came to his feet behind the swinging Krogg, his sword slashing angrily across the alien's back.

The Krogg pitched forward and Lupus fired into the wound, vaporizing several internal organs. The alien fell limp.

Then the rest of the squad hit the Kroggs like a whirlwind. Again, Lupus saw the strengths of his well-honed, elite recon unit: they were light, fast, and tough. His wolves hacked apart the charging Kroggs, severing limbs and slashing through carapaces.

Seven more Kroggs came down the depression's side now, and Lupus turned to face them. The pulsar lashed out from behind his squad, quickly knocking down one Krogg. As the squad braced to receive the rest, a massive volley erupted from the direction of the camp.

Four Kroggs pitched forward as raw energy cracked open their backs, the last two reaching the squad only to meet the wolves' blades...

And that was all of them; in a blinding moment of action, the recon squad had dealt with this Krogg ambush... But the Earthers couldn't afford to push their luck — surprise had been on their side here, and luck wouldn't hold forever.

Lupus sighed and keyed off his sword, then sheathed it and holstered his pistol. He turned and softly spoke to one of the squad Privates, "Pawman, could you get our rifles please?"

Nodding, the marine turned and retraced his course up the gentle slope, passing Howler as the Corporal descended to stop before his Sergeant.

"Fine shooting, as usual," Lupus nodded to his friend, and Cadmus Howler smiled in thanks.

Humans swarmed the depression, holding their rifles close, some looking nervous, others carrying themselves with the confidence of experience. Lupus recognized a number of them, and he noted the relief on many of the human faces as they saw him. Then ArcColonel Forbes picked her way through the crowd.

"Sergeant Major Lupus?" she trotted down the depression and came to a stop in front of him, not even bothering to try to hide her relief.

He nodded with a kind smile, "ArcColonel Forbes, it's very good to see you.

We've come to bring you back to the mountains. ArcBrigadier Conroy is setting up a secure camp there with a handful of survivors."

Forbes' eyes brightened, "Good to hear. And glad you came along too — thanks for the help."

Lupus nodded, "We'd better get in before it gets dark."

Forbes bobbed her head in reply, and the Earthers and humans collected themselves, their wounded and dead, then headed back to the camp.

"Silent routine established, skipper. Field at 200 percent and holding, I don't think they've seen us."

Chronos Claw nodded evenly as his Master gave the report, then he came from his seat and frowned at the plot on *Flame's* bridge. They'd energy-hypered to a spot far enough from the Krogg base system to avoid detection and then cruised the rest of the way under conventional drives. Now *Flame's* ability to see without being seen would be put to the test.

Or *not*.

Keying the intercom, Claw frowned at what his sensors were showing him of the system, "Sensor Control, confirm what I'm seeing here — there's nothing in the system."

There was a pause on the other end of the line, then a sensor technician replied, "About a dozen ships that I can make out on the far side, sir. But definitely no fleet... wait a moment..."

Cocking an eyebrow, Claw glanced to the Master, then the battle plot shifted as Sensor Control fed it new data.

"Sir, there's a big hyperspace wake there. You mightn't be able to see it in the plot, but we're detecting enough spatial distortion for a fleet the size we're looking for."

The report drew a frown from Chronos Claw, and he rose from his chair and paced to the plot, examining the thin bands representing the wake, "So what's that tell us, Sensors?"

There was a pause, then a few new elements popped up in the plot, "Theoretically speaking, the wake fades within a day of departure... well, theoretically for a fleet this size. We've never tracked this much wake before — we didn't know to look for it after Genesis."

Indeed, hyperspace wakes were only mildly more tested on the theoretical side than energy- hyper. Commodore Ami Cairn had been the first to discover them when her frigate had been pushed out of energy drive by one... hopefully the science she'd discovered would pan out on the larger scale.

With that in mind, Claw straightened up and looked to the overhead speakers, "So they left within the past day? Where are they headed?"

"Couldn't say, sir. But whoever's receiving will have a bit of time to get ready for them."

Well that was something anyway. *Flame* could go looking for the Kroggs, but with a day's head start on their side, the aliens could easily lose the sloop in space... or worse, catch it and realize they'd been made.

No, Caine would need this information most of all. He'd figure out who they were attacking, now that he knew when...

"Alright, thanks Sensors," Claw hit the intercom key on the plot's side and turned to his Master. "No point trying to track them and getting caught... let's get out of here. Regular drives out of sensor range, then energy-hyper to Gibraltar."

The Master nodded, "Aye sir."

Flame turned and left the system that had consumed Pat's Pirates.

CHAPTER 24

Archangel Sword slid out of flux at the head of the Freetown Squadron, *Atlas* and *Vulcan* having come out of energy drive seconds earlier.

"Convoy dropping out of energy drive. Nothing foreign on scopes, skipper."

James Stanton looked up from his pad and nodded, absently considering how meager that good news seemed when contrasted with the dire situation at hand. Fox Magnus had been good enough to beam a copy of the most recent Earther deployments to *Archangel Sword*, and for the past two days James had been trying to figure out a way to mount a defense against the sort of force the Kroggs had put together.

Unfortunately, he wasn't coming up with anything.

Of course this was really Caine's problem, not his, but he still felt somehow obligated to lend a hand. He wanted to make some positive contributions, and to ease the First Lord's burden.

"I'm reading seven squadrons in system," *Sword's* Sensor Officer reported with a frown.

Stanton looked up, "That's three more than I would have expected. Numbers on the newcomers?"

The officer paused, "The 132nd, 112th, and 309th. Sixteen 74s and a squadron of 44s."

Stanton cocked an eyebrow. For those formations to have made it to Gibraltar this quickly, Chronos must have made incredibly good time to the system… and the drones would have had to make exceptional time reaching their picket systems…

That was usually half the trouble with deployment, after all; it took twice the transit time to get a squadron where you wanted it because communication wasn't direct — a courier had to find the squadron first. That travel requirement meant there were a number of squadrons actually within three or four days of Gibraltar that would take a week to reach the system. So what had Claw managed here? He'd cut the transit times for these squadrons right in half, based on the deployments Fox had passed along.

Claw had either figured out a way to travel a few days' distance in a minute, or Caine was more on top of the situation than James would have thought possible.

Well he could pretty much rule out the former — unless the sloop commander had tried that insane energy-hyper thing he'd mentioned once at the *Pulsar*.

Probably the latter.

James turned back to his pad.

On the bridge of *Orion*, Caine watched the convoy arrive with more than a little relief. With crews working hard, the cargo haulers could dump their unassembled stations and engineers could have the orbitals running inside five days — well before the Kroggs were expected to arrive.

The situation certainly could have been worse.

The 74s that had been escorting the convoy would be useful as well, though their contribution was not so dramatic as that of the heavily armed *Gibraltar* stations. As for the Privateer Squadron... well, it would probably have little practical use in a slugging match, as much as Caine wished otherwise. Lacking capital ships of their own, the Freetown renegades would simply be slaughtered in the crossfire if it came to a major broadside battle.

Caine would probably just ask them to go home as soon as they could stock up on requisite supplies... Give them a chance to get out cleanly and protect their planet, or find a new one if further Krogg raids had wrecked the first.

Because the Kroggs were operating back there... they had even attacked Caine's home space.

Only hours earlier, sloops had brought that information back from Genesis: Earth had been attacked. So much for his hope that the Kroggs were being kept busy by the Allied efforts out here... Earth had been lucky so far as he knew — there'd been no follow-up to the initial attack, and Draco Maximane, a fine officer by all accounts, was hunting down the Kroggs who knew where the Earther homeworld was...

But as far as Setter Caine was concerned, it was still a failure on his part. His strategy had opened Earth to attack, and had now seen one carried out. So it was no longer just a matter of him having failed his Navy by scattering them across broad front lines; he'd nearly failed his home, and his family. He'd narrowly avoided paying for that failure with Earther civilian losses, but only through luck.

And he was beginning to deeply fear the moment when that luck ended. The Kroggs couldn't be stymied any longer by Earther momentum — if the tables turned and his planning was as inadequate as it seemed to be right now, the war effort might collapse.

But Caine knew he couldn't think about that — if he dwelled on the possibility of defeat instead of working against it, he'd be as good as surrendering. And there were opportunities to take advantage of now.

Chronos Claw had brought *Flame* back from the Krogg base hours earlier, and the report that the Krogg Fleet was indeed on the move surprised no one. At least the Allies had eight or nine days, just as Felix had suspected — so long as the assessment of the age of that hyperspace wake was correct... Caine had to assume it was. And with that assumption came the most crucial decision he might ever make: to protect Gibraltar, or to rush every ship he had home to protect Earth. The Krogg Fleet could be going either way, there was no way to track it...

He still wasn't certain of what to do. He was collecting strength at Gibraltar, but with the firepower of the stations now moving into place, he could conceivably send every mobile unit he had to Earth's defense...

Caine sat back in his chair. He had to make a decision, and soon.

Audrey strummed her fingers on the arm of her chair as *Grendelsbane* led *New Cashtown*, *Forton* and *Vance* into smart anchoring order alongside James' ships. The squadron's grav anchors — Earther devices they'd elected to install in their ships to replace the temperamental human station-keeping thrusters — dropped simultaneously, and each ship's main drives went to standby.

Despite the time they'd spent relaxing at Freetown, the squadron was still smartly honed for combat.

Audrey, however, was nervous about being at Gibraltar. Part of the uncertainty could be simply attributed to loneliness — she hadn't been with James for weeks after being spoiled by a routine of constant contact with her co-commander, and it was wearing on her just a little. Added to that was an uncertainty about the Krogg threat, and what it meant not only to the stability of the front lines but to the security of the home planets of the Alliance...

"Haulers are moving into orbit and beginning their unloading procedures. Flag is transmitting orders to *Atlas* — looks like Captain Magnus will be heading to *Orion* for a debriefing," the Signal Officer announced as he eavesdropped on Earther ship-to-ship traffic.

"Anything for us yet?" Audrey asked quietly, and the Lieutenant shook his head.

Well they'd have to wait then...

Audrey sighed and rubbed her forehead ruefully. She wanted to do *something...*

"He did *what?*"

Fox tried to contain his grin in front of the flag officers in *Orion's* briefing room, but it was really just a half-hearted attempt. He'd assumed Chronos Claw had been just telling stories at the *Pulsar*... That devil.

Fox had thought *Flame's* commander was *sane...*

Well, wrong about that one I suppose.

Ursla was sitting on the edge of the briefing table, and she offered a grin in reply to his remark, "Indeed, *energy-hyper*. Scared the hell out of us — we thought the Kroggs were here."

Fox snorted a laugh, "Typical of him. But marvelous all the same. Sometimes I miss the life of a cruiser..."

Ursla nodded knowingly, "Some days you just want the speed back, I know. Though I don't miss the low deckheads."

Fox nodded with a smile, "True enough..."

Caine cocked his eyebrow and cleared his throat.

Fox sobered and Ursla shrugged, "Sorry Setter, it's a cruiser-skipper thing."

The First Lord harrumphed, "Been a battleship fellow all my life. And I like it that way. In any case, Fox, Savanna's said he'd like to reattach you to the 301st, but since you've been out on your own for so long I've convinced him to let me keep you on hand for any special assignments that come up. I may be needing scouts soon."

Fox nodded with a bit of a frown, "Where is Admiral Felix, sir?"

Caine smiled wryly, "Meeting an old friend."

Fox's frown deepened, and Ursla grinned, "The pre-fab defense station."

I thought I'd finally gotten through this phase of my career.

Felix sat on his bridge as *Tonnant* came alongside *Gibraltar Two*'s floating components. As one of the Admirals who, in his desk days, had supervised the deployment of both the new *Mars* and *Asteroid* stations, he'd been given charge of the quick setup of the *Gibraltars*.

He knew what corners to cut.

And time was certainly of the essence...

"Alright, here's what we do," Felix turned to the team of engineers standing around *Tonnant's* main plot. "We don't pressurize until the last phase, guns go in first, then C&C. Modules six and fourteen are nice, but we won't need them until the very end... and as for the triple-bolting thing, *don't*. I've never seen one of our bolts give out, so double redundancy is more than enough..."

As the Admiral spoke, the engineers listened intently.

Fox left *Orion's* briefing room an hour after he arrived, and as the Commodore went, Caine leaned back in his chair and hefted a weighty sigh.

Turning slightly towards her friend, Ursla cocked an eyebrow, "What?"

Caine's eyes fixed on the holo projection that was glowing at the center of the table, noting its information on the dispositions of the Allied front line and the placement of the Krogg base relative to both Genesis and Earth.

After a moment he shrugged slightly, "You tell me what you'd do, Andra, because I'm not sure yet."

Frowning, Ursla leaned forward and planted her elbows on the table, "Not sure of *what*, exactly?"

Caine leaned forward as well, cocking his eyebrow, "What to protect. It was easy enough to go with Savanna's conclusion that they'd come for Gibraltar *before* Claw arrived with word of the raid... but they've already hit Earth once. The fleet they've put together could overwhelm Earth and take most of our infrastructure out of the war."

"Ah," Ursla's eyes shifted to the plot.

"At the same time, they can't afford not to use that sort of concentrated firepower to come after us, to stop their immediate problem. They knock Gibraltar out of the war, they buy themselves the time they need to consolidate their forces on this front..."

"Ah," Ursla repeated the sound, and Caine's eyes drifted to her.

"So," he said quietly, "what call do I make? I can trust my head or my instincts, but either way I don't think I'll be fully convinced."

Ursla's eyes fell to the table — it was quite the question. Earthers were great thinkers, and yet they were also great *feelers*... Forced to choose, which should they rely on to make a decision like this?

"Well... if Savanna were here I think he'd say instinct. I'm sure he would, actually. And I'd agree. I don't think we've been trusting our instincts enough lately, but when you and I went with them about that pod we were right. So follow your instincts."

Caine blinked and his ear twitched. He looked from Ursla to the plot, and his gaze found the glowing blue orb of Earth on the holo's far side before tracing its way up to Gibraltar.

"Indeed," he said quietly. "Then they're coming here. My instincts say they know we're here, and they're coming for us with everything they have. There's no evidence of that whatsoever, but it's what they're doing."

Ursla looked from the plot to Caine's solemn face and then nodded, "So we better be ready for them."

Caine blinked again, then looked at his friend, "And we'd better hope my instincts are right."

They sat in silence.

Sarah watched the renegade — *privateer* — squadron maneuver into parking orbit near Gibraltar. She was still feeling ashamed after Caine's pleas — she knew he needed her, and the thought of leaving him now was so much harder because, as much as she resisted the notion, she sometimes let go of her longtime orphan mindset and thought of the Earther as a father. Graham did too, or so he'd told her once; Caine was so well-meaning, so paternal, so wise...

How could she fail him?

Well she knew precisely how she could — she could abandon her post and go after Pat. She could follow the deepest feelings in her gut, trust her instincts and forget her responsibilities.

That'd disappoint Setter Caine, and the Alliance, rather spectacularly.

And yet, as much as she knew that, the deepest fibers of her being still told her that her very survival depended on doing it. And while her rational side argued that this was overly-emotional dribble drawn from a lack of experience in love, she still had to go.

Even if she'd regret it for the rest of her life.

And even if Setter Caine, her veritable father-figure, begged her not to.

She *had* to find Pat. He was out there somewhere, and he needed her.

So sitting in her cabin on *Joseph Barron*, she let a plan coalesce in her mind, and as it did, she keyed her comm.

"I need a secure channel to *Archangel Sword*."

"How about brunch tomorrow?" Ursla stretched her massive arms as she stood, and Caine smiled and nodded as he came to his feet. They'd spent enough time working on this problem for one evening — the situation was well in hand... at least the aspects that could be put in hand.

"Indeed, brunch sounds–" the chirping intercom cut Caine off, and he frowned curiously at Ursla as they waited two seconds for the Signal Officer to speak.

"Signal Officer here, sir. We just picked up a strange comm call... looks like *Joseph Barron* sent a signal to *Archangel Sword* on Batron 54."

Caine cocked an eyebrow, "A coded signal?"

"Yes sir," the Signal Officer replied. "Just thought you should know, sir."

Nodding, Caine addressed the ceiling speakers, "Yes, thanks Signals."

"Yes sir," the intercom cut.

Ursla frowned as Caine looked down at her again, "Why would Sarah want to talk to the privateers... she wouldn't want to scold them for anything..."

Caine's ear flicked again. Looking back to the plot, he let out a short sigh, then keyed the holo projection off.

"I told her to make a choice. She may just have done that."

CHAPTER 25

James was on his way to *Sword's* landing deck when the intercom chirped in the corridor ceiling above him, "Bridge to Captain Stanton, we're receiving a signal for you from flag."

Eager to meet Audrey as she came across from *Grendelsbane City*, James didn't slow down with the announcement. He was only a few seconds from the flight deck anyway — he could take the call from there.

It was probably Felix or Ursla — two Earthers he certainly would be happy to talk to again, but two who would never be greeted on the flight deck as *enthusiastically* as he'd be greeting Audrey. If he tried to hug Ursla the way he was about to hug his fellow human Captain, it would be both highly inappropriate and entirely back-breaking.

Snap.

Grinning at his mused joke, James rounded the last corner and came to a stop at the flight deck door, stepping through after some spacers exited. He was not taking himself altogether seriously enough these days — he certainly shouldn't be thinking about *hugs* on flight decks, that just wasn't appropriate for a professional spacer...

But then again he *was* a renegade. He could be sloppy, inappropriate and downright unpleasant if he wanted to be — no one could do a damn thing about it...

Ah, but there wasn't much chance of him or his people taking full advantage of that latitude, because despite calling themselves renegades, the privateers of Freetown shared a common agenda with the Earthers... and they *liked* the Earthers. But then who wouldn't appreciate a race of beings that was good-natured to a fault and that had released the Freetowners from their snares among the Genesis Fleet. The privateers wouldn't even dream of doing something that would somehow harm or hinder the Earther efforts — that'd be ungrateful in the extreme.

Besides, if it was going to annoy the Earthers, it probably wasn't a smart thing to do — not because the Earthers would retaliate, but because Earthers tended to have a pretty good grasp on the limits of right and wrong.

And so did the privateers. So much for being wild-eyed renegades...

But James was still going to hug Audrey.

Ooh a hug... scandalous.

Biting back a chuckle, James arrived at *Sword's* spotless, tightly-run deck, then marched across to the comm terminal that sat opposite the door behind the control station. Keying the console as he stopped, he waited for the line to open, then queried his Signal Officer, "What have you got for me, Jenn?"

The Signal Officer looked up into the monitor abruptly, "ArcGeneral Manchester on *Batron 54*."

James cocked an eyebrow at that — what did the ArcGeneral want with him? As Hastings had so well demonstrated, most Genesis personnel didn't take too warmly to the Freetowners. Granted, meetings with both Manchester and Pat Conroy had gone well enough during the Genesis campaign, but surely the commander-in-chief of the Genesis Fleet had people she'd rather meet with than the privateers... especially after losing Pat.

Unless she wanted to chew them out for something, which he supposed was entirely possible. She couldn't be taking the tragedy well, and after so long at the front without seeing so much as a single privateer ship helping with the Allied effort...

Even stranger, James abruptly realized, was the choice of signal frequency. Batron 54 had been the designation of Sarah's squadron back during the Earth campaign, months before James and *Sword* had struck out on their own. This signal was thus coming in on a secure combat frequency — tightbeamed and encrypted, and as far as James knew, entirely out of use since the 54th had been turned into the 444th — Pat's Pirates.

What was Manchester up to?

James blinked, realizing he'd been staring at the screen for almost a minute, "I'll take it in the conference room down here."

The Signal Officer nodded, blanking the screen, and James turned from the monitor just as Audrey's pinnace set down. He walked towards the vessel as it came to a halt, and waited as she descended the ramp.

He then hugged Audrey.

"A summons," Audrey tapped her boot steadily on the deck of her pinnace, grinding her jaw as she looked across at James.

He shrugged in reply, "Pretty much. She didn't say anything else."

Audrey scowled, "I know that. It was a rhetorical comment."

James cocked an eyebrow, "Well... yes."

"Maybe I'm just frustrated... we have plans and then she suddenly needs to talk to us..." Audrey let her head flop back against the headrest and James nodded.

"I'll definitely second that."

Grendelsbane's Captain's pinnace angled upward away from the privateer squadron, climbing towards the flight deck doors of the Superdreadnought *Pope Joseph Barron*. Sarah's message had been short indeed, requiring the presence of the two privateer Captains on her ship immediately. She hadn't hinted as to her motives, and James wasn't willing to guess.

Somewhat nervous and otherwise frustrated, he sat in Audrey's pinnace and waited to land on *Joseph Barron.*

Sarah had thought about meeting the privateers on the flight deck, but she felt too troubled — her emotional turmoil would be impossible to hide, no matter how much she tried to bury it. No, she'd wait for her guests to come to her, and then ask this favor of them in private...

She would beg if she had to. She couldn't go this route alone, and she couldn't ask any serving officers in the Genesis Navy to betray their fleet...

But James and Audrey didn't owe her anything. They'd only served with her once.

What would they say?

Sitting in the darkened conference room near the flight deck, Sarah stared at the screen on the far wall — the one displaying the final seconds of the drone's data on *Harbinger Bishop.*

And the planet that *Bishop* had fled to before dying...

Sarah had to go there, and the only people she could possibly take with her were the renegades...

James ignored the stares directed at both Audrey and himself. The spacers of *Joseph Barron* were clearly not accustomed to seeing humans wearing Earther uniforms, and perhaps even more to the point, weren't pleased by the presence of those who hadn't been fighting the Kroggs for the past eight months.

The ArcLieutenant guiding the human Captains was doing her best not to be discourteous to the pair, keeping a turned back and a quick pace between herself and the two renegades.

It seemed to take a painfully long time for the Freetowners to arrive at the door to the briefing room, and as they did the ArcLieutenant stepped aside and gestured James and Audrey through it, standing back as the guests entered the darkened room.

Audrey was the first in, immediately squinting through the darkness but then stopping a few meters from the door to stare at the projection on the monitor of *Bishop's* destruction. The visual of that sad scene was the only source of light in the room... so what exactly was going on here? There was no way Manchester could hold them responsible for Pat's death...

"James, Audrey, thank you for coming. Have a seat please."

Sarah's voice had a haunting edge. Audrey had to suppress a shiver as she preceded James to a chair at the table in the center of the room, facing the ArcGeneral hidden in the shadows. The two Captains seated themselves anxiously, Sarah not taking her eyes from the screen.

"I'm sorry my summons was so abrupt and inconsiderate, but... but I need to move quickly, before Setter hears of this. Please don't tell him, even if you say no..." Sarah turned awkwardly to look at her guests, her strained expression and gaunt, exhausted features shocking both Captains.

"We're glad to help, ArcGeneral... but neither of us is entirely sure what you want," Audrey said stiffly.

Sarah nodded very slowly, "I appreciate that, and I appreciate you coming. You see... you see I must..." she paused and closed her eyes, taking a centering breath before looking at them again. "It's so hard to say it. But I *must*. I'm taking *Barron* out of the line, and I'm going out to search for Pat. And to do that... I'm going to run up the pennant of a *privateer*."

The Captains froze.

"Setter pleaded with me not to go. I can't face him to tell him... but I can't stay... So I won't order *Barron* out by itself, I'll take it out of the service and do this on my own. I'd need Liz to approve me detaching myself if I stayed in, but I can sign my own letter of marquee. And Earther policy is that privateers can rejoin the service at will... I can use that gray area, I must... because I *know* Pat is alive. And I will find him..."

Sarah's voice trailed off, and James swallowed hard.

This was insanity — Gods' honest, grief-driven *insanity*. This was a *fleet commander* talking. This was *Sarah Manchester*, the woman who had lived and breathed duty for over a decade...

"Ma'am, this is a very serious consideration. You need to address any sort of issue like this with your crew... and I don't know that the Fourth could survive without you in command..."

Sarah quickly held up her hand and shook her head, "There are plenty of fine officers to command here, James. Setter's here, and he's the best I've ever known. He can handle any problems that cross him. But I'm no good to him like this — look at me... I know I *shouldn't* go... that it's unreasonable... and that I mustn't... but I will. I have no choice..."

The words coming from the ArcGeneral were sharp and pained.

"Pat's... well, you two surely know how it is. He's been too much of a pillar for me. With him out there, I'm closer and closer to collapsing every day. It's too much for me to go through without him. I can't desert him when I can *feel* him out there... I *can't*, you understand..." Sarah's words were stable but laced with desperation. "Setter asked me to stay, but he told me it was my choice. He asked me to stay, told me he'd understand if I didn't. And I can't... I just... *can't.*"

"Ma'am," Audrey took advantage of Sarah's brief pause, "For all you know ArcBrigadier Conroy is *dead*. Would he want you out there looking for him at a time like this... and in a Krogg-infested region?"

James winced at the question, and Audrey regretted it almost instantly —

wrong tack, bad timing...

Sarah's eyes — her pleading, desperate, dying eyes — grabbed hold of Audrey's, "If James was out there, wouldn't you go?" Her question seemed half rhetorical, half a plea for approval. "Could you just let him go? Can I?"

Audrey stiffened again and Sarah leaned back into the shadows, her chair turning from her guest as her breathing quickened slightly. James and Audrey exchanged a nervous glance, both unsure what was to come next...

But the privateers felt some of Sarah's pain... or at least understood it. Torn between duty and a love that she'd come to depend on, Sarah was convinced she couldn't go on fighting this war without Pat there to bolster her. Whether that was true... well, it seemed she was determined to make it the truth — it didn't seem she'd *allow* herself to get past Pat's loss, to move on.

"I'm losing it, James, Audrey. My rational side is telling me not to try this, but I... I can't... *not* try. Do you understand? I have no choice..." Sarah spoke from the darkness. "I have the support of my crew. I've spoken to them over the past few days. I've had little else to think about... and the Earthers have the defense well in hand."

Sarah turned her chair back towards her guests, "I know this is the irrational choice, and I know precisely what I am surrendering by going. I know what I'm jeopardizing, and I'm trying to minimize the damage I do... That's why I need you both, and your ships."

Ah, so that was it.

James cocked an eyebrow, "You need *us?*"

Sarah nodded slowly, leaning forward in her chair again, "I have one Superdreadnought, I need a good cruiser escort. If I write my own letter of marquee, I'll be a privateer as well... but that doesn't necessarily mean we fly together. I need to know whether you're willing to help me. To go there–" she bobbed her head at the screen "–to find Pat."

Audrey and James glanced slowly at each other. It was a compelling plea... but if they agreed it meant they'd be joining a suicide mission against the wishes of the First Lord. The pained eyes that Sarah let settle upon them both could only build so much sympathy — they couldn't go chasing across the cosmos with a renegade ArcGeneral just because she was heartbroken.

That said, it wasn't easy to say something like that to her face, and James' eyes conveyed that measured reluctance to Audrey in a slim few seconds. The latter looked back at Sarah with as much sympathetic concern as she could muster.

"It's not a decision we can make this instant... we must discuss it and consult our crews..." Audrey's words seemed to make Sarah's face tighten further, and both Captains ground their jaws against the ArcGeneral's grief.

"We'll talk to our Captains, and I'll have an answer for you first thing in the morning," James added quietly.

Sarah stared at them both, unsure how to feel. She leaned back in her chair, her eyes shifting momentarily back to the screen, and then she offered a few jerked nods, "Yes. Yes of course, do let me know."

Containing relieved sighs, Audrey and James both came to their feet, the former taking her turn to speak again, "We'll get back to our ships, then. We'll speak in the morning."

Sarah held up a hand to wave them away, "Yes. Thank you, yes..."

The two Captains abandoned her to the dark room.

"She's having serious trouble... but I suppose it's in character. She *is* the fleet commander who landed for a major *ground action* at Antarctica, remember. She's definitely a risk-taker... a gambler, even..."

James nodded at Audrey's conclusion, watching as *Archangel Sword's* landing deck grew before his pinnace.

It was hard to put into words just how much anguish the ArcGeneral must be feeling... James couldn't understand all of it himself. He was standing on the outside and looking in; if he were under similar circumstances, he couldn't be certain of just how he'd react.

So he sympathized with the ArcGeneral... but he just couldn't risk his loyal crews for her ill-advised mission...

Sword's landing bay swallowed the pinnace, and James let out another sigh, drawing a glance from Audrey.

"Tough, isn't it?" her question was answered with a tired nod.

"And just an hour ago I was loving the renegade life," he added after a moment.

The pinnace set down in its usual slot, the ramp dropped, and the pair of Captains stood and slid out of their seats before pacing to the hatch and walking down the ramp.

As they were both nodding to the deck crew, neither noticed the gray wolf standing at the bottom of the ramp until they virtually walked into him. That brought him to an abrupt halt.

"Sir! Lord Caine sir..." Audrey snapped to attention and saluted.

Realizing just what she was saying, James mirrored the action, "Sir, welcome aboard."

Caine's expression had been studied, but now he cocked an eyebrow, "Stop that, both of you. And call me Setter, because I'm certainly not here in an official capacity."

Lowering their salutes a bit more nervously than would usually be the case when they met Earthers, the two Captains uneasily shifted their weight from foot to foot.

"Um. What can we do for you, sir?" Audrey's question felt awkward, but Caine didn't seem to notice.

The First Lord simply tilted his head and let slip a sigh, then glanced up at them as they stood uncomfortably on the ramp, "Sarah wants to sign her own letter, does she?"

Both Captains' eyes widened and they immediately glanced to each other — how did he know...

"It was rhetorical, I expect she asked you not to tell me," Caine's eyes flickered to the floor for a moment and he blinked thoughtfully. "It's the only way she can detach herself from her fleet without being AWOL or without Liz's authorization... a lovely gray area that basically gives her de facto Earther authorization to go out there..."

"Yes sir..." James had to admit he was impressed by the First Lord's logical abilities. "But how'd you know..."

Caine cocked an eyebrow, "Batron 54 is a coded frequency, and it isn't very common. When she called you it lit up my Signal Officer's panel, and he let me know. After that it was fairly straightforward. Now, if I was to guess, I'd say she asked you to cruise with her, because she needs help saving Pat."

Both humans nodded again, still trying to fully process that the First Lord was talking to them so candidly.

"You're both reluctant, though, because she told you I asked her not to go... and because all the evidence says Pat's dead..." Caine looked to them again, and the pair suddenly wondered whether they were under disapproving scrutiny.

"We told her we'd tell her in the morning... but we weren't planning on saying yes..." Audrey tried not to sound like she felt bad about the decision.

Caine seemed to study them both for a moment, his deep amber eyes scanning them as they stood perched on the last meter of the pinnace ramp.

"Then I need a favor."

Both humans' brows arched as he said it, and their minds leapt to logical predictions of their own... James caught on almost instantly.

"You can't afford to lose Sarah... you need someone to look after her out there?"

Caine nodded, approval slipping into his expression.

"And you don't have any other ships to send yet..." Audrey completed the thought.

A small smile crept onto Caine's face, and without nodding he reached up and placed a hand on each of their shoulders, "It's been a pleasure meeting you both."

With that, he turned from the bottom of the ramp and walked back to his pinnace, parked on the far side of the landing bay.

James looked at Audrey as both of them stood in disbelief.

It wasn't until the ramp on Caine's pinnace rose that words finally came to James, "I suppose I'm calling Sarah in the morning."

CHAPTER 26

Ursla was sitting quietly in the lower deck officers' mess on *Gibraltar One*, eating a hefty slab of salmon and looking through the grand windows at *Joseph Barron* and the other Superdreadnoughts of the 401ˢᵗ Battle Squadron. Though Ursla still preferred the simple and effective hull lines of Earther vessels, the human ships were impressive enough.

The mess was almost abandoned at this mid-morning hour, most of the station's crew working round the clock either on gunboat production or bringing the rest of the *Gibraltars* online. The quiet pleased Ursla — her own stress had admittedly been mounting of late, so this brunch was going to be therapeutic. Nothing like salmon in mid-morning to right some of the universe's wrongs. Frankly she wasn't sure how she'd ever survived without a fish meal between her salmon breakfast and salmon lunch.

And there were many Earthers who would agree with her wholeheartedly on that count.

"Slow today, isn't it?"

The comment from nowhere caught Ursla by surprise, and her eyes shifted up to the speaker as she bit down painfully on her pitchfork.

Pulling the fork awkwardly out of her mouth, Ursla offered a warm smile, "Setter! You snuck up on me!"

Caine laid his own plate of food on the table opposite Ursla, "You looked a bit preoccupied. And far be it for me to get between you and fish — especially when you're eating with *that* weapon."

Ursla chuckled, dropping her hefty pitchfork to the table as Caine sat, "You know me too well."

Caine smiled and settled himself into his seat, "Well, it's good that we're in shape now to sit and eat. Better than a day ago, I think."

Ursla nodded, her smile fading. The *Gibraltar* stations were coming online, and because of Chronos Claw's daring efforts, more ships were arriving than they'd thought possible. Though there was still plenty of uncertainty.

"Still confident they're going to hit us here... not send those ships to Genesis, or to Earth?"

Reviving the discussion wasn't going to make for pleasant conversation, but it seemed necessary to be certain about this particular decision.

Caine nodded slowly, "My instincts... and yours I think... say it's us. They can't go after Earth until Gibraltar's gone — we must be threatening their home space from here, so they have to deal with us first…"

Ursla watched Caine's eyes as he spoke, and sensed his mix of assurance and doubt. She nodded slowly.

"And," Caine added quietly, "Draco Maximane might well have convinced them it's not worth the risk of going deep. No, they must know we're here, know we're weak…"

As he spoke, Ursla shoveled more food into her mouth, then nodded again, "Fair enough…"

There was silence for a moment as both Earthers chewed, then another thought crossed Ursla's mind. What about Sarah?

"And that issue's settled. Sarah's making some decisions for herself, and honestly not ones I'd prefer. But I visited DeBrooke and Stanton last night. She'll be kept alive… in body. The mind part is up to her," Caine made his report quietly, seemingly able to read Ursla's thoughts as he forked more fish into his mouth.

Ursla cocked an eyebrow, "You're sure she can cope? I don't mean to be inappropriate, but what if it were Elandra out there?"

Caine stared at his plate as he chewed — that was a question he'd put to himself more than once, "I'd have gone out after her already, privateers backing me or no."

"A fleet commander using the gray area between our two Naval policies to go on a personal mission…" Ursla thought out loud as she loaded another fork-load of fish. "Honestly didn't see it coming."

Caine swallowed and his ear twitched, "If she was in our fleet she wouldn't need the gray area."

In *Gibraltar One's* upper officers' mess, Graham stared across at his dinner date with a somewhat longing look on his face. Well, it was lunchtime, but this was probably their last chance for a meal together before he left to go aboard *Gibraltar Two* to set things up. That'd mean days apart, at least until she moved her office over as well…

"What?" Commandant Gillian Hodge cocked her eyebrow at Graham's strange expression.

"It's a tragedy, really," he said with a foolish smile. "We'll be thousands of kilometers apart, separate stations and all. Bugger of a thing."

Gillian smiled and sipped her water, "For what, a week? And I'll be ten minutes away by pinnace. You *really* want to make something of this?"

Graham grinned, "You marines and your practicality. One must embrace the sadness of it all!"

Gillian shrugged, "There are certainly *sadder* things in the universe."

As she said it Graham's eye caught sight of *Joseph Barron* floating beyond the windows of the mess. She was right — he suddenly felt a pang of guilt for his foolishness.

"Sadder things indeed," his tone darkened.

Gillian leaned back in her chair and sighed, "How's your sister doing?"

Graham stared out at the Superdreadnought and tilted his head, "She's miserable... but she couldn't be much else, I suppose."

He scratched his chin thoughtfully, then turned back to the Commandant, "*That's* a true tragedy. Only eight months in... it's hit her hard. I've never seen her so... well, so strained. I really worry about her."

Gillian sighed in reply, "Pat meant a lot to her. He was always a nice guy. Kept calling me 'lass'. I'd say it's war and we have to move on... but I know I probably wouldn't be able to if you... er... if similar circumstances befell me."

Graham was only partially paying attention to his companion's words. Was that light on *Barron's* hull supposed to be flashing?

"Indeed," he said after a pause.

Captain Fox Magnus sat with Captain Thena Venus of *Vulcan* in the briefing room of *Atlas*. Both vessels were lying off *Gibraltar One*, still not having been reattached to their squadron — Felix had his 74s tasked with towing components together for the construction of the rest of the *Gibraltars* in a bid to accelerate progress.

Venus, a young red fox whose ancestry was not unlike Fox's, sat back in her chair and sighed as Magnus explained what the First Lord had told him: *Atlas* and *Vulcan* might be required for 'special' operations in the coming days. Operations beyond the fleet were generally of great interest to these two — plum assignments like the operations at Galahad Belt...

But neither Captain was particularly pleased with the dire circumstances they'd be operating under.

"Well, recon would probably suit us best," Fox concluded his comments. "I figure we might get sent out to take a look around, see when the Kroggs are coming..."

Thena cocked an eyebrow, "That *is* the closest to what I'd like to do. And we might get to take *Flame* with us. You'll like that, won't you?"

She grinned at Fox and he smiled, "Yes, indeed I would, Captain Venus. I just wish the situation wasn't so grim. For now we can get some lunch and have a look at reconnaissance routes."

"And that'll be so much fun."

Fox's eyes narrowed slightly and his smile broadened, "Cynic."

Stepping out onto the bridge of *Pope Joseph Barron*, Sarah stood before the eyes of the command crew who had served her for what seemed an eternity.

"Give me intercom. Ship only," she nodded to the Comm Officer and spoke in low tones.

The ArcLieutenant complied, keying the comm, "All hands stand by for a message from ArcGeneral Manchester."

In her hand, Sarah tightly clutched a pad. She'd signed the letter on its screen five minutes before, and now she held it up in front of them all.

"I have in my hand the letter of marquee for *Joseph Barron*. I've signed it and this ship is now officially a privateer vessel. Two hours ago, Captain James Stanton of *Archangel Sword* and Captain Audrey DeBrooke of *Grendelsbane City* pledged the support of the Freetown Squadron to my mission. I intend to head for the system in which *Harbinger Bishop* was last seen."

The crew had been consulted about this possibility, but most were still shocked to see it actually happening. Officers and spacers on the bridge — and all across the ship — were abruptly silent.

Were they to stay with *Barron* they would be renegades, just like the Freetowners who would join with them. There could be few remedies to such a designation; they would hang under a cloud of ignominy unless circumstances turned to their side in dramatic fashion.

They would be shamed, like the Freetowners.

It was no mean request, then, that Sarah was about to make of them. She knew that as well as they did... and perhaps because they knew she knew it as well as they did, or perhaps simply because she was a well-loved ArcGeneral and had the absolute loyalty of everyone — yes *everyone* — on this ship, none even hesitated at the prospect of exile. Too many of *Barron's* crew had been on *Warlock Prophet* with her, or through too much more during these past months of war.

They wouldn't leave her side now.

"As a privateer, I am now taking control of this ship. Any officers or crew who do not wish to be a part of this expedition or who do not wish to withdraw from their place in the Genesis Fleet should take this opportunity to leave immediately. The pinnaces on the flight deck have been instructed to carry away any who wish to leave. You have ten minutes to reach them."

No one on the bridge moved.

"If you could also report your intention to the bridge; we need a record of the crew to ensure operational stability."

No one on the bridge breathed.

"Do so now please."

Sarah's heart was thumping fast in her chest, despite her attempts to slow it with controlled breathing. Over a decade of her life had just come to a close.

But she'd ended it for Pat's sake. And because of that it was alright — she could leave this life for him, and for herself.

"Anything, comm? Reports?" her question came uneasily after moments of silence.

The Comm Officer shook his head.

"Very well, all hands, prepare for flux."

As Sarah stepped forward to her chair, she let her hands find the back of the comfortable old seat. She'd been with *Barron* through plenty of hard times, though none would compare to this...

No... no dark thoughts now; she had her ship, and she had her crew... but as she looked around the command deck at those who'd agreed without reservation to join her, her gaunt face seemed to dim even more.

Her crew was going to share her fate with her. It was viciously bittersweet that ones so loyal would have to suffer, perhaps die.

She owed much to these men and women, and she knew it all too well.

"Thank you," her words were barely audible.

Barron prepared for flux.

James sat nervously on the bridge of *Sword* and watched as *Joseph Barron* fired up its flux drive generators. The Superdreadnought would be ready to accelerate in about two minutes — it would take that long for the drives to come to full readiness after so long in orbit of Gibraltar.

So anyone paying attention had two minutes to see exactly what was going on and to move to stop them...

"Orders to squadron: start spinning up flux drives," James said in low tones, as though a loud voice on his own bridge might somehow cause the expedition to be caught. "Get us ready to move out."

The Signal Officer passed the orders to the rest of the ships of the Freetown Squadron, and James held his breath.

The intercom on *Gibraltar One* chirped, and for some reason Caine's ear twitched as the announcement chime began.

"Alert status, First Lord Caine and Admiral Ursla be aware, we've just seen *Pope Joseph Barron's* pennant go narrow and teal."

With those words Caine let out a short breath and his head turned up, eyes fixed on the speakers in the ceiling. Teal... he rose from his chair and faced the window — sure enough, the dark green lights that ran along the hull of the Genesis Superdreadnought were changing color in sequence...

To teal — the color that had been assigned to the pennants of the Freetown Squadron after the Genesis campaign. It was a color that *no* other force under Allied command used... if *Barron* was flying a teal pennant, then Sarah had indeed gone through with it and signed her own letter.

Ursla rose to her feet behind Caine, "You called it."

Caine nodded very slowly, "I..."

He paused and felt a stab of worry.

"I hope she stays safe out there."

● ● ●

"Gods' dammit, what are you doing Sarah?" Graham hammered a fist into the mess' windows and screamed at the Superdreadnought now maneuvering out of formation just beyond the station. The Earthers and humans in the room, including Gillian Hodge, sat stunned by his outburst.

Not that he gave one sweet damn about what they thought...

She was going after him. Sarah was going after Pat... with the damned renegades helping! Dammit!

He turned and marched in long strides to the comm terminal mounted on the wall on the mess' far side. Roughly palming the hail key, he waited an impatient few seconds until the Signal Officer appeared on the screen. Graham nearly snarled at the Earther, "Link me to *Barron!*"

The Midshipman blinked once in surprise before keying the signal, and almost to Graham's surprise, Sarah's face appeared on the screen a second later. Her gaunt features were as strained as before, but a new shadow of confidence seemed to be cast over her expression.

"What is it, Graham?" her voice was calm.

"Damn you, I *forbid* this! Stand down!"

Sarah stared at him, her eyes trying to harden but failing in the attempt. She could only shake her head slowly, "I'm sorry Graham, but no. Just... wish your big sister luck, okay?"

Before he could say anything else, the comm link cut, and he watched helplessly as *Barron* slowly moved away from *Gibraltar One*.

Graham was frozen in place and scarcely breathing... what was she doing? Setter had asked her not to go — told her that they couldn't do without her... how could she leave after that plea? Why was she so determined to fly off to her death?

As *Barron* accelerated from the station, Graham ground his jaw. He'd see to it she didn't get far...

"Skipper..."

Fox looked up as the intercom speakers addressed him, then with an eyebrow cocked towards Thena Venus he activated his comm link to the bridge. The holo tank at the center of the Captain's desk glowed to life and *Atlas'* First Lieutenant appeared, shock etched on his face, "Take a look, Fox."

The face of the Lieutenant vanished abruptly, to be replaced by a visual of *Pope Joseph Barron*... running with a narrow teal pennant and accelerating away from *Gibraltar One* in the company of the Freetowners.

It took Fox's mind a minute to process what he was seeing, and then something inside him shivered. ArcGeneral Manchester was going out after ArcBrigadier Conroy.

CHAPTER 27

"Send them to bring her *back*!"

Caine stiffened as Graham roared at him, surprised at the anger erupting from the generally pleasant junior Manchester. There was a serious amount of concern underlying the spite in Graham's tone, and it was concern that Caine shared... but there was nothing to be done about it just now.

"She signed her own letter of marquee, Graham," Savanna Felix said quietly. The white cat had come aboard *Gibraltar One* to meet Caine as soon as he'd learned the Freetowners had left the system with Sarah. His relief had been little short of immense when Caine informed him of the request to James and Audrey to go along... after all, it had been Felix who had first commissioned those privateers.

So the Admiral of the Earther Third Fleet pressed on, leaning on the briefing table in *Gibraltar One's* main conference room, "You *know* Alliance policy as well as the rest of us, Graham. We don't attempt to stop anyone from leaving the fleet. Your sister is well within her rights — she had the authority to write her own letter, and because she did we'll have the leverage with Liz to see her reinstated when she comes back..."

Graham's eyes shifted to Felix, his glare icier than anything the tiger had expected to see, "Damn the policy, this isn't some Battlecruiser, Savanna. You bloody well know that! We hold Fleet Commanders to a different bloody damned standard! We can't just let Sarah walk off the job!"

Caine cleared his throat and Graham's gaze shifted back to the wolf. The redness in his face startled the First Lord...

"I can't have her hauled back here, Graham," he said in a frustratingly quiet, paternal way. "I told her I'd respect her choice, and knowing her as we both do I don't expect she made this decision lightly. Whether we like it or not, the choice was hers to make..."

The younger Manchester's eyes widened, "What's this? More of your self-enlightened idealist *bullshit*? Perhaps the reality of the universe hasn't penetrated your psyche just yet through that Earther utopia you hide behind, but she's going to Gods-damned well get herself killed out there."

Felix's eyebrows went up at the outburst, and he tried to hide his patent shock at the outrageousness of the comments being leveled at the *First Lord of the Admiralty* as he looked towards Caine... But the First Lord's eyes merely settled on Graham, his demeanor totally calm while Graham loaded another verbal salvo.

"You Earthers, always the do-gooders, never dealing with the hard consequences or facing up to unfair *reality*. I could live with that *quaint* eccentricity up 'til now, even with thousands dying, but Sarah's too important to sacrifice for your blind idealism. Go *get* her, or I'll bloody well *make* you!"

In his now-seething rage, Graham made the mistake of taking a step forward to emphasize his ambitious threat. Savanna Felix wasn't a great sparrer by Earther standards, but his hand still found the back of Graham's collar before the human saw any sign of movement. Like a parent handling his cub, the cat lifted the junior Manchester by the veritable scruff of his neck and held him steady a few centimeters off the ground.

"You *watch yourself*. No one talks to the *First Lord* like that, least of all one of his own," the cat's voice was sharp, and as he met Graham's eyes the human's rage stalled for just an instant. "You blame our idealism, do you? Think we're too good to deal with reality? Think we don't realize just how lucky we've been so far, that we don't know or don't care about what this war has cost you and yours? You're more wrong than you can know, my friend. So *stow* that garbage."

Graham's breathing was still ragged, and he strained against Felix's grip. The Earther's eyes narrowed, "And *enough* of this 'too-good-to-be-true' foolishness. You'd better stop assuming the entire universe is *unfair*. You don't get to blame those things you don't like about human nature on the *universe* being evil, you have to blame them on yourselves. And don't expect us to apologize for not doing things you'd consider bad and for not failing just to make you feel a little more comfortable in this Alliance. We're doing what we promised you we'd do because that's in *our* nature. Stop expecting us to have *your* flaws, Graham — we're not human, and despite what you might like to see, we don't have to abide by the rules of *human nature*."

The junior Manchester bristled at the scolding, and Felix's eyes narrowed further, "You hear me, Graham? We done?"

Graham's breathing slowed marginally, though his glare remained fierce.

Caine looked up at the human, a tired but otherwise unreadable expression on his face.

"We all have our own flaws to deal with, Graham," both Felix and Graham turned their eyes back as Caine spoke, "but that's a discussion for another time. It's your choice whether you want to try to go after Sarah... I just hope you don't make the same decision she did. I need you here. Particularly now."

The junior Manchester's breathing remained huffed, and he tugged his tunic back into place jerkily as Felix lowered him to the ground, "No, I won't go out there. But with or without *human* faults, if you don't do something about this, I'll hold you accountable. She's my sister. If something happens to her I'll take it out of *your* hides."

Graham's icy eyes lashed into Felix's, then he turned and let them stab into Caine.

"*Clear?*"

Caine tilted his head slowly, but Felix took a short step forward, forcing the human back a pace. The Third Fleet's Admiral's eyes narrowed, "You've crossed a line here, my friend. You really don't want to use insolence to start probing — you'll do damage that can't be fixed."

Before Graham's angry retort could leave his throat, Felix took another step forward and his tiger eyes narrowed, "But since you're so determined, you should know that Setter asked the Freetowners to go with her. The decision to leave was hers, but they wouldn't be there to support her if Setter hadn't gone to *Sword* himself and *asked*. Now I think the lines you've crossed start somewhere on the other side of that door. I suggest you cross back over them and take some time to calm down."

Those stern words finally sparked the revelation that Graham might just be chewing out the choir, and with a huff that was both angry and awkward, he turned and stormed from the briefing room.

As the hatch closed, Caine looked to Felix with a slowly shaking head, "If *he's* bitter about our relative losses, I don't want to know what general opinion in their fleet must be like."

"They'll come around," Felix turned from the hatch, forcing the tension from his face. "That or our luck will run out and they'll be... I hesitate to say 'happy', but I get a sinking feeling that'd be the word for it."

Caine's eyes drifted momentarily to the floor. Perhaps their luck was already turning. The Kroggs were coming and the frustration of the humans seemed to be growing because the Earthers weren't losing or suffering as much, even though the Earthers were doing a proportionate share of the fighting.

'Proportionate' meaning the majority.

Alas, Setter Caine still didn't understand that human equation he'd once spoken about with Ursla. Not when it could set even good people like Graham against their trusted friends.

Heaving a weary sigh, Felix hopped back up to sit on the edge of the briefing table, "But are we going to send anyone else out after Sarah? I realize you couldn't have assigned Fox to her without knowing whether she was going... and without seeming to be involved in convincing her to go. But I know you've got *Atlas* and *Vulcan* set aside for something."

Caine cocked an eyebrow at his friend's insight, "I didn't think it was that obvious."

Felix smiled, "You *wouldn't*, but those are nominally my ships. And that's Fox Magnus skippering them. No way you were just going to tell him to fly recon."

A small smile slid onto Caine's face, despite the still-heavy atmosphere, "Andra's on her way to talk to Fox right now."

"I'm good," Felix grinned. "So they're out there to be discreet escorts, and to be scouts too?"

Caine's smile faded and he nodded, "To keep an eye out for the Kroggs, yes. But I want Fox looking after Sarah. In case things get rough."

Fox Magnus had his crew preparing *Atlas* for an out-of-system expedition, and as he moved swiftly through the corridors of his 74, it seemed that such a mission was coming to meet him. After what he'd just seen, he expected to be going after Sarah Manchester and the Freetowners immediately, but evidently Caine and Ursla had wanted to keep that mission off the comms, probably due to the potential sensitivity of the issue — the human fleet commander had signed her own letter, after all.

So Ursla had just landed to meet Fox personally and to sort out this operation...

A huge bear appeared in the far end of the corridor Fox was rushing down — he'd promised to meet Ursla in the main briefing room, but it seemed now they'd meet in the corridor outside.

As the two officers paced quickly towards each other, Ursla offered an amiable wave of greeting to the intrepid Captain, and he returned it with a smile. They reached the briefing room door at almost the same time.

"Sorry I didn't meet you down there — I didn't have time to..."

Ursla held up a hand to stop Fox's apology, "Nothing to worry about, let's go in."

Fox nodded and opened the hatch to the briefing room, letting Ursla enter first. The Earthers wasted no time finding seats and as the hatch closed Ursla activated the table holo plot. A map of the front, with teal markers showing the projected course of the renegades, formed in the display. Fox eyed it closely.

"We're handling this delicately, Fox, as you can well imagine. Graham's apparently breathing fire... and we're concerned about the potential reaction of the Genesis Fleet if we're seen to be encouraging Sarah. A lot of tension bubbling under the surface, I'm afraid... Hence my visit instead of a set of orders over the comm..."

Fox nodded, "Thought so. Thena and I are going out then?"

"Indeed... as close support."

Cocking an eyebrow, the Captain looked from the plot to his Admiral, "Not to bring them back... but to make sure they make it home in one piece?"

"Exactly. We're sending you, *Flame* and *Vulcan* out after them. Your orders will be to catch up with them and to look after them... and while you're out we'll also need you to give us warning if you come across the Krogg force on its way in. That's what *Flame* will be for — real time communication."

"Of course..."

"And," Ursla held up a halting hand, "You should know that the reason James and Audrey went out there is because Setter asked them to. Personally, last night."

"Ah," Fox had wondered just what Sarah had said to get the privateers on side — it seemed a little out of character for them to join up with the fleet commander of a service that had rejected them just because she changed her pennant...

But that didn't change his mission at all.

"Alright," Fox said after that moment's thought, "I'll signal *Vulcan* right away. We cleared to weigh immediately?"

Ursla nodded, "At your discretion. I imagine they'll be moving fast though, so the sooner the better, I'd guess."

Fox nodded thoughtfully, "I don't expect tracking them will be a problem but catching them might take some time. James likes to move fast, and I don't expect *Barron* is going to be slow."

Ursla came to her feet, "Indeed, I'll get out of your way, then. Safe journey, Fox. Good luck."

Extending her hand as Fox stood, the two Earthers — one tall, one much shorter, and both brilliant cruiser officers — nodded to each other. Then Ursla stepped quickly out of the room, heading directly back to her pinnace.

Fox stood silently in the briefing room for a few seconds, contemplating his mission, then turned on his heel and headed quickly for the bridge. Time to talk to Thena...

Graham sat stiffly in his desk chair and stared out the window in his quarters. The enhanced visuals supplied by *Gibraltar One's* sensors displayed an impressive menagerie of ships, but none of them was the ship Graham wanted to see. Sarah was gone off to die for love. It wasn't a worthy trade, and even now, after Graham had managed to calm himself, the prospect of Sarah being out there with only those renegades looking after her was bloody terrifying.

She was his big sister. She'd virtually raised him. But she did this too often — she jumped into the fray, dove into the breach... did all those Gods-damned poetic things that won storied deaths. And she did them all the time.

Usually Pat kept her out of the worst of the messes, but he was dead and his death was drawing her to a brutal end. The universe had a brilliant sense of irony.

The *universe* had a sense of irony...

The comment reminded Graham of Felix's words — the *universe* couldn't be blamed for bad things, it wasn't a 'cruel universe'. Humans just liked to say that to get out of owning up to their own mistakes and foolishness.

Yes, Graham understood what the Earther cat had said to him, though he wasn't fully ready to accept it.

He just hoped that incredible Earther luck Felix had mentioned panned out for his sister.

And as that thought crossed Graham's mind, two 74s and a sloop that had been mixed into the menagerie of ships beyond his window collapsed into energy drive and raced away.

CHAPTER 28

Lupus sat silently, observing the crew of *Bishop's* camp as they went about their business beyond the central canopy. The 'tent' he occupied was of ramshackle but effective construction, built out of a tarp stretched over four shrapnel posts in the center of the perimeter formed by the three crashed pods... and it was serving as ArcColonel Jessica Forbes' new 'bridge'.

With the shield up around the camp, Lupus could feel reasonably safe, especially since they'd gotten the boat ashore and into the protected zone. Pawman and a couple of human engineers were now looking over the impeller damage, though Lupus wasn't too optimistic about their chances of putting the engine back into full service.

One fortunate Krogg had sent this entire rescue plan awry. Despite being a very experienced soldier, Lupus honestly hadn't expected to lose the *engine*. But things could be worse — at least the camp was reasonably strong... Which was actually something of a curiosity in itself.

Why had the camp been allowed to remain? It was wide open in a field and its shield wasn't reinforced by the generator of an Earther dropship like the one at Pat's camp would be... In essence, then, this camp could be vaporized by a single volley from one of those orbiting Destroyers.

It was as though it had been left out here as bait for the Earthers...

"Well, I'm certainly glad to see you here, Beckett," Forbes rounded the tilted table in front of Lupus' chair and seated herself, interrupting his pondering. "We've been trying to consolidate our camp — get things in order. I was going to get us moving towards those mountains asap, but you seem to have beaten us to the punch."

Lupus nodded, "Pat's up there with about twenty *Bishops*. Nice strong camp, though we could certainly toughen it up some more with your shield generators. That's not to complain, though — our dropship got off the deck cleanly, so we've had a fairly good resource base."

"Hell of a riverboat you've got yourselves," Forbes smiled. "And you got the ArcBrig off — I should stick with him next time I flee an exploding ship!"

Lupus smiled, "You seem to be doing well enough for yourselves here... actually, I should tell you I was wondering about that..."

Forbes frowned slightly as Lupus' smile began to fade, "I'm not sure I follow."

Leaning back and thinking, the wolf looked to Forbes, "You know there are two Destroyers in orbit? I don't imagine there's any way they haven't seen your camp from space, what with your shield up. So — and you'll have to pardon my frankness — why haven't you been vaporized?"

Cocking an eyebrow, Forbes leaned forward in her seat, "Two *Destroyers*? I... I don't know why, then. They've stayed out of it... they must have left us here for a reason..." she paused and looked up at Lupus, her eyes narrowing. "As bait for you, maybe? They figure they can kill most of us in one shot, and if they get you the rest of the crew is an absolute write off..."

Lupus slowly shook his head as she suggested it, "If that was the case, I don't see how they could have waited this long to open the attack on us. We weren't subtle in announcing our arrival."

Forbes' frown deepened and she nodded, "I suppose so... then maybe they're looking for more prisoners."

Lupus' eyebrows shot up instantly, "Excuse me, *prisoners?*"

Forbes looked up at him and blinked, "Right, you wouldn't know. They took my XO prisoner the day after we got down here, and two more of my crew in that week. We actually saw them being hauled off — they weren't killed... I'm guessing they're looking for intel. Interrogation, I expect. It's probably how they found out enough about our front lines to position that fleet we found... they know our biology and our technology because we worked for them for so long... now they're getting information out of us."

Lupus' eyebrows stayed up. He'd heard nothing of humans being taken prisoner over the past months, though it certainly would explain a few things.

But why would they leave this camp intact when it was loaded only with men and women who probably wouldn't know anything new? It could be a ploy, or bait...

Bait.

Bait for Earthers.

A trap.

"They want to take one of my squad prisoner... that must be it. They leave us an inviting base to rescue and know we'll try, then move to cut us off and take one of my team hostage."

Forbes' own brow raised, "That'd be huge for them... even though they wouldn't get anything out of one of yours, I mean... But if that's the case what do they do next?"

Leaning back in his chair again, Lupus sighed thinly, "The ball's in our court. We've got to break out of here, and all they have to do is have a force in place to stop us. The good news is they won't use orbital strikes against you because it'd risk eliminating us as an information source."

"You're worth more alive than we are dead," Forbes' words drew a somewhat surprised glance from Lupus, then he tilted his head and looked momentarily at the river.

"We really must move you..." he paused again and blinked a few times to clear his mind of less-than-immediate concerns. "We'd planned to construct makeshift rafts for us to tow your crew back up to the mountains, but with our impeller down I doubt we'll be going anywhere."

Forbes frowned again, "I'm no engineer, but shouldn't the thing be pretty fixable?"

Lupus shook his head and shifted in the chair, "If we had a pre-fab plant with us, I think it would be. But we left all the construction gear with Pat."

A smile temporarily brightened Forbes' face, "Well, see, I just happened to pack one."

Lupus paused, then leaned forward with an approving nod, "I see. Then you've done *very* well for yourselves, ArcColonel. So that's problem number one looked after. Now we just need to come up with some lightweight, high-capacity rafts to get your people upstream."

Forbes frowned, "You know, I thought about packing those, but I brought my bathing suit instead."

Lupus cocked an eyebrow, "So you're offering to swim back and pull the rest of us along with you?"

Forbes chuckled.

Pat huffed loudly and collapsed back against a tree, wiping his brow on the back of his sleeve. Gods wept, this was bloody hard work!

"We've almost got everything hooked up now, sir," Raymond Keats said cordially, and Pat winced into the bright sunlight as he looked up at the Spacer First Class.

"A bloody miracle, that is. Gods though, you'd think Cuttar would be up here running the bloody cables himself, wouldn't you?"

The spacer smiled politely, "I suppose so, sir."

Pat nodded, satisfied. The Earther was actually down in the dead ground below the mouth of the camp's cave, helping a number of other *Bishop* spacers dig the bed for their gun. Because it would almost certainly be firing at high trajectories if at all, the engineer needed to make sure the bed was steady and well-lined to deal with the harsh recoil of the Sixth Rate-sized energy cannon.

That left Pat and Spacer First Class Keats to read the manual and actually connect the gun's energy matrix... barrel... targeting... everything... *whatever.*

Pat had seen enough colored linkages and matching geometric figures to make him a happy vegetable — all the foolproof coordination made life easy for figuring out the gun, but... But. One could only look at bright happy triangles that told one to hook coupling 'a' up to reactor 'q' for so long without going batty.

It was like assembling furniture. Except it lasted for over fourteen hours. Straight.

Oh well.

Pat had made this gun the business of the camp. With Lupus off in search of survivors, he had to expect attention to be drawn to their base — even if it only came when the Sergeant Major returned. It'd be easy enough for the Kroggs to follow that Earther boat along a river, especially given their added advantage of orbital surveillance, so if they did find the camp it seemed a good idea to have a weapon ready to shoot back at them.

The Mark XII wasn't much of a gun for battleship fighting, but firing from the ground under good cover, Pat was willing to bet it could play hell with the Destroyers in low orbit — particularly since they'd have no idea it was down here. And there was one thing Pat could always count on about Earther guns: they had a splendid 'raw destruction' quotient.

Heaving a sigh, Pat glanced back up at Keats. The spacer was standing awkwardly under the shade of the cave entrance, looking out and down at the pit. The barrel of the big — or at least *relatively* big — gun was sticking out in the same direction. It had been assembled in the cave to avoid complications, they'd float it down later on a grav cart...

An odd, random thought crossed Pat's mind as his eyes shifted from the ground beyond the cave to Keats and back. There'd been something familiar about the spacer from the moment Pat had seen him, but he'd simply assumed it was passing recognition — the man served aboard *Bishop* after all...

But no, something about the way the spacer was now standing... it was oddly reminiscent of a more specific entry in Pat's memory...

"Keats, have we worked closely together on any operations in... oh, say the past year?"

The spacer suddenly stiffened, "Um... not exactly sir."

"And what did you say your post was... laser maintenance?"

"Yes sir."

Pat frowned thoughtfully, "Then why am I remembering you, spacer?"

Keats shrugged awkwardly, "Um... we did meet once, sir, outside the *Bloody Pulsar*. I was... um, well, it was about nine months ago now."

Cocking an eyebrow, Pat gestured for the tense fellow to go on, "Spit it out, man!"

"Well, I... ah, you and ArcGeneral Manchester were looking for ArcGeneral Manchester... the other one..." Keats let his voice trail off as Pat's eyes lit with the memory.

Sarah had gone off to the *Pulsar* and gotten herself a bit drunk, and he and Graham had been looking for her. He hadn't been in a particularly good mood at the time either. Right... the spacer had been on the boardwalk with his mates, talking about having spoken to Sarah.

'Spoken like a bloody Krogg,' right.

Pat grinned to himself at the memory. This poor fellow had caught him and Graham on a very bad day. Graham had just informed Pat that the whole Alliance was waiting for him and Sarah to get together... Then Sarah had found a hole in the Allied Fleet's battle plan.

As he recalled, when Keats had bumped into him, the instinct had been to toss the lonely spacer across *Genesis One*. Well, probably a good thing he hadn't done that — he'd have had no company putting this gun together.

Ah what a small world... or galaxy. Whatever. Stupid clichés. Shouldn't think in clichés — it makes me feel like I'm in a bad novel with a lazy author. And why does everyone speak English... shut it!

Even as Pat started to force his mind back to present matters, he began to chuckle.

"You're the spacer who hit on my lovely Sarah Manchester that day! Gods wept, man, we've had some laughs about you!"

Keats reddened.

"You must be glad I didn't know you were on *Bishop*! I'd have had you skinned and spaced! Good Gods!"

Pat's chuckle developed into a laugh, and Keats stood awkwardly, hoping this wasn't a precursor to his death. Accidents could happen in crash landings on planets...

But Pat sobered — after a while — and looked up at the man, "Oh don't worry now, Keats my boy. So long as you never try a stunt like that again I've got no reason to kill you. Well, not a good one, anyway. And as much as I wish I could say lack of a good reason hasn't stopped me from killing before, I can't, but that's mainly because the Church and the Kroggs were ordering me to shoot Larosians. So you're safe..."

Keats didn't quite follow that last comment, but at least the 'no reason to kill' part did manage to get through. That was good...

Grinning, Pat got to his feet and patted the spacer on the back, releasing a bit more of the man's tension, "Come on, let's finish this damned thing, eh?"

Keats nodded blankly and avoided eye contact.

CHAPTER 29

Commodore Draco Maximane leaned back against his bunk and sighed. *Engadine's* darkened flag cabin was proving an all too familiar refuge for the lion — he'd taken to spending his off-duty time here, shutting out all distractions as he tried to decide how much further he should go with this mission.

Two Carriers — *Engadine* and *Monarch* — were chasing a rather sizable force of Krogg vessels through deep space, intent on catching them when they decelerated but *before* whoever they happened to join could intervene. All this in hope of protecting Earth's location and the existence of the Carriers for a short while longer — at least long enough to get some of their new ships deployed to the front.

Maximane rubbed his eyes wearily. Some plan, this.

The Carriers were making remarkable time chasing the Kroggs. By now, after over two weeks of hard travel, they were far out on the wings of the front, probably beyond any active units of Allied vessels. Maximane's two sloops had already fallen off the pace and were cruising to Genesis with updates on the situation out here... but he had to contemplate turning around. He simply *had* to.

The risks were becoming increasingly obvious to Maximane as time wore on. If two Carriers joined action against a superior fleet and were captured, the damage could be far worse than a betrayal of their existence. The technology, the information — things that were keeping the Earthers ahead of the Kroggs in this fight — could fall into enemy hands. No, it would soon be time to abandon this effort — chasing from afar had seemed a good idea days before, but too little had come of it to warrant persisting.

Maximane's mulling was interrupted by the chirping comm, "All hands, beat to quarters! Crews to your boats, clear for action!"

Maximane was out of his cabin before his hand left his eyes.

Sarah refused to switch uniforms. She didn't know if this privateer guise was going to be permanent, and she couldn't cast off what she felt was her only hope — and her *crew's* only hope — of redemption. Not yet, anyway. Even days out of Gibraltar, running with a squadron of self-professed renegades, she couldn't break down and trade in her Genesis greens for Earther blues.

Old ways died hard.

Sitting in her cabin, she stared blankly at the cover of a book Pat had given her. *Garnan's Military History of Pre-Omega Earth*, reputed to be a definitive survey of all the ways humans could kill each other, and *why*! Brilliant. Just what she wanted to think about now...

Grinding her jaw, Sarah laid the book on the table next to her bed and sighed. She wasn't sure what she wanted to think anymore. No, she knew that she wanted Pat to be alive, and she wanted that more than anything.

But the rest made no sense...

She was essentially resigning herself to the reality that she wouldn't work things out until Pat was found. And she just had to believe — as she did — that he was there to be found...

The intercom buzzed, rescuing Sarah from her thoughts, "Ma'am, we're seeing some anomalous readings. Could you please come up?"

"They've got us in their crosshairs, sir. And they've met up with a few more friends to make trouble for us."

Maximane nodded at the report from Captain Ronax Hobbes. The Kroggs had turned to take advantage of the Carriers' relative weakness, just as he'd feared. The four Dreadnoughts and six Destroyers he'd been chasing had been reinforced by another light raiding group — a Dreadnought and three Destroyers — and now the weight of broadside was seriously in the Kroggs' favor.

And evidently, despite stretched drive fields, they'd seen *Engadine* and *Monarch*.

Normally, in ships other than Carriers, a situation like this would warrant a simple solution: turn and run like the wind. Unfortunately, with their fields stretched to such excesses, and evidently without the benefit of stealth on their side, there'd be no way to change course before Krogg ships moved to ram *Engadine* and *Monarch*.

Months ago, Commodore Ami Cairn of *Inferno* had discovered just what a 'ramming' by a ship in hyperspace could do to a ship in energy drive — the hyperspace wake, or more properly the distortions in the subspace layers created by a ship in hyper, could have a destabilizing effect on energy drive fields. Cairn's 38-gun frigate had enjoyed an impromptu run in with a Krogg Superdreadnought... *Engadine* and *Monarch* were staring at a similar challenge, and they probably couldn't run...

No, we won't have the chance to show the Kroggs a clean pair of heels. We'll have to try to buy a head-start...

Maximane didn't relish that thought, but he turned to the Captain all the same, "Tighten the fields, then drop out of energy and run out the guns. Launch all boats as soon as you can."

•••

Sarah frowned at the monitor as *Joseph Barron* slipped through space with the Freetown privateers. In a system somewhere on the edge of detection range, what looked like a Krogg Dreadnought group was rendezvousing.

Sarah's first instinct was to engage, but she quickly remembered *Joseph Barron* was the only capital ship she'd taken out of Gibraltar. Trying to mix it up with some Krogg capital ships would simply be asking for trouble.

"Kroggs," she said quietly as she thought. "Tightbeam a signal to *Archangel Sword*. Adjust course relative by four degrees port. Let's try to stay out of sight as best we can."

"Yes, ma'am."

Aboard *Sword*, James squinted at the Krogg icons on his own monitor. Defeating the group probably wouldn't be *impossible* for the privateers... but they couldn't afford to try when they were this far from help, and when they could just as easily avoid the mess.

Well, at least they knew they were heading in the right direction... and as soon as he got out of sensor range of the Kroggs, James would have to send a pod to warn Caine.

"Direct squadron to alter course–"

The Signal Officer cut James off, "*Joseph Barron* is directing us to veer four degrees port and avoid action."

With a surprised but pleased blink, James nodded, "Pass on the orders. Helm, you heard. Four points to port."

Maximane had heard many stories about Earther luck. Fox Magnus' run home from Genesis had just happened to cross paths with Admiral Felix's 74s. Caine had been able to arrive at the Battle of Genesis just in time to turn the tide. At Nova Star, the flying 111th had come in at just the right vector to see the Kroggs' trap before it was sprung...

So far the Earthers seemed to have things work in their favor a lot of the time... at least some of that was good luck, but somehow Draco Maximane thought it wouldn't be perpetual. That said, he needed a bit of it right now.

Well, a *lot*, actually.

"Boats launched, skipper. We're cleared for action and holding the range open as ordered."

Maximane nodded. He knew the Carriers didn't have a hope if they came in close, so he'd have to use their speed to keep them out of range of the Krogg spines while his boats battered the alien capital ships. If he could hold things open enough, the boats could destroy all the Dreadnoughts before any could return fire on the *Engadine* or *Monarch*... but it was the Destroyers that worried him.

His swarms of boats might be cut up by those escorts, if they were deployed properly. Or, barring that, the littler ships could swarm the Carriers themselves, and if all the gunboats were out dealing with Dreadnoughts there'd be no protection for the Earthers' large berthing ships.

Come on great celestial luck-giver, let's have some.

Any time now.

Please?

"Just moving out of extreme range now," *Barron's* ArcColonel said softly, and Sarah nodded. Nothing was going to get between her and a chance to find Pat. It was time for her to hang up her impetuous shoes and go straight for what she wanted without distraction...

Which actually meant she was still being impetuous... by definition. But that was irrelevant.

There'd be no stops, no detours.

Who cared about a handful of Dreadnoughts anyway?

CHAPTER 30

"I hope the Freetowners avoided them," Fox's First Lieutenant said quietly, and Magnus nodded.

His detached force was still trying to catch up to the privateer squadron, but it remained beyond *Flame's* scanning range. The little sloop, like all ships of its type, maintained an impressive suite of detection gear, and while it still wasn't seeing the Freetowners, the gear was definitely paying off.

Big time.

'Big time' enough to warrant the use of such a cliché.

Because it had detected Kroggs.

No, *the* Kroggs. Their *whole fleet*.

"Check their numbers — are we seeing everything *Bishop* detected?" Fox asked quickly, and the First Lieutenant keyed his pad for a moment.

A new window opened in *Atlas'* main bridge holo tank, and figures began to scroll across it. The projection paused with two groups of ship numbers highlighted in red, indicating a discrepancy, a third in blue, indicating an exact match.

"This fleet has all twenty of the Motherships, 200 of the 203 Dreadnoughts, and 400 of 414 Destroyers. It's a safe bet this is all that the Kroggs are sending... and vector confirms, they're headed for Gibraltar."

Fox nodded to his First Lieutenant, then turned to his Signal Officer, "Tightbeam Captain Venus and Commander Claw, let's angle away slowly."

"Aye," the Signal Officer began strumming the keys on her console.

Fox turned back to his Cruising Master, "Got that clearly, Mister Gunth?"

"Already maneuvering, sir," the grizzled old Master said with a grin, and *Atlas*, cruising with an open field under energy drive, slid further down below the Krogg Fleet.

The attack force passed safely by in hyper, not even noticing the energy fields of the three Earther ships. Sometimes the single-mindedness of the Kroggs was quite self-defeating.

"*Flame* reports we're clearing the Kroggs' detection range. Commander Claw says there's no sign of battle — looks like the Freetowners got past cleanly."

Fox withheld a relieved sigh — he wouldn't have expected James or Audrey to get caught... then he nodded in reply to his Signal Officer, "Have Chronos return to Gibraltar to warn Caine. *Flame* is to rendezvous with us when possible."

The signals crossed space, and *Flame* quickly split away from its two larger consorts. Fox watched silently as his former ship turned from the pair of 74s and began generating a hyper point… then the point abruptly died and *Flame* turned back.

"Sir… *Flame's* picking up more Kroggs. Edge of scope…"

Fox frowned and turned back to the plot. A few more after all then…

Wait a minute…

"The Destroyers are closing, sir."

Maximane nodded as he quietly eyed *Engadine's* main battle tank. The Kroggs were going to try to break up his gunboat cover and then sweep in on him when the Carriers were vulnerable. This was the trouble with small strike craft in the sphere of three-dimensional warfare: they lacked the inherent advantage altitude had given old air fighters and thus were only really useful in massed waves.

But they could still swarm, and pack quite a punch when they did. Maximane was counting on them to do exactly that right now… they'd have to try to go out and meet the Destroyers as the Kroggs crossed the space gap to the fleeing Carriers…

"Order the boats to interpose. Try to hold the Destroyers back."

"Aye sir."

Maximane scowled and turned to watch in the boat plot as the hundreds of small craft turned back to chase the pursuing Kroggs. Chances were good most of those boats would be destroyed in this sort of stern chase situation, and without even considering the massive number of Earther lives that would be lost in such a scenario, it would be a disaster for *Engadine* and *Monarch*.

"A little bit of Earther luck… come on…" Maximane said the words softly to himself, and his ear twitched.

"Looks like a heavy raiding force. Five Dreadnoughts and nine Destroyers. They're certainly formed up to attack *something*…"

Fox frowned as his First Lieutenant used his finger to point out the Krogg ships. If the whole fleet was going after Gibraltar, the only excuse these ships would have to break formation would be an Allied presence nearby…

"The Freetowners are clear?" Fox asked.

The First Lieutenant turned quickly to the Sensor Chief for confirmation, then nodded to Fox.

"Who'd be this far out… must have been a Genesis-based force pursuing a raiding group. They must have gone quite a ways to get here…" Fox's words faded and his frown deepened. Very odd that they'd just happened to run across each other in deep space, too…

Well whoever it was, the Allied force couldn't be all that big to have only five Dreadnoughts sent after it. Maybe a mixed frigate force... but then why were they accepting action? Plenty about this seemed strange...

"Master, change course to come up on the Dreadnoughts' flanks. Signal Officer, send our new vector to *Vulcan* and *Flame*. Ask them to clear for action. Lieutenant, beat to quarters, if you please."

The Destroyers charged like elephants through the ranks at Zama — several gunboats exploded violently, a few were clipped by neuro pulses and corkscrewed out of formation, but for the most part, the Destroyers passed straight through the boat wave with minimal effect, clearly having been ordered after the Carriers. The Kroggs had evidently realized the boats were vulnerable without their base ships...

During that first charge the boats had held their fire, hoping they'd survive the run-in and have a chance to reply. They'd been given that chance. With the Destroyers past them, they put their helms hard over and rushed back to confront their relatively large foes. Presenting their sterns, the Destroyers were rather vulnerable to the attacks from the small ships' heavy guns.

One exploded in a cloud of gore, two more were seriously wounded and staggered aside. The last six realized their mistake in letting the gunboats see their backs. While Larosian fighters were only moderately effective against heavy vessels, gunboats packed a corvette-like punch. There could be no ignoring them...

As the Kroggs turned, the boats scattered by squadrons, their guns cycling as they swept themselves clear of the Krogg counter-fire. The Destroyers turned away from their target Carriers and began intensifying anti-small-craft fire, a half dozen more boats being shattered by focused neural energy.

Maximane watched with a frown — the remaining Destroyers were not as easy targets for the boats as the Dreadnoughts might be... They could *really* maneuver, and now that they were turning their attention to the boats, they were faring better against their tormentors.

Another handful of boats was consumed by silent fire, with no Krogg casualties to offset the loss.

The boats couldn't do it all... it would take broadsides.

"Send to *Monarch*, reverse course and engage enemy with guns."

Atlas slowly closed with the stern of the lumbering Krogg Dreadnoughts. Still cruising with an open field under energy drive, the 74 was actually moving at sub-light speed as it maneuvered into a place in the center of the Krogg formation.

"We'll have to pull the field in quickly," Fox said again to the Cruising Master, and Gunth nodded.

"Not a problem, skipper."

Fox took a deep breath. Though both he and Thena Venus were veteran campaigners, the odds of two 74s stopping that many Dreadnoughts weren't spectacular... so they'd have to improvise.

"In position, sir. Matching speed."

Fox nodded at the report from his First Lieutenant, then met the Master's eyes, "Ready both broadsides and carronades. Mister Gunth, at your discretion."

The Master nodded, turned to his helm, took a rugged-seeming breath, and then touched the cougar who sat there once on the shoulder. *Atlas* shuddered hard.

"Sir! New ship in range... *Atlas*, 74!"

Maximane heard the report and already his eyes were searching *Engadine's* main battle plot for the ship. Earther luck paying off again after all... but what the...?

Cruising right between the two central Dreadnoughts in formation, *Atlas* drew in its field and dropped into matter almost in the blink of an eye. The Kroggs tried to sheer out of formation as they recognized the arrival, but *Atlas'* guns were already running out and firing.

At virtually point-blank range, the heavy broadsides cut smartly through the Dreadnoughts, immediately crushing the two Krogg ships that Cruising Master Gunth had maneuvered *Atlas* between. The 74 then cut starboard and loosed its heavy carronades on a third Dreadnought.

Even as *Atlas* dove relatively downwards to pass beneath the Krogg ship, *Vulcan* exploded from energy drive on the far side of the formation and sent a broadside into each of the two remaining Dreadnoughts.

Captain Venus hadn't been able to come in as close to the Krogg formation, but one of the Dreadnoughts still came apart beneath the weight of her powerful energy salvoes. As those ships exploded, *Vulcan* pressed in close to the last unengaged foe, carronades cutting into the Krogg armor at point-blank range. It was torn into quarters almost immediately.

Flame slipped from energy last, its target the marauding Destroyers instead of the capital ships. As *Atlas* and *Vulcan* lunged after the last fleeing Krogg Dreadnought, *Flame* crossed the bow of a Destroyer and loosed a small but potent broadside, backing it with carronades.

The gunboats, given sudden relief by the confusion, dove towards their targets, spraying the Kroggs with shot. Three more Destroyers were put smartly out of action in a matter of seconds, two of the final three veering back into clouds of boats as they tried to escape.

One pressed on towards *Engadine*.

Driving hard, this last Krogg Destroyer was determined to take at least one important Earther ship with it — death was certain at the hands of the boats, and so ramming was the most productive course of action. The huge Earther ship was hardly a subtle target.

With this in mind, the last scraps of energy left to the Destroyer were thrown into its drives, and it pulled away from both *Flame* and the boats as they pounced on its consorts.

Maximane saw the Destroyer coming fast, and since *Monarch* and *Engadine* were turning to join the action, there wasn't enough time to reverse course and get out of the way.

"Port guns fire!" he roared abruptly, and the shot of *Engadine's* broadside tore outward, *Monarch's* firing in support. The converging energy sliced the Destroyer apart, scattering debris in all directions...

A piece of carapace somersaulted toward *Engadine*, moving as quickly as a kinetic missile thanks to its progenitor's incredible velocity. One of *Engadine's* carronades took a fruitless shot at it, but it was too fast. It slammed hard into the Carrier's shields and disintegrated.

For a brief second that seemed like the end of the action — debris was absorbed by shields all the time, and often more debris than this...

But *Engadine* hadn't finished shaking down just yet, and one of the brand new power couplings in the massive ship's forward grid had developed a minor flux in its regulator.

In other words, it overloaded, just as *Gargoyle's* had back at Earth.

Perhaps it was a bad batch of regulators...

Maximane didn't realize something had hit the shields until the battle plot's display flickered once. He started to turn to ask for a damage report when the entire tank exploded in front of him, victim of a massive power surge.

He hit the deck hard, and *Engadine* slewed to one side as part of its power grid went down.

CHAPTER 31

"Lightweight, high capacity... more than adequate to cram 200 humans into for a week," ArcColonel Jessica Forbes tapped the alloy hull of one of the three so-called 'river runners' with her fist.

Lupus cocked an eyebrow at the huge barge, then glanced at its bigger brother. Both had been cobbled together by Bishop's crew with the help of his Earther squad and the pre-fab plant Forbes had so thoughtfully provided.

The giant rafts looked more like tanks than boats. None too easy to propel, one might suspect... but then there was a new impeller to haul them. It had taken three days to assemble that new unit, even with the manufacturing plant working round the clock, but they'd made its completion their main priority, second only perhaps to bolstering the staunch defenses of the camp against further Krogg raids. Things hadn't gotten any quieter in the past four days.

Once the impeller had been finished and assembled, they'd gathered the parts from the crashed pods, and in a single day, managed to weld together these rafts out of the remaining pod scrap. They were massive flat-bottomed beasts, and as Lupus looked at them, he began to doubt his estimates about transit time back to camp.

Hauling barges that big against the current... well, it wasn't too speedy a proposition. At least it didn't seem to be one.

"What?" Forbes frowned at Lupus' seeming lack of enthusiasm.

Lupus ground his jaw and shrugged, "Might be just a bit heavy... I mean to tow. We could have some problems with the new impeller."

Forbes' bright expression sobered, "I thought you said your engine could handle it."

"Our old one could have, but the one we put together out here mightn't be as reliable. We scraped the parts together from crashed pods, after all."

Forbes released a thin sigh and nodded, turning away from the wolf and staring at the larger barge. Lupus frowned thoughtfully at the broad thing, then looked closely at the other two beached craft. They were essentially sea anchors — if only they could do more than just float. Pawman had already explained there weren't enough materials available to build a second impeller... but what if they went lower-tech? Maybe not as low-tech as oars or paddle wheels, but...

"What if we lash them all together and form a single huge hull, then build a few banks of simple propellers to add more thrust?" he suggested, crouching to look for potential engine-mounting space on the smaller barge's flat bottom.

Forbes paused thoughtfully, trying to remember if she actually knew anything about watercraft propulsion. The Earthers had overseen the impeller's reconstruction, piece by delicate piece, but the humans probably knew more about simple propellers. And a single big hull...

"We could build it to be about thirty meters long, four wide... the barge that is. Fit the pulsars on the quarters like a broadside... maybe even use our portable shields to defend it. With enough propellers we might even get up to forty knots," she said thoughtfully.

Standing up again, Lupus nodded at Forbes' comment. They could turn this into a *super-combat* barge.

Ooh, the Navy will surely be lining up to adopt that class name for something...

Wisely choosing not to voice his amusing musings, Lupus nodded, "We could make it back up river in five days. Still arrive back when Pat expects us."

Forbes nodded again, and Lupus caught Pawman's eye as the wolf passed behind the ArcColonel with an armful of parts.

"We need propellers!"

Joseph Barron continued silently through the darkness of space, unnoticed by the Kroggs it had just passed. Sarah sat in her equally silent and dark cabin aboard the Superdreadnought — she hadn't bothered to turn on the lights. Her green tunic sat folded in her lap, and as her fingers traced the seams of the cloth, her mind continued to bombard her with the reality of what she'd just done.

She'd just *avoided* the enemy. And worse than that, she hadn't sent Caine word. And she wasn't going to. She couldn't afford to send any of her small squadron back to warn him — they were too far from Gibraltar and if they tried to split up the Kroggs would probably kill the messenger long before it got near the system. Pods would betray her location, and...

And Caine might send someone out to bring her back...

Sarah shook those thoughts out of her mind...

Caine's scouts would have to locate the Kroggs for themselves... and it wasn't as though she had passed the whole fleet and not warned Gibraltar. No, that fleet was still ahead of her, and she'd need every Freetown ship she had if she was going to be able to succeed in this surgical expedition to a system supposedly beyond its pickets.

Sarah rubbed her eyes in the darkness — for now, at least, she was done with the Navy. Hopefully it would outlive her...

Almost symbolically, Sarah lifted the tunic from her lap and heaved it over the arm of the chair. The dull thud of the fabric bunching on the floor seemed altogether too loud, and she closed her eyes as it reached her.

She was done with the Navy. She was now a renegade, looking for Pat Conroy. For love.

• • •

"Good work!" Forbes eyed the rough-looking outboard motor with a grin. "Record time too — what sort of speed can it make?"

Grinning, *Bishop's* surviving engineer offered a shrug, "The Earthers say it'll do thirty knots cruising, forty in a pinch."

Lupus came to a halt next to Forbes and eyed the small propeller assembly as the engineer explained its expected performance. It wasn't as impressive looking as the impeller, but then he tended not to be fooled by appearances.

Glancing from the engineer to Forbes, the wolf nodded, "They aren't a third as efficient or quiet as the impeller, but we're not looking for stealth or economy. We've got enough power between the packs we brought and the ones you've got to keep this contraption cruising for a month."

Forbes nodded to the Sergeant and then peered past him at the barges — the squad was welding them together and to their own impeller boat. It had only taken an hour and a half for the pre-fab plant to cobble up the outboard, and now that the plans were fixed in its computer, it would take less than that for every subsequent motor. With all the outboards built and installed, they'd be able to push this giant super barge pretty fast.

And then they'd have to leave relative safety... well, as much safety as Lupus could conceive of in the middle of an open plain on a planet he'd crash-landed on with a Krogg army trying to take him prisoner...

Before Lupus' musing wit could involve itself in that dire thought, something tweaked his instincts. He stepped lightly away from the ArcColonel, wandering towards the shield with squinted eyes. It was midday, and the blue vegetation seemed to glisten under the natural light. There was nothing in sight — the human sentries were lined up at the perimeter of the shield keeping a close eye out for the Kroggs...

But something definitely felt wrong.

Squinting towards the river, Lupus' eyes followed the flowing stream from the bank near the human camp towards the mountains, carefully examining every curve. At first nothing seemed out of the ordinary, but then, as the water curled into the trees, something made Lupus pause and look more closely.

What *was* that?

It looked black, shiny... and it was floating in the center of the river...

Hastening his pace, the Sergeant Major moved further down towards the water, trying to get a better view... aha. Oh dear. With a claw dug into each bank to serve as a tether, it sat in the water. And there was what looked like a neuro pulse weapon protruding from its nose. It snorted.

By the Earth, it was a *Krogg boat*. Its genetic plans must have been stored in the bio banks of the Destroyers in orbit, they must have *grown* it to command the river after the Earthers had arrived down here in their boat. Judging by its size relative to the river, the Krogg water vessel wasn't small. It looked at least as big as a dropship... far larger than the boat the Earthers had used to come downstream, maybe even bigger than their makeshift riverboat.

And it housed a *corvette*-sized weapon.

Earther portable shields were designed to handle just about anything in the way of land weaponry — artillery included — but a Krogg neuro pulse was not traditional in the infantry sense. In space, it was like a carronade — deadly at close range and very persistent in its output.

Clearly, this wasn't the same weapon, but it appeared to be quite similar. Chances were it could command the river, and very likely kill all of them.

"Jessica!" Lupus called to the ArcColonel and she looked up.

Pointing upriver, Lupus turned back to eye the strange craft again, his brain ticking over quickly in hopes of finding an obvious counter. The Kroggs didn't seem to be coming down to the *Bishop* base — probably wise considering the volume of fire the humans could pour from behind the Earther shields during that cruise through confined waters.

But if the Kroggs were really hoping to catch Earthers, then cutting off their obvious avenue of retreat was perfectly sensible. They were playing a craftier game than Lupus was used to seeing from them.

"What's up, Beck?"

Forbes came to a stop next to Lupus and the taller wolf pointed to the Krogg boat, "A blockship. At least one, maybe more. And there's a neuro pulse on its bow. They know where we're headed, by the looks of it."

The human stiffened, "Can shields handle a neuro pulse?"

"On land, fully powered and interlocked, probably," Lupus wasn't sure whether that bit was true or wishful thinking, "but definitely not in the water, with shaky power and stretched interlocks."

His words had been quiet, so most of the humans around hadn't heard him, but four of his marines had been close enough to catch the comment and now they gathered behind him and the ArcColonel. This *was* a problem...

"Can the pulsars crack that thing?" Forbes asked softly, squinting to see it more clearly.

Lupus ground his jaw, "I wouldn't count on it. We only have anti-soldier patterns, not anti-vehicle."

The pair stood silently for a moment, Forbes' hopes beginning to sink again, Lupus simply frowning. In order to crack that sort of obstacle they'd need heavier weapons... and since that boat was a Krogg organism, the Earthers probably couldn't just go out and capture it.

No, they'd blow it completely out of the way so it didn't block their own voyage.

A plan slowly formed behind Lupus' eyes, and he turned towards Corporal Howler and Private Pawman.

"Either of you know anything about *torpedoes*?"

CHAPTER 32

Caine stood alone on *Orion's* upper observation deck, counting all the vessels that were visible. Dozens of Earther warships had dropped their grav anchors and were floating in orbit of *Gibraltar One* — ships of the line and frigates all clustered together, awaiting action.

As Caine took some comfort in the familiar sight, a new component of naval warfare crossed his vision — a flight of four gunboats. The formation was slipping between a handful of 74s, flying fast in a vertical diamond pattern, its pilots practicing maneuvers to improve their comfort with the new ships. All the trained boat pilots were with the Carriers now rushing to Gibraltar's aid from Genesis. The Earthers flying these boats were pinnace pilots who'd volunteered to learn the controls of the new ships — who'd volunteered to commit to action despite significant lack of experience.

And so far, there was no pilot shortage; *Gibraltar One* had been holding pilots for six stations of its size, and virtually all the pinnace crews off arriving squadron ships were volunteering. That being the case, there were enough crews available to assign one to each new gunboat as it came off the production line.

All Caine had to do was figure out how best to use these boats in action.

In addition to the flag squadrons that had already been at Gibraltar, four Allied squadrons had arrived, two of them composed of Third Rates. That infusion of capital ships could, based on his discussion with Graham, provide a large number of launching platforms for the boats in Gibraltar space... but Caine wasn't enthusiastic about that idea. Loading boats onto ships of the line might not be the best approach for the defense of Gibraltar.

In simplest terms, the problem the Allies faced here wasn't one of deck space, but one of effectiveness. Though Felix was close to putting the finishing touches on the balance of the *Gibraltar* stations, the boats were, for now, flying exclusively off the decks of *Gibraltar One*. The station could hold a remarkable number of these small fighting ships, and Caine was feeling inclined to take advantage of that.

Putting boats on ships would be useful when the fighting was away from the concentrated boat umbrella that a station like *Gibraltar One* could provide, but in a small planetary system with stations to carry the boat load, it seemed as though cramming boats onto ships would be an unnecessary complication.

Gibraltar One could effectively serve as a huge, stationary carrier...

The doors behind Caine parted, admitting a lone figure into the room. Expectantly, Caine turned to face Graham Manchester.

The young human's eyes were sunk deep in his head, and they avoided contact with Caine as Graham came to a stop in the room. His anger at the Earthers was subsiding... somewhat. But he was still angry enough at himself and worried enough about Sarah that he wasn't ready to reconcile with his Earther comrades just yet.

He fully *realized* that his outburst had been wholly needless; he'd attacked some particularly fine Earthers because he'd found himself wounded and hurting. It was neither a correct nor fair reaction, but there was nothing he could do about it now.

He didn't deny a meeting with Caine, but he wouldn't be particularly open during it... And damn Sarah for bringing this on...

Dammit Sarah, what were you thinking?

Caine watched the junior Manchester as the human stared at the floor, then took a few steps towards the ArcLieutenant-General. Clasping his hands behind his back, the First Lord made sure he was noisy enough in his movement to draw Graham's eyes to him.

The human's face seemed relatively impassive, "You wanted to see me, Setter?"

Caine cocked an eyebrow at the stiffness of the question — his instincts were telling him Graham was calm, but it seemed the junior Manchester was well aware of the rift he'd opened between himself and Caine... he just wasn't ready to attempt to bridge it yet.

That was fine, and there was no point dwelling on Graham's dark mood, especially since he was already fully aware of his mistake, "I haven't heard from Fox's group yet, but it seems pretty evident that your sister is going to be out of Gibraltar for the battle."

Graham ground his jaw and nodded slowly, "So?"

Caine tilted his head at the cool remark.

"So I need *you* to fill a gap in my higher command, Graham. I need you to serve as a senior flag officer in the coming fight," Caine's words betrayed some of his own strain.

"I'm a desk officer, Setter. I'm not trained in mobile fighting," Graham replied, pacing ahead and passing Caine to stare out at the assembled ships beyond *Orion's* massive hull.

"Savanna was an administrator too, Graham. Now he's one of the best squadron commanders in the fleet," Caine turned after the human and spoke to his back.

Graham silently gazed through the glass. He'd been in war-games three times in his life, and he'd gotten himself thoroughly thrashed the first two times. The third... well, the third he'd pulled through on luck and guts.

He wasn't a good fleet commander.

"Felix is an Earther, Setter. He has the natural ability."

Nodding slowly, Caine paced to the glass and stopped next to Graham, "I suppose he does. But so do you, I think. You don't have a spectacular war-gaming record, I'll grant you, but simulations aren't the extent of warfare."

Graham snorted dejectedly, "Regardless, I'm not the one to control a quarter of your force, Setter. You'll have both Ursla and Felix to do that, and I heard that Caitlin Hargreaves will be coming in the day after tomorrow with the 427th. She was with Sarah at Genesis — she'd be far better suited."

Caine tilted his head slightly, "Hargreaves is good, but like the rest of us, she's been fighting the same old war since Genesis."

They'd *all* been fighting that war... what was Caine getting at...?

Frowning now, Graham turned to the First Lord, "I don't see quite what you're saying."

With both eyebrows arched, Caine tilted his head, "Carriers, Graham." The First Lord bobbed his head toward a diamond of gunboats sliding through space outside the glass. "We all think in terms of broadsides and volleys, and it's a hard habit to break without any contrasting combat experience — especially in such a short time span."

"And you think I'm a clean slate? You want *me* to command the boats because I don't know any better."

"That is probably the basest interpretation I can think of," Caine's brow creased into a frown again. "You're the one who suggested the whole ship-equipping thing, and you've plenty of system-defense experience. What I need you to do is make sure they head to the right part of the battle at the right time."

Graham winced. Back in the good old days, less than a week ago, when he could fall off a chair, laugh, and make sense of things without a missing sister and a dead almost-brother, he would've loved a job like this. He was starting to get pretty damned annoyed with the universe.

"Unchecked common sense, then?" he said somewhat bitterly after a moment's thought.

Caine contained a sigh at Graham's cynical tone and answered with a shrug. He then lifted a tentative hand and pointed to *Gibraltar One* in the distance, "The boats are all based on that station right now. I've been trying to figure out whether I should leave them there. Quite frankly, I can't decide."

"So you want *me* to tell you."

"These short, cryptic statements really don't suit you, Graham," Caine consciously lightened his tone and turned to his friend. "Yes, I want you to figure it out. Work from scratch — I've been trying to work from history but the situations aren't quite the same. The Larosian tactics don't take into account the firepower our boats provide, so it'll be a new school of development."

Grinding his jaw again, Graham turned back to Caine, "What about the tactics you've been developing at home. Your Carriers should be here in time for the action, why not wait for the professionals?"

Caine shrugged again, "Two reasons. First, our Carrier skippers are trained in *tactics*. I need a strategy to employ our boats in support of the fleet, not a tactic for beating a single Krogg formation. The only one working on strategy was Commodore Maximane, but *Engadine* is missing."

Logical enough, Graham mused. But he still didn't want the job. Gunboats be damned, he ran space stations, managed docking routines and got the occasional chance to shoot down intruders. Not orchestrate a massive gunboat screening movement.

Then Graham frowned — the wolf hadn't finished yet.

"That was only one reason, Setter."

Raising his eyebrows, Caine turned to the window again, "I need you to do this for me, Graham. You're one of our very best, and I need your help."

An unimpressed expression formed on Graham's face, "Keep the boy busy so he doesn't stir up trouble, then? Think you can keep me from riding you about Sarah because I'll be too tired out by days of play..."

Caine cocked an eyebrow, "You need to back off, Graham. We're not out to get you, you know that."

The junior Manchester's cold eyes found Caine's tired ones, and the much younger human jerked a single nod, "Fine. Send me your info and I'll get going on it."

Caine nodded slowly, "Very well."

That was one more weight off the shoulders of the First Lord.

CHAPTER 33

"Commodore?"

"Grrrrmmmpphh."

"Commodore. *Commodore Maximane!*"

Draco Maximane heard his name in the distance. He wasn't sure just where he was, but it sounded like the person calling his name was getting closer... perhaps he should see...

Rather weakly, the lion forced his heavy lids back from over his eyes.

"What is it?"

Startled by the coarseness of his own voice, Maximane tried to sit up, only to have two big hands push him back down to his bed. Blinking in surprise, his vision cleared enough to see a fox and Doctor Talous, *Engadine's* surgeon, standing over him.

"Sir?" Talous asked quietly.

Maximane nodded, "Would you unhand..."

Something felt wrong... or *didn't* feel at all. Draco's mind began running through a veritable system's check — no feeling in his chest or his right leg, only a familiar stasis patch tingle in his neck. He was in *Engadine's* infirmary then, and he was wounded. Ah, the action with the Kroggs — he must have taken shrapnel hits... or something along those lines.

Bad luck.

"What have I missed?" he let his head fall back against his bed's pillow and released a tired sigh.

Standing above him, the fox — a Post Captain by his pips — saluted respectfully, "Captain Fox Magnus, sir, of *Atlas.*"

Maximane frowned slightly at the vaguely familiar names, then squinted in realization, "You were on one of those 74s?"

Fox nodded, "Aye sir, I'm in command of that division. We're out here to locate the Krogg Fleet and to warn Gibraltar before it attacks... among other things..."

Maximane was nodding slowly at Fox's report, then his mind fully grasped what had been said — *Krogg Fleet?* There was no concentrated Krogg Fleet... but then Magnus had no reason to lie... and a strong Krogg force might explain the attack on Earth... partially.

"They only hit Earth with a light force. Why would they... I mean... what..."

Draco Maximane didn't usually do well trying to think on his back, and as he spouted frazzled ideas he made an effort to sit up again. The hands of the surgeon quickly righted him, "Stay *down*, sir. You're in rough shape."

Ignoring the words, Maximane leaned up and eyed the Captain, "A Krogg heavy force out here?"

Fox nodded, "The Kroggs have hundreds of ships advancing on our flank. Caine is at Gibraltar, rallying what he can to fend them off. My division is his picket..."

So that was it then — the Kroggs were playing the Battle of the Bulge and Caine was trapped at Gibraltar with nothing but a scraped-together force. Maximane had spent long enough in Earth space reading campaign reports to know the Allied Fleet was spread to hell's beyond — there'd be no concentrating it in time...

"Did the group that attacked my Carriers get in touch with the fleet? They were carrying..."

Fox was already shaking his head, "I already spoke to Captain Hobbes. We read no signal traffic between the picket group and the main fleet — they probably didn't want to tip you off to what you'd run into, in case you had a way to get word out. That or they were just so annoyed with you they forgot protocol... So the Krogg Fleet shouldn't know about Carriers."

Maximane let out a relieved sigh — they'd pulled it off after all... albeit in the last few minutes. Nothing to be displeased about though, just Earther timing in action. But now there was a Krogg Fleet heading for Gibraltar...

Well, they could add *Engadine* and *Monarch* to the defense.

"How far from Gibraltar are we... how long until we drop anchor there?" Maximane let his head loll back again.

Fox frowned, "Sir, we're a picket... a long range one at that. We're not going back — it'd take days."

The Commodore matched Fox's frown — that was a good point... now that he thought about it, he hadn't taken the Carriers anywhere near Gibraltar. What was a picket doing out this far... and what was this about not going back...?

The lion's eyes found Fox's, "Why are 74s on this picket... and why out so far. You're not going to be able to give much warning... if you won't go back..."

Nodding again, Fox let a bit of a smile creep onto his face, "Suffice it to say that we've discovered a new way for sloops to go *very* fast. We send them into hyperspace under energy drive."

Even Talous cocked an eyebrow at that — it didn't exactly *sound* safe. And by pre-war standards, Maximane somehow doubted it could be called prudent. But in time of war, it did sound incredibly useful...

Closing his eyes for a second, Maximane processed the news, "So you'll let Gibraltar know... then we're on our way to port?"

It was Fox's turn to frown, "Sir?"

"Well what else is there to do, Captain? There's a Krogg attack heading towards Gibraltar... unless some commander went off half-cocked I don't expect there's cause for us to stay out here while the fight's on at base."

Fox shook his head slowly, "It's funny you should mention half-cocked commanders, sir... but either way, I don't expect there's any way we could get around the Krogg Fleet now — they have too much of a head start, and from what Captain Hobbes has been telling me, they saw right through your stealth. Our working theory on that is it's the distribution of the power in your reactors — you have a much higher energy output in *Engadine* than in any conventional ship in the fleet. Makes you visible where we aren't."

Maximane's eyebrow arched, "Lovely... so what then? Do we have other orders?"

Taking a breath, Fox plunged into the tale of Pat's loss and Sarah's renegade actions, gauging Maximane's reaction as he did so. The Commodore, for all his injuries, was quite alert, drawing certain conclusions about Caine's decisions long before Fox got to them.

At the end of the explanation Maximane's mind continued ticking over, "So you'd recommend my Carriers join you in assisting ArcGeneral Manchester, then?"

Fox shrugged, "I can't see anything else for your ships, sir. You'd probably get caught if you tried to slip around the Kroggs, and thus far, they don't seem to know about our Carriers. It would be more useful if you stayed out of their hands..."

Maximane forced another jerked nod — Captain Magnus was quite right, there was nothing they could do to get to Gibraltar in time. They wouldn't turn the tide on their own, and if the system was to fall, better that they inflict any damage they could on the Kroggs' own base...

And that last thought gave the Commodore an idea, "We could attack *their* flank."

Fox frowned — attack what flank? The fleet when it hit Gibraltar? They'd be overwhelmed, boats or no... so what was he talking about... "I don't know if I take your meaning, sir."

Maximane struggled to sit up a bit straighter again, Talous' hands letting him rise enough to emphasize the point, "Where the Kroggs came from, Captain. Their base. I suspect that would be where they're launching their raids from, and if they were able to pool hundreds of ships there, as you say, it must be fairly well developed... With their fleet out it could be vulnerable."

A streak of enlightenment crossed Fox's face, "Indeed, sir. *Flame* located that base with the help of energy-hyper, and it was only lightly protected... We're too weak to hit it ourselves, even between both our commands. But if we can get ArcGeneral Manchester and the Freetown Squadron to assist us, we'll be in better shape to give it a try."

Maximane nodded in agreement, letting his head fall back to the pillow, "So let's alert Caine and get after the privateers."

Fox nodded again, then paused with a frown as a thought crossed his mind, "I don't mean to remove you from your command sir, but the doctor says you could use treatment at *Gibraltar One*. We could send you back with *Flame* for care... and you'd be in a good position to command their boats during the action."

A thoughtful look formed in Maximane's eyes, but he shook his head, "We'll be against worse odds out here, I think. And I'll live. If it's all the same to you, Captain, I'll stay." He paused, lifting an arm gingerly. "In this state, though, it'll be more of a symbolic gesture, I think. You were given command by Caine, so I'll turn *Engadine* and *Monarch* over to you, at least for now."

Fox abruptly cocked an eyebrow, "Uh... yes sir. Thank you..."

"It's 'Draco', Fox. Now go tell your sloop to head for Gibraltar."

"The reactors are starting to take this personally, Chronos," Lieutenant Lang Sandpelt met the eyes of *Flame's* Commander somewhat skeptically from across the bridge.

Claw could only sigh and offer a shrug, "We absolutely *must* get this word back to Gibraltar, Lang. That's what we signed on for."

The young Lieutenant cracked a small smile, "I don't recall the part of the application form that listed insane cruises at ridiculous speeds through a lower layer of subspace. What page was it on?"

The Commander smiled in reply, "I never read the forms, just sign them. But it was in there. Trust me."

With an over-deep breath, Lang nodded, "I figured. Alright, I'll get down to the engine deck and make sure everything's welded down. Let me know when you want us."

Claw nodded slowly and watched his junior leave *Flame's* cramped bridge, empathizing with him as he went. On the now-famous run from Genesis to Earth — or rather, almost to Earth, as circumstance proved — it had been Claw himself who'd been down there watching the engines, keeping the sloop's speed at a then unheard-of velocity. If anything, Sandpelt's stress would be greater, as, before a week ago, no one had ever pushed a warship through hyperspace at faster-than-light relative speed for a prolonged period.

Somehow Claw doubted the new drive configuration *Flame* had pioneered was going to be the cure for all the Earthers' long-range travel problems... which was almost just as well. He could accept everybody speaking English, but if some great force in the universe had made point-to-point travel so instantaneous, it'd take the fun out of life.

"Skipper," the Signal Chief chimed abruptly, "Captain Magnus for you... signaling from *Atlas*."

Blinking himself into reality, Claw nodded to the Chief and Fox's smiling face appeared in *Flame's* main battle tank. The positive expression immediately inflated Claw's hopes for the coming mission — Fox had the instincts of a sloop commander, and if he was smiling it was a good omen.

"What news, Fox?"

On the other end of the line, Fox bobbed his head to his own Signal Officer, and the orders he'd quickly written up on the way back from *Engadine* burst through space on the energy comm, reaching *Flame's* main computer.

"We're heading after ArcGeneral Manchester and then we'll be looking for whatever forward base the Kroggs have been using to launch these attacks. *Engadine* and *Monarch* will stay with us since there isn't much chance of them getting to Gibraltar in time or without being detected," Fox's words were quick, and Claw replied with a thoughtful nod.

"You'll have to move pretty quickly to catch up with Sarah," the cougar suggested after a moment, and Fox bobbed his head.

"We're clearing for high speed now. *You* need to get that news to Gibraltar, and then I want you to meet us here..."

A star chart suddenly appeared next to Fox in *Flame's* main tank, "The last system we suspect *Bishop* to have been in."

The system from *Bishop's* sensor logs flashed red in a cluster of white stars.

"We won't be there for at least three days yet, so keep yourself safe for that long, but when we get there I'd like to have some information about what's going on... if anything."

Claw frowned, "You sure you don't want us to try to rendezvous with you before you get there?"

Fox shook his head, "We probably won't be moving direct, if we're following the Freetowners. You might miss us and get caught by some Krogg heavies. Just as well you stay put where you know we can find you."

Nodding slowly in agreement, Claw glanced at his Cruising Master, "Get us ready for energy-hyper."

"Good luck, Chronos. And look after *Flame*," Fox's face sobered slightly in the plot.

"You know I will," Claw smiled.

With a parting nod between both maverick officers, the link cut. Claw settled himself in his seat as the Master announced to the ship their intention to engage energy-hyper, and *Flame's* crew hurried to their stations and found something solid to hold on to.

"Engine deck reports ready, sir," the Master said after a brief pause. "Field forming ahead of us."

"Wyndhymn generators online, bring us into energy drive. Set speed for 200 pls, set course and calculate exit point..."

Moments later *Flame* slid into the subspace layers.

CHAPTER 34

"Hyper footprint, Captain. The hyperspace distortion pattern looks like it's *Flame.*"

Karl Kandam looked up from his panel in *Gibraltar One's* C&C, "Send to the First Lord. Clear traffic space around the hyperpoint, and have Thirteenth Gun Squadron move to escort."

The last order — one to deploy gunboats around the sloop as it arrived — was unnecessary from any tactical perspective, as *Flame* was a friendly ship entering friendly space. But with battle almost certainly on the horizon, Kandam was inclined to use every opportunity to give some of the boats maneuver experience. The twenty-boat Thirteenth Gun Squadron was the newest and least experienced of the commissioned units thus far built in Gibraltar — it could use the practice.

Caine reached the bridge of *Orion* just as *Flame* burst from hyperspace, a red grow slowly fading from around the edges of the small sloop's slender hull.

Forepaw turned to the First Lord as he came to claim his seat, "Sensors read a spike in the energy field when they came through that time. Looks like the strain of energy-hyper is beginning to wear on the ship."

"Well that would make sense, wouldn't it," Caine frowned. "Any indication that they're close to breakdown?"

Forepaw turned briefly back to one of *Orion's* engineering officers, who shrugged helplessly, "No idea, sir. Could go either way. I'd advise caution though — we put enough strain on our Wyndhymns when we're cruising at normal space speeds."

Caine nodded at the suggestion, then turned to the Signal Officer, "Has Commander Claw hailed yet?"

The panther shook her head, "They seem to be experiencing comm interference, sir. The energy spikes have disrupted Fleetcomm..."

A deep sigh escaped Caine — this energy-hyper system was fast, but it was also draining the life out of little *Flame.* The ship had done the most runs so far, so it stood to reason it'd be the first to exhibit side effects–

"Sir, have a hail now. It's Commander Claw," the Signal Officer interrupted Caine's musing, and he turned to the battle plot expectantly.

Commander Chronos Claw appeared, looking only *slightly* disheveled after what had evidently been a rough transit, "Sir, dispatches from Captain Magnus are beaming to you now. We encountered Commodore Maximane's Carrier division, and now all units are in pursuit of ArcGeneral Manchester."

Caine cocked a tired eyebrow — Maximane was out that far?

"I take it there's detail about that in your dispatches, Commander?"

Claw nodded dutifully, "Direct from Captain Magnus, sir. We've also sighted the Krogg Fleet approaching. I'd say three days out, at most. They essentially number what *Bishop* detected — just short by a handful of ships."

Nodding, Caine tapped a few keys on the plot's console and began opening Magnus' message. After a moment he looked to Claw, "Commander, our readings show you're in rather rough shape. I think it's time you stand down and join the fleet. You've had enough hopping about at that speed — at least until your reactors can get a refit."

Claw blinked in surprise, "Sir, I'd respectfully request permission to refuse that order. Captain Magnus is expecting me to scout the system where we think *Bishop* was lost — he's counting on *Flame's* intelligence about potential survivors to help determine whether he should commit to a move there. He and Commodore Maximane also indicated they were going to attempt to destroy the Krogg base. I'd like to assist, sir."

Again Caine frowned... these young officers were so committed to their work. Surely he should tell Claw to stay, but here, now, one sloop could make no difference. And while it was still a risk, Fox could use *Flame's* abilities, "Even with ArcGeneral Manchester, he'll only have three capital ships. He's of the opinion that will be sufficient?"

"He and the Commodore seemed to concur, sir," Claw's answer was quick. "I'd like to join him in any attempt."

With a thoughtful blink, Caine slowly met Claw's gaze, "I'll leave it to you, Commander. Don't put your ship at unnecessary risk, though."

"I won't, sir." Claw turned to his Master, "Recharge the drives."

Caine straightened slightly, and looked at the young commander with both pride and respect, "Be careful, Commander. Good luck."

"Thank you, sir. And to you."

Caine nodded and the link closed. As much as he feared for *Flame*, the sloop was not his greatest concern now that word of the Kroggs was finally concrete.

Glancing sideways to Forepaw, Caine narrowed his eyes, "Call a meeting of the senior commanders here in half an hour. I'll be in the main briefing room."

"Two hundred Dreadnoughts, 400 Destroyers, and twenty Motherships. That's quite the attack force," Felix said quietly, gently strumming his fingers on the main battle plot's console.

"No half-measures, they're coming at us with everything they've got," Ursla nodded in reply.

"Well, we expected as much," Caine said with dark finality. He stood, hands linked behind his back, looking over the images *Flame* had provided. It was a *massive* armada... at least for this time in the war. Ten months ago, it would hardly have been adequate for action — the Battle of Genesis had been fought by *thousands* of vessels. Today, though, with both the Allied and Krogg Fleets scattered across hundreds of systems on this massive spatial front, this was a heavy concentration.

Not what Caine wanted to see.

Nonetheless, he had to keep reminding himself that it was expected, and that he'd have a sizable force of his own standing by to meet it. Thanks to Pat, they had a chance here... albeit not a great one.

Two more squadrons had reached Gibraltar earlier that very morning, one of Second Rates and one of Sixths. The next day was expected to bring three more to the system, then the day after Admiral Varnon Broadpaw and his four squadrons from the Oxford's Star station — including the 111th Flying Squadron under Commodore Dran Nightclaw and Varnon's own First Rates of the 202nd Battle Squadron. In addition to that force, ArcLieutenant-General Caitlin Hargreaves was bringing in two Genesis squadrons, one of Superdreadnoughts and the other of Battlecruisers. That infusion added twenty-three more vessels, and significantly increased the number of ships he could marshal in Gibraltar's defense.

Indeed, best-case estimates gave Caine over 300 vessels — many of them capital ships — before the Kroggs arrived...

Still, the Kroggs had twice that number of combat vessels — even if he didn't include the corvettes, which, like the rest of these Krogg ships, had doubtless been redesigned to better cope with Allied vessels. Perhaps that would make them vulnerable to the gunboats, but either way, those corvettes posed a serious threat.

"This is going to be a brutal fight. We'll need any scrap of luck we have left to win it... hopefully we haven't used it all up by now..." Caine's tone lacked its trademark certainty, but the assembled commanders nodded in silent agreement.

Graham was the first to reply, his quiet tone no more confident than Caine's, "So what of that base? The one Sarah, Fox and Maximane are going to destroy?"

Ursla quickly keyed in a few commands and the computer ran comparisons between the scans from *Bishop* and *Flame*, "They'll be facing three Dreadnoughts and a dozen Destroyers at least — plus the fixed weapons on the facilities there."

Graham's impassive face seemed to darken, and he turned away from the glowing blue holographic tank, "Two 74s and a Superdreadnought, a Battlecruiser, some heavies and lights, and the Destroyers... plus *Flame*... that seems to be almost a match for the base."

Felix detected the worry in the junior Manchester's voice — as he had in just about everybody else's — and he rounded the plot to join the human, "They've also got *Engadine* and *Monarch*, and the Kroggs don't know about the Carriers yet. They'll do well, I think."

"The Kroggs won't be ready for them," Ursla chimed in helpfully, sounding reasonably convinced of the conclusion. "So as long as Sarah agrees to help Fox, that base will be looked after..."

"She will," Graham leaned back in his chair. "She'll realize Pat is dead and she'll want blood."

Caine cocked an eyebrow at that, "I expect she'll help."

Graham ground his jaw at the measured comment, then nodded in spite of himself. That'd be... alright then. Sarah would be reasonably safe, especially once *Atlas* and the squadron caught up with her.

Something that almost felt like relief washed over the junior Manchester — no weight was lifted from his shoulders, but he surely felt stronger as he tried to hold up what was already there. The enemy had missed Sarah's privateers, and now she had even odds, Earther help, and the chance to make a difference again. He could live with that.

"Very well then," he said after a long pause. "So now we must figure out boat tactics, mustn't we?"

Felix gave a quick nod, and after a shared glance, Ursla and Caine mirrored the gesture.

"Certainly," the First Lord said quietly after a moment.

They had to protect Gibraltar.

Wreckage orbited the system's fourth planet — remains of *Harbinger Bishop*. Two Krogg Destroyers also sat in orbit, casting their attention groundward as the hunt to capture Earther prisoners continued. Human prisoners had told the Queen of Earth and Gibraltar, what useful knowledge could be extracted from the fur-bearing aliens?

Then, rather abruptly, a hyperpoint formed on the system's far side, and the Destroyers took notice. An Earther sloop exploded from the point... and immediately two of its reactors literally flew apart in its belly.

The small sloop bucked and began somersaulting through space without power, three of its crew dead and nine wounded. Its faster-than-light drives — conventional or otherwise — were completely offline, its shields and guns without power.

Ordering their units on the ground to continue the operation to capture the Earthers, the Destroyers broke orbit and headed after the wounded sloop.

Helplessly spiraling through space, *Flame* was the first victim of energy-hyper.

CHAPTER 35

"We've got three of them."

Lupus nodded slowly as the human engineer waved her arm to indicate the three silver tubes sitting in the grass next to the barge.

"They're each using some of the fuel from our pod thruster packs for their warheads, and a simple contact detonator. We arm them by pulling out that pin and we send them ahead by hitting the red button on this," the engineer held up a simple remote control that looked as though it'd been cobbled together from the parts of one of the pods. "Its fins should keep it running straight, and the engine we hitched to it should do almost thirty knots."

"Will it strike bottom?" Lupus asked with a cocked eyebrow, circling the cylinders as he wondered why they were different lengths.

"Hopefully not," Howler said with a skeptical smile. "Comp says they're neutrally buoyant, but we might not have accounted for current and such."

Forbes, standing next to Lupus, huffed a sigh, "How much punch?"

The human engineer grinned fiercely, "Enough to blow that boat right out of the water. Literally."

A slow smile spread across Forbes' face, "That'll work, I think."

Lupus nodded, "My team will take care of our watcher, then. You folks get to the boat and get ready to float it. We're expected back at Pat's camp in four days, but if your estimates are right it'll take five. Best we hurry."

The Krogg boat held tight to its moorings as night fell over the blue planet. The Krogg soldiers were out in the forest, watching the camp for an attempted overland escape. In the fading light, the glowing fires of the human survivors were clear. Yet again, the humans were too afraid to come out...

Lupus moved low and fast, three of his squad with him while the other three — Howler, Pawman and Canit — hefted the torpedo silently to the river. With its tendency to bend, the meandering stream wasn't particularly torpedo-friendly — in order for the straight-running warhead to strike its target, it would have to be let loose almost two kilometers upstream from the camp, with a direct line to the target.

Which meant the Earthers would have to get through a Krogg picket and into close range to release their weapon.

"Graxton, Villar, Fineclaw," Lupus whispered almost inaudibly to the three marines with him in the open meadow, and each murmured back soft replies.

They were in a single cluster, moving loudly out from the Bounce Hole. Normal procedure would have seen them spread out, moving silently and blending with the ground...

But now they *needed* to draw attention so that Howler's team, which was creeping along the bank with the more typical Earther stealth, would not be seen by the Kroggs in the twilight.

"Fan out, pulsars to the rear."

Villar and Fineclaw separated from the back of Lupus' group and planted themselves in the flanks of the Bounce Hole, propping their heavy weapons on the rim and setting sights on the dark blue jungle. Graxton and Lupus, for all their attempts to be noisy, slid almost invisibly forward.

"Ready on my signal," Lupus said loudly.

Stopping and dropping to one knee, he was acutely aware of his wide open position in the field. The Bounce Hole was only two dozen meters behind him. Graxton was thirty to his right.

Hefting his rifle to his shoulder, Lupus searched for a patch of shifting black in the dark blue vegetation. After a moment his eyes settled on what had to be a patrolling soldier. So far, despite his attempts, he hadn't been detected. Typical *good* luck for–

A Krogg popped out of a fold in the ground ten meters ahead of him.

And another.

Another *four*.

"*Fire!*"

Clamping down on his trigger, Lupus was already on his feet, pulling one arm from the stock of his rifle to clutch his short sword.

The first Krogg in the charge succumbed to the persistent energy streaming from the Seargent's weapon, but in the seconds it took for the shot to crack that leader, the rest covered the gap between their hiding place and the wolf.

Both pulsars were channeling bright energy into the attackers, and over a dozen more Kroggs were emerging now from their hiding place, still more erupting from the jungle beyond.

It was too late to try to stop them with rifles.

Letting go of his gun's grip, Lupus drew his blade and keyed it active in a fluid motion, raising it just in time to meet the first swing of a Krogg's mighty arm. The Earther-made weapon sliced right through the Krogg's bone, lopping the appendage off altogether.

Drawing away smoothly, Lupus keyed on his shield and brought himself into a fighting stance, sword held before him. Graxton joined him quickly, her own blade shimmering angrily in the darkening evening. Together, they braced as the next Kroggs sprinted into the fray.

•••

Down near the bank, Howler looked up slowly to observe the field and the pulsar bursts. He then noticed the flash of two polished blades in the twilight and realized the Kroggs must have been waiting for Lupus to sortie.

Hopefully they weren't expecting a water attack at the same time.

Hefting the biggest torpedo of the set, the remaining three Earthers slithered along the wet grass that edged the darkening river. They were coming to the last bend now, and they'd soon have to stop to arm their weapon.

With a glance at his two companions, Howler had his party stop in its tracks and lower the silver, finned tube to the ground. Carefully, then, they guided the weapon into the water, wading into the murky current to the stream's center. Cautiously checking that it didn't sink immediately, they held it fast while Howler removed the arming pin.

The small metal strip came from the tube's top, and once removed, the contact triggers were fully open to each other — the detonator could now spark the fuel and create a rather large bang on impact. Silently aware of this imminent danger, the trio of Earthers pushed their weapon through the water by hand, carefully avoiding the head.

Rounding the bend, they lined up the Krogg boat, gingerly letting go of the tube's sides as it came correctly to bear. Before the current could shift its trajectory, Howler hit the red button on his control box.

A loud whine filled the air, originating from the river. Lupus took the legs off a Krogg just as he heard the torpedo and then spun to eye the river. The Kroggs slowed to do the same, droning pulsars knocking many down as they did, and Lupus quickly swept forward again, slicing into one who had been distracted.

Pausing, Lupus listened as the whine turned into a deeper growl, and squinted at the river in hopes of seeing the torpedo cruise into the Krogg boat.

He waited a few seconds, but nothing happened. So he brought his blade back up and stepped closer to the distracted Kroggs.

Howler, Pawman and Canit flung themselves into the water beyond the bend. At such speed, the torpedo should have slammed straight into the boat. Holding their breath in the churning current, they waited for the telltale 'boom'.

And waited.

After a moment they surfaced, flung themselves against the bank facing the boat and peered over. The motor on the torpedo was droning, fighting the current angrily as it crawled up to the Krogg craft. So perhaps it wasn't a full thirty knots after all.

Then again, it was built from scrap metal and rocket fuel; it deserved some slack.

On the plain, the elite Earther wolves were desperately clinging to their ground, but there were dozens of Krogg reinforcements pouring from the blue forest to drive them back, and their shields were in danger of failing. Forbes and the humans were all packed up on the barge, waiting to take them off...

"Get your shields up and your swords out. We better go help Beck," Howler said quietly.

The three Earthers shifted from the bank, their shields shimmering into existence as they ran crouched over the grassy shore, in the direction of their Sergeant. If the torpedo failed, they'd have to get the Recon Squad safely back to the barge, then figure out what to–

A huge explosion erupted from the river, followed by terrific shrieks of anguish from dozens of Kroggs also caught in the blast. The concussion flattened vegetation all along the riverbank for nearly 100 meters, and the waters themselves sprayed upwards and outwards, raining back to the ground in thick sheets.

The vegetation began to burn, and the Kroggs on the plain froze in shock at the gruesome purple flames.

Howler and his marines were well within the blast radius, but the Corporal's order to activate shields saved them. Flung forty meters through the air, they landed on the soggy bank of the river with little more than bruises and minor fractures — nothing that would keep them from fighting.

Lupus and Graxton finished off their nearest adversaries, then snatched up their rifles and fell back to their pulsars. Seconds later, both Villar and Fine-claw hefted their heavy guns from the rim of the Bounce Hole and sprinted for the river, angling towards Howler's battered trio.

Firing parting shots, Lupus and Graxton turned after them, sprinting away from their slightly slower Krogg pursuers.

Jessica Forbes saw the massive explosion, *"Go!"*

The barge lurched painfully forward, its shields shimmering as the sloshing water began to spray up against them, its engines humming as the Earther power cells silently fed them a vast supply of energy. The prow of the boat lifted out of the water as speed built up, and soon the craft seemed to be cruising at a brilliant clip.

They'd be to the mountains in no time... after one stop...

Villar slid to a halt at the crest of the river bank, then dropped and propped her pulsar on the gentle rise. Fineclaw swiftly joined her, and both began pouring energy fire out past Lupus and Graxton as they sprinted to the water.

Howler shook himself from his bounce and groaned a moment. Seeing his squad mates at hand, he drew his sidearm from its holster, propped himself on the crest of the bank and added to the fire.

Slightly further towards the old camp, Canit helped Pawman out of the water. Both then drew their own pistols and slid up the bank to join Howler.

The Kroggs were sprinting hard towards the river, and even with pulsars slicing them down in scores, it was becoming apparent that the wait for the boat would be a rough one. They were farther away from the barge than planned — owing to the impromptu flight of Howler's team.

Moving now would just give the Kroggs more time to close unchallenged, so the Earthers would have to hold on...

Just over two kilometers for the barge to cruise... how long would it take for that big tub to get up to speed?

Lupus and Graxton slid down the reverse slope of the bank and opened up with their rifles, the energy slashing out to join that of the rest of the squad. The Krogg frontrunners were dropping fast, but they were still making up a lot of ground on their approach.

There was a growl from the direction of the camp — the boat's engines were straining for the first time. The marines continued to blast the Kroggs apart as best they could... but their killing field was down to less than 100 meters — and it was shrinking *very* quickly.

"At fifty meters we retreat across the river — clear?" Lupus growled to his squad, and they offered guttural sounds of acknowledgement as they kept up their intense fire.

The loud growl closed now, but Lupus continued to ignore it. Catching the Kroggs wading through the broad river would allow them to mow more down before blade range was reached–

A staccato of energy eruptions sounded from behind the Earthers, combined with the sizzle of energy fire slashing through a one-way shield. The growling softened as the barge reduced its speed to a crawl and dropped one of its shields.

"Get aboard Beck!"

The massive barrage of energy fire coming from the bow-mounted pulsar and the forty-odd human-hefted energy rifles was loud, but Lupus could just make out Jessica Forbes' words.

"To the barge, pulsars first!"

Villar and Fineclaw pulled their hefty guns off the bank and ran quickly into the water. Human hands helped pull them over the metal sides of the riverboat, then they turned their guns back on the plain.

Rushing to close with the Earthers, the Kroggs had ignored the human boat. Now they were stunned by the sudden energy barrage and their charge was slowing.

Howler and his group fled the bank, wading out to the boat and holstering their pistols. Graxton and Lupus backed away last, keeping the fire from their guns constant.

"Hurry!"

Already the Kroggs were advancing again, and even the fire from the boat wasn't slowing them now. Their objective, the Earther squad, was on the big makeshift river craft — they weren't going to let the wolves slip away...

Graxton was next to Lupus as they backed away, and just as she was about to climb aboard the boat, she froze, "Beck!"

Lupus turned at the warning and dove into his marine's back just in time to get her out of the path of a flying spine. Three more slashed into the rear shields of the barge, weakening its protection considerably. A second Krogg watercraft, somewhat smaller but of the same breed, was swimming up river behind the *Bishop* survivors.

A *second* boat... well it only made sense, now that he thought of it — two Destroyers, two boats... the smaller one hidden behind a bank downstream, where they hadn't bothered to look...

Graxton came up for air without her rifle, but before she could grab it from the bottom of the river, Lupus literally tossed her up into the boat.

"Give me the shortest torpedo!" he roared over the drone of energy fire.

The humans at the boat's side gaped at him in surprise, but Howler and Canit replied with practiced calm, hefting the heavy cylinder from the bottom of the barge and leaning over the side with it.

Aside from the purple fires in the forest, the sky was dark now, and as Lupus slowed the fall of the torpedo into the water, he looked up at Howler, "Your command, Cadmus! Get them to Pat!"

Cadmus Howler, a member of Lupus' squad for a dozen years, met the Sergeant Major's eyes, then nodded solemnly, "I will, Beck. Good luck."

Leaning back over the side with Canit, Howler keyed the shield up, "Go!"

The barge's engines roared and the makeshift craft shuddered and leapt ahead, its helm replying somewhat sluggishly, but more than adequately to get around the gentle river bends. Lupus watched it go, the brilliant energy fire rippling from behind its shields shifting to hit the Krogg boat approaching from astern. The whole Earther squad was on the back of it now, pouring energy into the bow of the alien pursuer that was coming up fast.

Slinging his rifle over his shoulder, Lupus turned the heavy torpedo to face in the direction of the Krogg vessel. There were bends in the river between the warhead and the boat, so he'd have to wait a moment...

And then he realized he had no control box.

Quickly opening the panel that lay over the torpedo's end, he reached in and found the manual trigger built into the engine. He'd have to stand here and wait for the Krogg...

Soldiers were gaining the bank now, but their attention seemed to be focused on chasing the escaping barge. He'd have a few seconds...

The Krogg boat was making at least fifty-five knots, and it turned the last bend with gothic grace.

Lupus glared at it for a second, centered the torpedo, and hit the manual start key.

The torpedo raced away from him, surging through the water with the help of the current, and Lupus dove down into the water, catching hold of Graxton's rifle–

"Where's the Sergeant Major?" Forbes came up to Howler as the barge passed the burning gore of the first boat. "I don't see him anywhere."

Howler turned to Forbes with a grim face and opened his mouth to speak.

The thunderous explosion of the second torpedo cut him off.

CHAPTER 36

"Report," Chronos Claw shakily forced himself to his feet and glared into a smoky bridge.

"Power grid offline. We've blown at least two reactors, and all the external systems are down. I can't tell you where we are skipper," the Master said gruffly, coming to his feet in the mist.

Claw grunted and offered a brief nod, stumbling to his chair. They'd been in hyperspace when something had gone wrong — one of the Wyndhymn generators, harshly overworked as it tried to hold *Flame's* field intact under the strain of energy-hyper's incredible speed, had finally failed.

He'd suspected it was inevitable — Claw was the first engineer ever to set foot on this diminutive sloop, after all — but he'd hoped one more trip was left in the little veteran. At least the Earther construction had held together well enough to get them out of danger alive... presumably.

"Internal comms are coming online — auxiliary systems are starting up," someone reported from the smoke.

"–onos, do you hear me? Dammit Chronos, are you up there?"

Claw quickly hit his comm key, "We're here, Lang. Report."

"Three dead down here. Parsons, Carster and Tremble. Two more wounded by my count. Probably more casualties outside the compartment," Sandpelt said grimly over the sizzling comm.

Claw's eyes closed, "Damn."

The bridge was silent. The romance of their maverick dashes across the stars had just come to an abrupt end...

"Alright. Damage, Lang? I have no idea where we are, so I'd like my sensors back. Then engines, shields, and guns, in that order," Claw's voice was reserved but persistent.

There was a pause clouded by some static, then: "Chronos, we lost Reactors One and Two. Looks like Two literally exploded and set One off right after. We no longer have enough power to run FTL — even standard energy drive."

Claw froze. Earther sloops, like all Earther ships, were built with one redundant reactor — most could run smoothly off three of the massive energy generators. But with two gone, there'd be no energy drive, and somewhat limited functions on the guns and shields.

"What can you give me?"

Sandpelt offered another brief pause, "By the looks of it, pretty much all engine power up to 98 pls, sixty percent on shields, sixty on guns. Our standard sensors are fried — the crash back into normal space cooked the receptors... but Bakon says she thinks she can get our long-range suite back online."

Like most sloops, *Flame* mounted a special sensor grid designed specifically for fleet recon. Usually left autonomous from ship operations, it was well protected and could, in a pinch, take the place of the regular ship sensor array.

But having only a little better than half strength on the defensive systems left Claw rather nervous. Wherever they'd come out of energy-hyper, chances were good the Kroggs were somewhere not too far away. And with a massive hyper-footprint augmented by a huge energy signature, *Flame* would look a lot like its namesake on the panel of any nearby Sensor Chief.

"Get going on it, Lang. Give Bakon whatever she needs and get the engines running. I'll send down the Master and all the idlers we can find."

"Aye."

The Krogg Destroyers hurried after the tumbling Earther sloop, keeping a close watch on it as they increased their gains. These were both new Destroyers — the faster breed capable of as much as .95 cee in normal space. The wounded Earther, even with the incredible speed of its hyperspace exit, was well within their grasp. It seemed only a matter of time before–

There was an explosion on the *planet*.

The first control boat — the only boat carried by one of the Destroyers — had been destroyed! The Destroyers slowed as information reached them... perhaps the Earther sloop was somehow a decoy — the Earther prey on the planet were going to escape when the orbiting ships were out of position and unable to support their landed units.

The Destroyers spun back, commanding the second water boat to pursue the escaping humans and Earthers as they turned. But then they saw the second boat explode as violently as the first, and many of the soldiers on the ground died at the same time.

The Earthers were escaping *very* quickly. Too easily.

But the Destroyers still had some indication of the location of the base to which the escapees were heading. The capture of Earthers from the planet could thus be carried out later. This Earther sloop, likely a mere distraction, should be dealt with now.

Turning back towards the Earther vessel, the Kroggs made a disturbing discovery: the Earther had slipped out of the range of their general scans — it was tumbling towards the system's star at a remarkable speed, and the electro-magnetic field of the bright sun was shielding conventional readings. It was unfortunate that Earthers could not be detected by telepathic probes — the intruding vessel would have to be found by other means.

Splitting up, the Destroyers plunged towards the star after their prey, hoping to see it more clearly from close range.

Lang Sandpelt fought exhaustion as he keyed his panel, the heat that now permeated *Flame's* engine deck coming close to smothering him. He'd already shrugged off the uniform tunic in favor of his light undershirt, but the heat was increasing exponentially.

"Lang?" Claw crackled over the comm.

"I'll have engines in three minutes. Bakon gives sensors another five," he was beginning to pant slightly, his body expelling heat as he breathed.

"I just came from a window. We're tumbling into a bright yellow star. Looks like we're getting pretty close," the implication was all too clear in Claw's warning.

"Give me a second, Chronos." Sandpelt turned to the Cruising Master, "Ready on Four, Caxton?"

The grayish cat nodded, "On your word, sir."

"I'm firing up Reactor Four right now, Chronos. I'll commit it to engines and that should get you pretty much everything. We can balance out the usage problems later when Three wakes up," Lang hastily keyed the power reassignments into his control console.

Usually engine power was drawn from a number of reactors — pulling too much speed on one alone had been known to burn it out... or blow it up. But desperate circumstances called for a bit of risk taking.

"Hit it, Master."

Reactor Four kicked into life, groaning its way into a soothing hum. On his panel, Sandpelt watched the engine readings climb slowly, the main drives beginning to surge to life as the flow from the reactor stabilized.

"You should have speed, Chronos. Don't push too hard though — Four's not exactly in perfect shape right now."

"Not a problem, I'll bring us up to 40 pls and hold at that until you can get me Three," Claw's voice was steady.

Escaping a star's pull wasn't a problem — even at 40 pls. It might take a little time, but it was simple enough.

The second Krogg Destroyer detected some sort of energy spike inside the star's aura. Slowly banking in that direction, it peered against the heat, hoping to catch sight of the disgustingly artificial hull of the Earther sloop.

The sun seemed too bright to get an exact position, but persistence would perhaps allow for detection...

"Bakon to skipper," Claw perked up as the bridge speakers cackled.

"Up to 40 pls now, skipper," the rating at helm interrupted quietly before

Claw could reply.

Nodding, the Commander keyed his comm button, "News, Bakon?"

"Give it a go, sir. I think we've got the suite running straight into the ship's receiver grid — you should see the readings up there," the engineer reported, the skepticism carried in her words bouncing off Claw for the moment.

If it failed, he'd be skeptical.

"Sensors up," Claw nodded to his Sensor Chief, and that console began to hum.

"I'm getting readings... wait... Krogg Destroyers, two of them on search vectors, homing in on our position!"

Claw's eyes widened, then he keyed his comm, "Beat to quarters! Clear for action! We have two Destroyers on approach. Lang, I need Three online *now*. Shields and guns too."

A harried voice came over the comm, "I've got it... *there*. Shields at forty percent is all I can promise until we rebalance the usage. I'll need us to be stopped for that."

A scowl inadvertently darkened Claw's face, "Can I have guns?"

There was a pause and another cackle, "One broadside at half and with a minute to recharge... or I can give you carronades at standard. The Master's coming back up to give you a hand."

Claw's scowl mutated into a frown and he turned to his Sensor Chief, "Do you think they've seen us?"

The Chief took a moment, "Looks like they know we're here... but I don't think they know quite *where*."

That was it then, "Carronades. And get Four braced for 95 pls."

Before Sandpelt could reply, the comm chirped off.

Claw turned back to the Chief, "Anywhere around here good for hiding?"

Another pause, then: "A ringed planet. Looks pretty big — we could mask ourselves in the rings for quite a while, I think."

"Do we have a clear route?"

The Chief frowned, "Past the second Destroyer. We go fast enough and they won't know for sure whether we're going that way or for the hyper limit... or for the other gas giant."

Claw nodded, "Good."

"Carronades and shields are yours, Chronos," Sandpelt reported over the comm.

"Gunner, get Midshipman Blackeye and two ratings, then get to the carronade turrets. I'll want you passing on targeting information if Bakon's link fails."

The lone Earther left *Flame's* smoky bridge, and Claw turned back to his helm, "Over forty degrees to starboard, up angle fifteen." He keyed the comm again, "Bakon, get ready to feed the carronades target info through the network.

If the link goes down, announce it over the comm."

"Aye. We're closing on the nearest Destroyer."

Claw took a breath, "Prepare to engage."

The second Destroyer finally thought it saw something... yes, moving on a controlled vector away from the star. The crippled Earther was less damaged than it had initially appeared. Signaling its cousin, the Destroyer pressed towards the cruising sloop, still unable to detect any particulars because of the interference from the star.

In reality, it couldn't even see how close it was to the Earther — it could just guess based on the fact that some of its senses were perceiving the metal beast.

Strange, one of those senses was sight — one usually not effective unless the target was at very close range...

Flame, like all ships of its 18-gun class, mounted four light carronades along its spine — two on top, two on bottom. At close range, each could do as much damage as a frigate's cannon, but usually they were used for point defense in concert with volleys of canister.

Now, they were *Flame's* best chance of survival.

The evidently half-blind Krogg was still vectoring in towards the star at less than 50 pls, expecting to find a wounded sloop tumbling helplessly. Claw wasn't about to give it the satisfaction.

"In range, skipper."

Claw took a breath and nodded, "Carronades, open fire."

Rolling slightly to present all four beams, *Flame* opened fire on its pursuer without the Krogg even realizing. Energy beams struck deep, viciously wounding the living vessel, slicing off parts of its sensor grid and disabling its weapons.

Flame slid past silently, and then the Destroyer released a terrifying telepathic shriek of pain — one that could be heard even in Earther brains.

Claw winced but remained focused, "Helm, ninety degrees port, down angle thirty-five. Up to 95 pls."

As its remaining reactors hummed in loud protest at the strain, *Flame* dove away from the maimed Destroyer, unwilling to wait for the Krogg's cousin to arrive on the scene.

Claw keyed his comm, "We got lucky, folks. They didn't see us. We're on the run now — stand down from quarters but keep everything cleared for action just in case."

"Rings of the planet in nine minutes, sir," the Sensor Chief reported.

The comm chirped again, "Skipper, Bakon. I think I have some good news."

Cocking an eyebrow, Claw came to his feet, "Don't hold me in suspense."

"We're right where we should be. I can see *Bishop's* planet out there, and I think I've got human bio signs on it too. The array is pretty rattled, but I'm also getting Earther-type metabolisms…"

A small formed on Claw's face, "And we've just drawn off their hunters."

CHAPTER 37

"Signal coming in from *Archangel Sword*, ma'am. They say they'd like to decelerate from flux while one of their Destroyers realigns its drives," ArcColonel... or was it now *Captain* Evan-Thomas... spoke up delicately.

Sarah blinked. She was on *Joseph Barron's* bridge, in a state that appeared to verge on catatonic. They were still a couple of days from *Bishop's* last-known system — a couple of days from Pat, she hoped — and she was too busy contemplating her own state of mind for cruising maintenance to really register as important...

"Which ship?" she asked quietly.

"*Vance*. They're afraid their flux field might go otherwise."

Sarah nodded, "Squadron to decelerate then. Right out here between systems — I don't want a Krogg picket to happen upon us. All ships to stand by alert in case."

Atlas, Vulcan, Engadine and *Monarch* hurtled through space at over 2,800 pls — a veritable sprint for ships of such massive size. The 74s were at their cruising limit, digging deep into the capabilities of their redundant reactors in order to hold their fields tight as they ripped across the void.

"Skipper! The Freetowners have decelerated ahead!"

Captain Thena Venus looked up from her status reports on *Vulcan's* bridge, "All of them?"

The Sensor Officer nodded quickly, "Looks like one of them is having a bit of engine trouble. Inevitable at these speeds, I suppose, especially for a human ship."

"All hands stand by for deceleration," Thena said to her Cruising Master.

The 74-gun sister to *Atlas*, heading the column of the four large vessels, let the speed begin to bleed out of its drives.

"All ships report safe deceleration from flux, skipper," *Sword's* Third Lieutenant reported to James in a sedate tone.

"Very good," the renegade Captain leaned back gingerly in his chair. "How long does *Vance* expect to be?"

There was a pause, "Only half an hour, sir. They'll just realign their field generat–"

"Skipper, four ships coming out of energy drive directly astern. Three 74s and a *massive* First Rate by the looks of it!"

James cocked an eyebrow as he abruptly leaned forward — so Caine had sent more help... but how had he managed to provide a First Rate? Could it be one of the Admirals?

"Squadron, stand down from alert," James' orders were smooth as he pondered the possibilities.

It was good to have a bit more help at hand — and powerful help at that. No Krogg Dreadnought squadron would be a match for this force now, with its mix of capital ships and cruisers...

"They're approaching at 55 pls, skipper. I can't see their pennants yet."

That drew a frown from James — he'd like to know who he was dealing with...

"Signal from one of the 74s to *Barron*... doubling it to us as well, sir," the Signal Officer keyed his console as he spoke.

"Check the signal tags — which ship is it?" James was already turning to face the monitor as *Sword's* Signal Officer examined the Earther message's headers. Before an answer could come, Fox Magnus appeared.

James had just enough time to recognize the face before the red-haired Earther grinned at him, "Leave *us* behind, will you?"

James wasn't sure exactly what he was looking at as his cutter slid silently towards the hull of *Atlas*, Sarah's pinnace already entering the Third Rate's landing bay ahead of him.

Atlas and *Vulcan* were obviously familiar ships to James, but the two vessels lying beyond the 74s were different than anything he'd seen. The transponders had marked them with the strange designation of 'CVA' — a reference James had never seen before. Earther ship transponder codes were always categorized by rate and number of guns — *Atlas* was '3-74', for instance.

But 'CVA'? James studied the Earther ships as the pinnaces approached. He couldn't see many gunports on their hulls, even on the massive First Rate.

Very strange.

Well whatever they were, Caine had seen fit to detach them to join Magnus on this mission... which meant they were probably either unimportant and served as good decoys, or they had some sort of unique capability better suited to independent operations than system defense.

And with hundreds of Krogg ships barreling down on Gibraltar, the latter possibility seemed highly unlikely just now.

Sitting in silence, James waited to land.

With Draco Maximane out of action and himself in charge, Fox had decided to hold the meeting with the Freetowners aboard *Atlas*. Bringing everyone to

Engadine would probably just have confused affairs, especially since James and Audrey likely had no idea what a Carrier even was.

Fox also wanted home-turf advantage when dealing with a significantly distraught fleet commander. He wasn't one of Sarah Manchester's close friends — that was Ursla and Caine territory — and he wasn't eager to meet the ArcGeneral's determination head-on in a place where he lacked circumstantial control.

"You're nervous."

Fox looked up from the blank tabletop and smiled at Thena Venus, "I was skippering a sloop a year ago, Thena. I'm not used to facing off with renegade fleet commanders just yet."

The slender red fox smiled coyly at her counterpart, "A year ago I was only a First Lieutenant in an 80. We're all doing well enough — I'm sure you'll figure it out."

Fox smiled in reply, but before he could press the conversation the door opposite his seat in the briefing room opened. Standing in the doorway was a slim, gaunt-faced human figure, flanked by two blue-clad human privateers.

Fox and Thena came to their feet.

"ArcGen… *ma'am*, please come in. James, Audrey…" Fox nodded to his two friends, and they nodded in return.

Sarah silently entered the room, finding the chair nearest the door and settling herself in it without ceremony. James and Audrey moved to one side of her, taking their seats equally quietly, their pleasure at seeing Fox tempered by the overbearing gloom emanating from the elder Manchester.

"Why are you here, Captain?"

Sarah's words surprised all present with their abruptness, and Fox quickly reseated himself before replying, "The First Lord sent us to catch up to you, ma'am. We had *Flame* with us until we ran across the Krogg Fleet a few days ago. Chronos went back to report in, but we're not under orders to return with the news."

It was said as quickly and as clearly as possible, and both Audrey and James had to stop themselves from releasing relieved sighs. Having Fox around to help watch Sarah definitely seemed to improve their prospects…

Wait just a moment, Fox had *found* the *Krogg Fleet*…?

Audrey was ahead of James on the question, "Where did you find the Krogg Fleet?"

Fox cast a cocked eyebrow towards Thena, "We were trying to catch up to you but you were moving too fast. They passed over us by a substantial margin. You didn't see them?"

With that James and Audrey exchanged nervous glances — so the Krogg Fleet had been within virtual spitting distance of them and only the luck of relative altitude in space had saved them.

Sarah just stared impassively at Fox, "The entire fleet?"

Fox shrouded his surprise at Sarah's stony face behind his own nod, "We picked up all but a few Dreadnoughts and a dozen Destroyers. The rest are probably at the base Pat discovered out here, getting ready to launch another raid."

"Like the one that hit Jardaw in *Highlander?*" Audrey chimed in soft reply.

Thena nodded, "And also the raid on Earth, Captain. That's why the Carriers are with us."

Sarah froze suddenly — a very slight distinction from her stony expression noted only by the Earthers. Caine... had sent *Carriers...?*

Audrey and James exchanged frowns, and after a second's confusion the latter looked to Fox, "I'm guessing you know that we don't have a clue about what you just said."

Fox let a small smile form on his face and he tipped his head jovially to Thena, who offered a smile in quick reply. Tapping the briefing room's tabletop console, she activated the holo generator and keyed it to display builders' plans for *Engadine* and *Monarch*.

"Each of them carries a good number of gunboats, though their signatures make them look like battleships on most panels we've found. Commodore Maximane was shaking them and their fellows down at Earth when the Kroggs hit. The Carriers made short work of the attack, but a Krogg Dreadnought got clear. He decided to pursue — he wanted to keep his new ships a secret. Two weeks later, we came across these two."

The privateers squinted at the schematics, noting the 180 boats that the two warships could deploy... a combat flight group that had more gun power than any *two* ships in this strange little renegade squadron. The Earthers sure knew how to build behemoths.

"Commodore Maximane is still aboard *Engadine*, but he was wounded in action and so he's turned his ships over to me," Fox concluded.

Sarah listened and nodded as she examined the two Carriers. So these were what the Earthers had been working on to counter the Motherships. She'd seen the preliminary plans, of course, but she'd never seen one of the behemoths up close...

They were more than a match for *Joseph Barron*, if they launched their boats. And backed by *Atlas* and *Vulcan* — two crack Third Rates with veteran crews — Sarah suddenly realized there was little hope of her privateers moving on.

She wasn't sure what her reaction to that was. But it wasn't happy.

"So you're here to take us back?" Sarah looked past *Engadine* to Fox, and the Captain locked eyes with her.

Fox frowned, "I'm sorry, perhaps I didn't make that clear enough to begin with... I'm authorized to support you. ArcGeneral Manchester — that is to say, *Graham* Manchester — wanted us to get under weigh for that purpose. Caine and Ursla's orders to me were a bit different; I'm to make sure you come back in one piece. Whatever you do out here is your business, I'm attached to *you*. Call us a Naval escort for a privateer squadron."

Sarah's expression seemed not to change, but James and Audrey smiled simultaneously.

"You'll assist us, Captain?" Sarah's tone was cool, but Fox could sense pain beneath it.

Fox nodded, "I've ordered *Flame* to scout ahead with energy-hyper. By the time we arrive in the system *Bishop* was lost in, we'll have good intelligence as to what we're facing, if anything..."

Sarah's eyes shifted from Fox to *Engadine* in the plot to the table top below. Even after his plea, Caine had honored her decision, and also sent her help. She had essentially betrayed him and yet he was still supporting her... how could she ever make up for this?

She didn't know.

But she still had something to do: she still had to find Pat. That was why she was out here. And after that she could try to rebuild the bridges she'd burned... or now it seemed, *hadn't* burned, on her quest.

She looked up to Fox again, "Thank you... Fox. Thank you."

Somewhat surprised by the earnest edge in Sarah's voice, Fox nodded, "It's our privilege, ma'am. And after we rescue *Bishop's* survivors, I think it might be prudent if we make a run at the Krogg base. Between both our forces, we can probably make short work of the defenses, and then whatever Krogg formation survives the fight at Gibraltar won't be able to replenish from this base and launch a second attack."

The typically-Earther idealistic confidence in Fox's statement — presuming both that there were survivors from *Bishop* and that Gibraltar would be a certain victory — was a refreshing change of perspective for the privateers in the room.

James and Audrey exchanged quick glances and nodded, then all eyes settled on Sarah. Her face remained gaunt and tired, but perhaps her eyes were a little brighter. She nodded.

CHAPTER 38

"By the looks of it, they've brought in three more Destroyers to search for us, skipper."

Claw nodded slowly and frowned at the sensor plot in the middle of the cramped auxiliary watch center. The sensors, jury-rigged though they were, offered a stable image of the entire system despite the interference from the planet they were hiding behind.

Four Destroyers, then, all scouring the system looking for *Flame* — and leaving the survivors alone. Two more days until Fox and his squadron were expected, and the Kroggs weren't even thinking about that planet anymore.

Despite his sloop's battered state, Claw couldn't help but smile to himself. It had been worth it after all. They may just have given *Bishop's* survivors a better fighting chance...

"Well," the Master said quietly, "I doubt if they'll be able to find us."

Sandpelt cocked his eyebrow at the remark, "You think this isn't a rather obvious place to hide, Master?"

The grizzled spacer smiled, "I imagine they'll look here first, but we've got a rather nice set of rings to maneuver through. They won't be able to keep up."

Claw ground his jaw, "Yes, I suppose so. Lang, what about the defensive systems?"

"Carronades up to full, shields are... *solid*. I can give you guns, but that'd be at limited intensity. And they might blow the reactors."

A soft growl escaped Claw, "It's that good?"

Sandpelt replied with a solemn nod.

Thoughts began to spiral through Claw's mind. They'd have to avoid action for two days... but still keep the Kroggs looking. The planet had to be *Flame's* first concern right now — the limited sensors showed human life amongst the mass of biomatter on surface, which meant that at least *some* of *Bishop's* crew had survived.

"Alright. Standard guerrilla tactics. Let's make life interesting for them. I want to give the survivors on that planet an even chance."

Pat sat in silence, looking out over the darkening forest. From his sitting position on a rock high up next to the cave entrance, he could examine just about everything there was to see in this area.

The river especially.

He knew it'd be impossible for him to detect the Earther boat coming up through all the dense vegetation, but for the past two days he'd been trying anyway. Lupus wasn't due back for at least another forty-eight hours, but Pat was hoping they'd somehow show up early.

Scratching his chin, Pat peered down the slope at the gun sitting heavily in its pit. Blinking lights made it stand out against the blue vegetation — an obvious target to anyone on the ground. An Earther camo-net and dampening field had been cast over it to shield it from the air, though its power signature was probably still somewhat readable from orbit.

To properly get a firing solution on it, though, the orbiting Krogg Destroyers would have to come in close and make visual confirmation... a range from which even this diminutive gun could do them great harm. Cuttar had already trained a number of *Bishop's* survivors to serve as a gun crew, and now they were drilling daily to make sure they could hit just about anything that came into range.

Besides that, the Earther shield grid that protected the *Bishop* camp would be at full strength. Though it was designed for anti-ground use, Cuttar had tapped it into the reactor on the dropship and thus had increased its strength substantially. It wouldn't last *long* against a couple of Destroyers, but it would allow the humans to get a few shots off in reply.

And that would hopefully be enough...

Pat heaved a sigh and came off the rock, rubbing his neck. One scuffle with a couple of Destroyers they could handle. But what about after that? The Kroggs would doubtless send more if the survivors killed the first force. And if they somehow lost their gun in the fight, there'd be nothing to do but run from the next attack — what else could they do against a dozen Destroyers or a Dreadnought?

And then there was an entirely different question to consider. So far planning had been easy — get things set so that survival was possible in the current climate. But what would they do if the Kroggs left or were defeated?

They could try running into space in the Earther dropship... but that was only sub-light and incapable of handling the large number of survivors Lupus would be bringing back. Waiting was the most practical option, hoping that an Allied ship happened across them one day.

Then again, what if the Allies had been smashed in an action at Gibraltar? There was no way to be sure whether anyone had gotten the telemetry he'd sent...

Pat drove his foot angrily into the large rock he'd been sitting on — and immediately regretted it.

"*Dammit!* Bloody damned hell's kitchen *rock!*"

Screwing up his reddening face, Pat hopped on one foot and morosely clutched his paining toes. That was the Gods telling him to stop worrying about what he couldn't control. Had to be.

"You alright, sir?" Cuttar came out of the cave with a light frown of concern.

Pat waved him off, "I hit my bloody toes Ernile, don't worry."

The Earther smiled politely and nodded, turning back towards the dropship and disappearing into the darkness.

Pat hobbled delicately down the slope a moment later, pacing towards the river. The only other thing left to think about was Sarah.

And that hurt much more than his toes.

Pat grimaced inwardly as he wondered where she was and what she was going through. Did she even know he was missing? He could still be on patrol with the Pirates, after all. The Kroggs could be nowhere in sight, and the 444th could just be doing a thorough survey.

Hell, if nobody had gotten the word, she could already be dead.

Floating in space, bloated and frozen, the wreckage of *Joseph Barron* spiraling around her in a tangled mess of destruction... he would never see her ag–

His foot caught something and he tumbled — "Oh damnati–"

Headfirst he somersaulted down the slope into the clear, cold water.

Further up on the slope, a dozen people heard Pat's cry, and grabbing the rifles they kept close at all times, they immediately charged down the slope after him.

Face down in the icy water, Pat flailed angrily until his feet could find the rocky bottom of the stream. The current had taken him down to within a few meters of the shield perimeter, and had left him in the middle of one of the broader points of the waterway.

Dammit!

Now he was all wet and cold, and that was in addition to being in a sorry state of mind. Pat swore at himself as he pushed back his hair and turned to wade from the water. But some instinct stopped him.

Out of the corner of his eye, the big Irishman noticed a lurking black and bladed figure slowly approach the edge of the stream. He immediately knew what it was.

And then there were four of them.

Seeing the vulnerable ArcBrigadier, the four Kroggs hissed and brought up their blades, edging towards him. Panic dissolved into calculation and Pat reached for his sidearm... but it must have come loose in the fall. It was gone...

His foot bumped it on the river bottom.

He froze for an instant, watching the unsettling eyes of the aliens. The exchange of glares lasted only seconds, and then Pat leaned forward and snatched his gun from the water.

The Kroggs charged as his head went down.

Coming up desperately to meet the attackers, Pat watched the first soldier lunge to within five meters of him. His pistol swung rapidly out of the water and he squeezed off a short burst of energy, but it went wide.

Stumbling backwards in an effort to avoid the Krogg, Pat fired twice more, one shot glancing off the thick Krogg carapace.

Cuttar's shot, however, punched straight through the alien's eye.

In typical fashion, the elite wolf had arrived just in time, and now he slid to a halt at the edge of the stream, rifle hefted in one arm and firing fast while he reached for and keyed active the perimeter shield that straddled the water. The powerful barrier hummed to life just in time to knock the next charging Krogg back into the woods. Pat forced himself to breathe as he brought his pistol up again and poured fire into the surprised soldiers, the one-way energy field humming as the bursts passed through it.

Shields began rising all along the perimeter as Keats led the *Bishops* in a mad dash along the long semi-circular line. As he neared Pat, Cuttar dropped one Krogg before the remaining two began to back away, and then fire from the rest of the humans caught those two from the flank. Now almost at the stream, the crew of *Bishop* got to vent some of their anger at their ship's loss and at the death of their mates — all at the two stricken soldiers. Energy fire sliced one of them apart after a moment.

The last Krogg crawled from the stream far from the shield, making the cover of the brush before fire could smash him as well. The crew stopped along the edge of the stream and watched Pat wade from its chilled waters.

"Good shooting, folks. I think that means they know we're here," Pat said jovially, masking his mild terror-of-near-death with a customary grin.

The humans nodded and began to smile back when a strange sound filled the woods... and then the shield shimmered.

Spines were slamming into it... from somewhere in the brush.

Pat whirled back to face the darkening jungle, and in just seconds he was able to spot the source. A Krogg... *thing*... some kind of gun-growth that fired spines.

"Take that thing out!" Pat roared, swinging his pistol up again.

The crew leveled their guns, but just as they began firing a second spine-gun opened up from a separate point... and a third... and a *fourth*. Krogg soldiers suddenly began stepping out of the brush beyond the shield. At least a hundred seemed to materialize, and the humans were frozen at the overwhelming number...

Pat stopped firing too, beginning to realize just how lucky he'd been to trip when he did.

Cuttar moved along the perimeter smoothly during this shocked second, his heavy rifle humming angrily and sending bolts of energy through the shield, scattering a number of Kroggs back into vegetation. The humans, shaken back into action, opened fire as well.

The first spine gun retreated out of sight as energy bursts glanced off it, followed by the other three. They continued spitting their deadly bone-bullet spines at the shield from the cover of the underbrush, but no one could see to fire back. The Krogg ranks evaporated into the blue jungle as well, leaving nothing in their wake but the implied threat.

Getting himself onto dry ground, Pat approached Cuttar, "This means a bit of a siege, I think. Never been so glad to fall on my head in my life. Gods wept, if we hadn't gotten that shield up..."

The wolf cocked an eyebrow, "Looked to me like they were lying in wait. Maybe they're after the boat, but they were willing to tip their hand for a chance to get you..."

"What an absolutely lovely thought... but no big guns yet, it seems," Pat grunted, sliding his pistol into its wet holster.

Cuttar nodded, then looked at the ArcBrigadier, "And they may not have any on the ground. But these soldiers can spot for the Destroyers if they come in for a strike."

Pat nodded slowly. The gun could be plainly seen from anywhere along the perimeter... and there was no way to hide it now. It was dug into a pit — they couldn't reposition it, and even if they could, the Kroggs on the ground would still see it. No, all that was left to do was crew it and still hope the Destroyers had to come close.

"Sir, what about the boat?" Keats spoke up quietly, approaching the pair from the group of armed crew.

Cuttar and Pat exchanged glances, and the wolf shrugged, "Beckett has shields, sir... but whatever he's cobbled up for the humans to ride may not."

Pat offered another thoughtful nod, "You're right then, Ernile. They're definitely after the boats... they're probably hoping to smash us all at once."

"What do we do, sir?" Keats' tone was grim.

"We wait. And keep guns all along the perimeter. I doubt the shields will get knocked out by those spine things — I've seen them hold against mass driver fire. We need to be ready to cause a major diversion, though. When we spot Beckett and the crew, we loose hell on our friends out there."

Keats and Cuttar were silent, peering out into the blue forest.

"Until then, we hope they can't find a way in."

CHAPTER 39

Orion's main briefing room was uncommonly busy. Thirteen flag officers now shuffled about the chamber, going over various details of their preparations, recalling past troubles, and generally trying to keep spirits up. Among them were Caine, Ursla, Felix, and Graham, and of those four, only Felix seemed his normal, confident self.

The Kroggs would be at Gibraltar in less than a day, so it seemed prudent to get the final strategy session moving. The last thing they needed was to have the Kroggs arrive while the major fleet commanders were in a meeting.

Caine took his seat at the head of the briefing table first, waiting silently for the officers to finish their business. He wouldn't call them to order — they would sit as soon as they were ready, and Caine trusted their judgment.

And he'd need the very best of their judgment, given the circumstances.

Gibraltar now boasted 303 warships, 196 of them capital ships and most of the rest frigates and cruisers. Only a handful of Destroyers had arrived, and most of the sloops were out on reconnaissance to watch for the Krogg arrival. In addition to these ships, the *Gibraltars* and the two shipyards had been brought online, the former providing guns, both producing a large numbers of gunboats. A total of almost 500 boats had been completed, and of those over 300 had modestly experienced crews. The rest of the personnel in the boats... well, Earthers were good at improvisation.

The Carriers still weren't in Gibraltar space, though — last report from a sloop picketing towards Genesis put Garvin Jardaw's Provisional Carrier Group some ten hours away. He might arrive in time, but the plans here had to assume the boats were going to launch only from the stations. If Jardaw did arrive, he'd be bringing a few hundred battle-tempered boats, and while they wouldn't win the battle on their own, they could certainly prove a great help...

Silence slowly settled over the room, and as Caine expected, the Earther and human officers began taking their seats. Aside from his core of three fleet commanders, Caine recognized many distinguished officers among them: the formidable Kella Felar, technically commander of the First Fleet; the venerable Varnon Broadpaw, wittiest of the fighting Admirals; Jax Furgus, the Admiral who'd had so many 64s shot out from under him Caine had lost count; Dran Nightclaw, of Ursla's old 111th, and the most elite frigate officer anywhere; and Caitlin Hargreaves, one of Sarah's chief officers from the Battle of Genesis.

Aside from those veterans of the Pluto Orbital Plane and Genesis, there were the humans Roger Sutton, Hoshi Chen, and Lynn Moureau, fine officers who had distinguished themselves in small actions between Genesis and this moment.

It was a team of strong officers, all things being equal, and Caine was relying on their skill — the plan he was about to lay out would be demanding, even for people of their talents.

"We all settled then?" he asked briefly, and everyone nodded.

Caine took a breath and keyed the table's holo. The light blue system chart shimmered into life, the planetoid, asteroid belt, and stations appearing first, followed by the icons of the squadrons in system.

"We're outgunned, as you all well know, so this isn't going to be nearly as clean a fight as Genesis," Caine kept any doubt out of his tone, and there were nods from the veterans of that battle. Furgus' ship had been shot out from under him in that action, and Varnon had sacrificed a leg. It had been a truly bloody fight.

Caine pressed on, "That said, I do believe we have a chance. Not a great one, but a chance." He chewed out that last comment. "We know the vector they're going to come in on, and we've got parity in capital ships. *They* have a clear edge on us in Destroyers and corvettes. Graham's been working hard to get boats ready for action, but not counting the Carriers that might arrive, it seems we'll have only 500 in any shape for fighting."

Graham nodded briefly to confirm the statement.

"As such, I'm electing to keep them out of the fight until the corvettes are well away from any support. We'll separate ourselves into three groups, one consisting of frigates, cruisers, and human capital ships, one a force of ships of the line, and the last consisting of the Destroyers and the *Gibraltars*. The stations will obviously stay in orbit of Gibraltar, but Graham, I'll want you to maneuver them into a line as best you can. Their station-keeping thrusters should be able to handle the move, and that'll bring their guns to bear."

"And their flight decks," Graham nodded, quickly tapping a note onto his personal pad.

"Now, I'll put the human capital ships under you, Caitie..." Caine nodded to ArcLieutenant-General Hargreaves, and as he tapped a key a marker some distance from Gibraltar appeared in the tank, "... and I'll station you here, where you'll wait with the frigates and cruisers. Dran, I'd have liked to turn the frigates over to you, but I'm afraid I needed someone a bit more senior for that many ships. Andra, you'll have to transfer your flag from *Agamemnon* to *Cerberus*. The rest of the ships of the line will be left to me, but I'll be dividing them into five main divisions to allow some flexibility. That puts Varnon, Kella, Jax, Savanna, and myself *here*."

Everyone sitting around the table expected the next icon to appear near the first — it would be common fleet practice to support the human capital ships, numbering only fifty-eight, with the Earther ships of the line. But the icon appeared far to the relative south of the human-frigate group.

"We'll open our fields and sit there, undetectable. The Kroggs shouldn't expect more than fifty capital ships in system anyway — we're so spread out and we have no warning, at least as far as they know. When the Kroggs arrive in system they'll detect Caitie and Andra's force, and the *Gibraltars*. They'll doubtless move to engage the mobile forces first, and that'll mean swamping them with about ten *thousand* corvettes. They'll be our biggest problem, I expect. I'm willing to bet they'll send them in from long range — they'll probably launch as soon as they come out of hyper. Even if they don't, though, they'll launch beyond gun range. They can't chance us smashing their Motherships before the corvettes get out... though with that many Dreadnoughts protecting them, I don't think we could manage it anyway."

There were nods around the table — Caine's predictions made sense given the Allies' experiences of the past months.

"When the corvettes launch, Andra and Graham will move their ships out to meet them. Not the boats, mind you, just the light *ships*. The Kroggs will probably send their Destroyers ahead to counter this move — they'll try to protect their corvettes as best they can before capital ships are engaged. Andra, your job will be to keep those Destroyers tied up... you'll be outnumbered four to one, so it'll be tricky, but you need to keep them as committed as you can."

Ursla nodded slowly, frowning at the plot as she strummed her large fingers on the arm of her chair.

"When the Destroyers clear out, I'll order the attack. The battleships will advance with stretched fields and then drop out of energy drive *inside* the Krogg Fleet. We can't let them see us coming until it's too late for them to disengage, and then we'll have to pound them. Caitie, you'll join as soon as you can, but if it looks like Andra needs you more, use your discretion. Once we break up the Dreadnoughts, we'll move back against the Destroyers and eliminate them — and hopefully the corvettes — in one push."

There was silence as the icons slid around in the battle plot, highlighting the intricacies of Caine's plan.

"Divide and conquer?" Broadpaw finally spoke up, and Caine nodded.

"The timing will be critical — I'll be running the battleship show, but the frigate movement will be up to you, Andra."

Graham cleared his throat, "And my boats?"

Caine blinked, as did most of the other officers — they'd all managed to forget to mention the non-conventional forces on hand. The gunboat was still such a new weapon...

Quickly keying his panel, Caine offered an apologetic nod to the younger Manchester, "I want you to hit the corvettes as soon as you think it's best — we need you to get a drop on them. The light ships will be trying to tie them up, so if you can come across the flank at the right moment, it could be decisive. Just remember that there'll be as many as ten thousand."

The comment forced most of the assembled officers' heads up. Setter Caine's plan had, a moment ago, sounded like a sure thing. It was complicated, seriously complicated, yet it had seemed practical enough.

But that was a *lot* of corvettes. And understandably, it sounded like too many.

"With attacks coming on all sides, we can try to split them up in the confusion and destroy them piecemeal," Caine added quietly. "And as I say, they'll be our biggest problem. If the Carrier group arrives the odds will be better, but we can't afford to bank on that. If we can maneuver correctly, we might be able to draw the corvettes onto the guns of the *Gibraltars*. Otherwise, we fight it out."

Caine's words drew further nods.

"And here's one thing to consider," Felix leaned forward and spoke for the first time during the meeting. "If we get beaten by corvettes today, then it's still a partial victory. So long as we kill their FTL ships we've secured the front. Even if their corvettes finish all of us off after that, they can't leave the system. We'll have them contained."

Glances shifted to the white cat, and Caine and Ursla both nodded slowly. That was indeed why Caine was willing to let the Motherships launch their craft — his first priority had to be the Dreadnoughts threatening the front, even if the corvettes proved a more immediate danger to Gibraltar.

Jax Furgus cocked an eyebrow and smiled, "And Graham just told me you were the *optimistic* one!"

Felix shrugged, "I call it optimism... we win even if we lose."

Caine let that comment sit for a few seconds, then blinked himself back into context, "True enough, Savanna. Anyway, we should all probably get back to our ships. See your commanding officers about the dispositions of your units — I'll have the ships of the line, Andra will have the cruiser assignments, and Caitie will have the Genesis capital ship groups."

Nods circled the table, the latter two commanders already beginning to consider their division assignments. Caine knew how his ships of the line were to be divided — he'd been thinking about it for a day...

But as he made to stand, everyone remained seated. What were they... ah. The meeting waited for a closing statement — Caine usually had something wise and inspiring to say before marching off to battle. But what?

"You know as well as I do that this could turn into a debacle. And it would be *my* debacle. My mistake for spreading us too thin; my fault. I'm sorry about that. But right now I need all of you, and all your crews to fight hard... and I know you will. I hope this is the Kroggs' last big push... but even if it isn't we'll have to keep fighting. And time will tell..."

Well that was less inspiring than had been expected.

So, being himself, Varnon Broadpaw leaned forward, "What our esteemed leader means to say is 'let's go beat them'. Caine, you must stop binge-drinking. Really now..."

There were nervous chuckles at the joke, and as Varnon's eyes settled on Caine's, the First Lord let out a long sigh. He couldn't afford to focus on his mistake right now. Varnon was right about that...

"Yes... well," Caine consciously fought to brighten his tone, "I guess we won't be drinking Scots together after we win, eh Varnon?"

There were further, lighter chuckles at the comment, and then Caitie Hargreaves leaned forward, "It's scotch, actually."

Caine shrugged, and with that last half-hearted attempt to brighten the atmosphere, the room began to clear.

CHAPTER 40

"I think they've got our number, skipper."

Claw looked up at the Sensor Chief's words, "How so?"

The rating waved his hand at the sensor plot, "One Destroyer is now returning to the *Bishop* planet, the other three are moving in a close trident straight for the rings."

A grunt was Claw's reply as he came out of his chair to see the situation for himself. In the past thirty-six hours of evasion and attraction, *Flame* had weaved in and out of the rings several times — each time attacking an isolated Destroyer in order to draw the rest back from the planet. The Kroggs had elected to concentrate their forces each time, leaving the planet completely alone.

Now they had clued in, and one Destroyer was about to menace the planet while the rest waited for *Flame* to try to intervene.

It was a perfect trap — one Chronos Claw couldn't *not* spring if he wanted to ensure the safety of the stranded survivors...

Though he had to remember there had been *two* Destroyers hovering over the *Bishop* crash site for days before he'd arrived... there was no reason to think this one would be anymore dangerous... especially for a period of only hours.

Fox and the squadron should be in system soon... assuming they hadn't been held up by something. It was always possible that they'd been delayed, and there was no way *Flame* could find out if they had been.

Wonderful.

"Have they spotted us?" Claw asked quietly after a moment.

The Master and Lang Sandpelt came to join Claw and the Chief at the sensor plot as the latter Earther shrugged, "I couldn't tell you, skipper. The jury rig can't get those sorts of specifics."

Claw nodded in silence, half surprised he hadn't asked about that before. *Flame* had been too proactive, never defensive. What he really wanted to do was go into energy drive and stalk the Destroyer heading for the planet... but that was impossible.

"Alright, we'll have to try and cut through that trident and get to the planet. Beat to quarters; Master, clear us for action. Alert the marines to prep their dropship, and have the landing bay get the pinnaces ready for orbital work. If we can get a good window, we should be able to drop them off to support the humans."

The assembled Earthers nodded at Claw's words, and Sandpelt replied first, "I'll head down to the engines then, Chronos. You'll have every scrap of power we've got."

Claw smiled thankfully at his long-time junior, "I always knew I would, Lang. Master, to quarters now, if you please."

"ETA is about half an hour, ArcGeneral."

Sarah twitched at the report. They'd been traveling hard for the past few days with the knowledge that *Flame* was in the system where *Bishop* was thought to have been lost. She would soon face the culminating moment — the one that justified or damned her choice to leave Gibraltar. Was *anyone* alive? Was *Pat*? He *had* to be. No story could have such a tragic end — surely life couldn't throw her such a bad hand.

And if it did... well, then she'd do her damnedest to get revenge... on the universe.

That thought cleared her head for a second, so she blinked herself back into reality and began tapping her fingers on the arm of her chair.

Flame broke from its shield of debris just as the Kroggs entered regular gun range. Having dealt with a number of such breakouts by the sloop in the past days, the Kroggs moved to intercept with the assurance of experience, bunching together and shifting their trajectory as a single unit to get in front of it.

Claw had been hoping they'd do just that, and as they angled around to face him *Flame* turned to meet them head-on, then accelerated quickly. The small ship lunged for the Kroggs and got to them before they quite realized the range had closed.

The carronade crews, now far more experienced than they'd been during the first encounter, sliced up the first ship, then the second. The Kroggs replied with respectable speed, dumping a dozen spines and a pair of neuro-energy blasts into the sloop's shields, batting it roughly off course.

On the bridge, Claw dug his fingers into the arms of his chair, "Roll and dive! Down angle thirty!"

The Master executed quickly and the carronades kept firing, but three Krogg Destroyers at point-blank range heavily outgunned diminutive little *Flame*. As the tight maneuver was executed, the ship bucked violently under the force of the incoming blows, one spine coming dangerously close to breaking the ship's make-shift shields.

"They're still coming on, skipper, right after us and accelerating..." the Sensor Chief reported nervously, and Claw nodded.

He needed *something*.

Keying his intercom key, Claw brought up his link to engineering.

"Sandpelt."

"Lang, I *need* guns — can you give them to me? Any of them?"

Sandpelt paused a second — he'd told his Commander repeatedly the guns were not a viable option. With only two reactors, they could do more harm than good... but the instinctive and obvious stress in Claw's voice forced the engineer to come up with something.

"If I take the secondary systems offline and slave Reactor Three directly to the guns, we can probably handle firing individual broadsides... but don't get ambitious. And we'll have to go to emergency helm control... lights, life support — *everything.*"

Claw ground his jaw for a second and then nodded, "Do it quickly. Helm, transfer command to auxiliary and get down there. Master, get ready on the guns. Sensor Chief, keep an eye on the Kroggs. All gun crews to their guns, immediately!"

"Move! Move! Move!" Sandpelt was keying in the last rewiring commands and getting his engineers away from the humming reactor. If it blew, there could be definite problems on *Flame.*

"Sir, what if it goes?" one of the engineers came to stand next to Sandpelt, and he blinked... they'd have to contain the explosion...

"Get to the armory and grab all the ground shields we have. The portable ones. Hurry up — we've got a minute at best."

The engineer sprinted away, calling on a few others to join her.

"They're right on top of us skipper..." the Sensor Chief looked up from the plot.

"Guns?"

The Master grunted and turned from his operations panels, "All manned, no power yet."

Claw nodded and keyed his intercom, "Lang? We need them."

"Charging now..." the Lieutenant sounded harried. "The reactor is theirs."

"Good work," Claw killed the intercom. "Master, run out the port broadside if you please." Again keying the comm, Claw continued, "Helm, hard to port, ninety degrees!"

Flame turned hard at full sub-light speed, its eight port-side guns revealing themselves. The Kroggs had correctly assumed all those guns had been disabled, but they hadn't counted on Earther ingenuity bringing them back online.

The aliens were heading straight into the path of the shot, and–

"Fire."

At point-blank range, even the light guns carried by an Earther sloop had an apocalyptic quality. As the first broadside raked the bows of three advancing Destroyers, *Flame* rolled fast and its starboard guns revealed themselves, sending a second scathing broadside through the reeling Kroggs.

Swinging back, the carronades added to the chaos, slicing angrily into wounded ships...

And then *Flame* was beyond the trident, cruising at full speed.

Claw sat in shock for a moment, then allowed himself to smile. They'd done–

The shield hummed into life around the roaring generator, and Sandpelt took a breath of relief.

That'll handle anything.

And then the struggling reactor finally overloaded and blew.

Flame lurched and the guns shut down immediately. There wasn't even power to close the ports; emergency generators kept the deck pressurized, and strained now to maintain the atmospheric integrity of the deck. Gun crews raced to the open hatches, accessing the manual cranks and leaning hard on the giant levers. The ports needed to be closed manually before those small power supplies keeping the vacuum at bay were drained of their power.

Claw gently slammed one fist into the palm of his other hand, "Damn."

Flame, running under a lone reactor, crawled toward the survivors' planet, entirely defenseless.

CHAPTER 41

"I think I've got something on the Skywatch, sir!"

Pat was crouching near the gun, watching the perimeter for the next Krogg concentration. Soldiers had been randomly focusing attacks and spine fire against individual sections of the shield grid for the last few hours, no doubt hoping to overload the barrier. That seemed an unlikely outcome, though Pat didn't want to chance it.

But now, a new problem... this was one well-coordinated assault.

Damn.

Cuttar joined the human at the gun controls and nodded, "Definitely a Destroyer. It's entering the atmosphere somewhere to the south... ETA about five minutes. Looks like it's already dropping more landers... probably another seventy Kroggs and equipment."

"Can we knock them out?" Pat glanced from Cuttar to the icons on the gunnery screen.

"I can try a shot," Cuttar was already keying in targeting commands and the Earther computer was lining up one of the descending Krogg troop craft in its active targeting memory.

The motorized gun carriage groaned abruptly, alerting everyone in the area to its activity. Moving at what seemed like a crawl, it settled on a trajectory and the screen flashed green.

"Clear the pit!" Cuttar called. "Fire in the hole!"

The human gun crew leapt from the pit and Cuttar and Pat followed quickly, the wolf drawing his personal pad and interfacing it with the gun computer.

"Firing!" he called as he hit the appropriate button.

Thunder filled the valley, and the gun shivered and spat out a massive ball of energy. Unprepared humans were flung to the ground by the shockwave of eruption as soon as the shot escaped the barrel, and the shields hissed angrily as the big burst passed through them. The shot was out of sight before Pat could look up from his position on the ground. Cuttar was already dropping back into the pit and eying the targeting panel.

"Missed! Damn! They're already too low, but I can take some shots at the Destroyer."

Pat nodded, "Do it."

His ears were ringing as he got to his feet, and he absently dusted himself off. He'd dropped his rifle in the blast, and now he gingerly leaned forward to pick it up.

"ArcBrigadier!"

Pat looked up abruptly at the hail, "Yes?"

The summons was coming from Keats in the cave — it was his shift to wait by the comm in case the boat was coming up the river and was in contact with...

Oh.

Grabbing his rifle hastily, Pat sprinted up the incline to the mouth of the cave, "How far out?"

"ArcColonel Forbes says she's got a fully-shielded barge. They're about three kilometers downstream, and apparently their contraption is too big to get through the narrows there," Keats reported excitedly.

Pat nodded, moving into the dropship and taking the pilot's chair. Keying the comm, he spoke up, "Jessica, that you?"

"ArcBrigadier?" Forbes' voice cackled over the comm, "Did you just fire a gun?"

"We've got a Destroyer trying to give us trouble, and we've got about 100 Kroggs in the woods around us," Pat didn't quite have time to process the relief he felt at hearing his flag ArcColonel's voice again.

Forbes paused, "We were about to try to reach you overland, but in that case we'd better sit tight. We're grounded pretty bad... although we could try to push ourselves off the bank... how wide is the stream up there?"

"Maybe ten meters... and pretty steady at that. Lupus should be able to tell you — and I'm sure he knows how to get the boat off the bank. Can you turn me over to him for a second, Jessica?" Pat leaned back in the pilot's chair and scratched his chin.

There was a pause.

A long one.

Well, it couldn't actually have been *that* long. But it felt long.

"Jessica, everything okay?"

"This is Cadmus Howler, ArcBrigadier. I'm afraid Sar-Major Lupus didn't come back with us."

Pat froze. That was *impossible*. Lupus was the best soldier Pat had ever known — not even the venerable Andros Grieve was quite so elite. What the hell could have killed him...

The gun thundered again, and Pat shook himself — he'd have to worry about that later.

"Can you get the boat upstream, Howler?" Pat asked quickly.

"I think so, sir. We can move fast when we clear the bank, so we should be with you in less than ten minutes."

Pat nodded to himself, "We'll be waiting. Be careful — there are Kroggs everywhere out there, by the looks of it."

"Yes sir."

The link cut and Pat took a heavy breath. Alright… now, the Destroyer…

Getting to his feet, Pat moved quickly out of the dropship and to the mouth of the cave. The gun crew was diving to the ground just as he did, and again Cuttar fired the massive piece. The energy bolt flashed through the air, leaving a smell of singed ozone as it went. It vanished over the horizon.

"How are we doing, Ernile?" Pat called anxiously.

As the crew began clearing the gun for another shot, the Earther turned, "We've registered one hit, ArcBrigadier. Nothing major, they're still closing."

Pat nodded, "Keep it up. Those transports on the ground yet?"

Cuttar nodded in quick reply, "Down a few kilometers to the west, best I can tell."

Double damned.

Another shot sliced the air overhead as Villar and Howler dove over the barge's side. On the other side, Graxton and Fineclaw dropped into the cool stream as well. The four couldn't hope to heave the massive, heavily-laden boat over the bank it was grounded on, but with their rifles they *could* move the bank.

"Now!" Howler growled as he found his place, and then opened up with his rifle on the innocent rocks and dirt of the streambed. The heavy energy quickly vaporized the ground, and he carefully swept his fire under the bottom of the barge to slice away the bar.

The barge shifted, Forbes firing its engines loudly in an attempt to push it over the obstruction. The fire of the four Earthers continued, until the boat lurched abruptly and hurtled upstream. The wolf marines didn't have a chance to get aboard.

"West bank!" Howler called to his quartet. He'd half expected this, and he'd told Forbes to leave the Earthers behind and go straight to the camp if it came to it.

A few kilometers overland wasn't a great challenge to them, even in Krogg-infested territory.

He hoped.

As the Earthers waded to the bank and formed their tiny diamond, another energy shot slashed overhead.

This one had a reply.

"Gods wept!"

Instinct forced Pat to throw himself to the ground as the first handful of Destroyer spines hammered into the shield. As big as tree trunks and moving at appalling speeds, those projectiles could have caused part of the mountain to vanish — had the shield failed.

A cackling neuro pulse slammed into the shield next, sliding along the barrier with a blinding glare that forced the eyes of all humans and Earthers away.

"The shield is holding," Keats called from the dropship, "but it's a hell of a strain on the reactor in here!"

Pat didn't bother to reply, spotting a black speck in the air way out over the horizon. The Destroyer.

Cuttar saw it too, and the cannon thundered again. The energy burst sliced right into the speck, and Pat was almost sure he saw it shiver. Another flurry of spines came in reply.

"How long can we hold against this?" Pat turned to the dropship even as another cackling neuro pulse smashed against the shields.

The reactor was already humming loudly. Pat didn't think Earther powerplants could explode, but this one sounded like it might be the first.

Keats, for his part, shrugged, "If I read this right, we might last five more minutes."

"Forbes to Conroy, we're a minute away!"

The static-masked alert came over the comm, and Pat just barely heard it thanks to his proximity to the dropship and Keats.

Wonderful timing.

Maybe they could all pile into the boat and run away...

Turning again down the slope, Pat yelled to Cuttar. The call was interrupted by the firing of the cannon, but as soon as the gun crew set about clearing the weapon for its next shot, the wolf vaulted from the pit and trotted up the slope to talk.

"The boat is a minute away, how can we get it in here?" Pat had to shout to be heard over the hissing shields.

Cuttar ground his jaw, "We'd have to drop the river shield... and that lets the Kroggs on the ground in... And if we unlink the grid now, a lucky hit from the Destroyer could finish us."

Pat swore quietly, then heaved a sigh, "Alright, we have to let them in — I can't abandon them after all this. Tell me how and I'll do it as soon as you fire your next shot."

Cuttar nodded, "The shield emitter — the silver box. Open the panel on the top and hit the red button. When you want it back up, hit the green one, same way I turned it on. It isn't too tough..."

"Gun clear, Ernile!"

Cuttar nodded quickly to Pat and whirled back to the gun, moving fast to his post. Pat turned to the cave, "Keats, I need you with me!"

· · ·

The barge slowed as it came to the shield, its pulsars slashing through the brush where the Kroggs were concealed.

"Someone needs to drop that shield before we can get through," Pawman yelled to Forbes over the roar.

The ArcColonel nodded in reply — while the shield was down, they'd need cover fire to keep Kroggs from getting into the camp.

"Everyone with guns get to the sides! If you see anything that looks like a Krogg, drop it!" she roared, and the nervous humans in the barge's center awkwardly came to their feet and moved to the sides of the craft.

If one of those spines went wide of the shield and hit them now, it'd be all over for the boat. Camp shields running off a dropship's reactor were reasonably tough... one boat with only energy packs providing the power wouldn't survive.

Pat was more careful on this descent to the river than he'd been two days before. Keats, following close behind, was equally sure in his footing. As the pair arrived at the stream bank, Pat paused a second to gawk at the massive barge that waited in the water, crammed tight with humans... a number of them armed.

"Keats, cover me! I must drop this shield!" Pat roared, and the spacer nodded calmly.

Finding the emitter on the side of the stream, Pat pried open the control panel and located the red and green buttons. The Earthers sure knew how to keep things simple.

Spines angrily smattered the shields down near the gun, and Pat held his breath. This was it...

The gun erupted, and Pat hit the red button.

The light blue energy-shield wall visibly dropped, and the Kroggs in the surrounding area launched themselves from their cover. Humans on the barge opened fire in immediate reply, pulsars and rifles forcing the Kroggs back from the breach. The big boat's engines kicked and the make-shift monstrosity of a watercraft slid into the security of the perimeter.

Pat slammed the green button and looked up. A Krogg was coming at him, but Keats was pouring energy into it... and then the shield was up, not a second too soon.

A half dozen spines slammed into the barrier just as it came online.

The force of that impact on the just-charging part of the barrier was tremendous — the collision produced a shockwave that knocked Pat and Keats back onto the ground. The emitter groaned, but took the punishment.

Struggling to his feet, Pat turned to the crowded barge. Two Earthers were coming off first, then some 200 humans. A huge smile formed on Pat's face as he saw some of his veteran crew.

It felt damned good, especially given the circumstances.

Someone called his name from the crowd of disembarking humans, "Three cheers for the ArcBrig!"

The new arrivals erupted in cheers as they dropped from the boat's side, and Pat grinned and reddened a bit at the reception.

Walking slowly into the midst of the survivors as they came off the barge, he was nearly deafened by cheering spacers and junior officers. Preparing to say something leader-like, he held up his hands to calm the reception.

As he finally quieted them, the shield unit he'd just reactivated exploded.

Cuttar's head snapped up. The river shield had overloaded... it hadn't been fully re-energized when it had absorbed the last hit, and a delayed catastrophic failure had resulted.

The wolf's thumb keyed the next shot from the gun and then he dropped the pad, yelling for one of his gun crew to take over. Pawman and Canit were on their way up from the river to the gun, but now they joined their squad mate on a run back down to the water.

Canit was the fastest of the three, stomping into the water and hopping up on the barge's side. He clutched one of the boat's shield emitters, tore it off and tossed it over the humans to Pawman who knelt with Cuttar at the river bank. The Earthers hurriedly keyed the shield active, and it reached out to the other perimeter shields and began to interface with the source of their power — the dropship generator.

The next volley was doubtless on its way... this shield *had* to get to full strength before it hit...

Cuttar held his breath, listening for the steady hum of a fully-charged field as he watched a volley of spines race from the rapidly-swelling dot in the sky...

At that second, the shield hummed at full strength.

Taking a deep breath, Cuttar flopped back on the ground.

"Been having fun, Ernile?" Pawman grinned, patting his shoulder jovially.

The wolf grinned back and sat up, looking to the humans.

None of them were standing.

CHAPTER 42

Flame slid painfully into high orbit over the planet. None among the original trident of Krogg Destroyers were capable of chasing the sloop, but there was one still here to be dealt with.

Not that Claw was sure he had any way of doing that.

Only quick thinking on Sandpelt's part had saved the last reactor, and the ship itself, and that power plant was currently responsible for the necessities: life support and engines. The gunports had been closed manually by determined crews, the last being shut by about forty Earthers just seconds before its accompanying atmospheric shield died. The carronades sat unpowered, but now that *Flame* was at its destination, perhaps some energy could be funneled into one of those weapons...

Basic sensor functions had been retained as well — only at *very* short range — and Claw frowned as he came to stand next to the sensor panel. The planet was already firing at the Destroyer... one gun by the looks of it.

But that didn't make sense, since Battlecruisers didn't carry Earther guns.

"Must be off their dropship," the Master commented quietly as he came to stand at the panel alongside Claw.

It wasn't common practice for human ships to carry any Earther personnel or gear, but *Bishop* had a recon squad and it seemed the Earthers on the ground were making a fight of it...

And the orbiting Destroyer was pounding them in reply. Claw could only guess that the survivors had some Earther shields too — and a big power plant supporting them. Even so, the Destroyer needed to be taken out before it could smash the fragile defense. A single ground-based gun could only do so much.

The intercom chirped, "Lang here, Chronos. I've cut engine power to orbital only. We can run one carronade at about half strength."

Claw grinned, "Read my mind. Master, move us in close."

"We don't have shields," Sandpelt added cautiously over the comm.

Sighing, Claw turned from the sensor panel, "Alright, all nonessential personnel move to secure areas. Marines, drop and look for the survivors' camp. Land in support. Everyone, prepare for damage."

In *Flame's* launch bay, the atmosphere vented through carefully controlled airlocks, and once emptied, the doors opened. The marine dropship — the same model as the one that had been aboard *Bishop* — slid into space and got a sensor lock on a trio of escape pods with Earther life signs among them. The Destroyer was pounding the mountainside and completely ignoring that near-abandoned camp, so the dropship moved quickly toward the life-sign reading.

"All hands report ready," the Cruising Master delivered the words somberly to his Commander.

Claw nodded, "Very well, mark course for the Krogg, down angle thirty."

Flame seemed to crawl now, its lone carronade swinging to aim at the Destroyer. They were almost in range...

The Destroyer, discovering its new stalker, turned to put the sloop out of its misery. The carronade cut out at it defiantly, adding another tear to its shiny black armor, but like the surface gun, *Flame's* single weapon could do little harm.

"Stand by to fire again. Master, we're going to need every maneuver you can manage for us..." a beep from the plot stopped Claw's words.

Then two thirty-gun broadsides flayed the Krogg vessel, and its wreckage fell limply towards the blue forests below.

Atlas and *Vulcan* had dropped out of energy drive almost on top of the Krogg, their starboard broadsides run out and charged. The alien hadn't even gotten a chance to fire as the two massive salvoes sent its broken hulk crashing into the surface.

On *Atlas'* bridge, Fox Magnus grinned to himself. When he retired, he was going to write a book entitled *Earther Timing: Damn It's Good*. And if people said it was all too predictable, he'd smack them.

Claw blinked at the sensor panel for a second, wondering whether the wounded system had finally given into delusions after the stress it had been under for that past two days.

No, that was *Atlas* sitting over them.

A grav tractor from the 74 latched onto the mauled sloop and drew it up out of planetary orbit, while the Third Rate's computer established a link with *Flame's*. Sharing the larger ship's sensor data, Claw saw the entire Freetown Squadron and two Carriers appear over the planet.

He grinned.

"Lots of Kroggs surrounding the main human camp, skipper," *Atlas'* Sensor Officer reported, and Fox nodded.

"All marines to their dropships. Have Thena drop hers as well. And send a pinnace to *Flame* with engineers and repair supplies — it looks like they've been through hell."

Brief acknowledgements came from around *Atlas'* bridge at the orders, and with a satisfied smile, Fox sat back in his chair.

Flame's marine dropship carried a single squad of eight. Composed entirely of cats much as Lupus' recon squad had been made up of wolves, it served mainly as a scouting force. Sloops seldom required huge parties of marines — major landing operations tended to be the business of capital ships.

The 74s, on the other hand, were each sending 150 marines to the ground. The Kroggs wouldn't be expecting *that* sort of infusion of strength and hopefully they'd be disorganized after the loss of their orbiting command ship…

Sergeant Major Ellanor Trix, commander of *Flame's* marine detail, watched the ground approach beneath the little craft. When closer inspection revealed that only one Earther was present at the open camp of human escape pods, she'd been tempted to change direction and strike the flanks of the Kroggs now moving against the main camp, but with the marines of the two Third Rates making that attack, she could afford to investigate the loner.

Sensors showed a dozen Kroggs in the general vicinity, a handful of them moving out toward the survivor over open plain. Whoever it was, company was coming.

The dropship came down in a depression some distance from the escape pods — interposing itself between the Kroggs and the survivor. Leaving six marines and the guns of the ship to hold back the aliens, Trix and one of her fellows stealthily covered the gap to the camp.

Pulsars and rifles whined as the cat marines sliced the Kroggs apart on their approach. There was little real challenge in the defense — Trix's troops were fresh and backed by a well-armed landing craft.

She completely ignored the skirmish as she came slowly to the side of the first pod. Her escort, Private Ellis, knelt behind her and offered a quick nod. Trix burst from cover and sprinted to the next pod, coming to stop behind it while Ellis swung around the side of the wrecked pod to cover her.

As Trix came to a stop, she swung her own rifle around the edge of the second pod and scanned the clearing for the survivor.

No sign.

Well, if it had been her, Trix would have hidden behind the most distant pod…

Nodding again to Ellis, Trix broke from cover and approached the last pod. Slowing her run on the approach, she bobbed her head in an attempt to see behind it.

Nothing.

"Where is this guy?" she muttered frustratedly to herself.

"I'm in *here!*"

Trix blinked.

"Who's that?" the voice was muffled.

"Sergeant Major Trix, off *Flame*."

"Oh good!" the voice sounded extremely pleased. "Get me out of here then, would you?"

Trix paused.

"*In the pod.*"

"Oh."

Trix slung her rifle and climbed up on the side of the big pod. Finding the panel controlling its hatch, she keyed it, waving for Ellis to join her. The door slid open and she let herself drop to the ground to meet the exiting Earther.

Emerging from the dark shelter, a piece of alloy bound to his right shin as a splint and his left arm blackened and burnt nearly beyond recognition, the Earther grinned.

"You alright?"

"Ever been blown up, Sar-Major?" the wolf joked pleasantly.

Trix's eyebrows went up and she shrugged.

Chuckling, Beckett Lupus hobbled towards the dropship.

CHAPTER 43

"You alright, sir?"

Pat groggily forced his eyes open ... what the *hell*?

Cuttar was leaning over him, "Good, sit up when you can."

The Earther disappeared from Pat's sight and the ArcBrigadier sat up painfully, "What happened?"

Pawman was alongside him quickly, "The shield unit overloaded. We interfaced one from the barge into the grid, and its drawing smoothly from the dropship generator, so we're still protected. The explosion killed at least seven people, and we have a lot of shrapnel wounds."

Pat nodded, rubbing his throbbing head. He'd only been saved by a crowding crew and a few seconds of walking... several times snatched from the jaws of death in one mission. He shivered subconsciously, then got to his feet.

Seven dead... and the rest would be too if the Destroyer wasn't stopped. Looking out into the sky, Pat saw the black dot of the Krogg ship joined by two much larger blobs... no, *six*... dear Gods! And they were coming closer...

"Dropships!" Cuttar called happily. "Whoever took out the Destroyer is landing support for us!"

Pat blinked. The Destroyer was gone?

As the dropships raced in closer to the perimeter, Pat could clearly make out their Earther shape. Help was at hand.

"Get your guns together and get on the perimeter!" Pat ordered, picking up his rifle. The crowd began to disperse, the wounded limping up the slope towards the cave while the rest of the humans gathered their weapons.

"Keats! Help them get the rest of the rifles out of the dropship!"

The spacer didn't answer, and Pat paused from checking his rifle. Keats was face down in the dirt, and he didn't look like he was breathing. Indeed, the large piece of shrapnel sticking out the back of his skull made breathing seem very unlikely.

Damn.

As foolish as the man had once been, he'd remained a reliable spacer.

Double damn.

"Ernile, give them that hand with the pulsars," Pat continued his words faintly, then looked to the humans who were standing, still somewhat shocked by the blast. "If you can't get a weapon, see to these people." Pat waved his hand over the dead.

Silently, he moved along the perimeter toward the gun.

Howler dropped his rifle and quickly swung his sword out of its sheath. The slightly curved blade took a Krogg's arm off, and with a quick redirection, sliced through the soldier's skull.

Behind the Corporal, Villar and Graxton maintained a steady fire from their rifles, driving back the dozen Kroggs trying to cross the stream to engage the surrounded Earther squad. Fineclaw, one arm missing below the elbow, desperately fired a sidearm in support.

As the first headless Krogg fell, Howler pushed forward swinging his short sword at two more who ventured closer.

They'd covered two kilometers on the trip toward the camp when they'd hit the thick Krogg lines. The fighting was so intense Howler didn't even notice the relative quiet overhead. Fineclaw had been blindsided just a moment ago, now the quartet was desperately trying to edge its way to the perimeter.

The odds did not look good, and the Kroggs who were clustering around them and staying just out of reach seemed to realize the much-desired capture of Earther prisoners was at hand.

Leaving the defense of the stream side to Graxton and Fineclaw, Villar maneuvered to support Howler. Relying on blades now, they both forced the massing Kroggs to fall back. Their shields were virtually untouched — each marine was only carrying one without reserve — but Graxton and Fineclaw had nothing left in their own belts.

It was all up to Howler and Villar on this front...

And then two Kroggs tried to grab Fineclaw. The first was halved by the wolf's sword, but as the veteran Private spun to get inside the guard of her second would-be captor, its blade — and not its hand — connected with her unshielded neck. Her head toppled to the forest floor, making her the second fatality in the history of Lupus' recon squad, behind only the Sergeant Major himself.

Howler's eyes drifted to his crumpling comrade and he ground his jaw. He turned fast at the Krogg who'd scored that kill, and as the soldier swept towards him the elite wolf went right under all four alien arm blades.

Howler's sword went into the Krogg at the groin, and with a fast motion it drove its way up to the alien's chest before he dragged it out and kicked the body aside.

Howler then covered Graxton as she took hold of the fallen headless body, and they dragged it behind them as they fought their way forward.

Seventy humans were stretched out along the perimeter, firing angrily into the brush. They didn't seem to be hitting anything substantial, but they were keeping the Kroggs from rushing the shields. The spine guns were focusing on the segment of shield protecting the gun, and the three Earther marines left in the camp were there with their rifles, firing back deliberately while the humans hefted the pulsars out of the barge.

The first of the heavy weapons was being carried across the slope by three *Bishops*, and was destined for the gun pit where Canit would use it.

Things were about to turn dramatically against the Kroggs…

At least thirty Kroggs were pressing in on Howler and his fellows, despite the desperate fight he and Villar were putting up. His shield was dropping below thirty percent… Villar's was just over fifty. Graxton was struggling to keep Fineclaw's body with them, but was batting Kroggs away with her sword in a desperate bid to buy time. Despite their efforts, they were starting to get overwhelmed on the stream bank…

It was going to end rather messily, then.

That revelation allowed a certain amount of calm to take hold of Cadmus Howler; the certainty of death, such as it was, cleared his mind. He didn't have to worry about moving, now, he'd just kill as many Kroggs as he could before the end.

And damn, this new group of rushing Kroggs looked a lot like bears. They were even wearing khakis…

Because they're marines.

A dozen grizzlies appeared around the remains of the squad. Carrying longer blades, they rushed into unsuspecting Kroggs on the wolves' left. To the right, another dozen bears appeared with similar long blades. The center was abruptly cleared by a pulsar blast.

Finishing the Krogg in front of him, Howler steadied himself as a company of bears surrounded his wounded party and then pushed past. And as they went on, more appeared. And more.

The perimeter near the river suddenly erupted in energy fire as a company of bears heavily hit the flank of the besieging Kroggs. The humans inside the shield cheered the Earthers as they set about their grizzly work.

In the confusion, the Kroggs tried to wheel, but they were instantly caught in a crossfire. Hundreds of heavy Earther marines were rolling up their line, and though half a dozen bears fell, there was little serious resistance to the overwhelming onslaught. Cuttar helped set up the second pulsar just as Canit opened fire on the spine guns with the first.

Then the heavy spine shooters turned on the bears and a dozen more were cut down, but Cuttar and Canit had already leveled their pulsars at the Krogg weapons, and the unshielded guns were cut apart before their damage could be crippling.

Pat rallied his crew, "*Bishops* to me!"

Seventy armed humans quickly congregated around their commander, and as one of them dropped the shield to the left of the gun, they set out into the jungle, massing their fire against anything that tried to rush them.

Shaking themselves into a line, the *Bishops* blocked the routed Kroggs as they tried to stream away from the advancing Earthers. The third pulsar, hefted by Pawman, quickly joined the open flank of the line, and the Kroggs were forced back into a pocket that rapidly became a killing field.

Major Colin Brawn of the Second Battalion, 54th Regiment of Marines dropped from *Vulcan*, met Pat twenty minutes later, finding the ArcBrigadier in front of the large, now well-used energy cannon. Snapping a salute, the young, two-and-a-half meter tall bear smiled down at the Irishman.

"Glad to see you alive and well, sir. We're loading up our ships to get back to the squadron now, but we'll leave a company to cover your camp until you're squared away to leave."

Cuttar joined the pair offering a salute to the Major, then turned to Pat, "Howler and the rest of the squad just came in. They lost Fineclaw."

Pat nodded, "We've got at least fifteen dead, many wounded, and one missing, Major. That's not including *Bishop's* losses."

The bear nodded, his face sobering, "You did the hard work for us, sir. We've several dead and about thirty wounded. Your stand here was brilliant."

Pat took a long blink and let his head tip to the side, "The architect is missing. Sergeant Major Lupus."

The Major nodded, "Yes sir, he's in *Flame's* dropship. They picked him up at a camp made of escape pods about half an hour ago. One arm gone and a broken leg, but still joking, Sar-Major Trix says."

Pat paused.

Well *damn*!

A smile crept over his face, and Cuttar straightened, "Excuse me a minute sir..."

The Earther turned and sprinted back to his squad, now clustering around the mouth of the cave.

When he arrived and delivered the news, a cheer — roar, actually — escaped them, and Brawn grinned at Pat.

"If you'd like sir, we can take you up with us. We're all heading for *Atlas* in orbit. You can go on to *Joseph Barron* from there."

The breath caught in Pat's chest. He blinked and mentally slapped himself twice.

"Who did you say was up there, Major?"

The bear cocked an eyebrow, "*Flame*, *Atlas* and *Vulcan*, 74s, *Engadine* and *Monarch*, Carriers, *Pope Joseph Barron* and the Freetown Squadron."

How had Sarah managed that?

Nodding quickly, Pat looked up at the Major, "Get me up there as quick as you can please, Major."

CHAPTER 44

Chronos Claw flopped into a chair and groaned, forcing a laugh from Fox Magnus. The secondary briefing room on *Atlas'* flight deck was cool, airy, and furnished. Claw enjoyed the change — *Flame* had taken rather a beating and the ship was neither cool nor airy. Nor were the furnishings generally where they were supposed to be.

"I told you to look after my ship, and you bring it in on *one reactor*," the red-haired Captain grinned, seating himself opposite the Commander.

Claw shrugged despite his exhaustion, "Energy-hyper has some hidden risks. Be glad we managed to stay together at all."

Fox nodded, "I am. You did some good work out here, Chronos. A kill tally of four Destroyers when you're at half power — very well done."

Straightening gingerly, Claw offered a weak, sad smile, "We did our best. Lost some of my best engineers though."

Fox's smile faded. He'd known every one of *Flame's* casualties personally from his days commanding the sloop. They'd died saving their ship; he knew that, and so did Claw. Neither of them were pleased by the reality.

But there was more to do, so Fox pressed on, "We might be able to rig you up with some fresh reactors from our machine shops, but I doubt they'll be too efficient. You won't be toying with energy-hyper anymore, my friend. But I will want you with the Freetown Destroyers when we hit the forward base."

Claw nodded slowly, "That'll be fine, I think. It'll be nice to have company again."

"Well, I hear ArcGeneral Manchester and James and Audrey are on their way over to receive the survivors, so I best go meet them. I'm going to send pinnaces for your crew — we'll put them up here and on *Vulcan* for the rest of the day and tonight. We can get a good start on repairs tomorrow," Fox came to his feet and nodded to his former First Lieutenant. "You go get some sleep."

"Go?" Claw grumbled and closed his eyes.

Flame's dropship came to a stop in one of *Atlas'* landing slots just as a med team arrived to take Beckett Lupus to sickbay. At the same time, Sarah descended the ramp of her pinnace and came to a stop on the busy flight deck. She'd heard nothing about Pat — she only knew that there were hundreds of survivors and that they'd held out against a large force of Kroggs.

Crossing the deck in silence, Sarah wasn't entirely sure whether her heart was still beating. The med team was unloading a half-charred figure from the dropship and she stepped quickly towards the wounded Earther.

As she came close, Lupus was settling himself into a hoverchair that would carry him gently to *Atlas'* infirmary.

"Sergeant Major Lupus?" Sarah called as he was turning to go.

The wolf, looking terrible, turned back with a smile, "ArcGeneral, thanks for picking us up. We weren't sure how things would go. I hear from Sar-Major Trix that the barge got its people back to the camp, though, so it seems a success... as many survivors as we could find."

Sarah tried to ask a question in reply but her throat wouldn't acknowledge her brain's commands. How could she ask it so easily — if the answer was negative she'd... she'd...

Lupus, despite his disfigured state and the evident pain he was in, immediately recognized what she needed to hear, "He's fine, ArcGeneral. And he's coming in on Major Brawn's dropship, or so they tell me."

Completely frozen, Sarah couldn't even offer thanks to the Earther as he was pushed away. Turning back to the opening at the end of the flight deck, she watched the Freetown pinnaces land with James Stanton and Audrey DeBrooke aboard, and then she saw the first of the Earther dropships come through the atmospheric shield.

She had no idea what to do. So she simply stood completely still.

Audrey descended the ramp of her ship in leaps, trotting across the space between her ship and James' to deliver a hug. James noticed Sarah standing near a dropship on the opposite side of the bay and pointed her out to Audrey.

"Is he alive?" Audrey asked. James shrugged.

"I think I heard someone say he was," Fox quietly appeared behind the privateers, and they wheeled to greet him. "He's supposed to be on the first one landing — Major Brawn's dropship."

"Ahh," Audrey murmured softly, then noticed how everyone on the other side of the flight deck was discreetly getting out of the way.

Even in the midst of a huge recovery operation, *Atlas'* main bay had ample room to allow a private moment or two.

The first dropship in line touched down in its slot, taking the space next to *Flame's*. The forward ramp dropped before the engines shut off, and the hatch swung open.

Sarah still hadn't moved so much as a muscle. Beckett had said Pat was alive. He was on this ship. Surely the Sergeant hadn't been wrong... surely...

An Earther bear stepped out through the hatch, and Sarah could distinctly feel her heart stop beating. If she'd been in a romance novel, Pat would've stepped out of the hatch at this point.

But another Earther limped out, and another after that. Sarah looked away. And then she looked back — surely he was there now. But no, a file of wounded marines was coming down the ramp, going to the medics and seeking attention. Maybe he was on a different ship. Maybe he was coming next...

Then Pat stepped somewhat gingerly through the hatch, nodding to an Earther in the dropship who was hidden from Sarah's view. She took two steps forward before she was able to stop herself, and then she stood still again. Her eyes met Pat's.

He walked down that ramp so slowly, hobbled across the deck... filthy, bloody, sweaty, and breathing... then slowed to a stop.

For all her logic, and her commitment to duty, Sarah suddenly knew exactly why she'd done all this.

So she wrapped her arms around Pat and closed her eyes, and he did the same, and they stood there silently as the marines filed past them.

"That's really nice," Audrey said with a touch of emotion in her voice.

James nodded slowly, glad to see Pat alive and pleased that Sarah had recovered him...

Fox cocked a thoughtful eyebrow, "Sarah's going to have a lot to work herself through, I fear. I hope she doesn't start vilifying herself for this... But we should get to the debrief. They'll find us when they're ready."

The humans turned and left the flight bay, just as Thena Venus arrived on the scene, her craft having landed a little further up the deck. She descended from her pinnace evenly as Fox marched up to her, and then her eyes settled on Sarah and Pat, still silent.

Fox smiled to her and bobbed his head at the pair, "We've done all we can to make this a happy ending, I think."

She grinned and nodded, and the pair of Earther Captains followed the privateers.

Sarah and Pat ended up on *Joseph Barron's* pinnace, the pilot and flight crew having discreetly absented themselves.

Pat collapsed into a chair as he boarded, and Sarah sat quickly on the floor next to his seat, facing him and never once letting go of his hand.

"How did you do it, Sarah? You got my telemetry... the attack and all..."

Sarah swallowed — that was the last thing she wanted to speak of. The thing she understood the least... but it was Pat asking. If anyone could understand...

She felt altogether too young, all of a sudden. And overwhelmed... "We didn't have any proof you'd lived... So Setter didn't want me to go... he begged me... but I couldn't not come. I *knew* you were out here... and I think Graham is going to kill me..."

So she began rushing through the story of the arrival of Pat's drones, and of the energy-hyper recalls of ships and squadrons to Gibraltar, and Caine's and Ursla's objections, and then of her solution.

As much as she wanted to look at Pat, she stared at the floor, "So I signed my own letter of marquee, and convinced James and Audrey to help me."

Pat's mouth opened, but he couldn't say anything.

"And then, even though he didn't want me out here, Setter sent Fox and his group to support us and to warn Gibraltar when the Kroggs were incoming, and then we happened across the Carriers…"

The whole story was hard for Pat to believe. Of course he was very, *very* happy that Sarah had come after him, but the tone of her voice, the exhaustion on her face… she was being slowly consumed by grief. And by *guilt*. It was obvious to him — he knew her so well. She'd given up her very life to come out here, and she felt as though that decision had made her both a failure and a disappointment.

And nothing Pat could say would convince her that she *hadn't* betrayed her friends… so for now all he could do was make sure he looked like a good reason to turn oneself into a renegade.

As much as he wanted to drift to sleep, comfortable in the reassuring arms of the woman he loved, he found his voice, and played his part with a soft smile, "You signed your own letter for *me*?"

Sarah shrugged almost sheepishly, "What else was I to do? I couldn't accept that you were dead, and I couldn't come out here otherwise."

That was her justification, and Pat could hear the conflict in her voice. She tried to hide it, but he heard it. She loved him, and that was tearing apart the fundamental pillars of her character.

He didn't know if it would destroy her in the end or not.

But that wasn't for now. Now they both needed comfort. So Pat's smile broadened, and he reached out and gently helped Sarah up into his arms again, "It's all turned out right then."

Sarah closed her eyes and rested her head on his shoulder, "It has."

"I don't expect we'll be seeing Sarah or Pat for a little while," Fox sat down in his main briefing room with the three Captains who'd joined him from the flight deck. "Once we get *Bishop's* survivors squared away, our next job will be dealing with any Krogg vessels left in system, and with repairing *Flame*."

Audrey cocked an eyebrow, "What happened to it, exactly?"

Fox frowned and shook his head once, "The strain of all that fast travel — Chronos says energy-hyper blew two of its reactors, and combat strain took out a third. We'll have to rig up something makeshift, but for now I'm getting the crew off the ship for a rest."

The other Captains nodded, James speaking up next, "I think we can take a quick sweep of the system to make sure it's clean. How long do we want to stay here?"

Fox leaned back in his chair, "The Kroggs are probably at Gibraltar right now, so if we want to find their base and take it out before their survivors get back, we'll have to move out within a couple of days."

There were nods again, and then Thena eyed Fox quietly, "You think the Kroggs are there now?"

Fox nodded, "I imagine they are."

CHAPTER 45

Orion sat with an open field well below Caitlin Hargreaves' human force, the ships of the line surrounding it divided between Setter Caine, Savanna Felix, Varnon Broadpaw, Jax Furgus, and Kella Felar. From the bridge, sitting next to Labrador Forepaw, the First Lord waited for the Kroggs to arrive.

Picketing sloops reported in at regular energy drive, moving relatively slowly to avoid detection by the Krogg Fleet. Caine watched them arrive in the system and felt his heart rate rising as he did. He forced himself to settle his mind as the last of those diminutive ships arrived and moved to join the Destroyers now floating around the *Gibraltars* — he needed to be confident and steady now, especially now, to ensure they maximized their chances of victory.

Since the meeting of the commanders, no new ships had arrived to support Gibraltar. Garvin Jardaw's Carriers were estimated to be two hours out — they could arrive during the battle but there was no certainty of that. No, it seemed victory would depend on the forces on hand, an unorthodox plan, bad odds and good luck.

Ursla somehow felt right to be sitting on the bridge of *Cerberus* again. The Fifth Rate — and its infamously low ceilings — had been her command for the years leading up to Pluto Orbital Plane, and now a force very similar to the old Exodus battle group was under her orders.

Through all the months of campaigning in a First Rate, the frigate life and style had never drifted far from Ursla's mind — that ability to avoid the enemy, to spring forth from nowhere and catch the foe at its worst possible moment... the tendency not to stand and just trade blows... things that sounded altogether more wolf-like than bear-like... those were the things she missed.

But not today — today she had her frigates back.

Now, screening for Hargreaves with frigates and cruisers, Ursla also waited for the Kroggs to show themselves.

The 301st Battle Squadron had been supplemented with the elements of three squadrons of 74s recently arrived from Oxford's Star, giving Felix a total direct command of twenty-three ships of the line. It seemed like a small number, but when put into the context of Caine's twenty-two, Broadpaw's twenty-three, Felar's twenty, or Furgus' group of smaller battleships — the older 64s and 70s that had been scraped together from various pickets — Felix considered his force solid.

He also liked the homogeneity that came with having so many Third Rates. *Tonnant* aside, all the 74s were basically identical, and that gave them some interesting advantages when it came to maneuvering. Better than that, though, was that two of these additional squadrons of 74s were not foreign to Felix. He had been fighting with the 301st for over a year, and two of the squadrons given to him, 346th and 319th, were veterans of his action at Arbalest Pulsar.

The Kroggs were going to get a nasty surprise.

Graham paced the deck of *Gibraltar One* so much he was almost making himself dizzy. He *wasn't* a combat commander, dammit! He shouldn't be doing this! This should be the job of an experienced battle officer, not an admin commander who had never so much as–

He walked right into Kandam's chest.

Looking up, he backed away, "Sorry Karl, a bit preoccupied."

The big panda Captain put a hand on his shoulder, "Settle down, you'll do fine."

Graham barely heard the comment as he went back to his pacing.

"Now reading a massive hyper point forming, sir," *Orion's* Sensor Officer reported calmly, and Caine nodded.

He'd toyed with the idea of sending a last message — something dramatic that would honor Nelson's last signal at Trafalgar — but had elected against it.

Aside from the fact that he wouldn't know what to say, he somehow got the impression that sending such a signal might tip off the Kroggs that he was there — that there were Earther battleships lying in wait, watching and readying themselves to pounce.

He didn't want to tip his hand, so he kept it simple.

"All ships beat to quarters," his words seemed understated.

The Allied ships prepared themselves.

The Krogg Fleet came out of hyper in one massive group, the Destroyers positioning themselves between the human vessels in the system and their own Dreadnoughts and Motherships. There was little delay: as Caine suspected, the whole fleet began to edge toward the visible mobile forces — the only Allied units that could be considered a serious threat based on what the Kroggs could see of the system.

The range was quite wide — the Kroggs had stopped short of the hyper limit in their exit from hyperspace, almost as if they were wary of a trap. Prudent, but the fact that they hadn't scouted the system beforehand demonstrated a certain lack of concern over the possibility of being caught out.

It seemed to be a Krogg tradition to charge straight in and deal with whatever fought back — a tradition which had been surprisingly effective in their centuries of conflict with the Larosians. Now, sliding through space easily, the fleet laid Hargreaves' force in their sights and prepared their massive onslaught.

Caine watched the advance silently from *Orion*; the evenly-numbered 400 Destroyers, 200 Dreadnoughts, and twenty Motherships formed into three waves, then the Motherships opened their eyelid-doors. Here, then, was the moment of truth: how many corvettes would come from each? Were the Allies damned already?

A surprisingly modest force of 250 corvettes fountained from each Mothership. Caine's eyes narrowed as the sensors began to pick up details on the small ships; they were slightly bigger and tougher... it looked as though their weapons were all slow-tracking and heavy — much better suited to dealing with Earther warships than Larosian fighters. Hopefully that meant they would be a bad match for gunboats. The increased size meant there were only 5,000 of these small ships... well, *only* not quite being the right word for it, but still...

Ten-to-one odds against the gunboats were better than the twenty-to-one they'd planned for... the frigates, cruisers and escorts would have to attempt to make up for the difference. But that would be Ursla's concern, so Caine forced his mind away from it. He had to contain his thoughts this time — he had turned command of different elements of this complicated operation over to different people, and he was himself commanding a component that would require his undivided attention.

The Krogg capital ships were stretched into a long thin wall, only two or three deep most of the way, and the Motherships were just slightly behind that line, their eyes closing after the not-so-massive launch.

Caine, and the battleships, watched and waited.

Ursla was to have the first move — something she was surprisingly accustomed to. She'd been first to meet the humans, first to meet the Larosians, and first to find Gibraltar. Hell, she'd been the first kodiak to attain flag rank. The only kodiak, actually.

A life of firsts, then, and she was about to add one more...

Whatever relevance that list happened to have was lost on her just now, as she watched a deathly cloud of corvettes coming her way. This would either be a magnificent Allied victory that would be made into movies... or a quick and altogether brutal end.

Just before she gave her first orders, she turned to Commodore Nightclaw and offered a thin smile, "Glad to have you here on this one, Dran."

The black panther, generally a reserved figure, offered a smile and nod, "It's good to be here, Andra."

Ursla nodded and turned to watch the corvettes advance on the monitors. "Frigates, cruisers, clear for action and advance by squadron."

Graham watched in *Gibraltar One's* main battle plot as Ursla and the 111th led the cruisers out from Hargreaves' position. That was his cue, and he looked through the holo tank to Kandam, who nodded.

"All Destroyers and sloops to advance in support of the cruisers," the big panda ordered in his smooth, rich voice.

With those commands, the escort ships clouding around the line of *Gibraltar* stations moved out... but they numbered only in the dozens where the Kroggs numbered in the hundreds.

Graham took a breath as they accelerated towards the fray, and then he watched as the Krogg corvettes began to cloud together. Corvettes didn't seem to abide by any specific formations or tactics, they simply engaged the targets assigned to them by their Motherships, and didn't stop attacking until their target was destroyed, or until they were told otherwise. They weren't easily distracted, even when being attacked from another direction... they just advanced as massive hordes and swamped defenders with chaos until the target or targets were gone.

Hopefully, the bait of capital ships and that single-minded, disorganized style of attack would give the boats the chance they needed.

"All crews to their boats, prepare for launch," Graham ordered quietly, and the flight decks of the *Gibraltars* sprung into action, 504 gunboats loading up with 2,016 volunteer Earthers.

Cerberus, known widely to be the best ship of its type in either Allied service, led the group of frigates and cruisers. The nine squadrons given to Ursla moved in separate lines abreast, maintaining their independence.

The sight was impressive in Ursla's plot on *Cerberus'* bridge... but what would the Kroggs do about them?

For a moment Ursla couldn't see a reaction, then the Kroggs evidently took notice.

Probably detecting the implied threat to their corvettes, and likely wary of sending 5,000 of these untested light ships to fight where 10,000 of the old ones would have gone, the Kroggs moved 300 Destroyers forward.

Ursla ground her jaw. They'd left Destroyers to screen the Motherships and some of the Dreadnoughts... enough small ships to conceivably cause problems for the battleships when Caine charged into the fray.

Graham's escorts, moving in a column three ships wide and seven ships long, were cruising in fast from the *Gibraltars*... for a moment Ursla considered going wildly off plan and sending them to support Caine's attack. Then the Kroggs committed forty more Destroyers to attack the sloops and Genesis Destroyers.

Glancing sideways at Nightclaw, Ursla offered a short nod. That was better...

The alien Destroyers raced out ahead of the corvettes, forcing every bit of speed they could from their black muscles. Ursla watched them quickly close the distance in their rush, and took a deep breath.

"Here we go again," she said softly. "Squadrons to operate independently. Commodore Nightclaw, fight your squadron..."

The panther paused, looked seriously at Ursla for a moment as the Signal Officer relayed the orders to her cruiser groups, and forced a cough.

"Pardon me, ma'am, but I feel rather ill. Would you care to assist me by taking command of the 111th?"

A number of the bridge crew smiled at the remark — almost all of them were veterans of the old Ursla days, and all of them would be glad to see the great bear taking the reins of the squadron, even from a master of the craft like Nightclaw.

Ursla smiled in reply, "As you say. 111th, stand by starboard broadside and prepare standard turn to port for line ahead."

The orders were relayed, and the Fifth Rates of the 111th prepared to meet their foe.

"Keep the speed low, move us towards the Dreadnought divisions," Caine ordered quietly.

As the orders were repeated to the ships of Caine's command, Forepaw instructed his Master to maneuver to specific coordinates. *Orion*, in company with the other fifteen First Rates and six Third Rates of Caine's group, slowly began to accelerate through space, its field open to 250 percent to avoid detection.

On his sensor plot, Caine watched Felix move with him, followed by Furgus, Broadpaw, and then Felar. The speed compared to the sprinting cruisers was almost nonexistent, but they couldn't risk being detected yet...

They had to wait until Andra had taken all of the Kroggs' attention. Caine watched Ursla's advance towards the firestorm, and he silently wished his old friend good luck. She could well need whatever luck the Earthers had left...

Then, abruptly but smoothly, the 111th executed a perfect turn to port, and fired the first broadsides of the battle at long range.

Ursla began giving squadron orders out of reflex. Conscious of the fact that her ships were now handier than the battleships she had become accustomed to over the past year, she rolled the squadron and vented another broadside, then wore her line around again and, at a good clip, chased the frigates' energy shot towards the enemy.

Salvoes of missiles and other broadsides appeared in her plot from the cruiser and frigate squadrons behind, and in their own order, those ships began to follow the 111th. The Allied cruisers ran down on the Krogg Destroyers...

"We'll be amongst them in forty seconds, ma'am."

Ursla looked up from her plot and gave a single nod to the Master, "Squadron stand by for division work and reassembly. At my mark, take two minutes independent."

She'd let her frigates fight in pairs when the chaos struck, then recombine them in the melee and let their concentrated fire crush the Kroggs...

In the battle tank, though, the Destroyers made their noisy reply. A massive number of spines — *showers* of the projectiles — clouded through space at high speed, and as Ursla took solid hold of the sides of the plot table, the 111th dove between volleys.

The elite Earther frigates weren't touched. Many of the Allied cruisers... mainly *human* cruisers... took the brunt of the first hits. No icons winked out of action on Ursla's plot, but two Heavy Cruisers slowed and started flashing in the holo tank.

Even considering those two damaged ships, the Kroggs weren't going to be able to do better than this Allied salvo — energy bursts and self-propelled missiles were more effective at this range.

Ursla watched as three Destroyers were crushed, a handful more badly wounded, and a small gap formed in the advancing Krogg Destroyer cloud...

And then Ursla's eyes shifted to a new wall of energy shot and missiles, not from her ships but from Graham's; the sloops and the Destroyers were now on the scene as well.

"In amongst them in fifteen seconds, ma'am," the next report caused Ursla's eyes to shift to her own command again. They'd have to drive in deep, split, then come back out...

The best chance she and the Allied escorts had of beating these Destroyers was simple: slowly draw the Kroggs onto the guns of the *Gibraltars*.

"Ready to engage. Carronades stand by," Nightclaw played his old, familiar role of Captain, and Ursla took a deep breath.

"*Fight.*"

The 111th slammed into the Destroyer formation, and as it did, its eight-ship line ahead shattered into fighting pairs of Fifth Rates. The elite frigates got into the Krogg echelons, and while many of the cruisers and even some of the other frigates that had followed Ursla to this place had stopped outside the Destroyer cloud, Ursla's ships ripped deep into the formation, and laid waste.

In a single minute, nineteen Krogg Destroyers had been eliminated.

Along with six human cruisers destroyed and two Sixth Rate frigates put out of action...

• • •

Caine watched the corvettes finish forming into their swarm beyond the fleet and noted the limited number of Destroyers remaining with the Krogg capital ships. Circumstances weren't ideal for his attack, but he needed to be sure he didn't give the Kroggs time to overwhelm Ursla and the cruisers.

"Close range and prepare to tighten and drop fields," he ordered quietly.

The battleships of Caine's groups began to accelerate, less concerned about detection than about simply reaching their foe.

"In range in... three minutes," the Master reported.

Caine offered a single nod.

Graham watched the battleships accelerate, knowing he'd have to hit the corvettes at just the right time to keep them from doubling back against Caine's ships of the line.

The corvettes were hurrying toward Hargreaves now... how long should he wait? He didn't know, he didn't have the experience for this job. So he'd just have to follow his instincts and hope they panned out...

Taking a breath, Graham looked up at Kandam, "Launch the boats, Karl."

The bear nodded, and the *Gibraltars* opened their flight deck doors.

CHAPTER 46

Lieutenant Trax Earon had been selected to command the gunboats from space. As the officer in charge of their construction in Gibraltar, he was the closest thing to an expert they had for this battle. That certainly didn't give him unlimited confidence, but he tried to ignore his nerves as his boat, *G101*, came first and fast out of *Gibraltar One's* bay. *G102* though *G197* were yet to launch.

"All boats form by Gun Squadrons, mark targets in the corvette groups and accelerate." Like all Earthers, Earon tended to sound calm even when under stress. The orders went through his comm directly to every boat that was now on the ready line to launch. There were no acknowledgements — having each boat individually accept the orders would have clogged the frequency. Instead, the marine system of silent acknowledgement was adopted, and the boats simply moved into position as they spilled from their hangers, forming giant claws in space and lurching forward at tremendous speeds.

They were on their way.

Caine watched the boats launch and wondered whether they were too early... but the decision on when to deploy was Graham's, not his. And looking at how far out towards the system rim the Kroggs had stopped, it made sense to give the boats ample flight time — they couldn't move faster than light, after all.

By the looks of things in *Orion's* plot, the Kroggs didn't know what to make of the boats. That was good — the corvettes weren't sure which threat was most pressing, and he was about to draw their attention with something clear and obvious.

Looking to Lab Forepaw, Caine offered a single nod, "Now."

The Signal Officer had also been listening, so that one word brought 138 Earther ships of the line out of energy drive *within* the formations of the Krogg Fleet. The chaos triggered by their sudden arrival proved they hadn't been expected. With their shields up and both broadsides run out, the battleships paused for an ominous second as they all emerged, then Caine nodded to Forepaw, and Forepaw nodded to his First Lieutenant.

Orion fired.

The whole force fired immediately afterwards, and at point-blank range the devastation was brutal. For every ship of the line, one Dreadnought was either heavily damaged or entirely destroyed, and while all the alien ships tried to wheel on their opponents, the Earther capital ships opened fire with their carronades.

Massive blades of energy criss-crossed in space and hacked Krogg Dreadnoughts apart, dismembering and murdering with disregard. Telepathic screams filled the minds of the Allies, but the slaughter continued unabated — there was no room for compassion here.

The seventy-odd unhurt Dreadnoughts began to congregate around their wounded fellows — a collection of some 140 ships, including the injured. In one swift move, the Earthers had evened the capital ship odds.

"Well done," Caine's comment was directed to the Signal Officer to be passed on. "Let slip the Admirals."

The Lieutenant at signals didn't recognize the allusion, but it hardly mattered. She keyed a message into her panel, and in every plot in Caine's force, the orders scrolled up.

Savanna Felix stood aboard *Tonnant* with Varnia Broadpaw at his side. He nodded to her when the words came up in his plot, then looked to his Signal Officer, "Orders to battle group, form on me."

Varnia ordered *Tonnant* into a charge, and the 74s of the 301st followed in the Second Rate's wake. Chase guns fired, and the Earther vessels surged ahead.

Caine nodded silently to himself at Felix's enthusiasm and watched his ships move in the plot.

Kella Felar, Felix's old war-games partner, followed the white cat scant seconds after *Tonnant* moved. Varnon Broadpaw and Jax Furgus attacked the opposite flank simultaneously, and so the only line of advance left to the First Lord was clear...

"We're going right up the middle, Lab. Copy those orders to squadron."

Mighty *Orion* lumbered forward.

Graham tried to keep track of just what the Earther ships of the line were doing... but it wasn't easy to follow the transponders of ships moving with such blinding speed. What he could make out was formidable...

Broadpaw's First and Second Rates rolled down to the farthest end of the Krogg line and began to bombard a half-dozen Motherships... but leaner and tougher than earlier models, the giant ships fought back with heavy spines and neuro pulses. They were suddenly outnumbered and grossly outgunned by Broadpaw's ships, but they struck back viciously, and a First Rate and a Second were lost in moments. Broadpaw's push, however, could not be checked.

Graham hoped, as he watched, that the pattern of Earther victory would repeat itself, so his eyes shifted to *Orion* and to the bright broad pennant of Setter Caine.

Orion and Caine's forces mirrored the operation on the opposite end of the line. With larger numbers of big ships at hand, Caine's battle group smashed more Motherships with the loss of only two 74s, and with two First Rates severely mauled.

The situation appeared to be unfolding to plan...

After the seeming clockwork elimination of the Motherships — *all* of them, just that simply — the First Rate groups turned on the remaining Krogg Dreadnoughts. Two Third Rates and a handful of smaller Earther battleships were destroyed on the turn, and another dozen heavily damaged, but many of the Dreadnoughts were completely destroyed in the crossfire seconds later.

The ships of the line, in just minutes, had broken the back of the Krogg capital ship lines... But Graham knew better than to celebrate. The main Krogg thrust today wasn't built on heavy units.

Orion drove through the last formation of Dreadnoughts left in its battle plot, forcing three of the Krogg capital ships to one side and two to the other. *Agamemnon* and six other First Rates were immediately in position to lay waste to those Krogg ships as they broke formation, and so as Lab Forepaw nodded to *Orion's* Master, the ship was able to decelerate and angle towards its squadron-mates without fear of reprisal.

As seemed the tradition, the great First Rate remained untouched by the fighting. It was a powerhouse of a vessel, after all, and it was crewed by the most elite Earthers in the service.

But in the plot, the flashing icons of at least forty of the Earther ships of the line that had just fought this action showed Caine that things hadn't gone as well as he'd have liked.

They'd eliminated the Dreadnoughts and the Motherships, essentially protecting the security of the frontier, and with five veteran fleet commanders on hand, that had been a remarkably simple accomplishment.

But eleven Allied ships had already been put entirely out of the fight, and they hadn't yet met the corvettes.

"Squadron reformed, ma'am," the Signal Officer repeated the report to Ursla and she nodded. They'd just witnessed Caine's trouncing of the Krogg battleship line with a relatively low number of casualties on the Allied side. Hopefully the rest of the Kroggs would lose their direction — become much easier to defeat...

Considering the situation, Andra watched the Destroyers and corvettes crowd closer together and made ready to attack.

"Let's get the cruiser force reassembled and back into order... I don't want those corvettes to get the drop on us..." Ursla turned back to the Signal Officer, who again replied with a nod.

The cruisers had killed as many as 100 Destroyers, and the rest of those Krogg ships were falling back to the safety of the corvette horde, avoiding the guns of Gibraltar... They might just have the time they needed. Ursla frowned into the plot. Her 111th was still virtually undamaged, but only seventy of the original ninety-seven cruisers remained, many of them badly shot up. They were pulling together now, and joining with the twenty sloops and Destroyers that had originally been assigned to Graham's stations... in just another minute they'd be an effective–

We don't have a minute.

Ursla's eyes settled on the *1,000* corvettes the Krogg Destroyers had called to their aid. It seemed there were at least a few tactical thinkers left with the Krogg ships in the system...

"Time to–?" Ursla bit off her question as the line of human Destroyers that was trying to join her formation ceased to exist.

All of them. The corvettes overwhelmed the human vessels and shredded them as Ursla watched. Eleven ships gone, just like that. The new heavy weapons on the corvettes were *devastating...*

Ursla shook herself out of the shock and turned again to her Signal Officer, "Everyone together, *now*! Concentrate point defense..."

The cruisers that had already managed to gather together fell in close with each other, and targeting computers linked and took command of human weapons, then were slaved to Earther gunnery Lieutenants.

As *Cerberus* joined a sphere of about fifty ships, Ursla watched any cruisers that had yet to form up be absorbed by the corvette wave. It was like watching piranhas feed. These were corvettes with powerful neuro pulse weapons and large spines that swallowed warships...

The 111th was suddenly taking damage, and that was a lesson in itself...

Ursla ground her jaw as icons winked out.

Caitlin Hargreaves, commanding from her Superdreadnought, *Pope Michael Dalton*, saw the situation develop.

She'd started this battle with the unpleasant stamp of 'bait' on her forehead, now she might have a chance to do some good. Those corvettes were overwhelming cruisers, but surely the greater armor protection and larger batteries would make her Dreadnoughts and Superdreadnoughts serve like castles in this fight — the small corvettes might be stopped, or at least stalled, if Caitlin brought her ships into the fight at just the right moment...

She nodded then to her ArcColonel, "Form up, let's try to take some heat off them..."

Formation was quick, and Hargreaves proudly watched as her ships came together and began advancing almost instantly under her orders. They quickly neared the corvette horde, and as they crept up behind the angry flock of enemy ships, Caitlin's eyes narrowed and she gave the order.

"Open *fire*."

Heavy lasers and missiles charged forth to cut swathes out of the Krogg cloud. Some took notice, but not enough. So focused were these Kroggs that they did not turn on the human capital ships.

So Hargreaves smiled, "We might just have them here..."

She was concentrating so completely on this 1,000, she forgot the other 4,000. But they didn't forget her.

Her flagship evaporated less than a minute later.

Krogg Destroyers were turning on Caine's force, trying to keep it from recombining.

But there were too few, and the Earthers were too determined.

Standing on the bridge of *Orion*, and staring at the plot, Setter Caine was beginning to realize just how well the Kroggs had adapted to defeat the Allied capital ships — those corvettes were feasting on his Fleet. And if any of the small Krogg ships survived, they could incinerate the Gibraltar stations and set the Allied war effort back by months.

Just the time needed by the Kroggs to consolidate, no doubt... things were more dire than he had first thought. Indeed, they were looking just as bad as he'd thought they could have.

So all he could do was try to get into that horde of some 4,500 corvettes to help Ursla. They had to kill as many of the small ships as possible, give the *Gibraltars* a fighting chance...

Caine watched in the plot as his formation reformed... he had sent the wounded ships to rally at the stations, so he now had a solid core of ninety ships of the line.

"Take us right through the Destroyers — we must get to Ursla!"

Tonnant bucked as two Destroyers lined up on the Second Rate. Savanna Felix's eyes narrowed as he caught sight of the two audacious little ships in his plot, then tried to determine where his closest support was.

Many of the ships of the 301st were severely damaged and on their way to the *Gibraltars* right now... Indeed, most of his battle group was out of the fight. He was staying close to Kella Felar's force, so as Varnia Broadpaw rolled *Tonnant* and incinerated the two gutsy Destroyers, Felix's eyes tracked back to *Endymion*, Felar's flag.

"Get me Felar on the comm," he looked to his Signal Officer, and with a nod the signal was sent to the large First Rate.

Kella's battle group was further ahead, about to engage some of the corvette stragglers to the rear, while Felix was trying to keep the Destroyers off them.

After a brief pause Felar appeared in the plot, "We're right on them now, Savanna. I think you can come up–"

The link cut. Felix had just been opening his mouth to speak when Kella's face vanished, and he looked quickly to the Signal Officer whose eyes had widened slightly. Felix looked back to the plot, then froze as *Endymion*'s broad pennant winked out and the ship heeled hard and began to spiral away from action.

Other ships of the line were working to protect the ailing oversized First Rate, but an arm of corvettes was reaching out of the cloud to seize it.

These corvettes...

"We need to get in there. Forget the Destroyers, move in *now*..."

Jax Furgus and Varnon Broadpaw were thundering ahead, and with some relief Caine watched as the two battle groups led by those well-seasoned commanders fought their way into the cloud of corvettes. Right now he couldn't think about what had happened to Kella Felar.

"Admiral Felix is rallying whatever's near him and moving in as well," Lab said softly from his position next to Caine at the plot, and the First Lord nodded.

"Let's get in there too."

Ursla vaguely noticed *Pope Michael Dalton*'s violent end, and she realized distantly that Caitlin Hargreaves had undoubtedly died on that ship. Sarah's elite 401st Battle Squadron died just as quickly — perhaps it was for the best that the ArcGeneral had left. *Endymion*'s severe mauling, and the seeming loss of Kella Felar also registered... but all of these revelations had to be set aside for the moment.

With the battle raging all around, there was just no time to feel. Two of the 111th's untouchable Fifth Rates had lost broadsides to severe damage, and were hiding behind their fellows as they desperately tried to survive. So far only about 700 of the 5,000 corvettes had been destroyed.

She'd started this fight with over a hundred cruisers, now she had only thirty-one. Nothing — absolutely *nothing* — of Caitie Hargreaves' force remained alive.

"Incoming to port, six of them... carronades tracking four!"

Cerberus bucked as neuro pulses scorched its shields, and another shot broke through the bow defenses and opened three more of the frigate's compartments to space. *Cerberus* lurched sideways and a ragged broadside smeared some corvettes out of existence... but there were more. Always more.

• • •

"Here we go — Lieutenant, all guns fire as you bear!" Lab Forepaw's orders carried an uncharacteristic tension, and Setter Caine took a deep breath as his ships slammed into the corvettes.

As *Orion* entered the cloud, the First Rate's massive broadsides slaughtered the first fifty corvettes that rushed forward. A further thirty slammed salvoes into the First Rate's shields, though they weren't enough to harm the mighty ship.

Under Artemis Tigar's command, nearby *Agamemnon* also fared well, as the wily tiger Captain swung his ship like a bat through scores of corvettes, unceremoniously crushing almost twenty with the hull. Then *Agamemnon's* 150 guns spoke, and more corvettes were destroyed... but again, as ever, there were more.

As they had at the Battle of Genesis, ships of the line began to pair off, and the veritable titans of the Earther Navy, *Orion* and *Agamemnon*, pulled together first. The only two ships truly able to absorb the heat of the corvettes, they tried to serve as a rallying point.

"Everybody *hold on!*"

Felix's head whipped up at Varnia Broadpaw's warning, and at the same time he took hold of the edges of the holo plot tank...

A corvette drove right through *Tonnant's* weakened port side shields and into the broadside, and *Tonnant* went sideways. The large ship was thrown hard by the collision, and worse, the Krogg corvette was sticking out the side of the Second Rate. Everyone on the bridge managed to keep their feet, and Varnia looked to the Master.

"Can you keep us steady with *that* thing in us?"

The gruff and experienced Earther nodded abruptly, and then the intercom cackled.

"Gun deck here ma'am, lower port side. We've got shields holding compression but there are *Kroggs* coming out of that corvette..."

Felix cocked an eyebrow, and Varnia gave the order, "Marines to the gun deck. Lieutenant, see if you can get some of those guns back in action..."

Tonnant slowly returned to the fight.

Caine cocked an eyebrow at Felix's predicament, "Lab, we better help him."

The Captain was well ahead, "Signals, tell Savanna to seal off that deck, we'll chop the back off that corvette for him. Get Artie to cover us from above."

Trying to follow the evolutions of this strange operation, Caine kept his eyes on the plot as *Orion* swept close to *Tonnant* and two carronades cut off most of the protruding corvette. The Second Rate seemed to right itself partially with the removal of some of the unexpected drag, then drifted up beneath *Orion's* bow with half its port broadside firing again.

* * *

Jax Furgus' flagship, *Grand Banks*, was maneuvering near *Tonnant*. Jax was a rough sort of character, and well-experienced in the war... but his 64 was not cut out for this.

He was standing on his bridge when the starboard shields caved, and as they did a volley of sixty spines slammed right through the gunports on that beam. In the blink of an eye, Earther gun crews were incinerated by acid, and *Grand Banks* developed an uncontrolled spiral.

"Abandon ship," was Jax's last order before racing to an escape pod — something he'd done all too many times.

Eleven gun crews — or parts of gun crews — were left alive on that starboard side, and they didn't leave their posts. Their deck was depressurizing, and they couldn't escape into the ship without decompressing it entirely.

So they fired off a last ragged broadside and then suffocated at their posts.

The rest of the crew boarded escape pods, followed at the last possible moment by Jax himself. He transferred his pennant to a life pod, then launched and looked for another ship from which to fly his flag. Varnon Broadpaw's flagship, *Algenon*, picked the pod up a moment later.

Caine watched the drama play out in his holo tank, and he realized that while there were now only 4,100 corvettes in the swarm, his ships were dying too quickly. He needed help soon, or there would be 3,000 corvettes left in the system after he went down...

If Caine's head had been clearer, he would have realized help was already on the way.

CHAPTER 47

Commodore Garvin Jardaw had been ordered to make the trip from Genesis to Gibraltar in eight days. It was a ten-day trip under good conditions, and only the fastest ships he'd ever encountered could make it in anything less than that.

Fortunately, he was cruising right now with those fastest ships. And while the Carriers, fast frigates, and two fast 64s couldn't make the journey in eight days, they had done it in *nine*... well, a few hours less than a whole nine, but that was splitting hairs.

Coming out of energy drive near the massive conflagration of corvettes and warships, Garvin Jardaw was glad they'd hurried. They wouldn't turn the tide on their own, but they'd certainly make a mark.

"Comm, send to the Carriers — launch *everything*," Jardaw turned from *Highlander's* plot to his Signal Officer, and the orders were repeated to *Diadem, Boadecia, Godetia,* and *Galatea*. Between them, these Carriers could put to space only 315 boats, but they had a certain advantage of surprise, not just in terms of when they were arriving, but in their very existence.

"Have the Carriers move in close to each other and order *Elephant* and the frigates to cover them. Drop us back to do the same."

There weren't any spare boats to protect the Carriers — that'd be up to the conventional warships. And so far the corvettes didn't look to be paying any attention to them...

That made sense, Jardaw realized; the last orders those corvettes would have gotten from their Motherships would have been to destroy the conventional ships they were now swarming. There was no one left to call them off... hopefully that would work to his Provisional Carrier Group's advantage.

Boats began hurtling out through the Carriers' launch tubes, their crews already tested once in battle at Earth. The crash launch put them all into space within a scant minute, and within ninety seconds the boats had shaken themselves into squadron order.

After two minutes, they were charging into the fray.

Caine had feared this fight would be like the Battle of Midway... perhaps, Graham realized, it was similar in some ways. The junior Manchester had read about the turning point in that centuries-past sea battle, and it did go something like this — strike forces off two Carriers independently found a much stronger enemy at just the right time.

It was a stretch, but as *Highlander* and its Carrier group appeared in *Gibraltar One's* battle plot, they might as well have been wearing United States flags instead of Earther pennants.

Well that's a bit much... but there's some irony there.

Because, it seemed to Graham, the Earther capital ships charging into that host of corvettes had forgotten entirely about the boats that were making the run from the *Gibraltars*. Graham had launched them just in time; after their sub-light flight, they were now entering battle range.

Looking to Kandam, Graham offered a single nod, "We've either got them or we're dead."

The panda cocked an eyebrow, "Right... Well then, all boats, *attack*."

Garvin Jardaw cocked an eyebrow at his plot; there were 504 new boats coming from the other side, cruising at the corvettes in squadron-sized claw formations.

Evidently Caine had supplemented his conventional forces with newly-built boats... which gave the Allies over 800 small attack ships in the system.

And perhaps a much better fighting chance than he'd first thought.

Indeed, thanks to Draco Maximane's effort to keep the Carriers secret, these corvettes probably didn't even know what was hitting them when the two large strike wings carved into the horrendous cloud.

Corvette casualty rates instantly doubled. Their heavy neuro pulses, adapted so they could easily smash capital ships, were far too slow to track the gunboats, as were their heavy spines.

And while the heavier build of the corvettes made them sturdier than most of their ancestors, a direct hit from a gunboat's cannon was enough to severely wound them. Had they been organized, massed fire could have compensated for these shortcomings... but they weren't. Their Motherships were gone, their Destroyers were gone, there was nothing left in their simple minds but chaotic destruction — albeit destruction of the surviving Earther capital ships.

They lashed out randomly at the boats, but there were 800 of the Earther small craft amongst them now. Operating in mutually supporting squadrons, using instinct to overcome inexperience, the Earther boat crews saw that they were the only chance for victory at Gibraltar. Weaving in and out of Krogg corvette clouds, the boats targeted independently in a manner impossible for broadside or turreted weapons on larger ships, and did great damage to the incredibly disorganized, seething mass of their foes.

This was the strength of the gunboats, and Garvin Jardaw was duly impressed...

But there were still 3,500 Krogg corvettes. And this was going to be a slugging match to the bitter end...

•••

From his place on the bridge of *Orion,* Caine watched in silence. His powerful unit of ships of the line, ninety when he'd entered this cloud, now numbered forty-one. Ursla's cruisers were down to seventeen, of which only two were Genesis ships. The gunboats from the *Gibraltars* and the Carrier group had arrived, but only in time to give them any chance of surviving this... at all.

"There was a crew of twenty on the Krogg corvette. They're all dead," the First Lieutenant reported to Varnia Broadpaw, and she nodded. The survivors of the Krogg ship that had crashed into *Tonnant's* side wouldn't be causing any problems aboard — the marines had done their work well.

But that was hardly the ship's only concern, and as Varnia glanced back at Felix he looked to her, "That's it for the 319th, they've all been destroyed."

The loss clutched at Felix for a moment, but even as it did he saw the importance of the sacrifice those ships had made. If necessary, every Earther vessel would go down fighting this cloud of corvettes; the Kroggs had to be stopped here and now. It was a sacrifice the Earther crews would make for the war if it was asked of them...

And it hurt him to see it. But it was required of those brave crews, and if need be, of him.

Varnia simply nodded in reply to her Admiral's words, then looked to the Master, "Looks like we'll want to move in alongside *Agamemnon* and *Orion.* Can you get us there?"

The gruff Master nodded, and as *Tonnant's* deck quivered, the ship edged its way even closer to the other two flagships.

Lab Forepaw's gaze moved from the holo projection to the Master and to Caine, while he continued to give orders in his controlled, smooth, almost patriarchal manner. Now the closing of the last ranks caught his eye — *Tonnant* and about thirty other ships were pulling tightly together, huddling up in another sphere and using all their guns to try to force the corvettes off.

"Setter, they're closing up with us," he looked to his First Lord as he spoke.

Caine nodded, "Indeed... Signal to Ursla, see if we can't move to merge with her formation... it's a matter of survival now..."

Both comment and order were in such quiet tones, and yet they were heard because unlike every other capital ship in this mess save for *Agamemnon, Orion* remained eerily untouched, its bridge deck silent and devoid of the rumbles of battle. It was as though the universe was saving something for the First Rate...

Or, Caine reflected as he tried again to pull his mind out of a pessimistic slump, it was because *Orion* was a massive beast of a ship, with more guns and a better crew than any other ship in the Allied Fleet, bar none.

"Looks like another strike wing's lining up for suicide runs on the bridge, skipper," the Third Lieutenant reported from the sensor console, and Lab cocked an eyebrow and nodded.

"Very well, Master give us a ninety degree roll... starboard guns stand by..."

Caine stood and watched this display — for the third time, fifty Krogg corvettes were trying to take their enemy's leadership out of the fight by destroying *Orion's* bridge. And for the third time, Lab Forepaw was meeting them with a broadside...

Orion rolled, and the corvettes crowded in too slowly. While their spines pounded *Orion's* shields, the guns of the starboard beam came up to meet them, and at point-blank range vaporized forty-six.

Four adjusted course to attempt ramming again, two instantly being shredded by carronade fire. One more was picked off, and the last charged madly for *Orion's* bridge.

Could this be the end, then — had luck finally turned against him, after all this time...?

No, of course not.

Because in rolling, *Orion* gave *Tonnant's* port guns a shot, and six of the cannon on the Second Rate's wounded side opened up on the corvette, and blasted it to pieces.

Space beyond *Orion* was rife with telepathic screams, and as Caine's eyes turned back to the great engagement in the plot, he found the corvette force was down to 3,000.

Earther luck was keeping their chance alive.

Ursla firmly held the sides of the holo plot. The last two human ships in Gibraltar space winked out of existence in that display, and she ground her jaw — so many brave humans, victims of the alien race that had given them their technology. She could only hope there were survivors...

From her own Earther ships too, in fact, since she was down now to twelve frigates, eight of them comprising the whole of the 111th. No ship was without damage, but they were fighting their way to Caine's position. They couldn't go to energy drive without abandoning five of their number due to damage, so they went together, the hard way.

And then they were down to ten ships. *Ten.*

It was worse than Genesis; losses were climbing past ninety percent for the Allies, and the Kroggs were persisting...

But the Allies needed this victory. So Ursla would die fighting if she had to.

Some moments later, the two squadrons of gunboats arrived alongside Ursla's frigates to escort them towards *Orion*.

•••

The desperate fighting went on for another twenty minutes. The Krogg casualties began to mount as the gunboats hit their killing rhythm, but the alien small craft would only die so quickly. Those that remained alive threw themselves angrily at an ever-shrinking cluster of Earther — no longer *Allied*, for the humans were all dead — ships.

Caine watched in silence as all the cruiser icons but for seven of the 111th disappeared from his plot. There had been over 100 cruisers in Gibraltar barely an hour before. Of his force of almost 200 ships of the line, there remained fewer than twenty, not including the handful of lucky wounded ships that had managed to escape to the *Gibraltars*. The gunboat numbers had fallen from over 800 to barely 600...

But the Kroggs continued to die. So long as any of his ships remained, Caine drew their fury, and gave the gunboats their opportunity. The Kroggs remained disorganized, and since the corvettes were a bad technological match for the Earther small craft, there still remained a chance of victory...

If one considered such enormous casualties to be acceptable. He was going to have to work on that particular notion — so much death didn't seem at all acceptable right now.

It took another half hour for the end to come.

Standing on *Orion's* still-untouched decks, Caine finally saw the turn he'd been hoping for: the corvettes no longer outnumbered the boats. Both groups of small craft were down to 400 — clearly the boats had done the work required of them by neutralizing the new Krogg ships. But barely in the nick of time.

Setter Caine had been right: this was a debacle.

And as much as he wanted to feel a certain sense of relief as the last of the corvettes were torn apart by now-bloodied wings of gunboats, he didn't feel positive at all.

If this was how his plan turned out when things went his way, how would things go when his luck ran out...?

With that thought gnawing at the back of his mind, Caine managed a nod to Lab Forepaw, "Let's stand down. Patch holes and get ready for search and rescue — we'll need everything that can fly out there looking for survivors."

Forepaw nodded and turned away as Caine, looking briefly back to the plot, closed his eyes. Only twenty ships remained from his original fleet of over 300.

This had been a 'victory'. A disastrous, horrid, bloody 'victory'.

The search for survivors began.

CHAPTER 48

Sarah had needed more time to collect herself than she'd expected. But she *had* pulled herself together, in spite of the emotional roller coaster she was riding with the joy of Pat's rescue, and the shame of betrayal borne out by her recent actions.

Right now she was fighting the internal voice saying she should hate herself, and only two things were keeping it from winning: the presence of Patrick Conroy and the promise of carrying war to the Kroggs.

Yes, fighting the Kroggs was perhaps the only thing that would help bring normality back into her life. There was family, of course — she'd been Graham's guardian since she was fourteen when they'd been in a foster home after the execution of their parents. But to her that'd been just another fight — one that had led the way to the Navy. So a fight now, perhaps, would help ground her.

And it would also help her make up for her failure to Setter Caine. Now that Pat was safe, redemption would be her greatest priority until the war was won.

So while Pat slept in her bed on *Joseph Barron*, finally having succumbed to the exhaustion of the last weeks, she sat in a pinnace on her way to *Engadine*. Since its boats would doubtless be decisive, the big Carrier was to be the site of this morning's strategy session, and they would discuss how to kill the Krogg base out here on the fringes of the frontier.

The location of the Krogg base was known, and finding it relative to this system was a matter of simple extrapolation from *Flame's* sensor logs. The matter of how to attack it, on the other hand, was less clear — but Commodore Maximane would doubtless have suggestions, and since this conference was to be in *Engadine*, the lion would be able to attend.

They'd find a way.

Draco Maximane carefully floated to the table on his hoverchair, and Fox quickly moved a seat aside to make room for him. The Commodore nodded in thanks and stopped his mobile chair in the empty space, shifting uncomfortably as it settled and he felt a flickering second of double-strength gravity. He disliked this hover device, but the doctors told him he couldn't be on his feet, so given a choice between not working and using this chair, the decision wasn't difficult.

Fox seated himself at the head of the table as the Commodore settled himself. Thena Venus sat to Fox's right, and Claw, looking amply refreshed, sat to his left. Captain Locke of *Monarch* was next to Thena, and next to him Hobbes of *Engadine*. The skippers of the Earther ships were to be joined only by the commanding officers of the Freetown force and Sarah Manchester — the individual human captains were still out sweeping the system, carefully looking around every asteroid just in case there were still Kroggs about.

Hobbes and Locke were discussing the tactics of boat deployment — and were diametrically disagreeing about them, albeit in a friendly manner — when the door at the far end of the room finally opened to admit Audrey and James. The two humans, still wearing their Earther uniforms, smiled warmly at all assembled and rounded the table, James taking a seat next to Maximane, Audrey next to her fellow captain.

As he settled in his chair, James cast his gaze around at all the familiar faces, then turned to the shabby-looking Earther next to him... he looked familiar...

"Commodore Maximane, isn't it?"

Nodding gingerly, the lion turned his chair to face the human, "It is, Captain Stanton."

James tilted his head awkwardly, "I'm sorry, sir, but I'm sure I've seen you somewhere before."

Despite the scorched fur across his face, Maximane managed a smile, "As I recall, I had to put my ship between you and ArcColonel Chen to make sure you didn't start firing at each other..."

James frowned briefly, then memories began slowly flowing back into his head... of *course*, "*Apollo*, you were in, wasn't it? A 74? Indeed, sir, it is *very* good to see you — I never got to thank you for your help that day."

Maximane shrugged and managed to stretch his smile, "You seemed nice enough."

Snorting a laugh, James smiled, "Yes well, I should clear something up: we could've taken that Dreadnought ourselves, straight up."

Maximane shrugged again, "Sure you could."

"Really!" James asserted in mock protest.

Deciding to pitch in, Fox leaned forward, "I don't know James, we're all well aware of how shabbily you renegades run your ships. Boots on tables, not addressing people by their rank... it's a travesty, eh Chronos?"

Fox hauled his boots up onto the table and leaned back in his chair as *Flame's* Commander turned away from his conversation with Thena Venus and frowned at his old CO, "What was that, Fox?"

"Renegades are undisciplined and disreputable by nature," Fox asserted with a grin.

Chronos cocked an eyebrow, "So what's your excuse?"

"Oof, that's the cue to start the meeting!" Maximane chuckled. "Now where's ArcGeneral..."

The door opened right on cue, and Sarah walked in with a face that was somewhat less gaunt and tired but just as determined as it had been days before, "Good day, all."

With virtually no ceremony she crossed the room and slid into the chair at the opposite head of the table to Fox, nodding in turn to everyone present.

"Well, time to start then," Fox dragged his legs off the table and leaned forward. "We're in no position to worry about Gibraltar, so as I understand it, ma'am, we're going out to do some base killing."

Sarah nodded, "So we are, Fox. If we take another look at *Flame's* scans of the system, we should be able to plan an effective assault."

Pausing to key up a map of the installation based on the scans made by Claw's sloop on its brief run to the system, Sarah's eyes drifted over all those assembled, "Now this is an approximation of the garrison based on the number of ships *Flame* detected and cross-referenced with those *Atlas* witnessed on route to Gibraltar."

Black icons appeared in the light blue holo projection that now floated over the table. Three were marked as Dreadnoughts, fourteen as Destroyers, and a half dozen appeared to be Krogg ship broods and grazing stations. It wasn't well defended — at least it didn't seem to be. And with the fleet out attacking Gibraltar, it was a particularly attractive target.

"Five of the Destroyers in the simulation are probably the ones we got rid of here," Claw suggested quietly, and Fox nodded.

"I doubt they'd weaken an assault fleet for the sake of one Battlecruiser," *Atlas'* Captain agreed. "And the rest of what we're looking at... well, it seems like it'll be pretty straightforward. We can set *Atlas*, *Vulcan*, and *Joseph Barron* up against the Dreadnoughts, the Freetown Squadron and *Flame* can take out the Destroyers, and the Carriers can launch against the base itself."

There were brief nods from all present, and Sarah leaned back thoughtfully, "You really think it'll be that easy, Captain?"

Fox shrugged, "Well, it seems unlikely the Kroggs will be there in much more strength than we've accounted for. Even assuming they have more ships than we're predicting, I expect we'll deal with them."

It didn't seem to be unreasonable confidence, even to Sarah. The Earthers *always* managed this — they did things that humans thought impossible, and they never seemed to doubt their ability.

They'd help her today, when she needed their support... in any number of ways...

So Sarah nodded, "Yes, I suppose so. That makes things easier... When shall we leave?"

Fox cocked an eyebrow at the question, but realized that in technical terms, he was the senior officer at the table — he was the acting Commodore of the squadron, and Sarah remained a privateer Captain...

"Ma'am, maybe you'd like to tear up your letter and make that decision yourself," he said in a lower, more somber tone.

Sarah seemed to stiffen at the suggestion, "Fox, I'll leave that for someone left in command to do. For now this is your force. Seriously, your decision..."

The Captain tried to glean the underlying meanings behind Sarah's words, but abruptly met with a solid wall of ice. Fair enough, he would make the call. Glancing from Maximane to James to Audrey to Thena to Claw, he frowned thoughtfully, "How's *Flame* doing, Chronos?"

The cat cracked a proud smile, "We're building makeshift reactors in *Engadine*, *Monarch*, and *Atlas*... I think we can install them and have sixty-five percent operating power in about a day."

"Makeshift? Are you going to be in fighting trim then, Chronos?" Thena leaned forward next to the Commander, and the cat shrugged.

"I was right about setting up energy-hyper; I'm right about jury rigging the reactors."

"Yes but energy-hyper blew you *up*," Fox didn't sound impressed and Claw grinned.

"See, it waited a while first. So I'm thinking we'll be fine at 2,400 pls with the make-shifts. Trust me."

Fox bobbed his head sideways and released a skeptical sigh, "Alright then. We go in a day... how are we doing with *Bishop's* survivors?"

Vulcan was running that show, and Thena Venus nodded at the question, "We're almost finished packing up camp planetside. We found six more survivors this morning, and we're running close scans to make sure we haven't left anyone behind."

"We're spreading the crew out among our ships," Audrey added. "There are too many survivors for just *Joseph Barron* to carry comfortably, so we've taken volunteers aboard *Grendelsbane* and *Sword*."

A few more nods served as acceptance of that report, and eyes shifted back to Fox. But the injured Commodore at the table elected to take his turn instead.

"Loose ends are being tied up, then," Maximane's voice was coarse as he projected it. "Good. Well, Tom and Ron," he looked to his two Carrier Captains, "it'll be up to the two of you to figure out with your flight teams how to crack Krogg installations."

The two officers nodded briefly... and then the room sat in silence. Come on, there had to be more that needed saying...

Finally, Sarah piped up, "After all we've been through to get here, this might prove a bit anti-climactic. So let's just destroy this thing and go home."

Fox grinned first, but James beat him to speaking, "Give the lady a gold star, she's learned her renegade lessons after all!"

There was laughter, and Sarah, contemplating the beginning of her redemption, replied with a small, polite smile.

CHAPTER 49

Caine sat silently in *Orion's* main observation lounge and watched wounded ships of the line and frigates drop anchor in orbit of Gibraltar. The carnage in the vicinity of the planetoid was minimal — most of the killing and destruction had been focused in open space, where the coagulate gore of the Krogg corvettes was now slowly diffusing among the wreckage of floating warships.

Caine found himself grinding his jaw as he thought of his losses — *massive* losses he believed, even though on paper the destruction of a couple of hundred ships was not a crushing blow to a fleet of thousands.

The scope of the action had been so small and *vicious*, and so very nearly a defeat for the Allies. By comparison, the actions of the Pluto Orbital Plane and Genesis had been large, with thousands, nearly *tens* of thousands of ships involved. Excluding the boats, there had been fewer than a thousand ships between both sides at Gibraltar, and for some reason that sort of intimacy made the fight seem much more brutal.

It had definitely been more desperate.

However he interpreted it, Caine knew one thing about Gibraltar: it had only occurred at all because he'd been foolish enough to spread his forces out over a broad frontier. The Kroggs had recognized this weakness and had very nearly exploited it.

They were losing an intergalactic war a galaxy away, yet they had been clever and tough enough to almost check him here. And they'd nearly gotten the best of him.

Caine turned his big black chair away from the pocked and battered Allied ships that limped about in orbit and closed his eyes.

He'd been outplayed, and only the sheer will of the Earthers and humans had pulled the situation back from the brink. They'd given him a chance to right his wrongs, and to make sure they got to see this war through to the end.

He'd better make their sacrifice worth it...

Caine could only continue with that in mind. He would begin to consolidate his force along the front. No more overstretched frontier — they had to be close enough to Krogg space now to drive ahead in just a few major thrusts towards the enemy's homeworld.

Until then, there was a base on the flank to be dealt with.

Caine took a deep breath and drummed his fingers on the desk before him. Reinforcement squadrons had arrived that morning — twelve hours too late for the battle, but just in time to refortify Gibraltar. The Genesis Home Fleet — twenty-four capital ships and twelve Destroyers strong — as well as the damaged ships rushed out of Genesis and a squadron of frigates from the Cambridge Nebula. Those fresh forces didn't even come close to replenishing the fleet's losses, but they did provide a nucleus around which a defense could be mounted in case of a second strike.

And more were coming. Esther Arbear was bringing in two divisions of 74s, Ami Cairn had her Flying Squadron on the way... there were Earthers coming too. More to fight and die, as needed...

Another attack seemed highly unlikely, though, so he was going to take a calculated chance and detach some of them...

"Setter?"

Caine blinked and looked up. Savanna Felix was standing next to him, a shallow frown on his face, "Savanna... hello..."

"Right, you and Andra both — you're looking awfully drained. I say get some sleep..." Felix shook his head and took a seat next to the First Lord. "Really, if you don't rest you'll be... consumed, let's call it, by all that's just happened."

Blinking a few times to make sure he'd heard that right, Caine frowned and looked to his friend, "Did I miss something? Isn't there still half a corvette sticking out of *Tonnant*, and over ninety percent casualties? Kella Felar is *dead*, the first Admiral we've lost since Andrea Talone at Genesis. Savanna, this was a death trap. We paid in *blood* for my mistakes–"

Felix's eyebrows rose slightly and he looked to his friend, holding up his hand, "We paid in blood to hold Gibraltar. 'Mistakes' are subjective designations, and we can't afford to sit around and wonder 'what if'. By the Earth, Setter, you want them to have died for nothing? You plan to sit here and brood about everyone who died to hold this place, or do you want to move on and make sure they didn't do it for nothing?"

Silence followed the statement, and Caine looked back out through the glass at the wrecked remnants of his Gibraltar force.

"You know better than this, Setter... you and Andra kept things in perspective after Genesis. You need to do that again. You need to remember why we're out here. We made promises and we're keeping them, and every Earther on every ship is willing to die to do that. We've always gotten past our losses before, you need to again."

Caine's gaze seemed to lock on the ruptured hull of one of the 111th's frigates, and he let out a long breath. Felix was right. They were out here fighting because they'd made a promise, and they wouldn't abandon their word lightly. Life wasn't cheap or easy to give... but sometimes it seemed so simply sold.

The Earthers — not just him, but all of them — were willing to give their lives because he'd promised the humans and Larosians they would join this war. Defeating the Kroggs was crucial to the safety of the Allies, and so the Earthers, the humans and the Larosians were fighting and dying. It would be a dishonor to those Earthers Caine had just lost if he failed to make good their sacrifice.

And, as recent events had proven, nothing short of victory would assure Earth's safety.

"So we keep fighting the war as Earthers do. We pay in blood, and we watch our human friends pay even more, but we keep going. Because we must... because we *can*... because we *must* fulfill our pledge," he said quietly after a moment, and Felix nodded.

"Indeed. Stay with it, we'll get this thing over with, one way or the other. And if we do it right, more of us will be going home than not..." Felix let his voice trail off as Caine offered a single slow nod, then the cat cleared his throat. "Anyway, the yards are working on repairs now. And Graham's outside. I wasn't about to let him in with you alone if you were... well, like this. Want me to tell him to go?"

Caine blinked a couple of times and sighed again, "No. I know what he wants, and we best get it over with. Bring him in."

With another nod, Felix stood and returned to the lounge hatch. Opening it, he admitted the somewhat disheveled figure of Graham Manchester into the room. The junior Manchester was exhausted — he had steadfastly refused sleep while his boats had been out hopping among wrecks to look for survivors and help escort search and rescue ships. But now the first three sweeps were complete, and he had to see to one more thing.

Caine watched as Graham walked wearily to the table, and sat facing the First Lord.

"I take it I may speak with you, Setter?"

Felix moved to stand at Graham's shoulder, and the human pretended not to notice the pseudo-guard.

"You don't look so well, Graham."

The junior Manchester cocked an eyebrow, "And you're a picture of youth and virility. I have a request."

The First Lord smiled sadly at the comment and nodded, "No need to ask, Graham. I'm removing you from command of the *Gibraltar* boats. Commodore Kandam will take over effective immediately. I'm also sending a task force after Fox Magnus, to make sure he has the firepower to deal with the Krogg base on our flank. I might have given it to Caitie Hargreaves, but her death notwithstanding, there are reasons I imagine you'd want to be out there."

Graham's passive face seemed to harden slightly at the prospect, and his eyes narrowed.

"You'll fly your flag from *Pope John Patrick*, and you'll take the 435th Super-dreadnoughts and Commodore Jardaw's Provisional Carrier Group," Caine continued. "You'll have to get out there fast, and give them a hand if they need it. They may already be engaged, or they could have already destroyed it. All our sloops were put out of action in the fight, so I can't find out easily. You'll have to find out for me, but you'll have plenty of firepower in case you need it."

Graham nodded slowly, "Very good. We'll leave immediately."

"You might want to sleep first," Felix offered from over his shoulder, but Graham shook his head.

"I'll sleep on the way. If that's all, then?"

As Caine nodded evenly, Graham came to his feet, "Fair enough. Thank you, Setter. Very decent of you..."

Graham turned away from the First Lord before Caine could say anything in reply, but came shoulder to shoulder with Felix. The cat nodded to him, "I'll walk you to the landing bay. That alright, Setter?"

"Indeed, thank you Savanna. And good hunting to you, Graham."

The human nodded once without looking back, then the pair left the lounge at a brisk pace.

Caine watched the ArcLieutenant General and his friend leave, then turned back to the window and took a deep breath as his solitude was restored.

Felix was right. They were making this fight as Earthers, he couldn't get caught in despair and doubt his own confidence or abilities. He had appointed himself to the position of First Lord because he was the best at his craft, and now all Earthers everywhere needed him to stand fast.

Nostalgia was beginning to stab at him, that was true. Part of him missed the old days when this had been a fight to save Earth, when he'd spent his work days at Admiralty House and his nights at home with his family... those were times when the cause was clear and death was easier to justify. Now things were increasingly complex, the threat to Earth's safety only one element among a myriad of reasons to press on. In so many ways, it seemed the basic tenets of Earther philosophy were all that was holding his mission together.

The Earthers were defending their home out here — even if it was a month away. And they'd also given their word to protect Genesis and help the Larosians; and when Earthers made promises, they kept them — no matter what. So Caine would work to his last breath to defeat the Kroggs, as would the Earthers. They had accepted him as their leader, and now as he made decisions on their behalf they followed him, trusted him, and died for him.

He had to justify their trust and their losses. And to do that, he'd have to win a war, and return his people to a time when concerns centered simply on living a good, happy life.

That was something he couldn't do if he was wrought with doubt. They'd have to fight on.

So *he* had promised, so *they* would do. And many would still have to die.

• • •

"You just about got to him, I think," Felix said smoothly as he and Graham walked through *Orion* to the flight deck.

Graham frowned slightly and glanced sideways at his Earther companion, "I don't take your meaning."

Felix donned a sad smile and met the human's gaze, "He's been doubting himself, doubting his suitability for his job. As though there's an alternative."

With something of a scowl, Graham looked away from his walking companion, "Well it was a bloody enough fight — surely the cost makes every Earther doubt."

"Makes us learn, Graham. How to do it better next time, but not how to give up. Remember we lost half the Second Fleet at Genesis, and today nine of every ten Earthers who joined the fight didn't come back. We don't overlook those numbers, believe me, but we don't brood over them either. Ours is a fleet of volunteers — everyone knows the stakes, and it makes it easier to accept sacrifice..."

"Slaughter, you mean?" Graham cut Felix off with a tone laced with fatigue.

The Earther Admiral cocked an eyebrow as they rounded the last turn in the corridor and arrived at the bay, "Yes, slaughter. But you know what, Graham, it's a slaughter that we endured because it furthered our objective. It helped us keep our promise to you, and to the Larosians, and to ourselves. Our people made that sacrifice knowingly and willingly, and we're not bitter about that."

Graham stopped as he passed through the hatch, turning to face Felix as the cat came through, "With respect, Savanna, you didn't see every last one of your ships wiped out. And for the record, as a human speaking, it's not your attitude that irks me. It's that you Earthers always have things work out for you. It's that you always have the cavalry show up in time to save the last heroic veterans, and that you don't lose Admirals hand over fist like we do. I think it's commendable that you keep fighting, but it'd be a hell of a lot more commendable if you did it after you suffered what we suffer."

Felix's eyes hardened slightly, "*Half* the fleet at Genesis, Graham. And this *slaughter* here. And attrition on this whole campaign. But we're in our first war, and we're living through it better than your people, the veterans of war. That's it, is it Graham?"

The junior Manchester nodded shortly, "Maybe it is. A slap in the face. Your first time out and you're not only idealistic and naive, you're making it *work*, while I'm off to chase my sister into the fringes and hope she isn't dead. And Caitie Hargreaves just died, along with every other flag officer and just about every other human in this system. And your folks lived, and are willing to do it again? You should bloody well know better than to want to keep going... I want to say that your idealism should be tempered by bloody damned reality..."

"But we're idealistic and still survive the reality. And that hurts," Felix quietly finished the thought for Graham, and the human, not quite realizing that his breathing was heavy, nodded.

"Indeed."

Savanna Felix released a deep sigh and looked across the flight deck for a moment. As easily as they communicated with these humans, there were still areas that didn't seem to connect. Perhaps in time...

"Well take solace in this, Graham. We're good fighters, and we know that. But we also know we're still riding a tide of luck. Personally I chalk it up to fighting an enemy that didn't know we existed until nine months ago, and was already losing a war anyway. But Setter's convinced, Andra's convinced, and I'm convinced, that our advantage is nearing its end. This fight proved that. The Kroggs have gotten our number, and they're going to make us pay even more dearly for each further step we take."

The human frowned, "You keep that quiet, do you? And what will you do when all your luck runs out? Will you understand what I'm talking about?"

Again Felix smiled sadly, "We understand *now*, Graham. And when our luck runs out, we'll keep fighting. We keep our word."

A bad feeling was starting to come over Graham as this conversation wound down, and he frowned now, "Without luck. And you think you were lucky today? With all these losses?"

Felix nodded, "We *were* lucky today. Maybe for the last day."

Graham then started to see what Felix was implying — the Earthers, the young, idealist race had been carrying this war effort squarely on its shoulders, fully aware of the ramifications. They were skilled and wise fighters, they were maddeningly idealistic some days, and they were *lucky*. But luck was like momentum — it changed hands.

"We're just trying to get as far as we can before our luck runs out," Felix almost seemed to hear Graham's thoughts, and the junior Manchester let out a sigh and nodded gravely.

"And when that time comes?" he asked in low tones.

Savanna Felix's sad smile remained, "Then we fight harder, Graham. We do what we said we'd do. And many more of us will die doing it... because it must be done."

The consequences of Earther idealism, Graham realized. They had made a promise and they *knew* the time was coming when they'd have to pay for it. Even more than they had today, perhaps...

"I... I'm sorry..." Graham frowned as he said the words, but Felix held up his hand and shook his head.

"You understand, I think. Now you best get going — good luck out there!"

Graham opened his mouth to say more, but Felix gave him a last nod and stepped away, heading for his pinnace.

At last Graham did understand.

But his heart was no lighter as he went to his pinnace.

CHAPTER 50

Flame slid out of energy drive with the slightest of tremors, three new make-shift reactors taking the strain of translation with only minor signs of potential explosion. Claw still didn't plan on pushing the sloop's field out to 200 percent to evade detection, or going into energy-hyper, so the quickly-built generators were more than adequate for *Flame's* tactical needs in action.

It felt good to have a working ship again. Even if there were some new holes in it.

"Telemetry coming in," the Sensor Chief reported in quiet tones. The sensor suite had been restored to its special work of long-range intelligence gathering, replacement parts for the main grid having been provided by *Atlas'* machine shops.

Claw watched quietly as the main bridge holo tank lit with the information the scanners were now bringing in. Three Dreadnoughts and eight Destroyers within sensor range — nothing unexpected there. Two Destroyers were far out from the planetary orbital planes, probably acting as pickets against any light force that might happen into the system.

Well, what was about to hit this base was anything *but* light.

"One of the Destroyers is turning to engage us, skipper," the Sensor Chief's voice heightened marginally.

"Beat to quarters," Claw turned to the Signal Officer. "Send our telemetry to *Atlas*."

Fox's eyes narrowed as the battle plot blinked into life showing the Krogg force in the system. The first time an Allied squadron had entered this region of space, it had been smashed by hopeless odds. Now the tables were turning.

"Carriers to hold to the rear, all ships reduce to normal drives."

Nodding at the Captain's orders, Mister Gunth, *Atlas'* grizzled Cruising Master, tapped the lion at helm gently on the shoulder, and the Third Rate erupted from an energy ball into real space.

Aboard *Vulcan*, Thena Venus acknowledged the orders with a simple nod to her Cruising Master, who in turn ordered the 74 out of energy drive. *Vulcan* and *Atlas* maneuvered smoothly into line abreast.

Captains Hobbes and Locke simultaneously brought their carriers — *Engadine* and *Monarch* — out of energy drive behind the pair of 74s, their boat crews sitting in their ships and waiting for the range to close.

Sarah gave the orders herself on the bridge of *Joseph Barron*, and the Superdreadnought smoothly eased out of flux drive, its tubes opening to space and missiles rolling into launch position. Edging up into the line abreast with *Atlas* and *Vulcan*, the Genesis ship slowed to wait for the Freetowners.

Standing on the bridge with her, Pat watched with a certain pride as those renegade cruisers and Destroyers slid into a line abreast ahead of the capital ships.

James commanded the first division of the Freetown Squadron from the bridge of *Archangel Sword*, his additional ships spreading in a line abreast to the advanced Battlecruiser's starboard side. His heavier group would be responsible for covering the Carriers if the Kroggs made a run at them.

Audrey sat in *Grendelsbane City's* command chair and directed the second division of the Freetown Squadron as it strung out into line abreast off her Heavy Cruiser's port beam. Since the Earther and human capital ships could likely handle themselves against the Krogg Dreadnoughts, her force would act as screening, leaving the larger and faster escorts to the more vulnerable Carriers.

And on *Flame's* bridge, Chronos Claw watched the Krogg picket Destroyer come into gun range. Unlike the last time he'd encountered Krogg escorts, his ship was in almost full working order today. 'Almost' meaning sixty-six percent of full, but all things being equal, he wasn't going to split hairs.

Well, that was actually more like splitting bricks, but who cared anyway. Stupid clichés.

"Turn us ninety degrees to port, run out starboard broadside," he said quietly, and *Flame's* Master turned the small sloop hard, taking advantage of its still-high maneuverability.

The Krogg Destroyer came straight in, spitting a half dozen spines at the sloop as it came around. Four missed, two glanced off shields, and then the little ship replied with its own tiny broadside. Energy shot stunned the Destroyer as it advanced, knocking it slightly off course.

Flame rolled hard, the port guns firing almost directly after the starboard, and as the Destroyer tried to right itself in space a second wave slapped it back.

As Claw ordered his ship around to engage his bow chaser, the competition came to an abrupt end — *Grendelsbane City* closed range and vented forty missiles at the small, battered Destroyer. The heavier warheads provided by the ex-Genesis vessel tore the small Krogg ship apart in a telepathic shriek.

Atlas, *Vulcan*, and *Joseph Barron* were already moving ahead fast, Audrey's ship rejoining their forward screening line as they did so. The Carriers and James' division followed behind at some distance.

Moving into loose formation to the starboard of *Grendelsbane City*, *Flame* continued to carefully scan the inner system. The three Dreadnoughts and the remaining Destroyers were coming out to meet their attackers. The Dreadnoughts looked to be smaller, older, wounded vessels — not fit for the long-distance drive to Gibraltar.

The Destroyers seemed to be equally inefficient breeds — they were the sort designed to fight Larosians, not Earthers. That would make things easier.

From the bridge of *Joseph Barron*, Sarah closely watched the movements of the Krogg defenders. They were abandoning their ship broods and feeding facilities entirely, expecting to meet two groups of battleships as they came out. The Carriers appeared from long range to be proper ships of the line, after all.

Glancing up at Pat, she smiled, "I think I've got an idea."

The big Irishman cocked his eyebrow — he'd never actually been on the bridge of a ship flying Sarah's flag, despite their close relationship. And she hadn't been smiling much lately either, for that matter.

Fox paid moderate attention as *Monarch* and *Engadine* dropped back into energy drive, gently letting their fields out to 140 percent — just enough to make precise detection difficult without putting too much strain on *Monarch's* reactors.

Accelerating past the rest of the squadron, the two Carriers followed Sarah's suggestion and entirely avoided any gun action.

The escorts that screened for the Krogg Dreadnoughts were coming closer: seven Destroyers menacing Audrey's division of four and *Flame*. Yet those numbers were misleading — two of Audrey's vessels were cruisers, and as James brought the rest of the Freetown force up to full speed and rejoined her, the Kroggs were suddenly outnumbered and grossly outgunned.

An advanced Battlecruiser, two Heavies, a Light, four Destroyers and a crack sloop against the runts of the Krogg Destroyer force.

The missile fire began at extreme range, the Freetowners forcing the Kroggs to break defensive formation to evade. Diving, peeling off, or climbing, the Destroyers were chased singly or in pairs by the Freetown ships, while *Flame* dropped back to take station just above *Atlas* in the center of the advancing van — just in case.

No longer divided by lighter units, the Dreadnoughts and the capital ships came together hard. Third Rates weren't traditionally gun-to-gun matches for Dreadnoughts, though that seldom mattered in action. Now the issue was even less pressing, as these Krogg Dreadnoughts were old and suffering.

As *Joseph Barron's* tubes vented missiles at the Dreadnought approaching opposite it in formation, the two 74s, well honed from months of work together in Felix's 301ˢᵗ Battle Squadron, came hard to port and let loose their heavy broadside into their opponents. Rolling to deliver second salvoes, the Third Rates found that their targets were turning and running before the tide of fire coming at them.

Shot slammed into their rear, as did missiles, but they retreated quickly, giving the Allies no time to follow up. Five Destroyers fled with them — only *Grendelsbane* and *Sword* scoring kills in the seconds-long melee. No significant damage had been suffered by the Allies.

But the Kroggs were hoping to consolidate and make a strong defense from their space broods and grazing yards. So he'd have to cope with that before deciding the Allied war effort was going to be fine.

Or maybe *he* wouldn't have to deal with it at all.

Captain Ronax Hobbes had a fundamentally different Carrier philosophy than Captain Tom Locke, but when it came to hitting stationary targets, the issues of deployment range, the role of the Carrier in a gunfight, and recovery speed were all essentially irrelevant.

For days, the elite boat crews on both *Engadine* and *Monarch* had seen no action, while the ships' machine shops had assembled replacements for the boats lost in their previous action against the Krogg raiding group. Now these boats hurtled from the sides of their vessels at high speed, their guns ready.

It took forty-five seconds for the boats to shake themselves into a solid formation, and then in waves they charged in on the Krogg base. Well-aimed strings of energy shot ripped into the stations from point-blank range, the anti-capital ship weapons on those installations swinging into action but helplessly missing the tiny vessels.

The Dreadnoughts were returning with the Freetown renegades and *Joseph Barron* chasing them closely. In the face of what appeared to be two large battleships, these old Dreadnoughts hesitated briefly, cutting their speed and allowing the humans to overtake their escorts for a second round.

With the heavy lasers of the Superdreadnought joining the fight this time, the five Krogg Destroyers were rapidly shattered. The elite Freetown forces, backed by the equally keen *Joseph Barron*, were simply too much for those small ships.

The Dreadnoughts ignored that fight to their rear and began to accelerate towards their base again, only to have their path blocked abruptly as *Atlas*, *Vulcan*, and *Flame* dropped from energy drive alongside the Carriers. Combined, the five Earther ships delivered an abrupt, heavy broadside.

The lead Krogg capital ship was torn apart by the massive volley, and the second was shattered by fire from the humans to the rear. The last surviving Dreadnought, least damaged of the trio, turned hard away and put on as much speed as possible for its older hull.

The Freetowners, their ships being the fastest, attempted to make chase, but the Dreadnought slipped into hyper.

As Fox watched all this from *Atlas'* bridge, he became aware of the Krogg installations now being strafed by the gunboats.

"All vessels, engage the stations," he concluded quietly, and both the First Lieutenant and the Signal Officer nodded in turn.

Atlas and *Vulcan* engaged first, hitting the large ship brood — the essential growth chamber where Krogg ships could be birthed. Impotent spines clattered off the 74s' shields as their broadsides opened up, and quickly *Joseph Barron's* missiles added to the fray.

The brood, massive and well armored, withstood the onslaught briefly, only crumpling when James moved his division into close range and began lobbing point-blank missiles and heavy lasers into its enormous womb.

As the brood began to come apart, Audrey's division joined *Flame* and the boats of *Monarch* in a fast run at the feeding facility — a massive unarmed ball of biomatter suitable for consumption by Krogg ships. Such 'grazing' stations substantially extended Krogg ships' range, but they were chronically vulnerable.

Firing upon it was like blowing up a sixteen-billion-ton ball of cheese.

These two installations quickly disappeared from Fox's battle plot, and as they did he glanced over to Mister Gunth with a nod, "Well, Master, we've done our bit."

The ever-grizzled Earther offered a nod in reply.

Just as long as the Allies had fared as well at Gibraltar... but surely they had.

They had Earther timing, Fox decided. *And some luck. They did fine.*

CHAPTER 51

Nine days after the battle of Gibraltar, *Pope John Patrick* came out of flux drive in the system that housed the Kroggs' forward base. With it, the 435th Battle Squadron and the Provisional Carrier Group under Commodore Garvin Jardaw were ready for action against a possibly superior force, but their preparations for action were entirely unnecessary.

Forton and *Vance*, pickets posted by the Freetown Squadron, met them as they formed up. The two Destroyers guided the Allied reinforcements further in system, where the renegade force and Fox's small squadron lay at anchor.

As the Carrier group slowed near *Engadine* and *Monarch*, and the 435th formed in two lines abreast and went to station-keeping above *Joseph Barron*, Graham Manchester sent a general hail to the detached forces.

Fox picked it up, and as Graham paced the bridge of his Superdreadnought, the young Captain appeared on his main screen, "ArcLieutenant-General, glad to see you!"

Graham was still the concerned, ever-worried brother who'd left Gibraltar. Eight days of hard travel hadn't done much to ease his fears about the fate of his sister, though he had at least gotten past his residual problems with the Earthers. Time and sleep did wonders... but seeing his sister alive and well would do more good than that.

With this in mind, Graham kept his tone taut, "Fox, what happen here?"

The dapper fox smiled at his counterpart, "We eliminated the base, sir. One Dreadnought escaped, but we had no losses."

Graham found his breath slightly short, "*None*, Captain?"

Felix's comments tried to sting at Graham's brain again, but he batted them away.

Fox shook his head, "None. We've also rescued ArcBrigadier Conroy, and several hundred survivors from *Bishop*. Right now I *believe* ArcGeneral Manchester is asleep on *Joseph Barron* — just about to end my night watch, you see."

Graham paused, turning from the monitor, "ArcColonel, have my pinnace prepared for launch."

Fox watched from the screen as the crew on *John Patrick's* bridge set about giving the orders, and then smiled as Graham turned back to him.

"Captain, I'll be going to meet my sister. If you'd like to conference with Commodore Jardaw of *Highlander*, it would be greatly appreciated."

Fox nodded, "I'll call the Freetown Captains and Commodore Maximane to the meeting. Just let me know when it'd be convenient for you."

Graham's eyes narrowed — not really at Fox, but at the thought of what would come before any meeting, "Garvin can go in my place, Fox. I've got some arguing to do, I think."

The Captain grinned and nodded, "Good luck."

The link cut, and Graham walked swiftly from the bridge.

Garvin Jardaw was last to enter *Atlas'* main briefing room for this early morning meeting, having come straight off his pinnace from *Highlander*. As the doors opened before him, he immediately recognized the figures awaiting him: the infamous Fox Magnus and–

"Garvin!" James came to his feet with a grin, Audrey following closely.

Both Freetowners extended hands to the polar bear, who took them each with a smile of his own, "We seem to be tied together by fate, us three."

Fox chuckled from across the room, coming to his feet as well, "It seems to be a pattern, Garvin. They saved me a year ago, and now I seem to come across them frequently."

The smaller Captain approached the broad-shouldered bear and offered his hand as well, "I just read your logs from *Highlander* — bad business at Gibraltar, but you did well."

The bear shrugged in reply, "We made good time and we got there when it counted..."

"How very Earther of you," Audrey patted him on the back as everyone drifted back to their seats.

Jardaw offered a somber smile, "Many still died, I'm afraid..." Then someone caught his eye, "I'm sorry, Audrey, excuse me..."

Draco Maximane was floating next to the table at the other side of the briefing room, and with an uncommonly broad smile, Jardaw lumbered quickly over to the Commodore and extended a hand, "Draco, it's so very good to see you! But you do look rather rough!"

The Commodore grinned at Jardaw and took the offered hand as soon as it was in range, "Didn't have you around to look after me, Garvin. But that's not a mistake I'll make again — I hear you're running 64s as escorts for Carriers now?"

The bear nodded, not noticing as the rest of the occupants of the room frowned at this friendly greeting with the Commodore.

"Well that's good," Maximane's smile broadened. "I'm going to request you be promoted up to Commodore to head my escort force then..."

Maximane detected the confusion on Fox's face as he leaned back and released Jardaw's hand, then he looked to James, "Garvin was my First Lieutenant in *Apollo*, James. He suggested we follow you that day with Chen..."

James opened his mouth, closed it, frowned, smiled, then rushed across the floor to shake Jardaw's hand again, "Damn me, I didn't even know! It's a small universe..."

They talked for ten minutes more before eventually finding themselves seats at the table.

"Well, we seem to have weathered the storms," Audrey began as they sat, still smiling at some of Jardaw's and Maximane's tales from their *Apollo* days.

Jardaw nodded slowly, his expression already sobering, "We weren't sure whether you'd done alright against the base, so the First Lord sent us to check."

Fox cocked a curious eyebrow, "He didn't send a sloop out first?"

Jardaw shook his head, "We only had a few at Gibraltar when the Kroggs hit, and they were all put out of action in the fight."

"Just as well," James said evenly, glancing at Chronos. "Energy-hyper can be moody."

Jardaw's eyebrows went up at the remark, and James nodded slowly under his questioning eyes.

Chronos Claw filled in the details, "Blew two of our reactors. The stress on them seemed to be cumulative — and based on the fatigue on the one surviving generator, it's virtually irreparable. *Flame* will need new proper reactors from the yards before I can head out for my next mission."

Jardaw absorbed the news silently, then nodded, "Seemed a bit too easy, the whole energy-hyper thing."

Maximane took his turn to shrug, "We contemplated trying to outfit a signal drone with it, but we don't have the equipment. We decided to stay here and wait for whatever was coming instead. There's a pod on its way to Gibraltar... actually, it's probably there by now. But we didn't want to go ourselves — in case the worst had occurred, and the Krogg Fleet was there waiting for us."

Jardaw offered another nod — it made sense to hold position in that case. Without knowing whether Gibraltar had been taken, it was safer for the mixed squadron to stay put and wait for some indication of the outcome than to run blindly into the unknown.

Fox was already nodding as Jardaw thought it, "As you understand, Garvin, we felt better being on the defensive here than trying a sortie."

The big polar bear nodded again, "That's part of what we were counting on when we came straight this way. Graham was betting you and ArcGeneral Manchester would hold your place and wait a while before moving, so he didn't slow to examine the systems along the way."

"Speaking of which," James frowned, "Where is the ArcLieutenant-General?"

"Open the damned door!"

Graham's fists pounded Sarah's hatch.

"Sarah, open this thing this *instant!*"

A few passing crew paused to look curiously at Graham as he hammered their fleet commander's door, but his sharp glare and ArcLieutenant-General pips sent them back to their duties.

"Open — *open!*"

The hatch abruptly slid open, Graham's fists swinging into unoccupied air before he could get them back to his sides in a less-than-graceful motion.

"About time... oh. Hi Pat."

The big Irishman, wearing a large, light-blue robe, stepped out into the corridor.

"Graham, how are you?"

Graham blinked, Pat's abrupt appearance seeming to neutralize his rage, "Um. Not too bad, I suppose. You look well."

"Yeah, I'm good, I think."

"All things considered, I suppose."

"Yeah, that'd be the way I'd put it."

"Good show. So she's sleeping then?"

Pat shrugged and nodded, "She seems to have been keeping herself up way too much over the past few weeks."

Graham nodded, "Know the feeling. Alright then... well, I'll call again later."

"Sure," Pat shrugged.

"Right. Oh, and when she wakes up tell her I'm going to take a piece out of her hide. You know the story, eh? Recklessly endangering herself and so on..."

Pat nodded, "I'd help, but I'm biased."

Graham grinned, "No offense to you, eh Pat. I just mean–"

The big Irishman held up a hand, "I know. We're fine."

"Good."

Pat nodded, "Okay then."

"Yep. We should get some food and catch up some time."

"I'm tired and wearing a bathrobe. So not right now," Pat didn't seem particularly conversational.

"Of course — I didn't mean to–"

"Have a good night, Graham."

"Er... morning?"

Pat shrugged, "Yeah, whichever."

Stepping back into Sarah's room, he closed the door.

And Graham, slightly flabbergasted, turned and walked away.

EPILOGUE

Orion took its place in line, its big engines humming as it prepared to accelerate away from Gibraltar. The 101st Battle Squadron was formed in a column behind the massive First Rate, but where in months past that unit alone had gone out to assault the Krogg lines, now 200 warships were moving into columns alongside.

A hundred ships would remain behind at Gibraltar, the nucleus for Ursla's newly-organized Second Fleet. Caine would take his 200-ship First Fleet out to a point only five days from the Allied forward base where he would engage a collection of Krogg raiding groups that had begun to assemble in the wake of their fleet's destruction.

By the time he returned, most of the fleet would be assembled at Gibraltar, ready to be reestablished into traditional divisions. Four spearheads would thus launch from Gibraltar in a couple of weeks' time. While only six weeks before this post had been home to only a few squadrons, *thousands* of Allied ships would be standing by there to press outward.

And a sizable force would *always* be kept far enough to the rear to defend Earth, Genesis, and Gibraltar.

Caine wouldn't be outplayed a second time.

Aboard *Tonnant*, Savanna Felix spent most of his time reassigning vessels from half-wrecked squadrons. There were so many below-strength forces now under the Allied command that the term 'squadron' was coming to mean anything from two to fifteen vessels.

A desk Admiral for so long, Felix was the best officer to remedy this, and he was glad to reapply his old skills after so long on a bridge. He wouldn't give up the Third Fleet command for anything, but he could set it aside for a few weeks.

Indeed, he'd have to get back out soon — check in on Caine and Ursla and everyone else, make sure they held their heads up and fought this war as the Earthers they were. He knew they'd be just fine if they did. It was his strategy, and he was sticking to it.

In the Gibraltar system itself, Commodore Karl Kandam took command of the *Gibraltars* in their entirety, while Captain Trax Earon was detailed Chief

Boat Ops Officer for the front. The contributions made by both Earthers had been amply recognized.

Commodore Garvin Jardaw retained not only *Highlander* but a squadron of 64s built around both his ship and *Elephant* — the vessels that had appeared at just the right time during the Gibraltar action. His orders were not to join a specific fleet, but instead to attach to the First Carrier Group, now under the command of a recovering and determined Rear Admiral Draco Maximane.

Campania and *Ark Royal*, the next two Carriers in *Engadine's* line, had been rushed up to join the fleet, giving it a combined Carrier strength of nine ships. The First consisted of the three massive *Engadine*-class ships and *Monarch* and *Diadem*. The *Boadecia*-class Carriers made up the Second Squadron under Commodore Dudley Revers, and were soon to be reinforced by further refitted ships of their class. And more Carriers were rolling from Earth yards.

Captain Chronos Claw got the new reactors he needed for *Flame*, as well as command of a sloop squadron attached to the First Fleet for reconnaissance and escort. While *Orion's* engines spun up and the Battle Squadron prepared to accelerate from Gibraltar, Claw and his sloops were already far out ahead of the force, advancing under standard energy drive to ensure a safe route for the capital ships and frigates.

An ambush wasn't expected, but as Caine was so ready to acknowledge, it remained *possible*. He wouldn't take a chance, and that meant Chronos Claw and his crew were sent straight from Gibraltar's yards to the front.

They would hardly say 'no' to the action.

To the rear, James Stanton and Audrey DeBrooke were leading their ships home, loaded with supplies for Freetown, including the first components for a complete orbital repair yard of their own. Their squadron of light ships was too mixed to integrate into any fleet, but as independent privateers, they could do much to protect the shipping lines between Earth and Genesis — a mission they had gladly accepted.

They had returned to their pursuit of swashbuckling romance, action, and a new life.

Major Beckett Lupus took command of the marines of *Atlas* on the same day Fox Magnus accepted his promotion to Commodore. The ex-Sergeant Major recovered from his wounds with remarkable speed, and after a very brief period of consideration, Caine took it upon himself to give the wolf a promotion suitable to his actions.

Bishop's former squad of wolves now served as *Atlas'* elite troop, and Fox was glad to have them aboard. He and Lupus, not well known to each other, were getting along quite well, despite the change in duties for both.

Fox's new squadron, the 186th, was part of Caine's fleet, and now it was to be the first in the column to launch itself outward. *Atlas, Vulcan, Fuji, Dominant, Téméraire, Jupiter, Lucifer,* and *Captain,* proceeding in that order, began to accelerate into energy drive at Fox's order.

On the newly established flag deck of *Gibraltar One,* Graham watched them go, then began to order the anchoring assignments for ships that were remaining. Gibraltar was his system now. Kandam commanded its stations, Earon its boats, and Gillian Hodge — who he continued to apologize profusely to for his inattentions during his *moody* period — its marines. But Graham was the one in charge of tying all those elements together.

Now that the world was marginally sane again, he could handle that. He kept ships rotating in and out of the repair yards, kept the yards going... well, he did everything the mountain of paper on his desk told him to do.

He didn't want to watch the luck run out just yet, so he'd do his very best to perpetuate it.

Pat's Pirates were gone, but a new force was assembled for the intrepid commander. Pat had mixed feelings about the whole idea — his ships, which had been passed to his command from Sarah after the defection at Earth, and had remained with him since, simply *couldn't* be replaced.

But in a time of war there could be substitutions, and he was willing to live with change for the sake of the war effort.

Though this time he wouldn't just get one squadron. The ArcLieutenant-General had amply proven his instincts by finding the Kroggs before the attack was launched, and his combat record was excellent. Both facts certainly warranted the thirty-six Battlecruisers now under his permanent command — the 444th, 445th, and 446th, 'Pat's Posse' of 'Pirates', 'Plunderers' and 'Pillagers'. He'd sat down with a dictionary for ten minutes before coming up with that little series.

Of course, anyone who didn't know Pat could easily assume his new command was granted him only because he was sleeping with the Fleet Commander. Literally, he was snoring on one side of the bed while Sarah lay contemplating her life on the other. Her letter of marquee had been torn up, and she was in command of the Fourth Fleet again — all Genesis ships, rallying now from every corner of the frontier. She wouldn't have to deploy forward until Caine returned, so until then she could relax and try to figure out exactly what was going on in her mind.

She'd been welcomed back by the Allied Fleet, but to her that charity was almost worse than a condemning of her actions. She'd run out on these people, her squadron and her ships had died without her, and she'd left Caine... she had to make it up to everyone. They said it didn't matter, but they were wrong. All of them.

And Caine felt he had gotten past his doubts. Standing on the main observation deck within *Orion's* superstructure, he forced his mind to press on. The 175-gun ship of the line was near the rear of the fleet, leaving it about twenty minutes from departure as he watched enhanced pictures of the ships departing ahead.

This time he would leave nothing to the Kroggs. He wouldn't be paranoid and refuse risk, but he wouldn't be foolish and generate advantages for his foe. He'd gotten carried away by success, then almost overcome by despair, and he knew it.

Now he had to steel himself. He would win this war, and do it as the Earther he was...

"You'll do fine, Setter."

Caine cocked an eyebrow and turned as Ursla came to a stop behind him. Surprisingly enough, he hadn't even realized his old friend had joined him here, and now he smiled warmly.

"Yes well, I hope I do a little *better* than fine, if that's not too much to ask. But there are days, Andra, when I just don't quite feel I've got it. Nothing I can't get past... but there are days."

With an understanding smile of her own, Ursla let her eyes drift to the images of the departing fleet, "Feel like there are more of those days lately, do you?"

A mild shrug came from the First Lord, "Lately, yes. But you know how that is; we just keep going, don't let them stop us from doing what we're out here to do."

"And remember the reason you named yourself First Lord, and the reason none of the other Admiralty Lords have superseded you is because we all know you're having fewer of those days than the rest of us. Don't doubt your position, you're the best we've got," Ursla's words drew Caine's eyes to the floor before him.

Noting her friend's quiet, Ursla elected to change her tack, "Usually at this point I'm the one coming to you for philosophy lessons — all those equations we keep coming up with, you know."

Despite himself, Caine smiled, "We should write a book."

"A series is more like it," Ursla said dryly. "And end each book with the equation we figured out."

Caine's eyebrow cocked, "Sounds sort of... cheesy. But we could put our pictures on the covers, that'd be quaint."

Ursla chuckled.

She was, in the end, right. There was no one else for this job but him

— he'd known that decades ago when he'd joined the Admiralty, and he knew it now. Repeating it to himself a few times would just keep it fresh in his mind.

"And if the humans are worrying you, don't listen to them. Savanna told me what Graham was saying to you, and it's all human-perspective stuff... they still can't accept that we're not bound by their nature," Ursla's words were somewhat unexpected, and they drew Caine's eyes back to hers.

"They're having trouble with that, but worse, they're being frustrated by the fact that we're having more success on the campaign than they are... and that we can be the young, idealistic race and still fight the bloodiest war in known galactic history. I hope they come to understand our commitment, and our willingness to see it through... but somehow I doubt they will until our good fortune fails and we keep going," Caine's words were darker than before, almost disappointed.

A slow nod was Ursla's answer, and for a moment the two stood silently on the deck.

The humans were such a paradox — even now, nearly two years after that supposed human equation had been formulated, Caine couldn't fully grasp their thinking...

"Hang on..." Ursla's abrupt words drew Caine's attention back to her. "The privateers get us. That's a start. I don't think they're fully comfortable with us yet, but look at all they did out here — they made sure we got the *Gibraltars*, they collected the working pod from *Bishop*, and they gave you most of the escort force you needed to send out with Sarah. They readily made choices the same way Earthers would..."

"Maybe for different reasons, though," Caine added thoughtfully, but Ursla shook her head.

"That's not the point. Graham wouldn't even have let Sarah go, given the choice, but when you asked the privateers to help, they *went*. They're human renegades, Setter, and not in the way all the Genesis people mean. They're a bit more like us, maybe they're a sign of what can become of this Alliance."

Caine's eyes lowered again. The Earthers had created the opening for the Freetowners, and Ursla was right, James Stanton and Audrey DeBrooke were certainly coming to understand the freedom and responsibility that came with the Earther-style life.

So perhaps awareness of that type of commitment on the part of the Earthers would spread among the humans over time. Perhaps Sarah would even understand it, given time to reconcile herself with her actions as a privateer.

Those renegade humans were a bridge between Earther ways and those of Genesis, and perhaps their success was proof that Caine wasn't getting things wrong after all. They'd broken free not only of their own society, but from some of its prejudices. They were rebelling against humanity's seemingly self-imposed anger at the universe.

"So this is our equation, then?" Caine finally looked up at Andra, and she cracked a smile.

"Yes, I suppose it is. When you can bring around the humans, even the privateers, then there's hope. What do you want, then... the *bringing-around* equation?"

Despite himself, Caine managed to smile at that prospect, "Well that sounds silly."

Ursla grinned, "So, wise gray one, what equation is it then?"

Chuckling softly, Caine glanced back to his ships beyond the glass.

"The renegade equation."

APPENDIX A: CHARACTERS

Hopefully you're getting used to this by now... these are the main characters to watch out for in *The Renegade Equation*, or if they don't figure prominently in this book, you can bet you'll be seeing them again in tales to come.

Broadpaw, Varnia – Captain
Recently promoted from *Orion's* lower port side gun deck, Varnia Broadpaw is an officer on the rise. Her leadership talents have been noted in many circles within the Navy, and led to her commissioning to Savanna Felix's *Tonnant*. She now serves as the Flag Captain of the 301st Battle Squadron, and the entire Third Fleet. And yes, she's Varnon's daughter. And no, nepotism didn't get her the command — she's one of the best ship-handlers in the service.

Broadpaw, Varnon – Admiral
A wolf who fancies himself one of the funniest Earthers in the fleet, Varnon Broadpaw had served as the commanding officer of the Third Fleet up to the Battle of the Pluto Orbital Plane, and second in command under Ursla with the Second Fleet at the Battle of Genesis. With his old Third Fleet now under the command of Savanna Felix, Varnon has taken up command of a battle group on the broad front line of the Allied advance. Ironically, the force he routinely has assembled and under his command is larger than what most of the fleet Admirals maintain, and he's making good use of the concentration. His flag still flies from the 125-gun *Algenon*, and he's a real bane for the Kroggs.

Caine, Setter – First Lord of the Admiralty
Setter Caine is still the most important officer in the Allied Fleet. His planning and insight have helped the Earthers and the humans carry the war to the Kroggs in such a way that the aliens have been unable to concentrate a defense. While the strain of constant warring is showing on both the fleet and on Caine himself, the reality is that he's doing the best possible job in a situation which is wildly unlike anything he'd conceived of only two years before. The humans trust him, the Earthers believe in him, and as he commands his 101st Battle Squadron from *Orion*, he is proving to the Kroggs just how vulnerable they can be.

Cairn, Ami – Commodore
This wolf's exploits aren't directly related to the course of events in this volume, though her name comes up a number of times. A leading frigate Commodore, she flies her flag from *Inferno*, 38. Wesley Prewer is the creator of this intrepid character; my thanks to him for her contributions to the storyline — she will be part of several important events in the Earthers' future.

Conroy, Patrick – ArcBrigadier
Over the months between the Battle of Genesis and the establishment of Gibraltar base, Pat Conroy has managed to improve his reputation as a cruiser commander from its pre-Genesis state of 'exceptional' to a level of 'absolutely incredible'. Skipping the hyperbole, then, the Irishman has remained one of the best cruiser commanders in either fleet, and thus his squadron, 'Pat's Pirates', is one of the most trusted formations available in the war for scouting and screening work. Still commanding his twelve Battlecruisers from *Harbinger Bishop*, Pat is a great space officer, and yes, he and Sarah are still together.

Claw, Chronos – Commander
Having once been First Lieutenant and chief engineer of *Flame*, this cat is the commander of the diminutive sloop. Claw is a fine officer, much like his friend and mentor Fox Magnus, but a little bit more technically inclined. He's been working with Fox over the months since the Battle of Genesis, continually putting *Flame* in the risky situations that have earned it its reputation of daring, and always finding time to tinker with the idea of energy-hyper, a system he's sure will work and everyone else is convinced will blow half the reactors of any ship that tries it.

Cuttar, Ernile — Private
The only reason this bio is here is this: "Ernile" is not pronounced 'Er-nile' with the last half sounding like the river in Egypt. It's pronounced "Er-nil-ee", and before you start wondering what sort of name that is, look up one the First Lords of the British Admiralty named Chatfield... who, now that I look him up again, spelled his first name "Ernle". Forget I mentioned it. But don't forget young Private Cuttar; attached to the most elite formation in the Marine Corps, he has a long future of distinguished service ahead of him.

DeBrooke, Audrey – Captain
Audrey DeBrooke was one of two cruiser ArcColonels saved by Ursla during the defection from the Church, and thereafter, she and her Heavy Cruiser, *Grendelsbane City*, elected to leave the Genesis Navy, owing to a dislike of the manner in which the fleet was seemingly becoming dependent on the Earthers. After joining up with fellow deserter James Stanton of *Archangel Sword*, Audrey

helped save Fox Magnus and *Flame* from Krogg pursuers during its courier run to Earth, and as a reward was commissioned as a privateer by Savanna Felix. After fighting in the Battle of Genesis alongside the Earthers, she and James elected to find a planet to set up as a privateer base. Shortly after the battle the pair located a system and have since been setting up their Freetown colony.

Felar, Kella – Admiral
Sharing command of the First Fleet with Caine, Kella Felar remains one of the Earther Navy's steadiest line admirals. A relatively young cat, she has retained command of a battle group during the campaign thus far, and her force remains one of the most reliable and hard-fighting formations on the Allied side. She flies her flag from *Endymion*, 125 guns.

Felix, Savanna –Admiral
Having proven his tactical skill beyond a doubt during the campaign and Battle of Genesis, this cat took command of Varnon Broadpaw's Third Fleet, once it had been reconstituted (Varnon was out for regeneration at the time). Now operating with his elite 301st Battle Squadron, Felix has a formidable battle record — even though he's fought most of his actions without his two star Captains, Fox Magnus and Thena Venus, who are usually detached for special operations. He still flies his flag from his trusty old 80, *ENS Tonnant.*

Forbes, Jessica – ArcColonel
Pat Conroy's flag ArcColonel in *Harbinger Bishop*, Forbes has been with Pat's Pirates since they were Sarah Manchester's Batron 54 during the Quest. She is a highly skilled combat officer, and over the past months she has proved indispensable to Pat and a great asset to *Bishop*. She is well liked by her crew and well respected by her peers.

Forepaw, Labrador – Captain
Skipper of the venerable 175-gun ship *Orion*, and by extension, Caine's Flag Captain, Lab Forepaw is one of the most trusted officers in the Fleet. Repeatedly rejecting promotion, this canine has remained with his ship in order to keep it in its best fighting trim for the campaign. He is one of the Caine's best friends, and his leadership skills have seen him marked as a First Lord of the future.

Furgus, Jax – Vice Admiral
Jax Furgus is one of those lions with a real reputation. He refuses to die, and moreover, he's just plain... curmudgeonly. Really, he can get as disagreeable as any Earther can get, which admittedly isn't saying much, but suffice it to say he's the rough-around-the-edges member of the inner circle of Admirals on the front line. Still commanding his notoriously short-lived 64s, he's managed to

get through the campaign to the establishment of Gibraltar without having to change ships. The Admiralty is still talking of requiring him to move up to a 74 next time he loses a vessel... he'll have something grumpy to say about that. And everyone will laugh when he says it.

Grieve, Andros – General
General Grieve doesn't factor into this volume much at all. Presently, he's conducting operations against a Krogg-occupied planet on the extreme left of the front with the Guards Brigade (both battalions of both the 1st and 3rd Guards Regiments). Like most of the operations to oust Kroggs from surviving planets along the front, this one is proving more protracted than the marines would like. But don't forget about old Andros — he's rather important.

Hargreaves, Caitlin – ArcLieutenant General
A veteran of the Genesis Navy, Caitie Hargreaves distinguished herself at the Battle of Genesis as one of Sarah's chief officers. Over the past months of campaign she has cemented her reputation as an excellent combat commander, and hers is one of the few consistently successful Battle Squadrons in the Genesis Fleet. The Superdreadnought *Pope Michael Dalton* is her flagship.

Hastings, Elizabeth – ArcGeneral
Liz is holding the war effort together from Genesis space with little short of a titanic effort of guts and determination. She knows better than most just how much the Genesis Navy is suffering at the hands of the Kroggs, and she's also well aware of how easy a time the Earthers are having in the war against the aliens. While she runs the home-side of the logistical effort keeping her fleet supplied, she's all too conscious of how little a difference her forces seem to be making, and the fact that she can do nothing to help them on the front lines is not sitting well with her. She continues to hope she'll be able to go up to the front for a line command as the campaign wears on, but whether that will be possible remains to be seen.

Hobbes, Ronax – Captain
Ron Hobbes is a steady cat who handles pressure very well, and handles a ship even better. Skippering a 74 over what's come to be called Grieve's Planet, he proved most adept at coordinating orbital-to-ground gun support of General Grieve's brigade-sized operations against a Krogg installation, and was most noted by the Admiralty for his ability to smoothly operate his ship alongside small craft such as marine dropships. These skills earned him reassignment to command of *Engadine*, as such skills will be most useful to the Carrier group. He is known to disagree on Carrier philosophy, however, with Captain Tom Locke of *Monarch*.

Hodge, Gillian – Commandant
The senior field officer of the Genesis Marine Corps, Commandant Hodge has spent much of her time over the months of the campaign supervising the situation at Genesis. With Bingham's government stabilizing and the front broadening, she has recently been ordered forward in order to oversee the employment of Genesis Marines in the field against the Kroggs.

Howler, Cadmus – Corporal
For many years, Cadmus Howler has been a member of Beckett Lupus' elite recon squad. An amiable and capable wolf, he has earned a great deal of respect throughout the fleet as being one of the Earther Marine Corps' best sparrers, and behind only the likes of Andros Grieve and his Sergeant Beckett Lupus, he has come to be renowned as one of the best sword-handlers Earth has ever produced. Perpetually at Lupus' side, he can be expected to rise in fame with the continued exploits of the wolf recon squad.

Jardaw, Garvin – Captain
As First Lieutenant of *Apollo* under Draco Maximane, this polar bear served well at the Battle of Genesis, and thus was recently granted promotion directly to Captain of *Highlander*, 64. As his ship has only just shaken down after a major refit in the Sol yards, he has been detailed to light duty — convoy escort — to give him the opportunity to get used to his new command.

Kandam, Karl – Commodore
Recently recovered from injuries sustained on campaign, Karl Kandam has found himself at the head of the new *Gibraltar* initiative. Over the months of the war since the Battle of Genesis, his 236th Battle Squadron was essentially destroyed in a series of very heavy actions, leaving only his own *Namur* and another 74 fit for service. When Caine required a seasoned officer for service in command of the *Gibraltar* stations, Kandam was both available and qualified, and so now he commands *Gibraltar One*, and will be in charge of all six *Gibraltar* stations, once they're assembled.

Karr, Farley – Captain
In command of *Diadem*, the first of the reconditioned Carriers to be put to space, Karr is a bear of excellent reputation. Having served as a First Lieutenant in Varnon Broadpaw's flagship for several months following the Battle of Genesis, Karr proved to be a highly adaptive and capable officer, and a generally excellent ship-handler. It is expected that he will be a great asset to the Carrier group.

Locke, Tom – Captain
Skippering the second (but fastest) of the reconditioned Earther Carriers,

ENS Monarch, Tom Locke is a very capable cat. His background is in frigates, which has led him to a Carrier philosophy that is rather opposite to that of his fellow Captain, Ron Hobbes, who began in Battleships. While the two disagree philosophically over several aspects of the employment of gunboats, both are excellent skippers, and for all their differences they work splendidly together.

Lupus, Beckett – Sergeant Major
This elite wolf is one of the Earther Marine Corps most seasoned non-coms. Commanding an excellent squad of recon wolves, Beckett Lupus had extensive experience in action at Antarctica, and an important role in the fruitless storming of the Queen's Hive during the Battle of Genesis. He and his squad have recently been seconded to *Harbinger Bishop* to serve as an intelligence-gathering unit for Pat's Pirates.

Magnus, Fox – Commander
Fox Magnus' reputation precedes him wherever he goes. He is the intrepid ex-sloop commander who made the daring run in *Flame* from Genesis to Earth — or almost, anyway — before the Battle of Genesis, and then more importantly (at least for notoriety's sake) was the first Earther to go to the *Bloody Pulsar* on *Genesis One*. Now a Post Captain commanding *Atlas* in Felix's 301st Battle Squadron, he is one of the rising stars of the fleet, and has been getting plum independent assignments, the most recent his operation with *Vulcan* and *Flame* at Galahad's Belt. Some think this dapper Fox is well on his way to being First Lord one day.

Manchester, Graham – ArcBrigadier
The junior Manchester sibling had been looking after Naval affairs in the Genesis system until recently; supporting Liz Hastings in her efforts to manage the war from the rear, he persistently proved his ability as an administrator in the orbitals over Genesis. Lately he's been promoted to be the senior Genesis officer in Gibraltar — a distinguished position that will move him closer to the action, and give his ample ability as an organizer plenty of opportunity to shine. He's also still a bit goofy, at least from time to time.

Manchester, Sarah – ArcGeneral
Sarah has taken full command of the Genesis Fleet on campaign, with Liz preoccupied in Genesis space and most of the old command cadre of officers in the Genesis Fleet dead. As is typical for her, she's taken on *all* the responsibilities of a fleet commander *without* devolving any authority to her staff: from fleet logistics to squadron combat command for her 401st Battle Squadron, she is doing it all on her own. She's been told this isn't wise for her health, but her ultimate concern is not for herself but for the survival of her fleet. Flying her flag still from *Joseph Barron*, she's finding that the war is really draining her.

Maximane, Draco – Commodore
An irrepressible lion, Maximane takes a keen interest in human Naval history, and after excellent service in *Apollo*, 74, at Genesis, he was returned home to recover from wounds. While in Earth space, he became the driving force behind the new Earther gunboat-carrier initiative, and has since been commissioned to the *Engadine* project. Lately, he has been overseeing the shakedown of the Earthers' new Carrier forces in Earth space, and looking forward to leading them into action.

Nightclaw, Dran – Commodore
With Ursla's rise to command of the Second Fleet, her once-Flag Captain Nightclaw was elevated to command the elite 111th frigate squadron. This panther's reputation as an Earther cruiser commander has since come to be heralded above all others — save, perhaps, for Ursla herself. Lately his frigates have been driving ahead of the Allied advance, looking for Kroggs and gathering intelligence for the fleet commanders. *Cerberus* is still his ship, and it remains the most storied cruiser in either Navy.

Peregrine, Kylie – Commodore
Kylie Peregrine is typical of the officers who form the backbone of the Earther Navy; she's intelligent, thoughtful, and when it comes to it, daring and courageous. Her service in the months after the Battle of Genesis upheld the Earther Navy's standard, seeing a series of solid victories with only moderate losses. Lately, her *Gargoyle* was rather badly shot up when her squadron was called in to assist a Genesis Dreadnought group in danger of being overwhelmed by Krogg Destroyers. The action was a success, but both she and her ship were severely mauled; she has returned with her ship to Sol for repairs. She has a very promising career ahead of her.

Redvers, Dudley – Captain
One of two bear Captains in the 901st Provisional Carrier Group (the other being Farley Karr of *Diadem*), Dudley Redvers is another quickly-rising officer of note. Having served as First Lieutenant of Kella Felar's *Endymion* for the entire period of time surrounding the Battle of Genesis, he proved quite adept at handling small craft during the landings of the Moustaffa Bengal's 3rd Guards Battalion at Z82-93. Shortly thereafter, he was transferred to the Carrier Group, and promoted to command of *Boadecia*, first of the larger series of reconditioned Carriers.

Sandpelt, Lang – Lieutenant
Lang Sandpelt joined *Flame* when it was under the orders of Fox Magnus, and when that intrepid commander was promoted up to *Atlas* after the Battle of

Genesis, Lang ended up being promoted as well — to the post of *Flame's* First Lieutenant. Taking the role of Chronos Claw, who was likewise promoted and thus given command of *Flame*, Lang now looks after the engineering section of the sloop — a section, admittedly, that gets plenty of hard work, thanks to *Flame's* reputation for speed and stealth.

Stanton, James – ArcColonel
The co-head of the Freetown Privateers, James has settled well into the renegade existence. Over the past months he's enjoyed the process of building up the privateer colony on Freetown — even the bureaucratic developments have intrigued him. He still hungers for action, though, and at some point he's quite certain he'll have to find his way to the front lines again. He and his advanced Battlecruiser, *Archangel Sword*, are certainly not finished with their Krogg-fighting careers.

Tigar, Artemis – Captain
A consummate professional, this tiger serves as Ursla's Flag Captain in *Agamemnon*. With plenty of experience in combat, including distinguished service in the 150-gun ship during the Battle of the Belt and at the Battle of Genesis, he has earned his posting as chief Captain of the Second Fleet. His remains one of the most prudent and skeptical minds in the Earther Navy when it comes to strategy — no mean claim, to be sure — but at the core, he's still a fighting officer. The Kroggs have learned to respect his ship-handling skill over the past months; he remains the only Earther skipper who has successfully been able to break a corvette formation by ramming.

Ursla, Andra – Admiral
Andra Ursla is the only kodiak bear to attain flag rank in the history of the Earther Navy, and she is Caine's right hand on this campaign. A savvy and highly capable line officer, she officially heads the Second Fleet, and over the past months has commanded *Agamemnon* and the 201st Battle Squadron to glory on many occasions. With the benefit of her experience in command at the Battle of Genesis, she has even more wisdom to offer the Earther service than she did at the Pluto Orbital Plane. The Allied advance has benefited immeasurably from her insights.

Venus, Thena – Captain
Skippering the 74 *Vulcan*, Thena Venus is Fox Magnus' division mate, and partner in crime. She also happens to be a fox, so her sense of adventure matches well with the former sloop commander.

APPENDIX B: EARTHER RANKS

It's become an oft-asked question among readers: how exactly do the ranks of the Earther Navy work? Is there a coherent chart somewhere, or do you make it up as you go? Well of course there's a chart! I just couldn't fit in here. But this will explain things...

First off, there are three tiers to the Earther Navy ranking system; the *Commissioned Officers*, *Warrant Officers*, and *Ratings*. Essentially, each section has its own role; the Commissioned Officers are those in command — they are trained specialists in Naval affairs, and thus they give orders and take charge of various sections. Warrant Officers are a specialist type; they're experts in a field that isn't exclusive to Naval service — Masters are great ship handlers and Surgeons (obviously) are medical practitioners. Ratings, finally, are the doers; they follow orders and run the ships and stations of the fleet, and thus are the true backbone of the Navy.

In terms of seniority, the Commissioned Officers are highest; in all matters, they are considered the experts in ship command, and so even young Midshipmen are given command over veteran Masters (though in a case where a Master is put under the orders of a Midshipman, it's generally considered a learning experience for that junior officer). Both Commissioned and Warrant Officers are within their rights to give orders to Ratings; as the doers, the Ratings facilitate the work of both types of officers.

Commissioned Officers
Probably the most confusing rank division is that commissioned officer; having inherited it — or more properly, borrowed it — from the Royal Navy's less well-organized period in history, the system still reflects some (thankfully not all) odd practices.

Midshipmen
Since no Earthers are technically 'men' — or 'women' for that matter — this rank title has survived without too much confusion in the Earther Navy. The Midshipmen are the first of the Commissioned Officers; Earthers entering the Navy who wish to be officers generally start here, and then work their way up

the commissioned chain. It is also often the starting point for Earthers raised from the Non-Commissioned level (Ratings and NCOs) who have been selected for promotion because of their ability.

Lieutenants

Pronounced in the more 'traditional' manner — *"left-tennant"* — these are the backbone of the officer corps. There are Lieutenants by the dozen in an Earther ship of the line, with the most senior five being designated 'First Lieutenant' through 'Fifth Lieutenant', and the rest simply all being called Lieutenant. This is a peculiar example of the reflection of Earther society in the Navy; in *Orion*, for instance, there are over 100 Lieutenants below Fifth, and yet they all cooperate without more definite hierarchical divisions. Lieutenants command and supervise all the general functions of a ship, from divisions of guns to sections of bridge command consoles (one usually finds a Sensor Officer overseeing the bridge sensor section, which is crewed by a Sensor Chief and Sensor Technicians).

Commanders

Here is a bit of a confusing rank; logically, it would appear to be a stepping stone between Lieutenant and Captain, but many Earther Captains (Garvin Jardaw for one) have skipped this rank. Essentially, Commander is a rank given to Lieutenants who have distinguished themselves but who might not yet have the experience to command a fully-rated ship of war. Invariably commanding sloops, these officers are often daring and clever, and as such the rank of Commander is perhaps most important as an opportunity for highly capable officers to further demonstrate their talents — think of Fox Magnus.

Captains and Post Captains

Officially on the Admiralty lists, there are two levels of Captaincy, though in effect the difference is not too great. In the original Royal Navy system, the rank of 'Post Captain' was reserved for Captains of a certain seniority; the Earthers borrowed that theory, but in retrospect they didn't need to. The differences between Captains and Post Captains are minute: any Captain commanding a Rated ship (a Sixth Rate or larger) or an orbital station is a Post Captain, but should a Captain be put in command of a sloop (or even a group of sloops) or in an administrative position (for instance, Chief of Research and Development Staff at Antarctic Base), he or she would just be a regular Captain. Post Captains are officially senior to regular Captains, but you know how the Earthers are: they really don't bother much with rank, just cooperation and ability.

By way of clarification, *Flag* Captain is not a rank, but a title; that is to say, any Captain (post or otherwise) could be named Flag Captain. The only requirement for the title is to be the Captain of a ship with a flag officer (Commodore or higher) flying his or her pennant from it. So Labrador Forepaw is Setter Caine's Flag Captain, but his rank is only Post Captain (though because of his great experience, he deservedly gets the informal respect due to an Admiral from his peers).

Commodores
Commodore is the next step up from Captain, and the rank comes in two grades of seniority, just as the rank of Captain does, except that the divisions here are more noticeable. Essentially, both grades of Commodore are squadron commanders; they are responsible for more ships than just their own (usually eight ships among the Earther fleets). The distinction between Junior and Senior grade Commodores is fairly simple: Junior Commodores don't have Flag Captains, Senior Commodores do. Thus, when Ursla was the *Senior* Commodore of the 111th, Dran Nightclaw was her Flag Captain, but when Dran Nightclaw was promoted up from Captain to *Junior* Commodore, he retained his position as Captain of *Cerberus*, and gained command of the rest of the 111th. Junior Commodores are thus concerned with both ship and squadron command, Senior Commodores are left to focus on grander affairs.

Admirals
There are a number of grades of Admiral (Rear, Vice, and just plain Admiral, moving from least to most senior) and they all have a theoretical importance related to the size of the force being commanded. Under the theory of the Earther Navy's officer structure, Rear Admirals should be commanding battle groups, Vice Admirals commanding Fleet Divisions, and Admirals commanding whole Fleets. That latter category has essentially been preserved, even on campaign, but Vice and Rear Admirals were being mixed through various command structures rather chaotically even before conflict with the humans began. Exceptions are still common enough, though; recall that Admiral Varnon Broadpaw (then of the Third Fleet) accompanied Ursla to Genesis as second in command of the Second Fleet, and that Kella Felar, Admiral of the First Fleet, essentially shares command of that Fleet with Setter Caine.

Admiralty Lords
The most auspiciously-titled rank in the Earther Navy, is unsurprisingly right at the top. The Admiralty (based out of Admiralty House, London) is the head of the Earther Navy, issuing orders that govern the campaign, but leaving operational command to personnel on scene. The Admiralty Lords are the most experienced Admirals in the Fleet, with the First Lord of the Admiralty a line officer, the Second Lord an administrator, and the seven other Lords selected from either side of the desk. Whether First Lords should accompany the fleet

on campaign is an open question; what Caine is doing works well, so while there might be adjustments to the structure of command in the future (the addition perhaps of another First Space Lord to carry the First Lord's duties on campaign, leaving the First Lord at home), no one's complaining just now.

Warrant Officers

The complicated distinction between Warrant and Commissioned Officers begins with the Boards who appoint them. The Admiralty Board, already discussed, is in charge of the Commissioned Officers, but the *Navy Board* is in charge of the Warrant Officers. So what's the Navy Board? Here's a simple way to understand just what the Navy Board does: while the Admiralty organizes the Fleet, sends it places and appoints its commanders, the Navy Board is concerned with making sure the ships of the Fleet actually *work*. Under a Comptroller, the Navy Board looks after supplying ships, repairing them, putting new equipment on them, etc. The Admiralty uses the Navy as the tool, the Navy Board maintains the tool. Unsurprisingly, then, the Officers warranted by the Board are those who are concerned with the operation of the Fleet.

Cruising Masters

Professional ship-handlers, the Masters are the ones who can be relied upon to move vessels in action. In theory, the officers (usually the Captain or First Lieutenant) give orders for movement that would contribute to a ship's conduct in battle — that is, they say "Hard to port" to avoid fire, or to present a broadside, or whatever. The Master is the one who knows how a ship handles, and who gives the more specific commands (the ones we never seem to hear in the pages for some strange reason!), like: "Back starboard three and four by fifty percent, fire thrusters ninety-six and ninety-nine at twelve point nine-four-two. Roll at axis point seventeen..." During regular cruising times, the Master and his mates (Ratings who are given certificates by the Navy Board) simply look after the conduct of the vessel through space, its helm systems and coordination with the engines... the mundane stuff never talked about because it'd be boring as hell. But crucial stuff, nonetheless!

Surgeon

If I said you'd need three guesses to figure out what the ship's doctor does, you'd probably smack me. Basically, it's as obvious as it sounds; ship surgeons are professional doctors (they could be straight out of civilian practice) who apply to the Navy Board for a warrant to serve aboard ship.

Overlap

This is a complicated system; the Earthers knew that when they borrowed it from the Royal Navy of the classic age of fighting sail, but they probably didn't realize just how messy it could get. Overlap occurs in a number of areas, the best example being in engineering.

Engineers are Commissioned Officers — consider Lieutenant Claw and Lieutenant Sandpelt as engineers in *Flame* — but in order to be certified for service as an engineer in any ship, officers must be awarded a warrant from the Navy Board. Thus, they get their Commissions — their permission to give orders and command ships in the service — from the Admiralty, but their authorization to work on the ships of the fleet comes from Navy Board. It's a needlessly complicated system but it works for the Earthers, because when it comes to dealing with each other, they do just fine.

Ratings

There are a plethora of different classes under the Ratings system; the name of the category suggests their first distinction from officers of either Warrant or Commissioned type. Once you sign on with the Navy in a regular spacer capacity, you're given a two-week course in spacecraft operation, then you're rated based on your proficiency. If, for instance, you're a spacer who decided to leave the fleet for a couple of decades to pursue an acting career (it *could* happen...) you can return, do the course, and because of your experience be rated Senior immediately. If you've got some space travel experience, but haven't served in the Navy, you're probably an Able Spacer, if you're just a regular sort who hasn't been to space much, you're probably a Regular Spacer. It's all skill-based, though, so it depends entirely on individual ability where you might end up on the ladder.

Non-Commissioned Officers

Appointed by Commissioned and Warrant Officers, these are the organizational heads among the ratings, who manage the on-the-ground operations as team leaders. They can serve as assistants (Sensor Chief, Master's Mate, Doctor's Orderly, etc.) and can be given certificates in various fields from the Navy Board, which may be applicable in case they are commissioned or warranted as officers. Because of the crucial level of organization they oversee, the NCOs are perhaps some of the most critical elements of the fleet structure — they turn officers' orders into a reality.

Conclusion

So that's a brief overview of the Earther Navy's rank structure; of course there are exceptions and contradictions, and particularly in wartime these come to light. However, the Earthers have a real knack for making things work, no matter what the bureaucratic circumstances. No worries, then — the Earthers will see things right!

ABOUT THE AUTHOR

Born in 1984 in St. John's, Newfoundland, Kenneth Tam holds both a Bachelor's and Master's degree in history from Wilfrid Laurier University in Waterloo, Canada. His MA thesis examined the creation and operation of the Caribou Hut, a hostel for Allied servicemen in St. John's during the Second World War.

In 2006, Kenneth received a prestigious Canada Graduate Scholarship from the Social Sciences and Humanities Council of Canada. He was also awarded a Balsillie Fellowship at the Centre for International Governance Innovation during 2006-07. In that capacity, he worked for Mr. Paul Heinbecker, Canada's former ambassador and permanent representative to the United Nations. He presently serves as a Communications Consultant for Kitchener–Waterloo's federal Member of Parliament, Peter Braid.

Since first releasing the first *Equations* novel in 2003, Tam has promoted his books across Canada, speaking with junior and high school students, delivering writing workshops, and doing book signings at bookstores and Iceberg-organized events. He frequently appears as a guest author at science fiction events across the country.

Kenneth is a partner in Iceberg Publishing, the company he and his family started in 2002. He has authored many of the company's existing titles, and is also responsible for graphic design, including the company logo, website, banners, advertisements, and other marketing materials. He acts as a primary contact with printers and suppliers, and is also key in new author development and recruitment.

He remains very lazy about writing his author bios. When they told him to make this one longer, he mostly copied and pasted it together from the Iceberg website, www.icebergpublishing.com.